HUCKLEBERRY HARVEST

Mandy watched Mammi leave with the empty jug. "I'm sorry we didn't save you any lemonade, Noah. You're the most deserving one."

"What about me?" Titus called. "It wasn't easy organizing everybody into typographical order."

Noah stopped throwing bales with all those muscles of his and curled his lips into a very attractive smile. "It's all right. I'm glad there was enough for your future husband, whoever he may be."

Mandy groaned. "Believe me. My future husband did not drink lemonade today."

Noah chuckled. "I hope he's not thirsty."

His eyes were such a warm shade of brown, Mandy thought she could very well get lost in them. But really, she needed to tear her gaze from his and go into the house and . . . what was it she needed to do?

Noah kept up his steady pace with the hay bales. Did he ever tire?

She should march out of the barn and away from the sight of Noah's chiseled arms and milk-chocolate brown eyes and go help Mammi do . . . something. Certainly Mammi needed help with something.

Instead, she leaned against the wall of the barn and watched Noah toss every last bale of hay.

The something, whatever it was, could wait. . . .

Books by Jennifer Beckstrand

HUCKLEBERRY HILL

HUCKLEBERRY SUMMER

HUCKLEBERRY CHRISTMAS

HUCKLEBERRY SPRING

HUCKLEBERRY HARVEST

Published by Kensington Publishing Corporation

Huckleberry Harvest

JENNIFER BECKSTRAND

ZEBRA BOOKS
KENSINGTON PUBLISHING CORP.
http://www.kensingtonbooks.com

ZEBRA BOOKS are published by

Kensington Publishing Corp.
119 West 40th Street
New York, NY 10018

All Kensington titles, imprints, and distributed lines are available at special quantity discounts for bulk purchases for sales promotion, premiums, fund-raising, educational, or institutional use.

Special book excerpts or customized printings can also be created to fit specific needs. For details, write or phone the office of the Kensington Sales Manager: Attn.: Sales Department. Kensington Publishing Corp., 119 West 40th Street, New York, NY 10018. Phone: 1-800-221-2647.

Zebra and the Z logo Reg. U.S. Pat. & TM Off.

First Printing: June 2015
ISBN-13: 978-1-4201-3651-7
ISBN-10: 1-4201-3651-8

eISBN-13: 978-1-4201-3652-4
eISBN-10: 1-4201-3652-6

10 9 8 7 6 5 4 3 2 1

Printed in the United States of America

Chapter One

The chickens gathered at Anna Helmuth's feet as she scattered scratch from her pail. "Oh, dear," she said. "I suppose I should have tossed it away from me if I wanted to keep my shoes clean."

"You're doing a fine job, Annie," her husband Felty said. "The hens are getting fat."

Anna tiptoed around the chickens as they pecked at the feed. Bitzy, the Plymouth Rock hen, put up a fuss when Anna accidentally stepped on her, but she recovered enough to squawk in disapproval before going back to her breakfast. "Did you bring the chopped carrots?" Anna asked.

Felty pulled a handful of carrot pieces from his pocket. "This is all we had."

"It will be enough." Anna took the slices from Felty's hand and tossed them into the small flock of chickens. She beaned one chicken in the head inadvertently, but surely a carrot to the head wouldn't have hurt anybody seriously. The chicken kept right on eating and didn't seem to notice. "I'm planning a special breakfast for Mandy's first day on Huckleberry Hill, and I want the eggs to be extra-bright yellow."

"What special breakfast are you making for our granddaughter?"

"She's only staying a month, so I want every meal to

be memorable. Tomorrow morning we're having Eggs Benedict. I've never made it before, but the picture in my recipe book looks delicious. I just have to figure out what a poached egg is, and we'll be all set."

"Do you still want to find a boy for Mandy while she's in town?"

"*Jah*. But don't worry. I'll see to it that any romantic goings-on will not be detrimental to your blood pressure."

"What about my ulcer?"

Anna propped a hand on her hip. "Now, Felty. You don't have an ulcer."

"I will by the time Mandy goes back to Ohio."

"We can't let Mandy leave Bonduel without a husband."

Felty stroked his salt-and-pepper beard. "It's a bit of a stretch to think Mandy will meet a boy, fall in love, get engaged, and plan a wedding in one month's time."

Anna bit her bottom lip. "Maybe we could talk her into staying an extra week."

"We better encourage the chickens to lay more eggs if we need five weeks of Eggs Benefit," Felty said.

"Now, Felty. We'll have enough time. Our biggest problem is finding the right young man for our granddaughter. Her plans for a visit took me by surprise. I haven't had the time to spy out prospective husbands like I usually do. I just don't know what boy in Bonduel would do for our Mandy."

Felty nodded. "She's a spunky sort of girl."

"Jah," Anna said, dumping the rest of the scratch from her pail onto the ground. "She needs a spunky, cheerful boy to keep her laughing."

Felty took the pail from Anna as they walked toward the house. "What do you think of Noah Mischler? He's as *gute* a boy as ever there was."

Anna furrowed her brow until the wrinkles piled on top of each other. "Noah Mischler? He's as solid as a tree."

"Is that bad?"

"*Nae*. It means he's not afraid of hard work."

"Being a hard worker is the most important quality for a grandson in-law to possess."

Anna ran her hands down the front of her apron. "Don't get me wrong, Felty. I adore Noah Mischler. Saloma Miller tells me he put a new gas stove in her kitchen last April that practically makes dinner by itself. Noah is smart enough to fix anything that's broken, and he's so gute to his *dat*. But I don't think he and Mandy would suit. He's gloomier than three weeks of rain."

Felty rubbed the back of his neck. "Maybe he don't have much cause to smile these days."

"Mandy won't look twice at someone like him. We've got to think of somebody else."

Felty opened the door for his wife of sixty-four years and followed her into the house. "How will we ever find someone in four weeks?"

"Five weeks. We'll talk Mandy into five weeks. And I'm going to pull out my new recipe book. The way to a man's heart is through his stomach."

"In that case, Mandy won't have a lick of trouble finding a boy. Nobody knows how to cook like you do, Annie." Felty paused inside the door, looked around the great room, and thumbed his suspenders. He grinned as an idea came to him. "Annie, how would you like a new gas stove for all this cooking you're going to be doing?"

Chapter Two

"Is this the house?" Mandy asked as she pulled Dawdi's buggy in front of the run-down shack with paint peeling off the siding.

"Jah," Kristina said, still sniffling after all the crying she'd done today.

Mandy set the brake and tied the reins. "Do you want to come with me?"

"No. Never."

"I'll talk to him. Keep an eye out. If he wants to apologize or get back together with you, I'll wave to you. Okay?"

"Be sure to tell him I still love him."

Mandy ground her teeth together. Kristina didn't have a lick of sense about how to handle such things. "Remember what we talked about? That will only make you sound desperate. You're not desperate." She patted Kristina's hand. "You've been treated very badly, and someone needs to put Noah Mischler in his place. If his conscience nags at him and he realizes he can't live without you, all the better."

"But what if he doesn't know how much I love him? Maybe he broke it off because he thought I was going to break it off first."

"I'll fix it."

"But how?"

"I'll make Noah Mischler see the error of his ways. Believe me, I know how to make a *deerich* boy feel guilty. He'll realize what he's done, and everything will be set to rights."

The grass in the front yard grew in tufts like the hair on a balding old man. Mandy tromped along the dirt path worn into the sparse lawn and climbed the two concrete steps to the small cement pad that served as a porch. Thick lilac bushes grew on either side of the house, creating a barrier as impassable as any stone wall. They grew tall and thick and undisciplined, as if they were trying to imprison the house. Without their blooms, they were quite unsightly. No trees or flowers graced the front yard, and a barbed wire fence, tangled and swaying, ran along the north side of the yard. The property looked sad, as if it had lived a long, difficult life and was ready to give up the ghost.

A droopy-eared hound lazed next to the door and didn't even bark when Mandy approached. He looked as if he had barely enough energy to lift his head.

Pausing, she took the dog's face in her hands and caressed his ears. "Pretty dog. Good dog," she cooed. The dog responded by attempting to lick her face. She dodged his tongue and gave him a swift pat on the head before squaring her shoulders and knocking on the door.

Time to show her angry-yet-ready-to-forgive face. Noah Mischler didn't stand a chance.

She waited for several seconds with no response from the inside and then knocked again—more forcefully this time. Six loud raps that told anyone inside she meant business.

A young man, sturdy and tall, answered the door. When he gave her a tentative smile, the air stuck in her throat, and she forgot to breathe. This pleasant-looking, muscular young man was Noah Mischler? The boy who had scornfully stomped on her best friend's heart? By the way Kristina had described him, Mandy had expected a scowling, sinister boy with fangs and bushy dark eyebrows.

The boy standing before her was not at all what she had pictured. His wavy hair was the color of wheat just before harvest and his dark, lively eyes called to mind the deep browns and rich greens of the forest. His face, lean and tan from the summer's work, looked as if it could belong to one of the statues standing in a museum in Milwaukee. No wonder Kristina wanted him back.

He tilted his head. "Can I help you?"

She realized she'd been staring and cleared her throat. This was no time to be distracted by a handsome face. *Pretty is as pretty does*, that was what Mamm always said. If Noah Mischler wasn't a godly man in his heart, it didn't matter how he looked on the outside.

"Are you Noah Mischler?"

"Jah," he said, holding out his hand. Instinctively, she shook it even though she had determined that she wasn't going to be friendly. Noah needed to see the stern side of Mandy Helmuth today. He must be made to understand the seriousness of his transgressions.

She quickly pulled her hand away. Puzzlement flitted across his face as he stepped out onto the porch and shut the door behind him. "And you are . . . ?"

"Mandy Helmuth." She cleared her throat again.

"Helmuth. Are you related to Anna and Felty Helmuth on Huckleberry Hill?"

"Jah. I am their granddaughter. I'm visiting from Ohio."

"Nice to meet you. Felty is . . . friends with my dat." His eyebrows inched closer together as he studied her face and waited for her to explain herself.

Suddenly she found the words harder to push out of her mouth than she had expected. He seemed so nice, the way he eyed her curiously but with no apparent ill will.

She took a determined breath and arched her eyebrows. Looks could be deceiving.

"Noah Mischler, I came to tell you that what you did to Kristina Beachy is despicable, and you'd better repent right quick."

His face immediately hardened like cement or, rather, like cold, hard granite. She'd never seen an expression so unyielding. "You don't know anything."

"I know that you flirted with Kristina for months and months and took her home from gatherings in your courting buggy and made her believe you loved her and then broke the whole thing off with a text message."

He stared at her with fire in his eyes even as the rest of his face could have been chiseled out of solid rock. "Like I said. You don't know anything about it." He stepped back and took hold of the door handle, as if he were planning to leave her standing there. As if the conversation were over!

"I'm not finished," Mandy said.

"I am," he replied, opening the door and stepping inside.

Mandy pointed to the buggy. "There is a heartbroken girl in there, wondering what she did to deserve such cruelty from you."

"Cruelty?"

"You treated her like dirt, and yet she forgives you."

The lines of his mouth twitched with simmering resentment. "Kristina has an overactive imagination."

"Don't you think she at least deserves an apology for how you treated her?"

"Nae."

"You won't even apologize? Kristina hasn't stopped crying since you dumped her."

His eyes narrowed into slits. "She's been crying for three solid weeks?"

Mandy shouldn't have exaggerated. It made her sound

childish. "All I'm saying is that she is devastated. You led her on. She has a right to an explanation."

"I said all I needed to say in the text."

She was losing ground. Not even the faintest hint of remorse tinged his features. "And that's another thing. Kristina told me you've been baptized. Why does a baptized member of the church have a cell phone? I can understand Kristina having one. She hasn't taken baptism classes yet. But why do you have one? What would the bishop think if he knew you were breaking the rules of the *Ordnung*?"

Nastiness crept into his voice. "Why don't you go ask him and find out?"

"Maybe I will. Maybe if you lose your phone, you won't be able to break more hearts. At least in a text."

He folded his arms, moved closer, and stared her down with those fiery brown eyes. She resisted the urge to take a step back. She wouldn't appear weak, not even if Noah Mischler was strong enough to break her like a twig. "Maybe, Mandy Helmuth, you should get your superior little *hinner-dale* off my porch."

She nearly choked on his words. How dare he? Fighting the urge to hiss like a cat, she wrapped her arms around her waist until she felt composed enough to speak. "So, you refuse to see reason."

"I'm not the one who refuses to see reason. You got precisely half of the story, which isn't true, by the way, and you aren't reasonable enough to ask my side. But it doesn't matter, because my side is none of your business."

"It's my business when a dear friend gets hurt."

He grunted so that Mandy knew exactly what he thought of that logic. "Why don't you stick your little freckled nose into someone else's life? I don't care what you think." He backed away and shut the door in her face before she had a chance to answer him. Before she could even give him a lecture about the proper way to treat girls and the punishments awaiting deceivers in hell.

Well then. If he refused to improve himself and repent of his wrongdoing, then his soul was not Mandy's problem. She'd done all she could. Even her dawdi, as kind as he was, couldn't have been expected to do more.

Mandy stomped down the stairs, gave the dog one last pat, and made a beeline for the buggy, not caring how many pathetic tufts of grass she trampled along the way. That lawn wouldn't last another winter anyway. If she were them, she'd till up the whole thing and plant new grass seed next spring.

She couldn't hide her indignation as she climbed into the buggy and got it rolling as quickly as possible. Noah Mischler would try the patience of Job.

"What did he say?" Kristina asked, as if Mandy held all her hopes and dreams in her hand.

"I don't understand why you like Noah Mischler. He has no remorse for anything. He's *doomkop*. Forget him, Krissy."

"I can't."

"Jah, you can. There's dozens of other boys who don't scowl and who don't say words like 'hinnerdale' right to a girl's face. You can do so much better."

"That's not true. Noah is the most wonderful boy in the world, and I think I'll die of a broken heart if he doesn't take me back."

Kristina always did have a flair for the dramatic. Still, Mandy sympathized with her completely. Insensitive, aggravating Noah Mischler had made her friend miserable, and Mandy had been left to pick up the pieces of Kristina's heart.

Mandy would be perfectly happy if she never laid eyes on that boy again.

Chapter Three

"*In heaven I know there'll be no weeping or dying, No chilly winds or tornadoes ever blow, It is a land of love and springtime beauty, Where purple flowers ever grow*," Dawdi sang as he swept the last of the ashes out of the wood box with a hand broom. Music floated around Dawdi like air floated around everybody else. He sang when he did his chores. He sang in the bathroom. He hummed while reading the newspaper. It seemed the only time he didn't sing was at the dinner table because Mammi had made a rule against it. "Enough of my boys are singers that we had to make the no-singing-at-the-table rule," she had told Mandy. "It's nonsense to try to eat and sing at the same time." Dawdi knew lots of tunes but often forgot the words. Most of his lyrics were made up on the spot.

The ashes from the cookstove floated into the pail, and Dawdi flipped the lid shut. "That's the last time I'm ever going to clean out that old stove. The new one comes today."

They'd eaten cold cereal that morning so the cookstove would be cool enough for the salvage men to haul away. Bran flakes weren't Mandy's favorite, but after something runny and gooey yesterday called Eggs Benedict, Mandy would have cheerfully eaten pine needles and twigs for the rest of her life.

"We've had this woodstove for forty years," Mammi said, taking a rag and wiping the top of it.

"Sixty-four," Dawdi said. "My dat gave it to us on our wedding day."

Mammi nodded and looked at Mandy. "Your dawdi is so eager for a newfangled stove. I hope I'll be able to get the bread just right in a gas stove."

Mandy smiled sympathetically at her mammi. Poor Mammi had never gotten the bread just right in the old stove. But it was okay. Everybody ate Mammi's cooking, no matter how bad it tasted. It gave Mammi so much pleasure to feed her family. A little dinner-table discomfort was secondary to Mammi's feelings.

Dawdi put his arm around Mammi. "You're the best cook in the world, Annie Banannie. A new gas stove won't slow you down."

"Of course not," Mammi said. "I can learn. My doctor says your brain gets old if you stop learning."

"When are they coming with the new stove?" Mandy asked. Lord willing, she'd get bran flakes two days in a row.

Dawdi glanced at the bird clock on the wall. "Should be here within the hour." He chuckled as at that minute, someone knocked on the door. "They're early."

Mandy was closest to the door. The moment she opened it, she wished she hadn't. Noah Mischler stood on Mammi's porch holding a large metal box that looked as if it weighed fifty pounds. That boy was as sturdy as a tree and as handsome as a sunset.

And she loathed him.

Noah nodded at Mandy, his eyes two chips of brown ice and his face devoid of expression.

She was stunned, simply stunned, to see Noah Mischler on Mammi's doorstep only a day after she'd given him a tongue-lashing and he'd ordered her off his porch. What was he doing here?

"I came to help with the stove," he said, not acting surprised or annoyed to see her. Of course he wasn't surprised. She had told him yesterday that she was staying with her grandparents. And even though his face betrayed no emotion, he was certainly annoyed with her. She'd called him to repentance. What boy would want to be in the same room with a girl who wasn't taken in by his good looks and rock-hard arms?

"Noah," Dawdi said, grasping Noah's hand and pulling him into the house. It seemed to Mandy that he came reluctantly. "If there's one thing I like, it's a man who's prompt."

Mammi's little white poodle, Sparky, waddled into the great room and nudged the leg of Noah's trousers with her wet nose as if she and Noah were friends or something. As if Noah deserved a friendly greeting. He bent over and casually scratched Sparky's curly head. "I thought I'd decide where to drill the hole before the stove gets here."

Mandy moved out of the way. She wanted to run for the comfort of her room, but opted to pretend that something at the sink needed her full attention. Only after she got there did she realize that such a move put her much closer to where Noah would actually be working. *Oh sis yuscht!*

Dawdi's eyes twinkled, and he thumbed his suspenders. "Noah, this is my granddaughter Mandy from Charm, Ohio."

"Nice to meet you," Mandy said, which was probably the biggest lie she'd ever told.

Noah merely nodded, which seemed to be all the response Dawdi expected. "She's not going to be in town long," Dawdi added.

Mandy could almost hear Noah giving thanks inside his head.

"You're here, and the stove isn't," Dawdi said, motioning

to the table. "Sit. Mandy made huckleberry pie. Have a piece while you wait."

"No, *denki*," Noah said, glancing at Mandy and quickly looking away. "I'm not hungry." He probably suspected poison.

"Stuff and nonsense," Mammi said, pushing a chair in his direction. "A boy your age is always hungry yet. And you only get fresh huckleberry pie once a year."

Looking about as stiff as an icicle, Noah hung his hat on the hook, set his giant box near the door, and sat at the table.

"We had our huckleberry picking frolic last week," Mammi said. "Most of the berries got made into jam. Mandy was kind enough to make a pie with the last of them. She's a very gute cook."

Mandy really, really didn't welcome the warmth that traveled up her neck and no doubt tinged her cheeks bright red. She couldn't have cared less if Noah liked her pie. Why should prickly Noah Mischler have the privilege of eating her pie anyway? He didn't deserve it.

Noah still looked as if he wanted to refuse. Did he think he was too good for Mandy's cooking? "I don't want to impose."

"No imposition at all," Mammi insisted, not guessing how adamantly Mandy disagreed with her. "I'll put some whipped cream on top." Mammi's baked goods always tasted better with several dollops of whipped cream. The Helmuth family used whipped cream like most people used salt.

When Mammi pulled the whipped cream from the fridge, Mandy realized that she was expected to slice the pie and serve a piece to Noah. Her chest tightened around the little pebble that must have been her heart. She'd be forced to walk over to the table and give him the pie with her own two hands. Would they make eye contact? Would he bite her fingers off?

Nae, he seemed the type to keep his emotions in check.

She just didn't know if she was capable of doing the same thing. She'd never been quite so uncomfortable. What would Mammi and Dawdi say if they knew what had occurred between Noah and Mandy yesterday?

Mammi would definitely be shocked that Noah had been so rude, but if her grandparents had known Noah's true character, they would never have let him set foot in their house, and they certainly wouldn't let him work on their new gas stove. He might get careless and set the house on fire.

She cut him a generous piece of pie, because she was a nice girl after all, and Mammi plopped a gute helping of cream on top.

Noah didn't smile at her, but he looked less like an angry badger when she laid the pie on table. "Denki," he mumbled resentfully.

"You're welcome," she mumbled, just as resentfully, while adding a twinge of disdain to her voice.

Mammi and Dawdi didn't seem to notice, but he did. He pressed his lips into an inflexible line and picked up his fork as if it weighed a hundred pounds—not that he would have any trouble whatsoever lifting a hundred-pound fork. He raised the pie to his lips as if he thought it might bite him.

She took comfort in the fact that he was as uncomfortable as she was. Gute. It served him right. He should feel uncomfortable for the way he had treated poor Kristina.

He closed his eyes and savored his bite. Mandy could tell he enjoyed it by the slight upward curl of his lips.

"Mandy made it," Dawdi said, in case Noah had already forgotten.

"All by herself," Mammi added.

"It's wonderful gute," Noah said.

Mandy immediately felt irritated at how pleased she was by Noah's compliment. One bit of praise, even from a boy she didn't like, was enough to send her floating to the clouds.

She turned her back on him. "Mammi and Dawdi, do you want pie?"

Mammi waved Mandy away. "I'll wait for the boys to get here."

Mandy poured Noah a glass of milk and handed it to him. She turned her back on him again immediately. She wouldn't do him the courtesy of paying him any more notice than she had to.

Once she put some distance between them, her mind caught hold of what Mammi had said. "What boys?"

Mammi's eyes twinkled as she clapped her hands. "All handpicked."

"The boys" sounded like a bushel of tomatoes. "What do you mean, Mammi?"

"We've got five eligible young men coming to haul the stove out of the house, and then we are going to feed each of them a piece of pie. While they eat, you are going to pick the one you want for a boyfriend."

Behind her, it sounded as if Noah were quietly choking. Mandy whipped her head around to see him tapping his chest with his fist. "Sorry," he managed to say between coughs. "Swallowed down the wrong pipe."

Mandy did her best to ignore him altogether. He was only here to install the new stove. She didn't have to speak to him if she didn't want to.

Instead, she focused on her mammi and tried to make sense of what she was hearing. "You want me to have a boyfriend?"

Mammi's grin was as wide as Shawano Lake. "I want you to have a husband, but I'm having trouble landing on just the right one yet. I'm going to let you have your pick."

Mandy feared her face might burst into flames at the thought that disagreeable Noah Mischler was hearing this entire conversation. "Mammi, I don't need you to find me a husband."

"Of course you do, dear. All *die youngie* need help with romance. You'll be pleased with the boys I've chosen. And you should feel special, because I haven't let any of the other grandchildren pick their own spouses."

"Do these boys know they are competing for my affections?"

"Nae," Mammi said. "I don't want the ones you reject to feel bad. They think they are coming to move the stove, but it's the perfect opportunity to meet each of them face-to-face and decide which one you like the best."

Mandy's throat constricted even as she pasted a pleasant look on her face. Mammi's matchmaking schemes were well known among the family. The dear woman couldn't resist meddling with her grandchildren. But Mandy refused to be meddled with. There were plenty of boys in Charm to spark her interest, and if the rest of the boys in Bonduel were anything like Noah Mischler, she was definitely not interested.

But she wouldn't for the world hurt Mammi's feelings. "It's such a lovely idea, Mammi," she said, "but I'm only going to be here for four weeks. Hardly enough time to find a boyfriend."

She glanced at Noah. He concentrated very intently on the last bites of his pie, avoiding eye contact like the stomach flu. She disliked him more than ever for making fun of her inside his head, because that was surely what he must be doing. A boy like him probably bullied small children and kicked puppies on a regular basis. Of course he'd be privately mocking Mandy and her grandparents.

"We hoped you'd stay for five weeks," Mammi said. "That should give us enough time."

"Please, Mammi. I'd rather not."

Mammi bustled over and patted Mandy's hand. "That's what they all say, dear."

Mandy looked to Dawdi for support. He merely grinned and winked at her. "Five weeks is better than four."

Mandy blew at a strand of hair hovering over her forehead. She didn't really mind the matchmaking. Mammi could do all the scheming she wanted. Mandy didn't have to go along with any of it. But it certainly galled her that Noah had heard their strange conversation. What would he tell his friends? *Helmuths' granddaughter is so desperate, she needs her mammi to find boys for her to date.*

Mandy frowned and shook her head. A boy like Noah Mischler probably didn't have any friends to tell. That thought made her feel a little better.

With that grin firmly etched into his face, Dawdi took Mammi by the hand as his gaze skipped between Mandy and Noah. "*Cum*, Annie, there's something in the bedroom I want you to see."

"Can it wait, Felty dear? I want to be here when the boys arrive so I can introduce them to Mandy."

"We won't be gone long. Besides, the boys are going to be late yet."

"Late?" Mammi said. "How do you know they're going to be late?"

"Because I told them to be late," Dawdi said, raising an eyebrow at Mandy, as if he were harboring a mysterious secret.

"Now, Felty, why in the world would you tell those boys to be late? You know we've only got five weeks."

Dawdi tugged Mammi forward. "Cum see what I've got in the bedroom. We'll be back soon enough."

"Now, Felty," she said, with a mild scold in her voice, "I've already seen your new toenail clippers."

"It's not my toenail clippers," Dawdi said, coaxing her down the hall.

Mandy thought she might be ill when she realized that Dawdi and Mammi had left her all alone in the kitchen with Noah Mischler, who had no reason to behave himself now that her grandparents were gone.

In desperation, she grabbed a rag, turned her back on him, and started wiping down the front of the fridge. Anything to appear too busy for idle conversation.

She heard him slide his chair out from the table and come toward her. *Oh sis yuscht!* Was he going to yell at her to mind her own business or tell her to get her little hinnerdale out of his way?

"Denki for the pie," he said.

Holding her breath, she turned her head and nodded slightly. That was all the acknowledgment she would stoop to give him.

She watched out of the corner of her eye as he turned on the water and rinsed off his plate. To her surprise, he found the dish soap under the sink, washed his dishes, dried them, and put them back in the cupboards where they belonged.

Had he done that to try to impress her?

Of course not. He despised her as much as she despised him. The cleaning up obviously came as naturally to him as walking. Whoever his mother was, she had trained him well.

She turned her attention back to the fridge. She refused to be amazed by anything Noah Mischler did or did not do. He was a low-down snake who'd broken Kristina's heart and then had the nerve to scoff at Mandy about it. His washing three measly dishes didn't mean much piled on top of his multitude of sins.

The tension between them expanded like a balloon until Mandy felt as if she were being squished into a corner by the silence. She glanced at him as he rummaged through that giant toolbox of his. Sparky the dog sat on her haunches a few inches from the toolbox and studied Noah with her black eyes as if he were the most fascinating thing in the world. Noah reached out and cupped Sparky's face in his big hand before turning his attention back to his tools.

He had been holding his temper well and didn't seem inclined to scowl at her. He *had* complimented her on the pie and been nice to the dog. Maybe he wasn't completely without feelings. Maybe he could still be influenced in Kristina's direction. "If you think my pie was good, you should try Kristina's soft pretzels. You've never tasted anything better."

He looked at her as if she'd just said something slightly rude. "Do you really think I want to talk about Kristina Beachy?"

She clamped her mouth shut faster than Mammi could click her knitting needles together. He might have said nice things about her pie, but why in a million years had she ever believed he might be a partially nice person?

Fine.

She would remain silent. Let him smell her disdain from halfway across the room like an *Englischer*'s cheap perfume.

He retrieved a tape measure and a pencil from his toolbox. After surveying the wall behind the old cookstove, he measured the distance between the stove and the wall. Jotting notes and numbers directly onto the wall, he made a measure of where the stovepipe went into the wall and how big the hole was.

Mandy quickly abandoned the refrigerator. It stood right next to the cookstove, and she couldn't bear the thought of being that close to Mr. Grumpy. Instead, she found some paper plates and napkins and set them on the cupboard. If all these suitors were going to come, she'd like to be ready to serve them pie. Too bad she hadn't known about Mammi's plans earlier. She would have invited Kristina to the party and let her take her pick of the lot. Mandy would have relished the satisfaction of seeing Noah's brown eyes turn green with jealousy.

Noah tried to measure the entire length of the wall behind the stove, but the fridge got in the way, and when he tried to lengthen out his measuring tape, it snapped in the middle and sagged to the floor.

"Here," she said, instinctively grabbing the end of the measuring tape. "Where do you want me to hold it?" She might not have liked him, but she was a very nice girl, after all.

Suspicion traveled across his face, as if he feared an ambush. Maybe he thought she'd try to bully him into a date with Kristina. Well, maybe Mandy had decided not to try to get them back together. What did it matter that Noah was handsome? Kristina could do much better.

"Denki," he said. He didn't make eye contact, but one corner of his mouth twitched slightly upward. It must have been as close as he ever came to a smile, considering his expression consistently looked as if he'd just come from a funeral.

He wrote down the measurements, she released the tape measure, and he let it roll back onto itself.

"Denki," he said again, as if it were the only word that was safe to say to her.

It probably was.

She nodded once again, all the while searching for an excuse to get out of the kitchen. Maybe she didn't need an excuse. Maybe she could just walk away.

Before she had time to put her brilliant plan into action, someone knocked on the door. She took a deep breath and tried not to hyperventilate. The first of Mammi's boys had arrived. Even though Mandy had no intention of getting together with any of them, her heart still raced at the thought that whether they knew it or not, they had come specifically to meet her. She felt like a cow at the auction, and she'd much rather not have been the center of attention.

Noah continued to jot his numbers and notes on the wall and didn't seem to notice that anyone had knocked. At least he didn't smirk or glare at her. She would have died of embarrassment if he'd even glanced at her the wrong way.

She smoothed her dress before she even realized she was

doing it, and opened the door. Her cousin Titus, with the ever-present toothpick in his mouth, smiled back at her.

She stretched a smile across her face. Surely Mammi had no intention of matching Mandy with her own cousin. Maybe Mammi had forgotten they were related.

"Mandy," Titus said, pulling her in for a bear hug. "I didn't know you were here. Are you in for a visit?"

"Jah, for a few weeks."

"Well, Mamm will be cross if you don't come down to the house for a visit. You can meet Ben's fiancée Emma."

Mandy nodded. "I'll be sure to come."

"I'll tell her," Titus said, gnawing on his toothpick. "Freeman Kiem told me Mammi asked him to come help move a stove today, and I thought, 'Who better to help my mammi than her own grandson.' So I invited myself."

"Is Freeman coming?" Mandy asked.

"I told him I'd meet him here. He's always late. Where are Mammi and Dawdi?" Titus strolled into the room and nodded at Noah. "Noah. I figured you'd be here. It seems nothing gets fixed in Bonduel without you being part of it."

Noah stowed his measuring tape in the toolbox and smiled that attractive smile he'd flashed at Mandy when she first met him, before she knew how unpleasant he really was. "How is the pump working?" he said.

The toothpick bobbed on Titus's lips as he spoke. "Better than new. Dat says we should have paid you double for all the money you saved us."

Noah lowered his head. "You paid me plenty. I'm grateful for the work."

"From what I hear," Titus said, "people like your work so much, you've got enough jobs to keep you busy for about thirty more years."

"God has been good to me."

Okay. So Noah showed a little humility. Maybe he wasn't completely beyond repair.

Mammi came bustling down the hall as if she were late for her own wedding. Dawdi ambled far behind. "Oh, Titus," she said. "It's only you. I was afraid I missed the introductions."

Titus took the toothpick out of his mouth and kissed Mammi on the cheek. "Good to see you too, Mammi."

She nudged his shoulder. "Don't tease me. I didn't mean it like that. Of course I'm happy to see you. You're just not who I was expecting."

"Freeman's coming soon," Titus said.

Mammi's eyes danced. "Actually, this works out better than planned. Mandy, come stand over here by me while Titus answers the door. It will give you a better view of each boy as he comes in."

Titus gnawed on his toothpick. "Is this a parade, or are you making matches again, Mammi?"

"Never you mind, Titus. Just do your job and don't ask any questions."

"What's my job again?" Titus asked, squinting in concentration.

Mammi went to her hall closet and pulled out five of her colorful hand-knitted pot holders. "Answer the door when the boys come, dear," Mammi said, handing the pot holders to Titus, "and give each of them a pot holder as a welcome gift."

Mammi took Mandy by the elbow and dragged her near the sofa. "You and I will inspect each boy as he enters."

Mandy couldn't help but giggle.

Dawdi didn't seem as interested in finding Mandy a husband as he was about getting a new stove. While Titus hovered near the door and Mammi clutched Mandy's hand, Dawdi had Noah show him where the stove was going to go and gave Noah his opinion on where to drill the hole for the gas line. Dawdi acted as if he truly respected Noah's knowledge, as if Noah were a close friend instead of a boy who broke hearts with his cell phone.

They didn't have to wait long for the first visitor. Titus, who obviously wanted to perfectly execute his responsibilities, opened the door almost before the knock came. Two young men stood on the porch, one tall with curly hair and the other shorter, with a mouth full of braces. He looked about fourteen years old. Titus invited them in and handed each a pot holder.

Mammi leaned to whisper in Mandy's ear. "That's Paul Zook. He's going to have nice teeth in seven to nine months. The tall one is Melvin Lambright. He's twenty-nine years old and has a gute farm with his dat, but he's lactose intolerant. Do you mind a husband with an acid stomach?"

Mandy couldn't do anything but humor her mammi, who took her matchmaking duties very seriously. "I suppose an acid stomach is better than a snoring problem."

Mammi raised her hand to her mouth. "Oh dear. I didn't ask about snoring."

Both Melvin and Paul immediately sought out Noah and shook his hand. Mandy heard Paul ask Noah something about a water heater, and both boys listened intently as Noah launched into an explanation that Mandy couldn't begin to be interested in.

Adam Wengerd arrived next. Stationed close to Titus, Sparky greeted him with a soft yip. Adam was almost as handsome as Noah Mischler. He had a good face and eyes the color of caramel drizzled over ice cream.

"Adam teaches school," Mammi whispered as they watched Adam slap Noah on the shoulder and join in a conversation about copper piping. "So he'd be out of a job if he married you. You might want to keep that in mind. But he has gute hair. I'm partial to wavy hair like that."

The last two boys arrived. One of them must have been Freeman because Titus greeted him with a warm handshake.

"That's Davy Burkholder and Freeman Kiem," Mammi said. "Davy hasn't been baptized yet. He is in love with his cell phone."

Mandy raised her eyebrows and nodded in disapproval. Noah Mischler had a cell phone too. She wouldn't give the time of day to a boy who had a cell phone.

"But Davy is a gute boy," Mammi said. "He loves to hunt. Think of the wonderful venison you could eat if you married him."

Mandy wrinkled her nose. Venison made her gag. She only ate it when absolutely necessary—like when Mammi served it and she didn't want to hurt her feelings.

Mammi hooked her arm around Mandy's elbow. "Freeman can crack nuts with his teeth."

And that must have been all Mandy needed to know about Freeman.

Freeman and Davy also immediately found Noah. Mandy's five potential husbands plus Titus gathered around Noah as if he were handing out free ice cream cones. They seemed to hang on his every word, acting like he had all the answers to every question ever asked.

Didn't they know that Noah Mischler slammed doors in the faces of unsuspecting girls?

"Yoo-hoo," Mammi called, waving her hand as if she were signaling a taxi. "Yoo-hoo, everybody. I'd like you to meet my granddaughter Mandy Helmuth." In unison, the boys stopped talking. Mammi couldn't leave well enough alone. "Mandy is only in town a short time. Any of you who would like to ask her on a date had better hurry up."

Mandy's face caught fire with embarrassment. The room full of boys stared at her as if they expected her to do a somersault or some other circus trick right there in Mammi's great room. She would have gladly crawled underneath the sofa and taken up residence with the dust bunnies.

Something akin to sympathy traveled across Noah's face. He thumped Adam on the back with his palm and nudged Freeman with his shoulder. "Quit staring and help me move this stove. I don't know about you, but I got other stuff I gotta do today."

Noah's unconcerned manner immediately dispelled the awkward tension in the room. Titus and Freeman laughed, and the boys turned their attention to the stove, acting as if they'd forgotten Mandy was in the room. She breathed a sigh of relief and felt almost grateful to Noah Mischler. Almost. He was in a hurry to move the stove, nothing more. He hadn't intended to help ease Mandy's embarrassment. But at least no one was staring at her anymore.

Mandy decided to stay out of the way and watch. She couldn't begin to help lift the old cookstove, and Noah would surely be annoyed if she tried to help.

"We need to shove the stove out from the wall and lift together," Adam said.

Noah shook his head. "Nae. Let's do it the easy way. Freeman, you and Davy detach the pipe and take it apart. I'll be right back. Adam, can you help me?"

Noah and Adam bounded out the front door.

"He's a smart one," Dawdi said, grinning and gazing pointedly at Mandy, as if Noah's intelligence were something she should know about.

Before Freeman and Davy had pulled the pipe from the stove, Noah returned with a strange cart that stood low to the ground and looked like a flat red wagon or a skinny lawn mower. Adam followed, carrying three or four sheets of cardboard.

"We can get the stove out of the kitchen with this," Noah said. "I'll need you to keep it steady and then lift it down the stairs and into my wagon."

Even though Mandy had determined never to speak to Noah again, her curiosity got the better of her. "What is that?"

Noah glanced at her. "It's a floor jack. It can lift almost anything."

"I should have thought of that," Titus said, forgetting that he mostly never had thoughts that deep.

The stovepipe squealed as Davy and Freeman tried to jiggle it loose from the cookstove.

"Wait," Noah said, reaching into his toolbox for a screwdriver. "You've got to unscrew the pipe from the ceiling support."

Davy and Freeman did as they were told, and with a little more coaching from Noah, detached the pipe from the stove. A cloud of black ash floated into the air once the pipe was off.

"*Ach, du lieva*," Mammi said. "Oh, my goodness. I should have cleaned that better."

Mandy put her arm around Mammi. "It's okay. We will give the house a gute dusting once the stove is in."

Noah took the sheets of cardboard and laid them over Mammi's floor, making a path to the front door.

"Don't want to hurt the wood," Dawdi said.

The other boys moved out of the way, and Noah deftly slid the jack under the stove. He pumped the handle up and down, and the jack slowly rose, lifting the stove with it. Adam and Melvin supported the massive stove on either side to ensure it wouldn't tip, and Noah slowly wheeled the jack with the stove to the door.

The boys followed Noah outside with Mandy and Sparky close behind. At the edge of the porch, Noah lowered the jack and slid it out from under the stove. Dawdi stood back. As much as he liked to do things himself, he was an eighty-five-year-old man who was wise enough to know he didn't want to strain his back.

The seven young men surrounded the stove and lifted it from the porch to the ground. Noah pumped up his jack again and pulled the stove over the grass to his flatbed wagon parked in front of Mammi and Dawdi's house. Again the team of seven was needed to lift the stove into the wagon. This was an amazing feat. That stove had to weigh at least eight hundred pounds. All the boys looked strong, but Noah was by far the most muscular, with arms as solid as good timber. In the tepid air of early September, sweat dripped down his face.

Once the stove sat in the middle of the wagon bed, Noah wasted no time. He pulled a pile of ropes from a box near the wagon seat and started securing the stove to the wagon. No wonder Noah had brought a team of horses. It would take quite a bit to get that thing down the hill.

With a bandanna, Freeman mopped up the moisture from his face. "What will you do with the old stove?"

"Noah's going to sell it," Dawdi said, overseeing proceedings from the porch with Mandy and Mammi.

Noah tied the stove to the wagon as if he'd done such a thing a thousand times. "If nobody wants it, I'll sell it for scrap."

Davy ran back into the house and emerged with the stovepipe. Noah secured it onto his wagon with his seemingly endless supply of rope.

"He's got gute hands for it, don't he?" Dawdi said as they watched Noah work.

"Noah's a gute boy," Mammi said, paying no attention to what Noah was doing. She nudged Mandy with her elbow. "What do you think of Davy? His ears stick out a bit, but he has beautiful long eyelashes."

Mandy gazed with concern as Noah tied knot after knot. Was he making them tight enough? Would the stove slide off the wagon the minute it got going down the hill? What man was ever careful about such things?

"Cum, everybody," Mammi said. "Let's have some of Mandy's pie."

The boys began to file into the house. Unable to resist, Mandy leaped off the porch, dodged Adam and Melvin coming the other way, and went to Noah's wagon. Starting at one corner, she tugged on the ropes and fingered each of Noah's knots to make sure they would hold. The ropes seemed to stretch sufficiently taut to hold the stove in place, and she wouldn't have been able to loosen those knots even if she had twenty fingers on each hand.

Noah seemed to sneak up beside her. "Checking to see if I did it right?" he said as he secured one last knot. There was more of exasperation in his voice than resentment.

"Just making sure," she said, lifting her chin slightly so he knew he couldn't intimidate her. So he knew there was at least one person who wasn't fooled by his big muscles and clever mind. "I don't know you very well. You might be careless."

Mandy glanced behind her. No one would hear their conversation. Everyone else was probably sitting at the table with their forks in the air, eagerly awaiting a slice of pie.

Noah's brows inched closer together. "You knew everything about me yesterday. Maybe you think a boy who treats girls like dirt is incapable of doing anything right."

She caught her breath when she heard her own words tossed back into her face. "You don't have to confess your sins to me. I'm already fully aware of what kind of boy you are."

He pinned her with a piercing gaze. "Are you?" he said, scorn dripping from his tone.

"You told me to get my hinnerdale off your porch."

He folded his arms. "You wouldn't leave."

"You insulted my freckles."

He rested his hand on the wagon and leaned closer. She leaned away. "I like freckles," he said. "It's your nose in my business I don't like."

They scowled at each other until Noah seemed to give up on the conversation. He gave the nearest rope one last tug and turned his back on Mandy. "You can be as indignant as you want," he said, "but I'm going to have another piece of that pie. The girl who made it has a sharp tongue, but her pies are sweeter than honey."

* * *

After her fourth morning of bran flakes, Mandy repented of ever thinking an unkind thought about Mammi's Eggs Benedict. At this point, she would have been content with a nice pot of boiling water just to break up the monotony. Last Friday, the new stove had arrived half an hour after Noah and the other boys had hauled the old one out of the house, but Noah had taken one look at it and insisted the deliverymen put it back on the truck. Dawdi had ordered a stove that couldn't be converted to run on liquid propane gas, so another one had to be ordered. No one in the Amish community would have allowed a delivery on the Sabbath, and today was Labor Day, so the stove would supposedly be delivered tomorrow after a very long weekend of cold cereal for every breakfast, bread and cheese at every supper, and tuna salad with pickles for dinner.

After milking and other chores, Mandy borrowed Dawdi's buggy and made a beeline for Kristina's house. Surely Kristina had a working stove and food in her fridge. Mandy thought she might die for a warm cup of cocoa with marshmallows floating on top or even a piece of slightly warm toast.

Hopefully Kristina would offer to feed her something. Anything. Especially if it hovered above the temperature of lukewarm milk.

Noah had stayed after the other boys had left, patching the hole in the roof where the stovepipe had been. Mandy's tongue had gone dry when she had overheard Dawdi asking Noah to reshingle the entire roof once he had installed the new stove. She was only going to be on Huckleberry Hill for a month. Would she have to endure Noah's presence for the entire visit?

At least he wouldn't be in the house making a pest of himself. She could easily ignore him altogether even if he clomped around on the roof all day. At least she wouldn't have to endure the painful silences that prevailed when he was in the same room with her.

Mandy turned the horse down the road to Kristina's house. She planned on spending the entire day with Kristina, offering her comfort and talking her out of ever trying to get back with Noah. Kristina and Mandy had grown up together in Charm and had been best friends for as long as Mandy could remember. Kristina's dat had bought a piece of land at a gute price and moved his family to Bonduel last year. Mandy had cried so hard when she said good-bye that her eyes had stung for days afterward. She and Kristina wrote every week and told each other the secrets they never shared with anyone else.

Mandy loved Kristina, even if she was a bit melodramatic at times. To Kristina, life was either absolutely, gloriously marvelous or dismally, depressingly horrible, with no emotions existing between the two extremes. Dat said Kristina was needy. Mandy was just happy to be needed.

As she got closer to Kristina's house, Mandy spied her friend ambling down the road barefoot with a sunflower dangling from her fingers. Mandy reined in the horse as she reached Kristina's side. Kristina paused and slumped her shoulders.

"What are you doing?" Mandy said.

Kristina sighed mournfully. "Just taking a stroll and thinking about the boy I love."

"Really, Krissy. You've got to stop. He's not worth the aggravation."

Kristina slid open the door, jumped inside the buggy, and pulled her phone from her apron pocket. "He won't answer my texts. I don't know what I'll do."

"How do you even get service out here?"

"They just put in a new cell phone tower in February. Almost everybody gets service now." She punched a few buttons on her phone before her demeanor altered almost immediately and she acted as if she'd just been invited to a surprise birthday party. "Oh, Mandy. I'm so glad you've come. We've got to get to Coblentz's pasture immediately." She shut the door and tapped impatiently on the dashboard. "Hurry. I don't want to miss him."

Mandy didn't even so much as jiggle the reins. "What is going on?"

Kristina was so eager, she seemed to bounce like a ball. "Noah. I found out he's helping Jethro Coblentz fix his corn picker. If we hurry, we can spy on him from behind the trees by the river."

Mandy's eyebrows nearly flew off her forehead. "You're not serious."

"I am too." She waved her hand in the direction of the horse. "Go, Mandy. I don't want to miss him."

Surprise rendered her incapable of movement. "Krissy, thirteen-year-olds spy on boys, not nineteen-year-olds. It's childish."

Kristina stuck out her bottom lip. "Dori Rose and me spied on Noah all summer, whenever he was out working someone's field or raising a barn or fixing a water pump." No one could whine at quite the pitch Kristina achieved. "Come on, Mandy. I want to see him. He's so handsome. I just want a peek."

"All summer? But why would you spy on him when you were courting and could have seen him anytime you wanted?"

Kristina suddenly became very interested in her finger-nails. "I just like looking at him. You understand, don't you, Mandy? You've seen him. You know how handsome he is."

Jah, she knew how handsome he was. She also knew how disagreeable he was. "I don't want to spy on Noah Mischler. You need to put him out of your mind, Krissy. He's no gute."

Tears pooled in Kristina's eyes. Big, plump tears that

splashed onto her cheeks and made her look utterly pathetic. "I love him. I want to see him again. You've never been in love. You don't know how it feels."

"That's true," she admitted. She might have had her eye on a boy or two back home, but romance was completely foreign to her.

Kristina sniffed and stuttered violently. "There's no harm in sneaking a look. He never sees us."

In truth, as reluctant as she was, Mandy would do anything to stop Kristina's tears. She hated to see her friend so unhappy, especially when she had the means of transportation to take Kristina where her heart wanted to go. Who was she to stand in the way of love?

Mandy heaved a sigh. "Okay. I'll take you."

Kristina clapped her hands and exploded into a smile. All was right with the world again.

Mandy raised her voice to be heard above Kristina's squeals of delight. "But I refuse to stay for longer than five minutes. Do you understand? Five minutes is all I'm giving you."

Nothing could dampen Kristina's mood. "Okay, five minutes. That's all I need."

Kristina pointed Mandy in the direction they needed to go. When they approached Coblentz's pasture, they couldn't just stop the buggy next to the field and stare at Noah from ten feet away. Oh no. Kristina knew a secluded trail near the river where they parked the buggy and then hiked ten minutes through the thick woods. Kristina giggled like a schoolgirl as they came to the edge of the woods about a hundred feet from the pasture.

To their left, Mandy could hear the river slapping against the boulders in its path. It ran alongside Coblentz's cornfields for nearly a mile. Three people stood in the field looking at the idle corn picker. Mandy and Kristina were close enough to hear muffled voices. Before Mandy got a good look at any of them, Kristina grabbed her arm and pulled her behind a maple tree at the water's edge.

"Stay behind the tree," Kristina said, giggling as if she couldn't stop herself. She was a little too excited about this whole spying thing. Did she really adore Noah that much? "We don't want them to see us."

Kristina leaned her head around the trunk to take a peek, gasped, and quickly pulled back. "He's over there," she whispered breathlessly. Mandy had to strain to hear her. The river roared not five feet away. "He's with Alvin and Jethro."

Mandy planted herself firmly behind the tree. Let Kristina look if she wanted to. She'd be mortified if anyone discovered her spying on Noah Mischler. Maybe she should hike back the way they'd come and wait in the buggy.

Kristina seemed to be having the time of her life. She peeked around the tree again. "He's holding up one side so Jethro can look at it. Oh, he's so strong. Look at those muscles." She turned to glance at Mandy and motioned for her to lean in. "Come on, Mandy. You've got to see his muscles."

Growing more uncomfortable by the minute, Mandy folded her arms and took a step back, being careful not to lose her footing on the riverbank. She'd already seen Noah's muscles when he'd hefted that stove onto his wagon. She didn't need to see his muscles ever again.

Why had she let Kristina talk her into this? It was too childish.

Kristina's eyes flashed with mischief. She puckered her lips and cupped her hands around her mouth. "Hoo hoo," she called, making her voice sound like some strange bird trying to lay a ten-pound egg.

Mandy grabbed her arm and yanked her back. "What are you doing?" she hissed. "We don't want them to see us."

It seemed Kristina would giggle herself to death. "I'm just having a little fun. Dori Rose and I made all sorts of noises when we spied on Noah. Dori does a very good dog."

Mandy had nearly reached the end of her rope. "This is ridiculous."

"Sometimes Noah would hear us and look our way, but we were too fast for him. He'd always be so confused." Kristina burst into another fit of giggles. Had she truly enjoyed teasing her boyfriend like that?

Mandy furrowed her brows and whispered, "It sounds like a very strange courtship."

Giggling harder, Kristina poked her head from behind the tree again and made another bird noise. An anemic bird.

Kristina gasped. "He's coming over here!" She turned abruptly, crashed into Mandy, and sent her flying head over heels into the river.

She heard Kristina scream as she tumbled into the water. It wasn't deep, probably four feet, but she went under before, coughing and gasping, she righted herself and found the bottom with her toes. Stunned and soaking wet, she anchored her feet on the pebbly surface below and stood. The chilly water came to just below her shoulders.

"Are you okay?" Kristina yelled from the bank. She didn't need to be so loud. She was only five feet away. "I didn't mean to push you in."

Mandy glanced in the direction of the cornfield. Noah, Jethro, and Alvin were still working on the picker, seemingly oblivious to Mandy's embarrassing accident. She sighed in relief even as she tried to drift downriver a little so they wouldn't see her.

She was going to get out of this water and go home. She'd never indulge Kristina in such foolishness again.

Her black bonnet floated lazily downstream, just out of reach. She tiptoed through the silt and pebbles in hopes of snagging the bonnet before it got caught up in the swift current. Her fingertips touched it before it bobbed away from her again. She redoubled her efforts, finding purchase on a sturdy boulder beneath her feet, but the boulder proved more slippery than she expected. When she pushed off from it and lunged at her bonnet, her feet slipped out from underneath her and she went below the surface once again, only this time, the current caught her and dragged her into faster-moving, deeper water. She couldn't touch the bottom anymore, and the water tossed her around like a beach ball in the tide at the lake.

Flailing her arms, she managed to catapult herself to the surface. "Help!" she screamed. The river pulled her under again, shoving her body against boulders on one bank and then the other. She reached out for something, anything to hold fast to. She clawed at rocks and overhanging bushes, but she was moving too fast to take hold of anything.

Almost as if in a dream, she heard Kristina screaming hysterically on the bank, now several yards upriver. The water pushed her farther and farther away from help.

She was going to drown in the deerich pursuit of Noah Mischler. If she got out of this alive, Kristina would get a gute scolding.

Chapter Four

Noah ground his teeth together. The irritating, childish spying started out like it always did. It wasn't easy to ignore. Kristina liked to sneak up on him with all the subtlety of a charging bull. He could always hear her coming from about a mile away.

Noah took a deep breath. He must learn to relax. His jaw would crack if he clenched it any tighter.

At least Kristina proved predictable. She wanted him to see her, even while she pretended to want to hide. Before, if he didn't look her way, she and her giggly friends would start making noises, hoping he'd look up and catch a glimpse of them. *Ach*, but he found it irritating. Why wouldn't that girl just leave him alone?

He was clenching his jaw again.

If Kristina insisted on her infatuation much longer, he wouldn't have any teeth left.

It galled him that when a pretty girl had shown up at his house four days ago, she had come to give him a lecture about being nice. He'd bent over backward to be nice to Kristina. But there was only so much a boy could take before he had to put a stop to the nonsense. If Mandy Helmuth was so willing to believe the tales of a silly girl like Kristina Beachy, then she didn't deserve to know the truth.

Kristina stood near the river behind a tall maple, but he couldn't tell if she had anybody with her. Out of the corner of his eye, he saw her peek her head out from behind the tree and pull it back again, as if appearing and disappearing would spark his interest.

When he paid no heed to that, she hooted like an owl. Jethro and Alvin Coblentz turned their heads in the direction of the sound, but Noah didn't even glance up. Let Kristina chirp, bark, howl, or oink all day long. He wasn't going to give her the satisfaction of looking.

Trying to be oblivious to all the birds dying behind that maple tree over there, he unclamped his jaw and got on his hands and knees to inspect the corn picker.

"Your axle's bent," he told Jethro. "You must have gone over a mighty big bump in the road."

Jethro, a sturdy, weathered Amishman of fifty-five, stroked his hand down the length of his beard. Jethro was missing both his middle and ring fingers just above the knuckles. Corn pickers tended to jam up, and farmers all too often were tempted to clear the machinery by hand. More than one corn farmer had lost a finger to the gathering chains of the picker.

"I guess I used it too rough," Alvin said. Alvin was Jethro's son, probably ten years Noah's senior. Alvin and Jethro farmed the land together, but Alvin tended to be careless with his equipment. The Coblentzes summoned Noah to their farm on a regular basis to fix something—not that he was complaining. He always needed the work.

Noah paused to listen. The screech owls had stopped. Maybe Kristina had given up early. "Your tires could use more air too."

The screaming made the hair on the back of his neck stand up. Kristina had never out-and-out screamed to get his attention before. She'd never charged at him like a wild woman either, but there she was, screaming hysterically and sprinting out of the woods as if she were fleeing from a forest beast. Noah leaped to his feet. Had she seen a bear?

"Noah, Noah. Mandy fell in the river. She's drowning!"

Noah didn't even stop to ask just how Kristina's pretty friend had happened to fall into the river. He raced to the maple tree with Kristina, Alvin and Jethro close behind. He got to the bank and focused his eyes downriver. "I don't see her."

Kristina sobbed uncontrollably. "She's under . . . she's drowned . . . I pushed her."

Knowing he'd get no help from Kristina, Noah shoved his hand into his pocket, pulled out his phone, and slapped it into Jethro's hand. "Can you call the police?" He pointed at Kristina, whose face was white as a newly washed sheet. "Find a place to sit down, Kristina. I'll go downriver and see if I can see her."

"I'm coming too," Alvin said.

Noah nodded. Without waiting for Alvin to keep up, he raced along the bank, keeping his gaze glued to the water for any sign of Mandy Helmuth. Lord willing, she had dressed in something bright today that he could easily spot. Did she know how to swim? Would she know to grab onto a rock or an overhanging branch to pull herself out?

Dear Heavenly Father, he prayed, *please spare her life and guide me to her.*

Noah put a lot of faith in prayer, even when he hadn't always felt God's answers in his life.

With his long legs and athletic stride, he soon outpaced Alvin, who was a little older and a lot thicker around the middle. Noah ran a few yards, paused to study the river, then sprinted farther downstream and paused again. He hoped she'd found something to grab on to. He couldn't win a race with the swift current.

In his haste, he almost missed her. By the grace of God, he caught a glimpse of her mint-green sleeve as she stuck her arm out of the water and clutched a boulder near the opposite bank of the river. Her hair splayed around her shoulders in an unruly tangle, her *kapp* and the pins that secured it long gone in the swirling waves. The boulder was tall and slick. She wouldn't be able to hold on indefinitely.

"Mandy," he yelled. "Don't move." She made no indication that she had heard him. He didn't wait to find out. Without hesitation, he stomped into the water twenty feet upstream.

Alvin, still several paces behind him, called out. "Don't go in."

"I'm okay. Stay where you are."

When Noah had ventured deep enough into the water, he leveraged his boots on the bottom, pushed with all his might, and plunged into the middle of the river. Letting the current carry him downstream, he paddled in the direction of the other bank, pushing the water behind him with all the force of his work-hardened arms. Gute thing he was accustomed to heavy lifting. It took all his strength to fight the powerful pull of the river.

Before the water could sweep him away, he caught hold of Mandy's boulder. He inched his way around it until he stood between Mandy and the rushing water. She had her back to him, hugging the boulder like a best friend.

"Are you okay?" he yelled above the roar of water.

Her teeth chattered and her eyes were closed, but she nodded.

The oncoming, relentless water pushed him into her, pressing her between him and the boulder. Anchoring his hands on either side of her body, he pushed backward. He'd rather not crush her just when they were so close to getting out.

"Can you push away a little? I'm going to put my arm around you."

"I'll lose my grip," she said.

"Just push away. I won't let you go. I'm strong enough."

"I know you are," she said, still not letting go. She turned her head to look at him. "I'm afraid."

"Do you trust me?" It was a dumb question. Of course she didn't trust him. She despised him.

She studied his face for a moment before releasing her grip on the boulder and grabbing his wrist. "I trust you," she said breathlessly.

He didn't expect the warmth that spread to fill every space in his chest. She trusted him. Gute thing. Maybe she wouldn't jump out of her skin when he snaked his arm around her waist.

"Put your arms around my neck and don't let go," he said, trying to make his voice reassuring. He didn't have much experience coddling girls. To Mandy, he probably sounded harsh and pushy.

Holding her breath, she turned, lunged at him, and slapped her arms around his neck.

"Not quite so tight. I need to be able to breathe."

She loosened her grip as he looped one arm around her waist and held on. He wasn't going to lose her to the river. Turning toward the near shore, he pushed the water behind him, taking wide strokes with his free hand, fighting against the current trying to pull them farther into the river. He kicked his legs, made extra heavy by the boots still on his feet. Should he have taken them off? When he had jumped in, he had thought it better to go in with the boots and avoid cutting his feet on the sharp rocks at the bottom. Now they felt like two anvils tied to his ankles.

"Kick your feet," he yelled. If she could help him just a little, it would be enough.

She realized what he needed from her, and she began to

kick her feet back and forth. To his surprise, her effort helped quite a bit.

His arms and legs were on fire, but he refused to let the pain overcome him. He grunted as he pulled strength from deep within his gut and struggled toward the bank.

Just as his arms began to shake, his foot found a hold as they finally reached shallow water. Gulping in air, he fought for every step as he pulled himself and Mandy out of the river.

He was glad he had his boots. The rocks were sharp, and he could plant his feet firmly without being injured or losing his balance.

His ragged breathing matched Mandy's as he half dragged, half carried her away from the water. He found a boulder at the river's edge where they could both sit.

Alvin stood on the opposite bank. "Are you okay?"

Too breathless to speak, Noah nodded and raised his hand as if he were asking the teacher a question. That's all he had strength for.

"I'll go back and tell them you got her out," Alvin called.

Noah feebly raised his hand again. He was too spent to lift it higher than his head. Hopefully Alvin could interpret the gesture as a sign of agreement.

They sat on the hard boulder, unable to speak until they had both taken in their fill of air.

He finally found the energy to turn his head and look at her. Her left cheek was lightly scraped where she had pressed it against the boulder, and her bottom lip oozed blood, but other than that, it didn't look as if she were badly injured.

He took a soaking-wet handkerchief from his soaking-wet pocket and handed it to her. "Your mouth," he said.

She hesitated for a split second before taking the handkerchief and dabbing it against her lip. "Denki."

"Are you hurt anywhere else?"

She brushed the side of her face with her hand, then squeezed out some of the water from her dripping hair. "My knee crashed into something hard under the water. Probably a rock. It's a little sore, but not bad."

"Can you walk?" he asked, eyeing her carefully. She seemed dazed, maybe in shock. She'd almost drowned. He'd be surprised if she wasn't in shock.

She tried to push herself from the boulder. "I have to get across the river to my buggy."

"Maybe we should sit here for another minute."

"I should probably get my buggy." She wouldn't meet his eye, as if she were embarrassed, maybe about falling into the river.

Okay, he could understand that. It was pretty hard to fall into a river if you were even a little coordinated. He wouldn't come right out and say it, but jah, she should be embarrassed.

She turned her face away and seemed to turn bright red. Was she blushing? Yep, she was definitely feeling the humiliation. "Is Kristina okay?" she said.

Noah leaned back, pressed his lips into a rigid line, and put two and two together. How dumb was he to not realize it sooner?

Mandy had been spying with Kristina.

His stomach felt as if he'd just swallowed a pound of lead. Even though he didn't like her very much, he had thought Felty Helmuth's granddaughter might have more sense than empty-headed Kristina Beachy.

He had been mistaken.

Mandy was a bossy busybody *and* just another silly girl who made a fool of herself by tormenting innocent boys. She'd been spying on him too, and somehow fallen in the river because of it.

She'd put not only her own life in danger, but his as well.

His gut clenched in disgust. Why wouldn't these girls leave him alone?

Was it too much to ask to be left in peace to live his life and take care of his dat?

"Come on," he said, standing abruptly. Without pausing to help her to her feet or to see if she followed, he hiked up the gentle incline to the stand of trees that ran alongside the river. "There's a footbridge just down from Coblentz's field where you can cross."

He looked back and watched as she carefully stood and tried to take a step on her shaky legs. He groaned inwardly. She wouldn't be able to manage one yard, let alone one mile. Immediately feeling guilty for not helping her the first time, he tromped back down the slope and offered his arm. Even if she was silly and thoughtless, she was a girl and she was hurt. His mother would have scolded him for forgetting his manners.

Pursing her lips doubtfully, she hesitated before hooking her arm around his. She took one step, and her knee buckled under her. Noah tightened his grip to keep her from falling.

"Maybe I hurt my knee worse than I thought," she said, trying to hobble up the slope on one leg. She winced every time she put weight on her injured knee.

They managed to make it to the top with a lot of leaning on her part and a lot of dragging on his part. He led her through the thin border of trees to a dirt road that ran alongside the river.

She let go of him and tilted her face toward the sun. She lifted her arms away from her body, probably hoping the breeze would dry her dress. They were both soaking wet.

Noah heard the wail of a siren across the river. "The police are here," he said.

"You called the police?"

"Jethro used my cell phone."

She frowned, no doubt remembering their argument about his cell phone. Well, her righteous indignation seemed a little foolish now, didn't it?

"You shouldn't have called the police."

Never mind. She'd probably been too busy making a tally of Noah's transgressions in her head to be grateful for his cell phone. "You almost drowned."

"But I didn't."

"Not for lack of trying," he said.

She got red in the face again. "I can't believe you called the police."

He felt a campfire roar to life inside him. She was more of a nuisance than Kristina. "Next time I'll let you drown."

She met his eyes, then looked away and seemed to come to rest even though she hadn't been moving. "I'm sorry."

"Are you?"

She raised her head and pinned him with a piercing gaze. Her eyes were the color of clear skies, but they flashed with all the intensity of a rolling thunderstorm. "I didn't mean to blame you like that. It's just that the humiliation is unbearable."

Her stare made him uncomfortable, as if he were discovering a deeper part of her that he didn't think existed.

"We should get back so the police know you're okay. They'll want to take you to the hospital."

Something fierce and sincere flared in her eyes. "Don't let them take me anywhere. I'm ashamed enough as it is."

"You should have them look at your knee."

She placed a hand on his arm. "Please. Don't let them. I just want to go home."

His arm seemed warmer where she touched him. He let it fall to his side and gave it a good shake. He turned away from those eyes and gave his head a good shake. He'd swallowed too much water.

Okay then. He'd send the police away. If she wanted her

leg to fall off in the comfort of her own home, then who was he to insist on anything different?

"Let's get back, then," he said. "Are you okay to walk? We'll go slow."

She nodded, took a step, and let out a little squeak as she lurched forward. Instinctively, he reached out to steady her. She took his hand and pursed her lips. "I think you'd better leave me here. I can't walk."

"You need a hospital."

"No hospital. I'm too embarrassed for a hospital. Don't let them take me to a hospital." She squeezed his hand. "Promise me."

He growled. How did she know that if she made him feel sorry for her, she could get him to agree to just about anything?

"I already said okay."

Her stubbornness might save her from a hospital visit, but it would serve her right if they had to amputate.

She tried to take another step and caught her breath.

He clenched his teeth. Dust. His teeth were bound to disintegrate to dust. "I'm going to have to carry you, you know."

"You don't know anything. I can manage."

He shook his head, folded his arms, and pretended to study her closely. "Nope. You can't manage."

"I'm going to sit and scoot all the way on my bottom," she said, with all the dignity she could muster.

He squeezed his lips together to keep from grinning at her stubborn independence. If she weren't so irritating in every way, she'd be sort of cute. "Much as I'd like to see that, you'd never make it, and you'd get slivers in places you don't want slivers." He shouldn't have said that. What would his mamm say?

Mandy's face glowed a bright shade of pink. "You just pulled me out of the river. You're as spent as I am."

"Nope, I'm not."

She took another step and nearly toppled over. He took hold of her wrist. She squinted as if trying to figure out an eighth-grade math problem and massaged a spot just above her eyebrow. "I'm the one who helps people. I don't like to be helped. *Ach.* I suppose I'll have to let you carry me."

"It's not as bad as all that," he said.

"But I don't like you."

If she didn't like him, then she should quit spying on him. He frowned. "I don't like you either, but I'm not asking for your hand in marriage. We've got to get you back to the buggy, and this is the only way I can think to do it unless you want them to bring in a stretcher and wheel you straight to the hospital."

"No hospital," she said, clutching a long strand of her hair.

"Okay then." In one swift movement, he scooped her into his arms, almost dropping her when her momentum sent her tumbling backward. She weighed less than a sack of flour. She caught her breath and threw her arms around his neck.

"I know you dislike me," she said, "but try not to kill me."

He merely grunted and frowned harder. Even for as low an opinion as she had of him, she should know he would make sure she came to no harm. He worked hard to be a credit to the mamm who raised him.

It wasn't far, and even after his exertion in the river, Noah found it relatively easy to carry her. She didn't weigh much, and he was used to hefting bales of hay.

She must have been exhausted. Her eyes fluttered, and even though she couldn't stand the sight of him, she rested her head against his chest, her warm cheek against his wet shirt.

He clenched his teeth as a strange longing attacked him like a punch to the gut. Mandy Helmuth felt oddly comfortable in his arms, like a warm blanket on a frosty evening or a mug of Mamm's hot wassail with cinnamon sprinkled on top.

He didn't like the feeling. Not one little bit.

So he talked himself out of it.

He'd just saved her life, so of course he felt naturally protective of her, drawn to her even though she was as immature and irritating as Kristina Beachy. Fixing things gave him a great sense of accomplishment. That was what he was feeling, merely the satisfaction of knowing he'd helped someone out by keeping her from drowning. Besides, she was a pretty girl. He'd have to be blind not to notice that.

If only she were as pretty on the inside.

He rejoiced when, after a long ten minutes, he crossed over the bridge. The Coblentz's corn grew tall to his left and the river flowed to his right. Once he'd cleared the row of cornstalks, Jethro, Alvin, Kristina, and the flashing police car came into view. They had their backs to Noah, looking downriver.

Mandy lifted her head. "You can put me down now."

"You suddenly found the strength to walk?"

"Kristina will have a heart attack if she sees me in your arms."

"We wouldn't want to do anything to hurt Kristina's feelings," he said dryly.

He expected her to scowl at him. Instead she furrowed her brow and frowned.

He set her on her feet, and she limped unsteadily toward the police car, wincing with every movement. Maybe he should insist she see a doctor.

The minute that thought came into his head, he shoved it away. He'd promised no hospital. Besides, he knew how futile it was to try to persuade someone to do what she didn't want to do. It wasn't his job to worry himself sick about her.

Kristina glanced in their direction. "Mandy," she squealed. "You're alive!" With arms outspread, she charged at Mandy and nearly knocked her over. Noah reached out to steady Mandy but thought better of it. She didn't want his help.

Kristina worked herself into hysteria in a matter of seconds. "I didn't mean to push you in. I was just so excited and I—"

Mandy patted Kristina's cheek. "It's all right. I'm okay."

Kristina abruptly released Mandy and threw her arms around Noah before he had a chance to defend himself. "Noah. You are my hero. I knew you could save her. You could lift a truck with those muscles of yours."

Noah raised his hands as if in surrender. Kristina might be hanging around his neck like a snake but he refused to touch her. And she didn't fool him. She was using Mandy's mishap as an excuse to get close to him. It was just another one of her tricks.

"Krissy," Mandy snapped. "Let go and leave Noah alone."

Kristina's suction-cup grip slackened, but she didn't back away.

"Kristina Beachy, let go this minute."

Kristina slid her arms from Noah's neck. Looking at Mandy with wide eyes, she twitched her lips and giggled halfheartedly. Mandy glared at her as if she'd just broken all the rules of the Ordnung.

Kristina stuck out her bottom lip. "You said you weren't mad at me for pushing you in the river."

Mandy's expression remained unyielding. "I'm not mad at you for the river," she said, pointing an accusing finger at Kristina. "You know why I'm mad."

Kristina batted her eyes innocently. "What? What are you mad about? I never did nothing wrong."

Mandy growled, took Kristina by the elbow, and practically shoved her in the direction of the woods. "We'll talk about it later. I'm taking you home." With Kristina in tow, Mandy stalked into the woods with a pronounced limp, like an old woman with two broken legs. She didn't even look at the policeman eyeing her curiously as she passed.

Kristina shuffled her feet as best she could while Mandy tugged on her arm and refused to let go.

"Don't you even believe in forgiveness?" Noah heard Kristina whine as she and Mandy disappeared into the thicket. "I guess my best friend has forgotten about forgiveness. If you don't forgive others, God won't forgive you."

Noah practically exploded with gratitude. It was about time someone put that girl in her place. He just hadn't expected it to be her equally silly and childish best friend.

The front door squeaked when Noah opened it. He'd have to take care of that later. At least a squeaky hinge was an easy fix. Jethro's picker was a different story altogether. Noah had ordered a new axle from Green Bay, but it wouldn't be here for at least a week. In the meantime, he'd jerry-rigged a couple of metal pipes and some baling wire so the Coblentzes would at least be able to start getting the corn in.

His Polish hound dog Chester came padding down the hall and greeted Noah with a wet tongue. "Any trouble while I was away?" Noah paused to stroke his dog's ears before hanging his hat on the hook near the door. It wouldn't be there long. He'd promised Tyler Yoder he'd be by at noon to help install a new LP gas fridge.

"Dat," he called.

No answer. Still asleep, no doubt. He'd had a rough night last night. Noah massaged his shoulder. Dat wasn't the only one who'd had a rough night.

Not to mention Noah's rough morning. He'd jumped into the river and swam until he thought his lungs would explode, pulled Mandy Helmuth out of the water, and hauled her in his arms for over a mile. That was a strain on even his strong frame.

Noah tromped into his room and shut the door. He usually avoided being at home during the day, but he needed a change of clothes. His trousers and boots were still damp from the river, and Tyler and Beth wouldn't appreciate his soggy feet on their new kitchen floor. Maybe he should do a batch of laundry before he left. Tyler didn't expect him for another hour.

He snatched the other pair of dirty work trousers from his basket and ventured into Dat's room for more laundry. Dat lay in bed on his side, in the exact same position Noah had left him last night. It looked like he hadn't moved a muscle. Noah picked up a pair of Dat's trousers from the floor and a navy blue shirt from the foot of the bed.

Dat stirred and rolled onto his back. Groaning, he laid his arm across his eyes to guard against the dim light filtering through the forest-green curtains in his bedroom.

A sharp knife twisted in Noah's gut. His dat was a mere scrap of the gute and strong man he once had been. Instead of letting Jesus take his pain, Dat had allowed his grief to bury him. When he could have opened his heart to the love of God and his family, he had instead turned to the bottom of a bottle for comfort.

Noah hated seeing Dat like this, beaten down, broken, a slave to his addictions, a man with no strength left to fight. The pity gave way to momentary resentment. Why wouldn't Dat stop? Because of him, Noah had lost everything important in his life.

Trust in the Lord with all thine heart and lean not unto thine own understanding.

"How do you feel, Dat?" Noah asked.

Dat lifted his arm long enough to take a good look at Noah, then he lowered it as if he'd lost the strength to hold it up any longer. "Like maybe I put up a fight last night?" he whispered.

Noah sighed in resignation. "Jah."

Dat's voice cracked. Because his arm rested over his eyes, Noah couldn't see the tears in Dat's eyes, but he knew they were there. "I'm sorry, son."

"Okay," Noah said, with no desire to make Dat feel worse than he already did. Dat's remorse overwhelmed him every morning but didn't stop him from drowning his sorrows in another bottle almost every night. "Do you want me to make you something to eat?"

"What time is it?" Dat said, moaning as if it hurt to blink.

"Eleven."

"Felty's coming at one."

Without fail, except when he was sick, Felty Helmuth came every Monday to eat lunch with Dat. By one o'clock, Dat was usually able to pull himself together and look almost normal. Dat looked forward to Felty's visits all week. Felty's concern hadn't slacked off as the years had passed, and he was one of the few people Dat would even let in the house anymore. It baffled Noah that Felty and Mandy were even related. He supposed that every family tree had a bad apple or two.

"Maybe a half a sandwich to tide you over?" Noah said.

"Jah, okay."

Noah gathered up the rest of his dat's clothes while his dat eased out of bed and shuffled to the bathroom, cradling his head in his hands.

The house was too tiny for a washroom, so Noah had set up the washer in his already small bedroom. While he filled the wringer washer, he could hear his dat through the thin walls heaving the poison out of his stomach. Noah turned on the machine to drown out the sound. He'd rigged up a compressor to run the washer and the wringer, so washing clothes was as simple and fast as turning on an oven. Mostly.

He closed his eyes and let the loud and steady rhythm of the machine calm him. Nobody but the bishop knew how bad things had gotten with Dat. Lord willing, nobody else would ever find out. Even Felty seemed oblivious to the worst. As long as Dat didn't show his face in the community, Noah could protect the secret.

Except for the rare gatherings he had attended this summer and the times when he was out trying to earn enough money for him and Dat to live on, Noah stayed at home and did his best to keep his Dat out of mischief. He'd rather keep his family's shame all to himself.

Noah lifted his arm up and down a couple of times to work out the stiffness. Gute thing the bruise was covered by his sleeve. He wouldn't be able to keep any secrets if the people at church saw a purple-and-blue mark the size of his hand.

In the kitchen, he grabbed a loaf of bread and a can of tuna from the cupboard. Would Dat be able to stomach tuna with a hangover? It would have to do. There was nothing else to eat. When Tyler Yoder paid him for working on the fridge later today, he would get some groceries. Maybe even splurge on a pie. Dat liked pie.

Too bad Dat hadn't gotten a piece of Mandy Helmuth's huckleberry pie. It was worth the trouble of actually having to be near her. He'd brave a hundred of those superior, self-righteous looks of hers for another taste of that sweet pie.

He might even let her spy on him if she promised him a piece of *snitz* pie in return.

His lips curled upward. A piece of pie and a look at those freckles.

He had a thing for pie.

And freckles.

Chapter Five

There were only so many amends she could make without an oven.

Mandy clutched her plastic bowl, waited for Noah to knock on the door, and steeled herself to be alone, completely alone with Noah Mischler. She hadn't been able to decide whether to be alarmed or relieved when Dawdi and Mammi had gone into town this morning, leaving Mandy by herself to let Noah into the house so he could hook up the new oven.

On one hand, there would be some immensely uncomfortable silences while Noah fixed the oven and Mandy cleaned the floor. On the other hand, she would be able to apologize for the river incident yesterday without arousing Mammi and Dawdi's curiosity.

On the other hand, what if he yelled at her? Or called her names? Or refused to speak to her at all? He'd taken a dunking because of her foolishness. She fully expected him to scowl and tell her she should keep her superior hinnerdale out of the river. She disliked him wholeheartedly.

She tested her knee by limping around the kitchen a few times. It was stiff and painful. If she concentrated hard on hiding her limp, Noah might not even remember she'd injured herself. She couldn't hope that he'd forgotten the entire incident.

Then again, he had risked his life to save hers. Reluctant as she was, she could not let his kindness go unthanked. But she'd rather not feel Noah's wrath today. She already felt deerich, foolish, enough.

She opened the door before he even knocked because she saw him coming from the window, and she'd rather not prolong her humiliation.

He stood on the doorstep with his toolbox the size of a car, looking intimidating and suspicious at the same time. She'd seen him only yesterday, but he seemed to be better looking than ever. Maybe it was because his hair wasn't dripping with river water and his face wasn't smeared with mud. That might have something to do with it. He had his hat in one hand, and his light brown hair fell playfully across his forehead, as if the wind had blown it there. His brown, intelligent eyes gazed at her as if trying to decide if she were the enemy.

"Is the stove here?" he asked, getting right down to business. No doubt he wanted to visit with her as little as she wanted to visit with him.

"It came this morning."

With the bowl still in one hand, she moved away from the door so he could come into the house. He set his toolbox next to the fridge and stepped back to take a look at the new stove. He examined it for about ten seconds before bending over to retrieve something from his box. It seemed as if he were in a hurry.

He wanted to get out of here as much as she wanted to get him out.

But maybe she should give him her gift before he got too far into his work. He already thought she was a nuisance. Interrupting him would only annoy him more.

She cleared her throat, which had dried up like a stale piece of toast. "Before you . . ."

He glanced at her as if she'd just done a cartwheel in Mammi's kitchen.

She cleared her throat again and held out her bowl for his inspection. "I made this for you."

He stood and came closer, rubbing his fingers across his jaw and studying her bowl as if it might bite him. "What is it?"

"I mean . . . it's chocolate chip and . . . I didn't have an oven this morning, so I made you some cookie dough."

"Thank you," he said. It sounded like a question.

"I can bake them for you after you hook up the oven, or you can take them home and bake them yourself."

He took the bowl and eyed her with heightened distrust.

She tried to twitch her lips into a smile. It didn't work. "I want to thank you for pulling me out of the river yesterday."

His expression might have softened around the edges a bit. "Don't mention it."

"You saved my life," she said. "I was terrified and exhausted. I knew I couldn't hold on to that rock much longer. I'm very, very grateful."

"If you must thank someone, thank God. He showed me how to find you and gave me the wisdom to help."

"Oh, okay. I will. I mean, I already have."

He stared into her face with those dark eyes until she thought she might crack under the pressure of his intense gaze. "How is your leg?" he said.

"Oh . . . fine. It's stiff, but I can stand on it just fine." She wanted to smack herself upside the head. He could see for himself that she was standing on it just fine. "They're chocolate chip. The cookies are. Or the dough is."

"Denki. I like chocolate chip."

"Bake at 350 degrees for eight to ten minutes."

"Okay."

She swallowed the lump of pride stuck in her throat. "I have something to confess."

He pressed his lips together, and she could see the muscles twitch along his jawline. "Okay."

"The reason I fell into the river is that Kristina and I were spying on you."

His expression didn't change. "Were you?"

"She wanted to see you something wonderful. She is very much in love with you."

His jaw muscles twitched again.

Mandy wrung her hands in agitation. "Not that I'm blaming Kristina for my own folly, but I was trying to be a gute friend. I'm embarrassed that she was able to talk me into such a childish, stupid scheme. I hope you'll forgive me. It won't happen again."

"I just want Kristina to leave me alone," Noah said, with more patience than irritation in his voice. That surprised her a little.

"I know. I'm sorry. Krissy is my best friend, and I want her to be happy. The spying was with the best of intentions. I didn't know it would get out of hand like that."

He palmed the bowl in his hand as one corner of his mouth quirked upward. "You didn't expect the giggling and the bird noises."

In mortification, she felt herself blush down to her toes. "Please don't mention it. It was horrible."

"She doesn't do a very good birdcall."

"When she started chirping, I decided to abandon her and hike back to the buggy by myself. Unfortunately, she pushed me in the river before I could leave."

Amusement flickered in Noah's eyes. "She pushed you?"

"She thought for sure you would come over to see what all the noise was about, and she panicked."

"Believe me," he said, "it never mattered how loud she

and her friends got. I was smart enough to know it would be hazardous to my health to ever actually catch her spying."

Mandy thought her eyes might pop out of her head. "You knew?"

"I always know. I spent a lot of time outdoors this summer. She spied on me almost every day of the week. It almost made me want to take up quilting just so I could stay inside and out of sight."

Mandy clapped her hand over her mouth before a giggle could escape. She immediately felt disloyal to Kristina for wanting to laugh.

Kristina's broken heart was no laughing matter. But what had that girl been up to? Mandy felt a glimmer of sympathy for Noah. Was that why he'd broken up with Kristina? If what he said was true, Kristina had certainly made a pest of herself. He'd told Mandy on the first day they'd met that she didn't know the whole story.

She felt more ashamed than ever. Had she accused Noah unjustly?

Nibbling on her bottom lip, she thought of poor Kristina. Her best friend had certainly made a fool of herself over a boy she loved, but who was Mandy to judge Kristina's behavior? She had no idea how silly she would be if she were ever in love.

And Noah *had* broken up with Kristina using a text message. His behavior was still inexcusable.

But so was Kristina's. Kristina might have been in love, but there were still certain acceptable behaviors toward boys, and spying on them was not an acceptable behavior. She'd told Kristina as much yesterday when she took her home in the buggy, soaking wet and mad as a, well, as a wet hen.

Kristina was fortunate that Mandy had come to Bonduel. Mandy knew how to fix things, make everything all better. She could teach Kristina the right way to attract a boy and the proper way to behave herself. In the end, Noah might decide he wanted her back. Mandy could be very persuasive.

"I truly am sorry, but you have to understand that Kristina is not thinking rationally. What girl in love is ever rational?"

At the mention of love, Noah's expression hardened to stone. The trace of softness that she had seen only moments before disappeared. She should have left Kristina's feelings out of it. She'd ruined the entire apology.

He set the cookie dough on the cupboard next to the sink. "I'll get to work on the stove. Denki for the cookies."

"You're welcome," she mumbled. She didn't feel any better than before Noah had come. She shouldn't have bothered making cookie dough. If Noah Mischler's heart could have been touched, he would have shown it by now.

She immediately grabbed the broom from the closet and began to sweep the great room. She promised Mammi that the floors would be spick-and-span by the time she returned home. Mammi had invited another set of boys over for dessert and games tonight. The floors had to sparkle.

Noah knelt down, opened the oven door, and shined a flashlight into the interior. He took a wrench from his box and tightened something at the back of the inside. He looked as if he knew what he was doing, but Mandy couldn't be sure. She wasn't altogether certain that Noah wouldn't blow up the house if he carelessly connected a pipe to the wrong thing. If he knew she was checking up on him, he might take greater care in hooking up everything the right way.

Leaning on her broom, she knelt next to Noah's toolbox on her good knee. She peered into the oven where Noah worked, unable to see a whole lot since his body was in the way.

He sensed her presence and turned his head to frown at her. "Don't like the way I'm doing it?"

She felt a twinge of guilt for offending him, but better a

little discomfort than a house fire. "I don't want an explosion in Mammi's kitchen."

He sat up and turned off his flashlight. "You promised not to spy on me again."

His accusation struck her nearly mute. "Oh . . . I wasn't . . ."

He sighed and slumped his shoulders. He didn't seem angry with her. "You don't think I'll do a good enough job for your grandparents."

"I just . . . I don't know you. Why did Dawdi hire you? Do you have any experience or training?"

Fire flickered in his eyes, but he smothered it and growled in exasperation. "Here," he said, handing her his wrench. "Come on this side, and I'll let you do this part."

She shook her head. "I don't need to do that. I just want to be sure . . ."

"If you want something done right, you should do it yourself."

She dropped the wrench into his box and stood up. "No, no. I'm fine. Just do what you need to do."

He took hold of her hand and gently tugged her back down.

Okay. He had nice, rough work hands. So. What.

Cradling her hand in his, he retrieved the wrench from the toolbox and laid it in her palm. "This is a wrench," he said.

"Seven-sixteenths," she replied.

He raised his eyebrows and flashed a quick smile. Actually smiled. He had very nice teeth.

She held her breath and commanded her heart to quit skipping about like a drop of water on a hot skillet. Who cared about Noah's teeth? Nobody should care about anybody's teeth. She didn't even care if Noah had real teeth or false teeth. It was none of her business.

"How do you know what size this wrench is?" he said.

She spoke slowly and loudly to keep her voice from shaking. "It says so right on the side." She pointed.

He kept smiling while keeping hold of her hand as if she needed help lifting the wrench.

She casually pulled her hand away. "With five sisters and two brothers, I tag along after my dat quite a bit. I helped my dat build a washhouse for my mamm. And my twin brother Max fixes old bikes and scooters and sells them. I help him out sometimes. I like to fix things."

"Okay then," he said. He pulled the bottom drawer from the oven and set it aside. "Look under there and see if you can find the air shutter."

"Nae. I don't need to."

"Cum," he said. "A girl who builds washhouses should know how to convert an oven."

"Because I never know how many ovens I'm going to convert in my lifetime."

When he scooted away and made room for her, she could tell he wasn't going to take no for an answer. This was all her own doing. She'd have to follow through.

She lay on her side with her face toward the oven. Shining the flashlight, Noah crouched beside her and bent over until his head nearly touched the floor. "Do you see that shiny pipe sticking down from the top?"

"Here?" she said.

"Jah. Tighten it down about two turns, but don't force it."

She did as he instructed, trying to keep her hands steady. She certainly did not want to be the one to blow up Mammi's house.

"Gute," he said.

"Do you want to make sure I tightened it enough?"

"Nae. I trust you."

She turned and studied his face, only a few inches from hers. Was he being sarcastic since she'd made it clear that she didn't like him? She couldn't detect any scorn in his expression. He seemed content to let her do it.

"Now, do you see the red cap to your left? You need to remove it with a crescent wrench."

She sat up, pulled a crescent wrench from Noah's toolbox, and held it up for his inspection. "Three-quarters?"

His mouth twitched as if he were resisting a smile. "I like you a lot better than I did five minutes ago."

She laughed softly as a warm liquid pulsed through her veins. "I'll take that as a compliment."

He erupted into a smile. "Okay. If you feel good about that."

The room felt as if someone had turned on the new oven. If only Noah would stop looking at her that way, her temperature would definitely improve. She lay back down with the crescent wrench poised for action.

"You need to remove the red cap. Give it a couple of twists. It doesn't take much to get it off."

Mandy twisted the cap off, and Noah showed her how to invert the regulator to be ready for LP gas. When they finished underneath, Noah slid the oven away from the wall and stepped into the space behind it. "Now I need to put on the fittings and hook up the gas line."

He pulled the balsa wood cork from the hole in the wall he had drilled on Friday. "Could you hand me the Teflon tape," he said. "Do you know what that is?"

She found the yellow tape at the bottom level of the toolbox and passed it to him. "Of course I know what Teflon tape is."

He smirked. "Of course you do."

Mandy grinned with her whole face. "We both know how smart I am, but I'm wondering where you learned to install appliances. Did your dat teach you? Did you work on things together when you were growing up?"

Noah's eyes were trained on the tape while he tried to

open the tightly wrapped package, and he acted as if he hadn't heard her. She bent her head sideways to meet his eye. "Tell me about your dat. Is he as handy as you are?"

Noah laid his arm across the top of the oven and turned his face from her. He let out a laugh, but there was only bitterness in it. "For a minute, I thought you were being sincere."

She furrowed her brow. What had she said to make him suddenly so resentful? "I am sincere."

He clenched his jaw and glared at her. "I don't believe you."

"What . . . what did I say?"

Clutching the tape in his hand until his knuckles turned white, he said, "I'm so stupid. The cookie dough, the wrench, the apology. They're all just more of Kristina's tricks. She told you to ask about my dat, didn't she? Did the two of you think it would be funny to humiliate me? To get back at me for hurting Kristina's feelings?"

Mandy wasn't quite sure what she was being accused of so didn't know how to defend herself. "I don't want to get back at you."

"Then why are you dragging my dat into this?"

Even knowing how disagreeable he was, Noah's reaction nearly knocked Mandy over. They'd been getting along so well. She backed away and leaned against the counter near the sink. "I don't understand. Is something wrong with your dat?"

Her question seemed to heighten his agitation. "Why does everybody think something's wrong?"

"You don't have to jump down my throat for asking a simple question." Why was she trying to reason with him when what she wanted to do was wring his neck?

And why was he so touchy about his dat?

She crossed her arms over her chest to push down the hurt that threatened to bubble up. She didn't really care why

Noah had erupted like a volcano at the mention of his *fater*. As he had told her, it was none of her business.

Still, she felt the need to defend herself. "Do you really think I would hurt your feelings just to get back at you for what you did to Kristina?"

"What I did to Kristina?" He spat the words out of his mouth as if they were too sour to taste.

"Do you really think I'm that petty?"

Noah studied her face as if he were evaluating her sincerity. Taking a deep breath, he ran a hand across his eyes and seemed to wilt like a flower in the heat. "I'm sorry. It's wrong of me to talk to you like this." He turned his back on her, which in the small space wasn't an easy task. "I don't need any more help with the oven. I just want to be left alone."

She shouldn't have given him that cookie dough. Noah Mischler was so prickly, he didn't even deserve a chocolate chip, let alone a whole cookie.

Mandy picked up her broom, walked to the corner of the room farthest from Noah, and swept as if all the dirt in the world were in that one little space. The floor had never been so clean.

Even with the swish of the broom, Mandy could have heard a pin drop three rooms away. Noah was so quiet, she wondered if he was breathing. How she wished she were anywhere but here!

Thank the good Lord for Mammi. She and Dawdi blew into the house like a fresh spring breeze and dispelled the stale air hanging between Noah and Mandy.

Mammi carried two bulging grocery sacks, her knitting bag, and a wide smile. "Look what I found at the store," she said, ushering three obviously uneasy boys into the room. "More prospects."

All three tiptoed just inside the door and fingered the brims of their straw hats.

"I invited them for lunch," Mammi said. She must have been desperate to find Mandy a husband. She had resorted to bringing strays home.

Grateful for any diversion, even an awkward one, Mandy leaned her broom against the wall and stepped forward to greet her guests, showing ten times more enthusiasm than she felt.

She shook hands with the first young man, who couldn't have been more than thirteen years old. He stood nearly half a foot shorter than Mandy.

Mammi placed her grocery bags on the table and pointed to the young teenager. "This is Benjamin Hoover, and this," she said, hooking her elbow around the arm of the middle boy and eagerly pulling him forward, "is his brother Stephen."

Stephen blushed so hard that his fair, freckly face turned purple. He was definitely older and taller than Benjamin. Probably just the right age for a wife. Mandy breathed an inward sigh of relief. Benjamin was Stephen's tagalong, not a potential suitor. Thank goodness Mammi wasn't that desperate.

Benjamin poked his brother with his elbow. "Me and Stephen are visiting from Greenwood to help our *Onkel* Perry get the feed corn in yet."

The third boy scratched his chin absentmindedly and looked as if he'd rather be anywhere but here. He was short and stocky, with a neck as thick as his head.

"This is Buddy," Mammi said. Her enthusiasm seemed to slag a bit. Buddy, with his blank stare and faint body odor, didn't seem the cream of the crop.

"Nice to meet you," Buddy said, snorting as if he were clearing his sinuses from the inside.

Mandy pasted a smile on her face and reminded herself that at least she didn't have to be alone with Noah. "You too."

Mammi patted Stephen on the back and motioned to a

chair at the table. "I promised these boys lunch and a pot holder if they came to Huckleberry Hill to meet you."

Realizing she'd been holding her breath in mortification, Mandy sucked the air into her lungs and forced it out again. It wouldn't be a good idea to hyperventilate just now. Mammi's three recruits eyed her tentatively, as if she had a dread disease. Why else would her mammi be luring potential boyfriends to Huckleberry Hill?

Being careful not to limp, she strolled into the kitchen to show her visitors she wasn't lame and took a stack of plates from the cupboard. Noah didn't look at her, and she recoiled at the idea of even glancing his way. "Noah has almost finished the stove," Mandy said, barely even coughing at the mention of his name. "When it's ready, I'll grill some cheese sandwiches."

Mammi clapped her hands. "I'll make Eggs Benedict."

"But, Mammi, it's not breakfast."

"Ach, nobody cares about that," Mammi said, as cheerful as a daisy. "And I've been saving up the eggs."

Mandy relaxed her shoulders and even managed a wan smile. She had no worries about running off this fresh batch of boys. One or two bites of Mammi's Eggs Benedict should do it.

"Hey, I know you," Buddy said, maneuvering his large frame around Stephen and Benjamin and pointing to Noah. "You and your dat laid the wood floor at our house."

Noah's dark expression descended even deeper into shadow. "We did?"

Buddy propped his elbows on the stove and leaned in for a better look. "It had to be eight or nine years ago. You were just a young teenager. Your dad brought you along and nobody's ever laid a tighter floor."

Noah fidgeted uncomfortably, glancing back and forth between Buddy and the roll of tape in his hands. "I recognize you. We did your house in Oconto."

"That's right," Buddy said. "There's nobody better with wood than your dad. How's he been?"

Noah didn't take his eyes from the yellow tape. "Fine. He's fine."

Buddy loudly cleared his sinuses again. "I understood he wasn't doing so good."

"Dat is gute. He has a woodworking shop behind our house." Was it her imagination, or had Noah turned deathly pale in a matter of seconds? He seemed uncharacteristically vulnerable, like a little boy afraid of the dark.

Buddy swiped his finger at a piece of lint on the stovetop. "I heard that after what happened to your sister he—"

"Buddy," Mandy interjected. She hadn't meant to be quite so loud, but at least she'd gotten everyone's attention. "I want to know more about you."

Buddy shifted his weight so that he was still leaning on the new stove, but he faced her and puckered his lips into a passable smile. He still probably suspected she had leprosy or something. "Well, what do you want to know?"

Her mind raced for an interesting topic of conversation. Anything to divert his attention from Noah, who looked as if he might pass out any second now. "I didn't know there was an Amish community in Oconto. How many families are in your district?"

Buddy twisted his wrist and waved his hand around. "There ain't any Amish folks I know of."

"Your family's without *gmayna*?" Dawdi chimed in, glancing at Noah and trying to help the conversation along.

Buddy pushed away from the stove and stood up straight. He folded his arms and looked at Dawdi. "Well, I ain't Amish. I'm a Mennonite. We've got a small congregation in Oconto, not far from the lake."

"Oh," Mammi said, twisting her lips into a crooked line. Nobody but Mandy and Dawdi would recognize that Mammi's feathers were ruffled by this news. If she'd been a chicken, no doubt she would have puffed up like a beach ball.

Buddy wore the traditional shirt and trousers with suspenders instead of a belt. He looked Amish enough. No one could fault Mammi for being confused.

Clutching a few tools in his hand, Noah slipped past Buddy and the other boys and out the door, trying to attract as little attention as possible. No doubt he was in a hurry to hook the propane tank to the stove and get away from Buddy and Mandy as soon as possible.

Buddy droned on and on about living near the lake and how he went fishing almost every day except Sundays.

Noah stepped back into the house. He glanced at Buddy. "Anna, do you want me to show you how to use your new stove before I leave?"

"Of course," Mammi said. "I want to make Eggs Benedict."

Mammi and Dawdi followed Noah to the stove. He pushed it against the wall and adjusted it until Mammi was satisfied it was straight. She pulled a notebook and pencil from the drawer. "I better write this down in case I forget."

Mandy sighed. She didn't need a stove lesson—she used an LP gas stove every day at home—but she would need to keep her potential husbands entertained while Noah explained the stove to her grandparents. She didn't want Buddy to have a chance to corner Noah again.

She walked to the table and smiled at Buddy as she passed him. Motioning to Ben and Stephen, she pulled a chair from the table. "Do you want to play Scrabble while we wait for Eggs Benedict?"

Ben shrugged. "Sure. What about you, Stephen?"

Stephen blushed and nodded. Stephen was either painfully shy or mute. He hadn't said a word since he'd gotten here.

Mandy got the Scrabble board from the closet and sat down at the table with her three suitors. Well, two suitors and one chaperone. Turning over letter tiles, she listened as Noah explained how to operate the oven. Mammi asked him to repeat every instruction three times, and he calmly walked her through everything she might need to know about the new appliance.

Mandy's mouth curled involuntarily. Even with his long list of bad qualities, Noah proved incredibly patient with her grandparents. Of course, that didn't mean he was patient with anybody else, especially girls with freckles. She'd personally witnessed how testy he could be. Still, she felt sorry about his dat. And what had happened to his sister? There was obviously a mountain of pain behind all that orneriness.

Benjamin was winning Scrabble handily when Noah finished with her grandparents. Mandy noticed how he carefully packed up his tools and wiped the floor and cupboards where he had left dust or smudges.

She heard Dawdi invite him back tomorrow to build a rain shelter for the propane tank. She was mildly pleased when she heard Noah agree to return and then chastised herself for being so shallow. He might be handsome and patient with old people, but Noah Mischler's faults would fill a bathtub to overflowing. She didn't need the aggravation he brought to her life.

As Mandy tried to form seven consonants into a word, she watched out of the corner of her eye as Noah carefully picked up her bowl of cookie dough and wedged it into his toolbox. He paused and looked at her, compelling her to lift her gaze to his face. He gifted her with a genuine smile, making her heart swell as wide as the sky.

What was that for? Wasn't he trying to avoid her?

Before she had a chance to figure it out, he snapped his toolbox shut and marched out the door.

Good-bye, Noah.

And good riddance.

She put her hand to her warm cheek. She really hoped

Noah liked the cookies. He had saved her life. He deserved something for that.

Mandy wasn't nearly as speedy a knitter as Mammi, but she would have been able to hold her own in a knitting club. Her fingers were nimble, and she seldom dropped a stitch. Mammi had taught her well.

Mandy and Mammi sat in the great room, Mammi in her rocker and Mandy on the sofa, knitting pot holders. Dawdi lounged in his new recliner and read the newspaper.

Yesterday, Mammi had given Benjamin, Stephen, and Buddy each a pot holder as promised, and found that she only had one left in her closet. Mandy had offered to help her replenish the supply, and right quick.

Mandy used a bicolored blue and green yarn. It made a pretty pattern on the finished pot holders. Mammi alternated between bright yellow yarn and fluorescent pink. She liked her pot holders to pop, she said.

For the three meals they'd cooked so far, the new stove and oven had worked wonderful gute. The kitchen had not caught fire, neither had it blown up. Mammi's Eggs Benedict yesterday for lunch was as runny and undercooked as if she'd made it on her old cookstove. Dinner last night had consisted of baked potatoes smothered in something Mammi called Thai peanut sauce, which wasn't too bad except for the layer of cooking oil that floated atop the mashed peanuts.

Mammi had made Eggs Benedict once again this morning for breakfast, and Mandy was beginning to hope that all the chickens would run away and there'd be no more eggs to poach. She feared if she had to eat another runny egg white, she might get deathly ill.

Maybe she'd volunteer to make breakfast tomorrow morning.

Every time she looked at that stove, Mandy thought of

Noah and the way he'd smiled at her when she picked up the crescent wrench. Her fingers paused in her knitting. She liked it when he smiled at her.

Wrinkling her nose in disgust, she concentrated harder on her task. Why did he have to be so aggravating the rest of the time? If he was going to take offense at every little thing she said, she wanted nothing to do with him, attractive smile or not.

Mammi pulled at the ball of yarn in her lap. "I was not happy about giving Buddy one of my pot holders. The Mennonites are lovely people, but if I'm going to feed a good meal to a boy, he'd better be someone my granddaughter can actually marry. He should have told me he was Mennonite before I invited him to lunch."

"Maybe he didn't think you cared," Dawdi said with his head buried in his paper.

"Of course I care. Any boy with a lick of sense would have been able to tell that. I invited him home to meet my Amish granddaughter. He should have known I'd want an Amish boy."

"You're right, Banannie. He did seem a little thick."

In between stitches, Mammi glanced at Mandy. "What did you think of Stephen?"

Mandy smiled a pleasant sort of noncommittal smile. "He's quiet."

"There's something very appealing about a shy boy," Mammi said. "It shows humility. Felty was shy when we were in primary school together."

Dawdi's paper rustled slightly. "Only shy around you, Annie. My tongue tied in knots anytime you came within ten feet. You were wonderful pretty. Still are."

"Now, Felty," Mammi scolded, but her eyes twinkled as she said it. She finished off another pot holder and clipped the yarn. "You must choose a boy soon, Mandy, or we'll be knitting pot holders till Christmas."

"How many more boys are you planning on introducing me to?" Mandy asked. Surely a dozen pot holders would be enough. They'd run out of boys before they ran out of pot holders.

"Maybe you've already met the right one," Dawdi said, still engrossed in his paper. It wondered her how he could follow the conversation while reading.

Mammi lowered her knitting and regarded Dawdi thoughtfully. "You could be right, Felty. Maybe she hasn't given them enough of a chance."

Dawdi peered over his glasses to look at Mandy. "Noah did a fine job with the stove, don't you think?"

"Jah," Mammi said. "Such a gute boy." She looked up at the ceiling, deep in thought. "Maybe I should have given Adam Wengerd a blue pot holder. I think he got brown."

"It was a very nice brown pot holder," Mandy said. On Friday before he had left the house, Adam Wengerd had asked Mandy to go riding with him this coming Thursday. She had agreed reluctantly. She didn't want a Bonduel boyfriend, but she couldn't very well turn him down when he'd come to Huckleberry Hill that day by special invitation from her mammi. But Mammi need never know about her coming date. Mandy didn't want her to get her hopes up.

Mammi was still deep in thought. "Davy Burkholder isn't fond of pie. Do you think we should invite him over for cake?"

"Noah loved Mandy's pie," Dawdi said.

"What if we had your cousin Titus put in a good word with Freeman Kiem?" Mammi said. "He probably doesn't realize we've only got four weeks left."

Mandy had a date with Freeman scheduled for tonight. She hadn't told Mammi about that one either.

"Maybe we should just forget about it," Mandy said. "I didn't come to Bonduel to meet a boy. I came to see Kristina and spend time with my grandparents."

Mammi leaned over and patted Mandy's hand. "That's sweet, dear. But don't you worry. I'm not giving up, no matter what."

Mandy hadn't expected her to.

Dawdi folded his newspaper and attempted to lower the footrest by pushing with his feet. He grunted a few times, but the footrest wouldn't budge. He finally reached down and pulled the lever on the side of the recliner. Mandy nearly jumped out of her skin as the recliner catapulted Dawdi into the air. For a brief second, he seemed to take flight before landing with his feet on the floor. "I love that chair," he said. "It always gives me a good push."

That chair might have been fine for Dawdi, but it had almost given Mandy a heart attack.

Dawdi plopped his paper in the kindling bin and thumbed his suspenders. "Noah's coming today to put up a shelter over the propane tank."

"Such a nice boy," Mammi said. Mandy wasn't altogether sure which boy she was talking about. Six of them seemed to be floating around in her head at the same time.

Mandy didn't like to gossip, but surely her grandparents could tell her something about Noah's dat. At least they could give her enough information so she wouldn't bring up a forbidden topic in Noah's presence. "Did something happen to Noah's sister?" she asked. "He seemed uncomfortable when Buddy brought it up."

Dawdi stroked his horseshoe beard, and a deep line appeared between his eyebrows. "Little thing died of a heart problem. I was still in my seventies. Maybe seven years ago."

"Oh," Mandy said. "That's too bad."

"Noah can't talk about it. I suspect that wound will be fresh for many years." Dawdi went behind Mammi's rocking chair and put a hand on her shoulder. She didn't stop knitting but tilted her head to nuzzle her cheek against the back of his hand. "We know a little of how that feels."

Mammi and Dawdi had lost three of their thirteen children. Andrew had drowned when he was just a toddler, and Martha Sue and Bartholomew had been struck by a car on the way to school. More than fifty years had passed, but Mandy could see plain as day that it still hurt.

"I'm sorry," she said.

Dawdi's lips curled into a sad smile. "We rejoice that our little ones are with Jesus. But we sure miss them."

"Is Noah's dat still grieving hard for his daughter?"

Dawdi nodded and looked away. "Real hard. His dat hasn't been quite right since then. Noah does his best to take care of him."

Mandy's heart sank, and she repented of every unkind word she'd said to Noah on his porch that first day. He might have been insensitive to Kristina, but his burdens were bigger than Mandy could have imagined. She was ashamed of herself. No wonder Noah had reacted so sharply when she had mentioned his dat. Not only had her question upset him, but he had accused Kristina of putting her up to it. What did the breakup with Kristina have to do with Noah's dat?

Mandy thought of their spying on Noah by the river and her surprise that Kristina would stoop to such childish tricks.

What about Noah's dat? Just how badly had Kristina behaved?

Her heart leaped into her throat as someone knocked on the door. That would be Noah. How could she face him, knowing how unfair she'd been? Would he recognize the sympathy he saw in her eyes and resent her for it?

If there was one thing she thought she knew about Noah Mischler, it was that he would not want to be pitied.

Mandy stayed glued to the sofa while Dawdi answered the door. Noah would be working outside. She wouldn't even need to make eye contact with him. She kept her attention on her knitting as Noah spoke to Dawdi.

"Just wanted you to know I'm here," he said. "I unloaded the wood to the side of the house."

"Okay," Dawdi said. "Holler if you need help."

Noah paused. "Could I talk to Mandy for a minute?"

Her heart galloped like a horse. What did he want with her? Just yesterday he'd told her to leave him alone. She knew too much about him. He'd get suspicious.

"Sure enough," she heard Dawdi say. "She's inside."

"Would you ask her to come out?"

Come out? He definitely wanted to yell at her.

Mandy laid her knitting aside and slowly rose to her feet. Why hadn't she gone for a long walk in the woods after breakfast? She could have avoided him all morning.

She dragged her feet all the way to the front door where Noah stood, looking too handsome to be real.

"Mandy," Noah said, with a hint of anticipation in his voice. Was he looking forward to yelling at her?

She found the courage to look him in the eye. If he was mad at her, she'd not back down. She'd admit her error and dare him to show her some forgiveness. When she met his eye, she didn't see anger burning in his expression like she thought she would. Instead, his eyes were tinged with sadness, as if he expected *her* to yell at him.

"*Gute maiya*," she said, feeling stiff and unnatural, as if he were a complete stranger she didn't trust.

He shifted his weight back and forth. "Could I talk to you for a minute?"

She nodded.

He attempted a smile. It came out more like a question mark on his face. "Outside?"

Mandy nodded again and pulled her black sweater from the hook. She put it on and stepped out onto the porch. She flinched as Dawdi, without warning, shut the door behind her. Alone with Noah Mischler again. How did this always happen?

"Hi," he said, as if he suddenly felt bashful in her presence.

"Hi," she replied.

With one hand behind his back, he fidgeted with his feet. "You know," he stuttered, "I am such an idiot sometimes."

"Okay?" she said, when it seemed he was done with the conversation.

"I am really, really sorry for getting mad at you yesterday."

Oh. He wasn't going to yell at her. "It was nothing."

"It wasn't nothing. I attacked you and assumed things that I shouldn't have."

She tried hard to keep the sympathy out of her voice. "You assumed that I wanted to hurt you."

He ran his hand across his eyes. "Jah, because of Kristina. But I'm not blaming her. There's no excuse for my behavior. I just don't like talking about my family, that's all."

"I wasn't mad." Well, not very mad.

"Because it's exactly what you expected of me. Because I've treated you rotten."

"I wasn't very nice either," Mandy said, cringing at the memory of their confrontation on his porch.

"You were acting off what Kristina told you. Of course you thought I didn't have a nice bone in my whole body."

She curled one corner of her mouth. "Maybe you do."

He studied her face before breaking into a cautious smile. "Maybe I don't." He pulled his hand from behind his back. He held a paper plate covered with tinfoil. "I apologize from the bottom of my heart."

Mandy took the plate and lifted the tinfoil to reveal two pieces of French toast smothered with syrup and powdered sugar. "Ach, du lieva. Oh, my goodness."

He grinned sheepishly. "French toast is kind of a weird gift, I know, but it was all I could come up with on short notice. I was going to bake your cookie dough and bring the cookies, but I ate every last one yesterday."

He must have liked them. She tried to ignore the tingle of pleasure skipping up her spine. "No, this is perfect." Looking at the thick, golden-brown slices of French toast made her stomach rumble from her lack of an edible breakfast this morning.

She sat on the top porch step and tossed the tinfoil from the plate. "You don't mind if I eat them, do you?"

"Right now?"

She grabbed the corners of one slice and folded it like a sandwich. The syrup dribbled off the French toast as she held the plate underneath her chin and took a hearty bite. She managed to keep the dripping syrup off her face and on the plate, but her fingers were a sticky, gooey mess. "Umm," she moaned.

Noah sat next to her with a look of restrained astonishment on his face.

"Delicious," she said between greedy bites of her messy French toast sandwich. "Crispy and soft with a touch of cinnamon and nutmeg."

Noah chuckled. "I'm glad you like it."

She giggled at his expression. "It's just that, well, we had Eggs Benedict for breakfast this morning."

He grinned. "Say no more. I'm glad you won't die of starvation."

When she'd polished off the second piece of toast and her plate was a pool of syrup and powdered sugar, he pulled four napkins from his jacket pocket and handed them to her. "If you need them," he said, taking her plate so she could wipe her hands.

"Denki." She swiped the paper napkins across her palms, but nothing less than a hose was going to wash the stickiness off. "I think I need some water."

His eyes seemed to glow as he studied her. "You are the strangest girl I've ever met."

"My freckles aren't that bad."

He smirked. "You know how to use a crescent wrench, you spy on people, and you're not afraid to eat in front of a boy."

"I don't usually spy on people."

"And you fall into rivers," he said.

She nudged him with her elbow. "I don't usually fall in rivers."

"Gute thing. I don't like getting wet."

"I'm glad you jumped in anyway." She thought of him cradling her in his arms and broke out with goose bumps. How far had he carried her? Her face flushed with heat. Far enough. "Denki for saving my life."

"You've already thanked me with a lump of cookie dough."

"But it's such a small gift in comparison."

He twisted his lips into a teasing grin. "I really don't want to speak of it ever again. And if you keep insisting on bringing it up, I will be forced to remind you of why you fell in the river."

She lifted her eyebrows. "The most embarrassing day of my life."

"So you see, it would be wise to forget it ever happened."

Mandy nodded. "I'm sure I'll be able to laugh about it in thirty or forty years. No wonder you think I'm strange."

"But it's not because of your freckles. I like your freckles." The way he looked at her made her feel shy— probably because nobody had ever complimented her on her freckles before. Suddenly, she was glad that three full summers of lemon juice and sitting outside in the sun hadn't faded them like Kristina said it would.

"I . . . I should go . . . do and go . . ." she stammered. What was it she needed to go and do?

"One more thing," Noah said, growing serious. "Thank you for what you did with Buddy yesterday."

"What did I do?"

"He asked about my dat. You diverted his attention." His chocolate-brown gaze pierced right through her. "Why did you, after how rude I was?"

"I could tell it made you unhappy. I didn't want you to be unhappy."

"Why?"

Her face got warm again. "I like helping people."

He nodded. "You like to fix things."

"I suppose I do. If people could just see how unhappy they are and how easy it is to make things better, there'd be a lot fewer problems in the world."

"So you came to my house to see if you could patch things up between me and Kristina because you thought it would make me happier?" he said.

Why did her face have to heat up every time he looked at her like that? "Well, it would have made Kristina happier."

"I know you don't believe me, but she wouldn't have been happier. Some things can't be fixed."

"Everything can be fixed."

He stiffened. "Nae. Most things can't. We must trust in God and let Him take care of the things beyond our control."

Mandy felt as if they were on the cusp of an argument. She didn't want to butt heads with Noah today. They were having such a pleasant time together. And she truly didn't relish the thought of talking Noah into getting back with Kristina. Noah and Kristina would never suit.

"You're right. We should never second-guess God." That gaze was too intense. She looked down at her hands. One of them seemed to be glued into a permanent fist with maple syrup.

Noah relaxed his jaw, eased into a smile, and took the

napkins she'd crumpled in her other hand. "We should get you to some water as soon as possible."

They stood up. "I'll wash at the kitchen sink," Mandy said. "Would you mind opening the door for me? I might get stuck on the handle."

He opened the door, and she took the sticky plate and napkins from his hand. He stood in the threshold and watched her as she threw the paper into the trash and washed and dried her hands.

Mammi still sat in her rocker knitting pot holders. "Noah," she said, "are you finished with the shed already?"

"Nae. Haven't started."

"You're a gute boy, to be sure. I'm sorry I can't offer you a pot holder, but we're saving them for Mandy's suitors."

He sprouted a self-conscious smile. "No apology necessary. I'm just here to build the shed."

"I knew you'd understand."

Noah looked uncertain as to whether he wanted to come in the house or go out. He nearly shut the door and then changed his mind and stepped back into the house. "I could use an extra pair of hands if you want to, Mandy."

Mandy felt as if she would burst. He wanted her help. She tossed the dish towel onto the cupboard and practically sprinted out the door, mentally reviewing the different kinds of screwdrivers, just in case she'd be called upon to use one.

She'd already impressed him with her wrench experience. He'd be doubly astounded by her screwdriver knowledge.

Noah was as meticulous as he was handsome. On the uneven ground, he insisted on using a level for every board, and screws instead of nails. Dawdi's shed would probably stand longer than the house. Mandy wondered why she had ever worried about the stove or the ropes or a house explosion. Noah worked as if a shelter for the propane tank was worth his best time and effort. He took great care with every corner and every surface.

Mandy handed him another screw so he wouldn't have to hold them in his mouth while he worked. In truth, Mandy was completely useless to Noah's project. He could certainly hold his own screws in the handy pocket in his tool belt. She saved him a little time by handing him tools and wooden slats, but she wasted more of his time with questions and idle conversation. Still, she kind of liked being with him, sometimes just being silent together, sometimes laughing at something funny.

She handed him another slat.

He glanced at her before screwing it into the frame. "I feel like I might be keeping you from something important," he said. "If your mammi needs you in the house, I can fetch my own wood."

"I'm okay," she said, rocking back and forth on her heels. "Unless I'm bothering you. You said you like to be left alone. I can leave."

A frown stumbled across his face. "I'm sorry I said that."

"And I'm sorry I spied."

The storm clouds parted, and he smiled. "We're not to mention the spying ever again."

"Or that you saved my life. Let's just leave it in the past. Everything."

"Okay. Everything."

Mandy grabbed another handful of screws. "You know, Noah, I'd be perfectly comfortable letting you raise a baby."

He snapped his head up and looked at her as if she'd eaten her shoe. "What are you talking about?"

"You're so careful with everything."

"I don't even know how to change a diaper."

"But if you had to, you'd figure out how to put one on. And then you'd mold it perfectly to fit the baby's bottom. Diaper rash would never afflict your baby."

His mouth curved upward. "If you gave me a manual I could probably do it. I'm not all that smart, but I know how to read directions."

He pulled his battery-operated drill away from the slat he was working on and knelt beside his toolbox.

Mandy stood ready with a board in one hand and a level in the other. "What do you need?"

"A different drill bit."

"I'll find it," she said. "What size?"

They both heard a bell. Mandy peered around the corner of the house and caught her breath. She'd been having so much fun that she'd forgotten about Kristina. Her best friend ambled up the lane walking her bicycle, occasionally flicking the bell with her thumb to make it tinkle. The lane was steep enough that most bikers didn't try to pedal up the hill.

"Oh." The word escaped her lips before she could pull it back.

"Who is it?" Noah said, squarely focused on his shed.

A thread of guilt wrapped itself around Mandy's throat. How would Kristina react if she knew Mandy was spending time with the "enemy"?

Or worse. What if Kristina knew Mandy was enjoying spending time with Noah? Kristina still loved him. Would she be jealous?

Should she be jealous?

Mandy tossed her handful of screws into the bucket. Of course not. She had recently come to think less harshly of Noah, but Kristina was still her best friend. Mandy would never do anything to jeopardize that friendship.

"It's Kristina," Mandy said. Did she sound disappointed?

Noah instinctively stepped back, even though Kristina couldn't see him from this angle. He crossed his arms over his chest so that the drill pointed into the sky. With the resentful frown etched into his face, he looked like a brick wall, impossible to topple. Whatever kind of attack Kristina planned to use, he was ready.

Mandy's mind raced for a way to make this awkward meeting less uncomfortable for everybody. Kristina still hadn't seen Noah. Maybe she didn't have to know he was here.

"Krissy," Mandy called, waving and skipping across the lawn to greet her.

Breathing as if she'd run a race, Kristina nudged the kickstand with her foot and parked her bike right in the middle of the lane. "That is a terrible hill. Somebody should make it flatter."

"It's not gute with a bike."

"Next time I'll ask Mamm if I can bring the buggy." She pulled a water bottle from her plaid bag and took a swig. "I'm ready to help with the spaghetti sauce. Do you have a gute recipe? My mamm makes the best spaghetti sauce."

"I don't know if it's a gute recipe," Mandy said, taking Kristina's elbow and guiding her in the direction of the porch and away from Noah's hiding place. "It always seems to taste the same no matter what recipe we use."

"Well, if you want, we can use my mamm's recipe. I'll show you how we do it."

"Okay," Mandy said, nudging Kristina toward the front door.

"What were you doing out here?" Kristina said.

"What? When?"

"Just now. What were you doing when I came up the hill? Something around the corner of the house."

Mandy tugged more forcefully on Kristina's elbow as she paused to peer in the forbidden direction.

"Are there still prickly bushes around that side?" Kristina asked. She slid her elbow free of Mandy's arm and marched around the corner of the house.

Mandy followed as if to catch her before she went over a cliff. "Krissy, wait."

Kristina stopped short when she caught sight of Noah, still standing as if he were rooted to the spot. She narrowed her eyes and lifted her nose in the air so far she might have been looking for birds.

Huffing her displeasure, she abruptly turned on her heels and hooked her arm around Mandy's elbow. With her back as stiff as a board, she marched to the house, dragging Mandy with her.

Mandy glanced back at Noah and shrugged before Kristina spirited her away. Noah remained immovable except for the twitching muscles of his clenched jaw.

Chapter Six

Kristina raced into the house with Mandy in tow. Breathlessly, she slammed the door and leaned her arms and cheek against it as if she had just run a marathon and was too exhausted to stand on her own. She panted with excitement as a smile formed on her lips. "Ach, he is so cute."

"I'm sorry if that made you feel uncomfortable. He's building a shed for—"

Kristina pushed away from the door, yanked on Mandy's arm, and dragged her to the kitchen window. She craned her neck to gaze around to the side of the house. Mandy heaved a sigh. Kristina wouldn't be able to see a thing from that angle. "Do you think he noticed how mad I was?" Kristina said.

"Maybe."

She planted her hands on her hips. "Gute. He'll not get one kind word from me until he apologizes for what he did."

Mammi stood at the sink up to her elbows in soapy water. "Hello, Kristina. It's very nice of you to help us do spaghetti sauce."

"I don't mind," said Kristina, turning her attention back to the window.

A row of quart jars sat next to the sink. Mammi dunked

each one in the soapy water, swished the water around inside the jar, and then rinsed them in the clear water sitting in the second sink. "How is your mother feeling?" Mammi asked without looking up from her task.

"She's getting her gallbladder out day after tomorrow," Kristina said.

The lines in Mammi's forehead deepened. "So soon? I'll have to think of something nice to bake for your family. Can people without gallbladders eat haggis? I've got a new international recipe book. Haggis is from Scotland. You use all the innards of the sheep that usually get thrown out."

"Oh, well, we don't need anything like that," Kristina stuttered, giving Mammi her full attention for the first time since she walked into the house. "My sister is coming up from Wautoma, and Aunt Esther will help for a few days. Esther makes gute potato soup."

A stack of newly knitted pot holders sat on the table. Mammi had been busy while Mandy had worked outside with Noah. Mandy smiled sheepishly. "Sorry, Mammi. I should have helped finish the pot holders."

Mammi waved away her apology, sending bubbles flying in every direction. "Felty's wonderful eager to get that shed up. He said Noah needed your help. I got seven pot holders done. That should tide us over for a few days."

"How many quarts are we doing, Mammi?"

Mammi took a paper towel and swiped a sticky spider's web out of one of the jars. "I've got two bushels of tomatoes downstairs, and Felty is out picking more right now. At least three dozen quarts. I hope the new stove holds up."

Mandy thought of Noah's careful hands. The stove would hold up just fine.

Kristina still peered out the window in hopes of catching a glimpse of Noah. It was no use. Unless he came around to the front of the house, she wouldn't be able to see him.

"We'll fetch the tomatoes," Mandy said, taking Kristina's

wrist and pulling her in the direction of the cellar. Kristina reluctantly followed.

"And I'll need more bottles. Another dozen will do it."

They tromped down the stairs, Mandy still holding on to Kristina's wrist just in case she decided she couldn't live one more minute without a glimpse of Noah.

"Do you think Noah will come in for a drink soon?" Kristina said.

The way Noah had reacted when Kristina came up that hill, he wouldn't even come in the house for emergency medical attention. "I don't wonder but he'll keep outside."

"I wish he were working right by the kitchen window. Then we could spy on him while we wash tomatoes."

"It's gute we can't see him, then," Mandy said, stooping to pick up one of the baskets of tomatoes. It wouldn't budge. "We've too much work to waste time spying."

Kristina gave Mandy a smug smile. "It's easy to spy while you work."

"It doesn't matter, because you promised there would be no more spying."

Kristina ran her finger along one of the shelves as if she were looking for dust. "Spying doesn't hurt anybody."

Mandy scolded Kristina with her eyes. "Have you forgotten that I almost drowned two days ago?"

"Nae," Kristina said, without a hint of remorse in her expression.

"Spying makes you look desperate."

"It does not." She smoothed her hand down her purple dress, leaving a smudge of dust from the shelf. Blinking as if holding back tears, she sighed dramatically. "Besides, I am desperate. I love Noah so much I think I'll die if he doesn't love me."

Mandy tried not to be impatient. Poor Kristina hoped for something that wasn't going to happen. Ever. Noah's heart was completely set against her. Mandy had seen it in his eyes a dozen different times since she'd met him. It was as if he'd never liked Kristina at all.

Mandy took Kristina's hand. "I think you're going to have to accept that Noah doesn't want to get back together with you." She felt a twinge of guilt. Was she glad that Noah didn't want to get back together with her best friend?

Kristina lifted her chin. "You're wrong. If he knew me better, he'd want to court me."

With all her might, Mandy tried to scoot a bushel of tomatoes toward the stairs. After she managed to move it about eight inches, she gave up. "I thought you said you dated over the summer. Didn't you get to know each other?"

Kristina suddenly became interested in the empty jars sitting on the shelves. "He drove me home hundreds of times in his courting buggy."

"But did he go to your house and sit with your parents and play Scrabble and Life on the Farm?"

Kristina picked up a jar and blew the dust off the top of it. "He doesn't like Scrabble."

"What does he like to do?"

Kristina's face lit up like a propane lantern, as if she were thinking about something else entirely. After returning the jar to its shelf, she pulled out her cell phone and started pushing buttons. "I'm going to text him. He'll die when he sees who it's from."

Mandy snatched the phone from Kristina. "You're not going to text him. That's ridiculous."

Kristina stuck out her lower lip. "I'm just teasing. Boys like to be teased."

"He doesn't. He'll think you're a nuisance," Mandy said.

"That's not true. We used to text each other all the time over the summer."

Mandy pressed her lips together. She wasn't as eager to believe Kristina's side of the story as she had been last week. "How often did you text Noah, really?"

"Twenty, thirty times a day."

Mandy's jaw clunked to the floor. "Twenty or thirty? And he texted you back?"

Kristina looked positively sullen. "Sometimes. And then he stopped responding altogether. I think he blocked my number or something."

No doubt he blocked Kristina's number. Mandy would have blocked Kristina's number. Mandy's throat went dry. She was beginning to suspect that she'd given Noah a scolding he hadn't deserved.

Kristina's eyes pooled with tears. She had a talent for turning on the water with only a few seconds' preparation. "He treated me so bad, but I still love him."

Even though her sympathy felt thin, Mandy snaked her arms around Kristina's shoulders. "Don't cry. Noah would no doubt make a fine husband, but there are plenty of other boys who might suit you better. If you stopped pining for Noah, you might find someone else."

"I don't want someone else," Kristina sobbed, compelling Mandy to lean away so her eardrum wouldn't shatter. "Noah is the only one. He knows how to fix anything. He takes his Bible everywhere he goes. He is the first one to help at the auctions and always goes to the barn raisings. He's wonderful. Wonderful. There's no boy in Bonduel even half as wonderful."

Mandy didn't know if she should pump Kristina with hope or serve her a dose of reality. It was plain that Noah had decided against Kristina. Mandy couldn't blame him. A girl who spied on a boy and texted him dozens of times a day needed to grow up before she ever thought about trying to find a husband.

She grasped Kristina by the shoulders and forced her to make eye contact. "Krissy, I know this is hard for you, but I don't think Noah is ever going to want you back."

"But why?"

Mandy cleared her throat. "He told me."

Kristina's eyes got as round as plump, juicy tomatoes. "He told you? When?"

"Today while I helped him with the shed."

"You and Noah talked about me? Behind my back?" Her voice rose in pitch.

"He said you'd be happier without him."

And he'd be happier without you.

Kristina narrowed her eyes into slits. "Last week you told me he was a *dumkoff*, and suddenly you two are building sheds together and gossiping about me? Are you trying to steal my boyfriend?"

Leave it to Kristina to blow things out of proportion. Mandy sighed to herself. At least she'd stopped crying. "Nae, of course not. Noah pulled me out of the river. I'm very grateful."

"Grateful enough to forget your best friend?"

"I would never forget my best friend," Mandy said.

"Then you shouldn't be nice to Noah. I promised myself I wouldn't even smile at him until he agreed to get back together."

"Noah and I are friends, Krissy." Mandy's heart did a little skip in her chest. Was she really friends with Noah Mischler, the boy who'd ordered her to get her hinnerdale off his porch? She swallowed the lump of guilt forming in her throat.

Kristina let out a squeak of indignation. "You can't be friends with someone who treated your best friend like dirt."

Nae. She couldn't be friends with someone like that, but Mandy was beginning to think that, as Noah had told her, she'd only gotten half a story that hadn't been true to begin with.

Kristina grabbed her phone from Mandy's hand. "I'm going to text him and tell him to help us carry the tomatoes."

"Don't, Krissy."

"They're too heavy to lug all the way up the stairs, and he has muscles."

The thought of Noah's muscles stole her breath for a second. "I don't want to interrupt him. I can carry the tomatoes upstairs. I just need a better grip on the handles."

Kristina made a halfhearted attempt to lift one of the bushels. "Come on, Mandy. We need his help for reals."

"If he blocked your number, he won't get your text."

Kristina's eyes sparkled playfully. "I'll go outside and fetch him."

"You said you weren't ever going to talk to him again."

She was already halfway up the stairs. "How I am going to get him to come in here if I don't talk to him?"

Dread settled like a pile of rocks in Mandy's stomach. Would it be better or worse if she went out there with Kristina? Would Noah accuse her of spying?

She had the almost overpowering urge to protect Noah from Kristina's attack, and yet her feet felt as heavy as a bushel of tomatoes. She didn't think she could bear to see the contempt or the betrayal on his face when Kristina asked him to do something that he knew perfectly well they could do themselves.

Maybe he would refuse to do Kristina's bidding. He avoided her whenever possible. Perhaps he would tell Kristina he was too busy to heft tomatoes. Mandy took heart at that thought. She'd rather not face him.

Her heart sank as she heard footsteps upstairs. Those heavy ones didn't belong to Kristina. When she heard Noah's boots on the stairs, she wanted to fold herself into a small pile and hide in one of Mammi's empty jars.

She stood there like an idiot watching as he clomped down the stairs with Kristina right behind him.

Kristina rattled on in that gushing tone she saved for babies and boys she was trying to impress. "Two whole bushels, that's what there is down here. Anna needs that spaghetti sauce done and we can't even get the tomatoes upstairs. But we knew you'd be able to do it. You're so strong, Noah." Mandy wished Kristina would make up her mind about whether she despised Noah or wanted to win him back. Mandy found it impossible to keep up.

They could probably turn all the lights off in the cellar and be able to see by the glow of Mandy's warm cheeks. When Noah got to the bottom of the stairs, his eyes met hers. He was grumpy, no doubt about that, but he didn't seem particularly angry with her, even though he should have been. She should have lugged the tomatoes upstairs instead of wasting time arguing with Kristina about it.

She raised her eyebrows and mouthed the word "Sorry." He turned his head slightly in Kristina's direction and smirked.

Kristina pointed to the tomatoes in case Noah didn't see them sitting in the middle of the floor. "There they are. I don't know how Felty got them down here, but you are the only one who can help us. We're just helpless girls, you know."

As easy as if it were a basket of feathers, Noah lifted one of the bushels and started up the stairs, frowning as if Kristina had asked him to marry her. Determined to pull her own weight, Mandy grunted as, with every ounce of strength she had, she lifted the second bushel.

Noah glanced back at her. "No, you don't. I'll come back for that one."

She ignored him, held her breath, and stumbled up the stairs. She thought her arms might fall off before she reached the top.

"Oh, Noah, you're so strong," Kristina cooed. "I'm such a weakling. It's so nice to have a big, strong man around to do the heavy lifting."

If Noah was even remotely impressed by her praise, he didn't show it. It was obvious that he was trying his very best to politely tolerate Kristina and her incessant chatter. After depositing his bushel on the table, he quickly grabbed

Mandy's. His hand brushed against hers, and she didn't even try to ignore the pleasant roughness of his calloused palms. "I told you I would get this one," he scolded mildly. "These probably weigh fifty pounds."

"I didn't want to impose. We are perfectly capable of carrying our own tomatoes."

His lips still turned downward, but she could have sworn he was smiling with his eyes. "I can spare an extra two minutes so you don't break your back." He brushed his hands together a few times. "Is there anything else you need, Anna?"

"Not a thing," Mammi said, dumping a dead beetle from one of the quart jars. They'd obviously been sitting in the basement a long time. "Denki for your help."

Noah turned his piercing gaze to Mandy. She held her breath. "If you need anything else," he said, "come get me. I'm happy to help."

"We will," Kristina said. "Canning is hard work. We will definitely need more of your muscles."

Mandy merely nodded.

Noah took his hat from the table and walked out the door. Kristina skipped to the window and watched as he tromped down the porch steps and disappeared around the side of the house. She pressed her cheek against the window. "He is wonderful. I want to marry him so bad."

Mandy bit her tongue. Kristina hadn't heard a word she'd said.

Kristina frowned. "But from now on, I'm not going to speak to him, not one word, until he apologizes for how terrible he was to me." She pivoted from the window and ran down the hall.

"Where are you going?"

Kristina turned back and put a hand over her mouth to

stifle a giggle. "There is a window that looks straight out where Noah is working. I'm going to spy."

"That's in my room," Mammi said, seemingly unconcerned that Kristina was planning to spy on Noah from her bedroom window. "Try not to wrinkle the curtains, dear."

Mandy gazed after Kristina with great concern. "Mammi, I don't think Kristina should spy on Noah. It's silly."

"Oh, it's all right. Noah is a gute boy, good-natured enough to bear a little bit of teasing from Kristina. It's just too bad Melvin Lambright isn't here. He could have carried tomatoes for us and then taken you for a drive. It would have been the perfect way to get you two together."

Mandy already had a date lined up with Melvin. She had agreed to meet him at a benefit haystack supper next week. Mammi need never know. She wouldn't be able to bear the disappointment when the date didn't work out. Mandy sidestepped the issue like she always did. "I'm not really interested in Melvin. He's almost thirty."

Mammi finished rinsing her bottles, dried her hands, and tapped her lips with her index finger. "Hmm. I see what you mean. It wonders me if you and Ephraim Glick would fit. He's your same age, and that skin condition is completely cleared up."

"I'll consider him," Mandy said, wishing her mammi wasn't so persistent. "There's nothing more attractive than a boy without a skin condition."

In truth, there was nothing more attractive than Noah Mischler, but seeing that look on Mammi's face, Mandy knew that now would not be the time to mention it.

Chapter Seven

"It wonders me what Noah is doing right now," Kristina said as she jumped into the car.

Mandy felt no need to respond as she slid into the backseat next to Kristina.

Their driver, Peggy Lofthouse, glanced at them from her rearview mirror. "How's your mom, Kristina? Surgery went a lot later than you thought."

"I hope it's not too late," Mandy said.

Peggy shook her head. "I always stay up to watch *Nightline*."

"My mamm's gallbladder came out just fine," Kristina said, "but she had a reaction to the medicine. It made her heart go all funny so they have to keep her overnight yet."

"That sounds scary," Peggy said.

"It was for a little while," Kristina said. "But she seems fine now, and she's none too happy about having to stay in the hospital for an extra night."

Peggy pulled onto the main road. "Better safe than sorry, I guess."

Kristina tucked her sweater around her neck. "Dat is staying at the hospital with her. Can you go get them in the morning?"

"Sure," Peggy said. "I'll plan on it. He has my number."

Kristina grabbed Mandy's knee and almost sent her to the moon. She had ticklish knees. "Where do you think Noah is? Do you think he's in bed?"

"It's none of our business," Mandy said, suddenly cross with her best friend. No wonder Noah didn't want anything to do with Kristina.

Kristina pulled out her phone. Seriously, that girl wouldn't know what to do with her hands once she got baptized and had to give up her phone. "I'm going to text him right now and find out."

Mandy didn't even protest. Didn't even remind Kristina that Noah never answered her texts, that he had most likely blocked her number and would never even have an inkling that Kristina was thinking about him. Instead, she surrendered silently and fixed her eyes on the dark road. Home was only twenty minutes away.

Kristina had wasted over an hour on Wednesday peeking out of Mammi's bedroom window, spying on Noah and punching the keys of her phone. Mandy and Mammi had been able to hear Kristina's giggling from the kitchen as they blanched and skinned tomatoes and chopped peppers and onions. Jah, Kristina had been a big help.

She had only joined them in the kitchen when her feet got tired and her cell battery died. She dutifully helped measure spices and stir the sauce, although Mandy had sensed that her heart wasn't in it. Her hopes had been dashed when Mammi informed her that they wouldn't need to summon Noah to lift the stockpot off the stove or to help them pull steaming jars from the water bath.

Noah hadn't come inside the rest of the day, and basically, Kristina's afternoon had been ruined. But they had managed to can thirty quarts of spaghetti sauce using Kristina's recipe. It hadn't turned out half bad.

"After Wednesday, I don't wonder if he'll want to get

back together," Kristina said, studying her phone as if it held the secret to her happiness. "He hauled the tomatoes up from the cellar for us. Boys like it when they have to rescue the helpless girls. If you hadn't insisted on carrying one of the bushels, we'd probably be back together right now."

Mandy stretched a smile across her face. She'd rather not argue tonight, rather not feel the niggling guilt that she should be less sympathetic to Noah and more sympathetic to Kristina. Kristina acted like a silly schoolgirl, but she was Mandy's best friend. Still, she was going to be bitterly disappointed when it came to Noah.

Mandy sighed and determined to make things right for Kristina. Maybe she could introduce her to some of the suitors Mammi had lined up for Mandy. After all, she couldn't marry all of them. She didn't want to marry any of them.

Freeman Kiem might be persuaded to give Kristina a chance. He had taken Mandy for ice cream on Wednesday night. A twenty-minute date. He was real nice, with a deep cleft in his chin that made his face look as if it had been molded out of clay. Freeman wasn't all that interesting to Mandy, and he hadn't seemed inclined to ask for another date.

On Thursday, her ride with Adam had been quite unpleasant. Adam had picked her up in his courting buggy, and Mandy hadn't been able to hide it from Mammi. As expected, Mammi had been rapturous that Mandy was going riding with Adam and was equally despondent after the date when Mandy had informed her that Adam wasn't the one.

Adam Wengerd was as handsome as the day is long, but he was also fully aware of his good looks. His arrogance was enough to give Mandy a headache. If there was anything she couldn't abide, it was a peacock. She much preferred someone like humble Noah Mischler, who had no idea how nice to look at he was, and wouldn't have cared if he did know.

"Ach, du lieva," Kristina said, so forcefully that Peggy slammed on the brakes.

All three of them jerked forward and back with the car. "What! What is it," Peggy said.

Mandy laid her hand over her racing heart. "What's the matter?"

"There he is," Kristina said, pointing out the window.

"Who?"

"Noah."

Mandy peered out the window. "I don't see him."

"Well, it's not him," Kristina said as if Mandy were dumber than a brick. "It's his courting buggy. See? At that bar across the street."

Peggy shoved her mouth to one side of her face. "I thought there was a deer."

"Sorry," Mandy said. "No deer."

Peggy let her foot off the brake and rolled forward a few feet to the stoplight, which had turned red during all the commotion. "Please try to keep boy sightings to yourself. I want my shocks to last for a few years yet."

Mandy knew it was none of her business, but she let her eyes stray across the street to the open-air buggy parked beneath the streetlight in front of the bar on the road near the airport. A second buggy, enclosed and black, sat to the side of the bar, partially obscured by the dark shadows of the night.

Was one of those Noah's buggy?

She folded her arms and sat back. She didn't really want to know. Her chest felt empty and her skin was cold. Even though they'd only known each other for a week, she had thought she knew him better than that. Noah wasn't a drinker, was he? Mandy wasn't so sure. He had a phone. What other rules of the church was he breaking?

Again her eyes drifted to the bar. Could Noah really be in there?

Jah, he could.

While they waited for the light to change, Noah emerged from inside, dragging someone with him.

"There he is," Kristina said. "I told you."

The other man's arm was draped over Noah's shoulder, and Noah had one arm wrapped around the other man's back. Noah's companion, significantly older than Noah, swayed unsteadily, as if standing on his own would be impossible. It was a gute thing Noah could lift a truck all by himself.

Suddenly, the staggering man shoved Noah away from him, swung his fist wildly, and caught Noah in the mouth. Mandy gasped as Noah stumbled backward. He met with the wall of the bar, and his legs crumpled beneath him. He slid to the ground and sat as if that was where he had intended to end up. The older man staggered back into the bar and slammed the door behind him.

"Peggy, wait," Mandy said as the light turned green. "We need to help him."

Kristina's eagerness over Noah vanished, and she folded her arms. "I'm not going over there."

"But Noah is hurt."

Kristina turned her face away. "Mamm wouldn't like it if I went to a bar, and Noah gets really mad if anybody knows anything."

Peggy hesitated for a minute before drifting into the left lane and pulling into the parking lot. She drove to the side of the bar next to the black buggy. Noah wouldn't even be able to see Peggy's car from where he sat. Mandy jumped out of the car and raced around the buggy. With his eyes downcast, Noah sat on the ground fingering his lip, which looked to be bleeding pretty good.

She squatted beside him. "Are you okay?"

He slowly lifted his head and focused his eyes on her. "What are you doing here?"

"I saw that man hit you. Are you okay?"

He covered his face and pressed his fingers to his temples. "Go away. I don't want you here." There was real anguish in his voice.

She didn't even flinch. He'd told her to go away before, yelled at her even. She wasn't about to believe that he didn't need her. "If you think all that bluster scares me, you can just think again. I'm not leaving."

His expression softened. "Please, Mandy. Leave me alone. I just want people to leave me alone."

She took a tissue from her coat pocket, congratulating herself that she always carried a few with her. "Here," she said. "Let me see."

"Mandy, you don't understand. You shouldn't be here. I don't want your help." He hissed as she dabbed at his lip with her tissue. "I'm not going to ask nice again."

"You wouldn't dare yell at me."

"Jah, if it would scare you into leaving."

"I'm not scared of you."

He took hold of her wrist and pulled her hand away from his mouth. "You should be."

His grip was strong, but not meant to hurt her. She tugged her hand out of his grasp. She told the truth. She wasn't afraid of him in the least. It was obvious that except for the blow to the face, he had his wits about him. He hadn't been drinking. But he was injured, and she was going to fix it. "You're harmless, Noah."

Surprise mingled with a bare hint of amusement glinted in his eyes. "Harmless?" He held up his hands. "I can lift four bushels of tomatoes at once." He winced as she tried to wipe the rest of the blood from his lip. "You, on the other hand, are going to kill me. Leave off. You'll make it worse."

This time he folded her hand in his. Their gazes met, and his brown eyes flashed as if he were trying to read her mind. His look sent the thoughts in her head tumbling like pebbles in a rockslide. At that moment, she didn't even know what she was thinking. He wouldn't have been able to read much.

He frowned as they heard a sound from inside the bar. Rubbing his jaw, he shot to his feet and pulled her with him. "Denki for checking on me." He nudged her in the direction opposite the bar. "You should go now."

"Do you need my help getting home?"

"*You* want to see that I get home safe? Forget it. I'll be fine." She heard something buzzing and realized that it was his cell phone. He shoved his hand into his pocket and silenced it without looking. He gazed around as if trying to find her buggy. "What about you? How did you happen to be at a bar in Shawano?"

"Oh, I . . . uh . . . was visiting someone in the hospital." She probably shouldn't mention that Kristina was with her. The mere thought of Kristina agitated him, and right now it was a good guess that he didn't need the added aggravation. "My driver is over there," she said, waving her hand in no direction in particular.

"Okay then," he said, acting as if he were about to jump into his buggy any second now. "We should both be going."

Mandy bit her tongue, resisting the urge to ask him what he had been doing in a bar and why that man had hit him and maybe why his brown eyes made her heart do somersaults inside her chest. But by the way he looked at her, she could practically hear the lecture that it was none of her business.

The door to the bar swung open, and a painfully skinny man with arms covered in tattoos stuck his head out. "Noah, you gotta come get him, or I'm going to have to throw him out."

Noah went completely rigid as if someone had rammed a steel rod down his back. Clenching his jaw, he glanced at Mandy before turning away and staring into the distance. "I'm coming."

The tattooed guy nodded and disappeared into the bar.

Mandy's heart sank to her toes. She should have listened when Noah had told her to go away. Now she had made him uncomfortable when she had just wanted to help.

"I'll go now," she said.

He nodded without meeting her eyes. "Okay."

The door swung open again, this time so forcefully that it crashed against the wall behind it. The man who had hit Noah staggered out of the bar.

Noah wrapped his arms around him in what looked like a bear hug, but it was meant to prop the older man up so he wouldn't fall over. It wasn't an easy task. The man was almost as big and as solid as Noah.

"Come on," Noah said. "Let's go home." He shifted, securing one arm around the older man so they could walk forward. Stunned and unsure of herself, Mandy stepped out of the way as they walked past. Noah barely gave her a second look.

The man reached out a hand to Mandy. "I'm sorry," he said, a look of utter despair on his face. "I'm so sorry."

Unsure of what to do, but feeling an overwhelming need to comfort him, she took his offered hand. "Everything is going to be okay."

The man stopped his halting shuffle and studied Mandy as if he were trying to bring her face into focus.

There was no mistaking the shame and grief warring on Noah's face. "Come on, Dat," he said, gently nudging him away from Mandy. "We need to go home."

Dat?

An invisible hand clamped around Mandy's throat. This broken shadow of a man was Noah's dat? Mandy almost cried out. She couldn't even begin to imagine the depth of Noah's pain. No wonder he hated the very mention of his family.

Noah's fater was an older version of Noah, with the same

solid arms and broad chest, except his dat had gone a little soft in the middle. There wasn't anything soft about Noah.

With surprising strength, Noah's dat shoved Noah away from him. "Leave me be," he groaned.

Noah stumbled backward but immediately returned to his father's side, taking his arm and pulling him more forcefully toward the buggy. His dat resisted and turned his eyes to Mandy. "I'm sorry, Little Rosie. Forgive me. Please, forgive me."

"Of course I forgive you," Mandy said, unsure who he was apologizing to but recognizing his need for reassurance. "Everything is okay. You're going to be okay."

His dat yanked his arm from Noah's grasp and staggered toward Mandy. "Take me home, Little Rosie. Please come home."

Noah immediately stepped between Mandy and his dat, enveloping him in another bear hug. "Mandy, go away," he pled, his voice cracking in a rare moment of vulnerability.

"Come home, Rosie," his dat repeated, reaching for Mandy even as Noah pushed him away.

Even though she'd seen him strike Noah, Mandy instinctively knew that Noah's dat wouldn't hurt her. He seemed so despondent, so damaged, that the only emotion she felt for him was profound compassion.

"Can I help you get him home?" she whispered, afraid her voice might give out on her if she spoke with more boldness.

Noah still would not look her in the eye as he took his dat's arm and draped it over his shoulders. "Nae. I can manage."

His dat stopped struggling. "Let her come home, Noah."

Noah pressed his lips into a rigid line as a storm raged behind his eyes.

At that moment, Mandy would have done anything to

ease the hurt she saw there. She pointed to the other buggy parked to the side of the building. "Your dat's?"

Noah nodded.

"I can drive one to your house if you drive the other."

His dat bent the arm that was slung over Noah's shoulder, pulling Noah closer to him as if he were giving him an affectionate hug. He furrowed his brow and seemed almost lucid. "Noah, don't you want your mama to come home?"

Noah bowed his head. "Come on, Dat," he mumbled.

"If you let Rosie come too."

Noah hesitated with one arm around his dat's back and his other hand gripped firmly around his dat's wrist. "Okay," he whispered.

"I'll tell my driver to go home," she said, hoping Noah wouldn't catch sight of who else was in the car.

She walked to the other side of the black buggy, where Peggy drummed on the steering wheel and Kristina sat with her arms clamped like a vise around her chest. The rear windows were tinted. Lord willing, Noah would be none the wiser. She opened the door and slipped into the front seat. "Peggy, I am going to help Noah. Will you take Kristina home?"

"What did he say?" Kristina asked. "He hates it when you tease him about his dat."

"Tease him?" Mandy said. "What do you mean *tease*? Kristina, did you say something to Noah you shouldn't have?"

She turned her face and stared at the stoplight. "He can't take a joke."

Mandy wanted to grab Kristina by the shoulders and shake some sense into her. She'd only been acquainted with Noah for a week but already knew that Noah's dat was a topic that should never be mentioned.

"I'll take her home," Peggy said. "Will you be okay?"

"Jah, I'll get home."

Peggy nodded and put the car into reverse. "If you run into trouble, call me. I always stay up late to watch *Nightline*."

"Please just . . ." She leaned toward Kristina. "Please, let's keep this between ourselves. It's pure gossip to spread someone else's misfortunes."

Kristina pinched her lips together and nodded. "Everybody already knows about Noah's dat."

Mandy glared at her best friend. "Promise me you won't say a word."

Kristina looked as if she might bite Mandy's head off. "Okay. Don't get huffy. I promise."

Mandy relaxed when Peggy pulled out of the parking lot and her car disappeared around the corner. Noah wouldn't have to know about Kristina.

Noah helped his dat into the black buggy. His dat lay down across the backseat and seemed to fall asleep immediately. Mandy grabbed a wool blanket sitting on the front seat and laid it over him. Noah risked a glance at her. "Denki," he said.

"I'll drive the courting buggy back," she said.

"It's cold."

"You need to be with your dat. I'll be warm enough."

Keeping his eyes down, he shrugged off his black coat and handed it to her. "Wear this."

"What about you?"

"I'll be fine."

His tone, almost resentful, shut down any argument Mandy might have tried to make. It was plain that he didn't want to be contradicted, didn't want to talk her into anything, and most certainly didn't want to spend any more time standing outside a bar where the whole world could see him.

She nudged her hands into the sleeves, and Noah's warmth immediately enveloped her. His coat smelled like him, clean and wintery, with just a touch of the deep forest lingering in the fabric. She rolled the sleeves twice and still the coat felt as if it would tumble from her shoulders if she breathed too hard. She buttoned it around her and climbed into Noah's open-air buggy.

"I'll follow you," he said.

She loosened the reins and with a flick of her wrist, got the horse moving. How far was it to Noah's house? Half an hour? Forty minutes? Her breath hung in the air. A little chilly for September.

She tucked her hand into one of Noah's coat pockets and found a pair of gloves. Sure to be too big for her, but better than hands made stiff with the cold. Keeping hold of the reins with one hand, she slipped each glove on in turn. Oversized, but they'd keep her hands warm. She had all of Noah's gear. Lord willing he'd be warm without it.

The horse's hooves clapping against the pavement lulled her into a sense of calm as they always did on a crisp, quiet night like tonight. She could hear the faint, comforting clip-clop of Noah's horse a few paces behind her. What was he thinking? Was he embarrassed about his dat? Grateful for her help? Mandy felt bad for Noah's dat, but was glad she had been there. She had always been able to make things better for people. Mamm said it was one of her gifts.

The darkness seemed to envelop her as she got closer to Noah's place and farther away from the lights of town. After half an hour of quiet solitude, she turned down the road to Noah's house. There was a little shed that looked as if it might be what Noah used as a stable a few hundred paces behind the house, but Mandy couldn't see how to get there from the dirt road. She parked the buggy in front of his house, and he pulled behind her.

She slid from her seat, eager for the warmth of the indoors. Noah didn't acknowledge her as he coaxed his dat to sit up and then climb out of the buggy.

"I'm sorry," Noah's dat mumbled. "I didn't mean it."

"Cum, Dat. I'll take you to bed."

His dat seemed to be walking and talking in his sleep as Noah put an arm around him and led him to the cement porch. Mandy went before him and held the door open as Noah led his dat up the step.

A floor lamp stood in the entryway, one of the kinds with a battery underneath the cabinet and a regular lightbulb on top. Mandy pulled the chain and turned on the light. The hound dog she had encountered here last week seemed to appear from out of nowhere. His collar jangled and his paws clicked against the wood floor as he bounced and fussed like a puppy, sniffing at Mandy and Noah and then Noah's dat.

"Down, Chester," Noah said as he struggled to coax his dat into the house.

The dog immediately backed away, rested his rump on the floor, and tilted his head to study the three people who had barged into the house.

Noah's dat paused in the entryway to take a blurry-eyed look at Mandy. "You remind me of my Rosie," he said. "She's a pretty gal."

Noah coaxed him down the hall to the left.

"Can I help?" Mandy said.

"Nae," Noah said. "You can't."

Feeling more than a little awkward, Mandy laced her fingers together and waited in the hallway with the dog as Noah took his father into what must have been a bedroom. The dog stayed put, quietly standing sentinel, waiting for Noah to return.

Mandy cautiously reached out a hand to pet him. He'd let her do it before, and he seemed gentle enough. "Chester," she said. "You are a very pretty dog." She scratched behind his floppy caramel-brown ears, and he nudged her fingers with his nose. "I have a cousin named Chester. He looks nothing like you."

After a few minutes of conversing with Noah's dog,

Mandy took a peek around the house. It looked even smaller on the inside than it did from the outside. In the shadows cast by the lamp, she could see three doors down the hall to her left that she guessed were bedrooms and a bathroom. The entry hall, which was about three feet square, opened into a small kitchen with a fridge and oven on one wall and a sink and window on the wall opposite her. A long gray counter came out from the wall behind the sink and divided the room in half. A square kitchen table, surrounded by three chairs, sat in the other half of the room next to a woodstove against the far wall. There was no sitting room to speak of, no sofa, no comfy chairs. Where did they wash their clothes? How could they hold *gmay* in such a small space?

Mandy took another step into the house. Chester twitched his nose, but otherwise didn't show any sign of objecting. It wasn't too hard to guess that this was one house where church was never held. Not only was it too small to fit a whole district, but Noah's dat had been allured by the evils of alcohol. A man like that wouldn't be in gute standing with the church.

Even though it was small, Noah's house was tidy. His mamm must be a gute housekeeper. Unless . . . What had Noah's dat said about his mamm? Mandy couldn't remember, but she'd gotten the impression that his mamm wasn't around anymore.

Was she dead? *Oh, please no, dear Lord.* Noah had already lost his sister to death and his fater to alcohol. Had Noah's mamm been taken too? Mandy couldn't bear the thought of more tragedy plaguing Noah's life.

She gazed down the hall. Certainly no more than two people and a good-sized dog could live in such a cramped space. Still, she didn't see how Noah and his dat would have been able to keep the house so clean all by themselves.

Finally feeling somewhat warm, Mandy began to unbutton Noah's oversized coat.

"Leave it on," she heard Noah say. She turned to look down the hall as he slipped out of his dat's room and shut the door behind him. He persistently refused to look her in the eye as he ambled down the hall and opened the front door. "Cum. I'll take you home." Chester's ears twitched, and he let out a soft whine. "Stay here, Chester."

The dog immediately came to attention as if he wouldn't dream of moving from his designated spot.

Mandy had the feeling that she was being dismissed. Didn't Noah want to talk about what had just happened with his dat? Didn't he want some comfort?

"What about your lip? We should put some ointment on it."

He rubbed his hand down the side of his face as if the weight of his dat's problems had fallen on his shoulders.

She rested her hand on his arm. He flinched. "It's going to be okay, Noah."

For the thousandth time tonight, he turned his face away from her. "What do you know about it?" His tone was mild but tinged with a bitterness that made her take a step back. "I asked you to go away. Why didn't you leave?"

"I wanted to help."

He ran his fingers through his hair. "Help? You can't help."

"He . . . he was so angry. I thought you might not be able to get him home by yourself."

He grunted his displeasure. "For five years I've managed to get my dat home all by myself. I've never needed your help, and I didn't need it tonight."

She swallowed the lump clogging her throat before she suffocated. "I'm sorry. I didn't know."

"No doubt Kristina's told you all about my dat, the drunk," he said, spitting the words out of his mouth. "You wanted to see for yourself, didn't you?"

Mandy tucked the collar of Noah's coat around her neck. His accusations chilled her to the bone. "I . . . I didn't."

"Kristina will love hearing about this latest incident, then, won't she?"

"I would never do that."

Noah took a ragged breath. "My mamm's gone, my dat's sick. Haven't you people made me suffer enough? Go. Please just go."

Mandy squared her shoulders and shook her head. "I'm not going. I'm still wearing your coat and I don't have a way home."

Leaving the front door wide open, he strode to the table and plopped into a chair with his back to her. He buried his face in his hands and acted as if he couldn't care less if she walked through that door and disappeared forever. Chester padded softly into the kitchen and stood next to Noah's chair, watching him expectantly as if to be ready if Noah needed him to fetch some slippers.

Mandy had never felt more miserable in her life. Somewhere along the line, her best intentions had gone awry, and there sat Noah, without a friend in the world, bearing a train-load of burdens on his shoulders. They were wide shoulders, jah, but a man could only take so much before he collapsed under the weight of it all.

Quietly, she shut the front door and tiptoed into the kitchen. She hesitated for only a moment before laying a hand on his shoulder. Chester sat on his haunches and licked the back of her other hand as a show of support.

Noah sighed, lowered his head even farther, and shoved his fingers through his hair. "You want me to say it? I'll say it. Seeing you there tonight, knowing what you know about my dat, I'm completely humiliated. I hope you're happy. You and Kristina will have a wonderful-gute time gloating."

Standing in Noah's quiet, dim kitchen, Mandy's heart broke for this wounded soul who thought that Mandy and

Kristina and maybe his entire community wanted to hurt him. Trying to keep some sort of connection between them, she left her hand on his shoulder and sat in the chair next to him. "Noah. I would never deliberately hurt you."

He lifted his eyes and studied her face. "I'm the boy who broke your best friend's heart."

"We've had our differences."

"We argue whenever we lay eyes on each other."

She shook her head. "I'm not afraid to tell you what I think, and I have certainly made some hasty accusations, but do you really think I would use your misfortunes for petty revenge?"

His eyes flashed, and his icy expression seemed to thaw momentarily, as if he believed her. "Kristina would love to shame me in front of everybody."

Mandy bit her bottom lip. Her best friend could be unpredictable and, yes, vindictive. Why had Mandy never noticed it before? They were definitely traits that Mandy found unattractive. "You keep talking as if Kristina and I have some secret plan to destroy your life."

He raised an eyebrow. "You spied on me. That sounds like a secret plan."

"She pushed me into the river. If it was a plan, it wasn't a very good one."

He let one corner of his mouth twitch upward. "Unless you planned that too. Kristina finagled a hug out of it."

Mandy frowned. "Jah. She did."

A shadow traveled across his face. "She's tricky that way."

That lump was still lodged in Mandy's throat. "You and Krissy were never boyfriend and girlfriend, were you?"

With his gaze riveted to hers, he rubbed the stubble on his jaw and shook his head.

Her face got hot. "And I came over and unjustly bawled you out."

"You believed Kristina's version."

"But why didn't you tell me the truth?"

He looked sideways at her. "Would you have believed me?"

She lowered her eyes. "I suppose not."

Noah leaned back in his chair and folded his arms. "She and her gaggle of friends followed me around all summer. There was the spying and the texting and the messages on my voice mail. She asked me to drive her home from a gathering. One gathering. She lives close. I was trying to be nice."

"She believed what she wanted to believe." Kristina had made a pest of herself for a boy who had no interest. She should have been unendurably embarrassed. Right now, Mandy felt embarrassed enough for the both of them.

"It's partly my fault. I should have put a stop to it sooner," he said.

"Nae. You are not responsible for Kristina's infatuation." Except he *was* to blame for his good looks. They were kind of hard to resist. Kristina's fascination was understandable. Her behavior was not.

"One day she . . . well, she did something that finally ended my patience. I texted her and told her to stay away from me and not to contact me ever again. I might have been a little harsh, but I wanted to make sure she understood. She's not one to take a hint." He let out a long sigh and rested a hand on Chester's head. "I suppose I should have had the conversation in person, but I didn't want to embarrass her and I didn't want her to blubber all over my boots." He inclined his head toward Mandy and pulled his phone from his pocket. "I apologize for doing it over a text. Somebody told me it's cruel to break up with a text message."

Mandy wanted to crawl into a tiny little hole. "Under the circumstances, I don't think it could be considered a breakup."

He frowned, concentrating on the phone as he twirled it

in his fingers. "The bishop consented to the phone. The bar calls me when I need to come get my dat."

Oh.

Mandy wanted to crawl into an even tinier hole and cover her head with dirt. "Sorry," she said, her voice cracking like a carton of smashed eggs.

He didn't reply, just played with his phone and kept his eyes away from her face.

Mandy leaned toward him and rested her hand on the table. "I won't say a word about your dat to anyone," she whispered.

"Denki," he said, still twirling his phone, still averting his gaze, but sounding as if he'd just released a breath he'd been holding for a very long time.

Her heart swelled in her chest. For some reason she couldn't explain, Mandy wanted Noah to share his pain with her, to express his deepest emotions. She wanted to laugh with him, be with him, understand him. Would he ever consider the possibility of being her friend? Did she dare invite him to? "I know this is none of my business . . ."

He looked up, probably expecting something horrible to come out of her mouth.

She cleared her throat. "If you don't like the question, you can kick me out of your house. But if you kick me out, I get to keep your coat."

His lip twitched almost imperceptibly. "Okay?"

"I barely know you. I know you don't like to talk about your family."

The muscles of his jaw tightened. "What do you want to know?"

"How long has your mamm been gone?"

He lifted his chin and seemed resentful of the question. "It's no secret. Your grandparents must have told you all about my family."

Mandy jiggled her head slightly. "My grandparents don't

tell tales on anybody except their grandchildren. When Mammi's scheming to make a match, all the grandchildren know about it except the grandchild she's scheming against."

He let down his guard. "Your mammi is scheming against you, in case you didn't know."

Mandy winced. "I know." She thumped her head down on her arm, which rested on the table. She bobbed her head up and down, lightly tapping her arm with her forehead as if she were banging her head against a wall. "She wants to make at least six more pot holders. You've got to save me, Noah."

He made a face. "I'll stay out of it. Felty asked me to fix his roof. He's not paying me to help you find a husband."

"I don't want to find a husband."

Noah rubbed his chin. "Davy Burkholder has three stuffed elk heads hanging in his living room. There's hardly room for furniture. And Melvin Lambright, he's nice enough, but he can't whistle a note. He'd make a gute husband if you don't mind that little disability yet."

"Ha, ha," Mandy said.

"The girls love Adam Wengerd."

Probably almost as much as Adam loved himself.

Noah's eyes sparkled with amusement. "Kristina says Adam's handsome. She spies on him too."

Mandy groaned.

"She was trying to make me jealous," Noah said. "But I wasn't."

The goofy look on his face made Mandy giggle.

He leaned closer. "I'll tell you a little secret. Adam Wengerd used to have the crookedest teeth you've ever seen. It took five years of braces. With headgear. If you marry him, don't be surprised if your children look like beavers."

Mandy playfully shoved Noah's arm off the table. "Stop it. I don't want to marry a Bonduel boy."

This news seemed to sober him a bit. "Why not?"

"Charm, Ohio, has a better selection."

"But we've got quality up here. What about Freeman Kiem? He's got that nice cleft in his chin."

"And I've got a face full of freckles. He doesn't want anything to do with me."

"I like freckles," Noah said. He cleared his throat and lowered his eyes.

Mandy rested her elbow on the table and propped her chin in her hand. "We've strayed wildly from the subject."

"What were we talking about?"

Ach. She should have been smarter than that. In an attempt to steer him from the subject of prospective husbands, she'd brought them right back to the question she shouldn't have asked. They had been getting along so well, and Noah had found his smile. Not an easy feat considering where they'd been an hour ago.

If Mandy had owned a third leg, she would have kicked herself under the table.

"It doesn't matter," she said. "Never mind."

Noah wilted slightly. "I remember. You want to know how long my mamm's been gone."

"It's late. We can talk another time. I should get home."

He reached over and laid his hand on top of hers. She didn't move a muscle. "It's okay. You might as well know. Then you won't be wondering, and I won't be avoiding eye contact every time we see each other."

She curled her lips and tried not to stare at his hand touching hers. "I guess that's so."

"My mamm's been gone three years."

"I'm sorry."

"Me too," he said. He seemed to remember that his hand still covered hers. He pulled it away.

"How did she die?"

"Die?" Lines of confusion appeared around his eyes. "Your grandparents really don't gossip, do they?"

"What do you mean?"

"My mamm isn't dead." His voice grew raspy and soft, as if the pain were too great to talk louder. He reached out and petted Chester again. "She left us. Took my five brothers and sisters and moved back to Missouri to live with her parents."

Whatever Mandy had expected to hear, that wasn't it. She caught her breath. "She . . . she left?"

He wouldn't look at her. "I don't blame her. She did what she had to do."

"Because of the drinking?"

He nodded. "My sister Edi died of a heart defect seven years ago. She wasn't yet one year old." He swiped a tear away and then tried to pretend he hadn't just swiped a tear away. "It was hard for all of us, but my dat especially. He didn't know what to do with all his grief. My mom gave hers to God, but Dat just didn't know how to do it. He had developed a taste for the alcohol during *rumschpringe* and went back to it to forget how sad he was to have lost Edi. The bishop used to come over every week, but he didn't know how to help. He quit coming after a while. My mamm put up with Dat for four years, and then she just couldn't do it anymore."

"So she divorced him and left the church?" Mandy asked.

"Nae. She wanted to stay in the church. They're still married."

Mandy sat with her heart in her throat, staring at Noah as if seeing him for the first time.

He didn't hide his distress now. Resting his forehead in his hands, he let his tears drip onto the table. "My mamm begged me to come with her, but Dat needed me. I had to stay here."

"Of course you did."

He glanced at her. "You think I did the right thing? My brother Yost says I should have come with them and left Dat to suffer the consequences of his drinking. But I just couldn't. I had to be the man my mamm raised me to be."

"She raised you to be gute."

He shook his head. "I'm not gute. I feel like I've been cut into two jagged pieces."

"Are you angry with your *mater*?"

"Nae." Noah rubbed the tears from his face with the back of his hand. "She was miserable. She did what she needed to do, what was best for my little brothers and sisters."

"And you did what you thought was best."

"Yost can't forgive me for it," Noah said. He ran his hand down the side of his face and nearly lost his composure. He looked so forlorn that Mandy couldn't just sit there and do nothing. Not caring if it was proper behavior, she scooted her chair close beside him, put her arm around his shoulders, and grasped his upper arm with her other hand.

He didn't acknowledge her gesture, but he didn't pull away either. They sat in silence until Noah regained the power to speak. "Yost hasn't had anything to do with me for three years. Mamm writes and calls once a week, but Yost hates me."

"I'm sorry."

"We used to be best friends."

"Is he close to your age?" Mandy whispered. Was she asking too many questions? She didn't want to upset him any more than he already was, but she knew from her experiences helping people that it usually did a person good to talk about their troubles. That was one of Noah's problems. He didn't seem to want to talk about anything.

"He'll be twenty next month. I knew he could take care of Mamm if I stayed with Dat. I thought he would see it as us working together. To him it was a betrayal."

"Does he have a gute job to help your mamm?"

"He works construction, but I want him to be able to save up enough money to buy his own farm someday. My mom and siblings live with my grandparents, so they don't have rent, and I send as much money as I can."

That explained the house the size of a postage stamp with the forsaken yard and peeling paint.

Noah pressed his fingers into his brow. "Yost is gute with a hammer, but he needs a big brother to show him how to do the mechanical repairs. I'm grateful to your dawdi for the job. Reshingling their roof will bring in gute money. Lisa is nineteen. I want her to have a beautiful wedding."

"My dawdi is a kind man, to be sure, but I know he didn't hire you out of pity. You are very talented. Everybody knows that."

Noah took a deep breath and looked into Mandy's face as he seemed to be considering something very carefully. He stood up, moved away from her, and came to rest leaning against the wall. Chester followed him. "I can guess what you must think of me now."

"What do you mean?"

"Godly men don't have fathers who drink or mothers who leave."

Mandy frowned. "That's not true. Everybody has problems. You're not less worthy because of your parents."

He looked away from her again, as if facing the truth were too painful. "Tell that to the old ladies at church who rattle their tongues about my family."

"Well," she said, looking at him as if he were deliberately trying to annoy her, "I haven't heard any tongue rattling. Maybe you're imagining things."

He slumped his shoulders. "It's out there. Kristina likes to spread it."

She bit her lip. Lord willing, Kristina would keep her mouth shut about tonight's incident. If they'd just kept on driving like Kristina had wanted to do, she would never have seen Noah's dat come out of the bar in a drunken rage. "I'm sorry I stuck my nose into your business tonight," she said. "You tried to tell me, but I wouldn't listen. I shouldn't have interfered."

"You didn't know."

"But I should have known. It's plain as day that you can handle your dat by yourself." She waved her hand in his direction. "You have all those big muscles and such."

He tilted his head and eyed her teasingly. "You like my muscles?"

She squirmed in her chair and cleared her throat. "I didn't say I liked your muscles. I just said you have them. Anyone with two eyes can see that."

"You have two eyes," he said, almost knocking her over with his piercing gaze. "Greenish blue. Like looking into an icy spring lake."

She might have shivered just a little.

He tore his eyes from her face, bent over, and stuffed a couple of logs into the woodstove. "Are you satisfied about my family?"

She crossed her heart. "I'll never mention them again . . . very much."

He cocked an eyebrow. "Very much?"

"I'd like to hear about your sister Lisa. She's only a little younger than I am, and if she's got plans for a beautiful wedding, I want to hear them. Girls love talking about weddings. I want pink and blue plates."

He shook his head vigorously. "Don't tell me. Talk of plate colors will send me running for the hills."

They laughed together, and Mandy thought she had never heard such an easy sound as Noah's laughter.

The small clock hanging on the kitchen wall chimed twelve times. Noah slapped his forehead. "Oh sis yuscht! Your grandparents are probably worried sick. I've got to get you home."

She started to unbutton his coat. "Leave it on," he said.

"If you freeze to death, who will drive me home?"

"My buggy is nice and warm. I installed a heater last winter."

"You're amazing," she said.

She could tell her praise pleased him, but he shrugged it off, as every gute Amish man should do. "None is amazing but God," he said.

"Will your dat be all right alone?"

Noah frowned and gloominess settled over him like a heavy blanket. "Once he's asleep, it's easier to wake a stone. Besides, Chester will be here."

"Okay," she said, sorry that she'd said anything to darken his mood.

After Noah gave Chester another order to stay put, they walked out into the crisp September evening. The two buggies sat side by side in front of the house. "I'll stable both horses when I get back," he said.

Noah took her elbow and helped her into the larger buggy. He turned on the floor heater, and Mandy was immediately impressed. Was there anything Noah couldn't do? She felt the warmth at her feet. In a few minutes, she would be toasty.

"Are you comfortable?" he asked.

"Jah. I might even consider giving your coat back." She settled into her seat, searching for a way to dispel the gloom that had fallen over him.

He jiggled the reins and started the horse forward.

"I'm looking forward to warm fingers and toes on the ride home." Mandy's lips twitched upward. "And if you don't mind, I'd like to talk about why you like my freckles."

His face lit up with a smile.

Who knew freckles could cheer somebody up like that?

Chapter Eight

Noah pulled the buggy in front of Helmuths' house, almost regretting they'd arrived. He never would have guessed that a girl could have made him smile that much. In their half-hour ride to Huckleberry Hill, they'd talked about freckles, near-drowning experiences, muscles, and Noah's purple thumbnail that he'd smashed with a hammer last week. Mandy told him about her twin brother Max, who was allergic to strawberries and had curly hair that he could barely run a comb through.

They'd even talked about his sister Lisa and what color plates she probably wanted at her wedding.

Noah hadn't felt this comfortable with anyone for years. Yost had always been his best friend, but when Mamm had taken his brother to Missouri, there hadn't been anyone to take his place.

Apparently Mandy felt comfortable with him too. Not ten minutes ago, she had nodded off to sleep with her head resting quite comfortably on his shoulder. He tried to relax so his shoulder would be a soft place for her head while at the same time doing his best not to move a muscle on that side of his body so as not to disturb her.

It wasn't easy. The thought of her soft cheek resting

against his arm made his pulse run faster than a racehorse. Even though he tried to distract himself with thoughts of flexible shaft wood carvers and zinc-plated grade-two steel hex bolts, thinking of tools only reminded him of the way Mandy could wield a crescent wrench like she'd been born holding one. The urge to brush a wisp of hair from her face became so overpowering, he clenched his hand into a tight fist and didn't release it until the horse pulled the buggy in front of Helmuths' house.

A small propane lantern hung near the front door, and Noah could see lights on inside. Someone had waited up. Noah chastised himself for bringing her back so late. He should have been thinking more about Mandy than his own problems.

Dropping the reins, he gently nudged her head off his shoulder. She woke with the dazed look of sleep in those aqua-blue eyes. "Did I fall asleep?"

He nodded.

She sighed. "I always seem to do embarrassing things when I'm with you."

He opened the door, climbed out, and took her hand. She slid across the seat and got out on his side. "I don't remember any embarrassing things," he said.

"Hmm, let's see," she said, lifting her eyes to the sky. "I lectured you on your porch and shamed you in front of your dog. I spied on you and then nearly drowned. I ate French toast with my fingers. Embarrassing."

Noah smiled. The French toast incident was one of his favorite memories. "Cum," he said, taking her elbow and guiding her toward the house. "I was raised better than to be thoughtless and bring a girl home so late at night."

"As I recall, I refused to leave your house and threatened to steal your coat."

"It is the man's duty to watch out for the women. I hope your grandparents aren't cross with me."

"My grandparents never get cross with anybody. And Dawdi thinks you are all pies and cakes. He brags about you as if you were one of his own sons. Besides, it's my fault I'm so late."

"I needed your help."

"You did not," she said, flashing him a self-deprecating smile.

He'd told her as much, but when he considered it, he realized that he had indeed needed Mandy's help. She'd made him feel like a person tonight instead of just a walking shadow. A warm sensation like pleasant summer air spread through his chest. How long had it been since he hadn't felt invisible?

They tromped up the porch steps, and Mandy opened the door. Light flooded from out of the house. Mandy's grandparents must have turned on every propane lamp they owned.

Anna and Felty sat at the kitchen table sipping something pink and steamy from their mugs. An imposing tower of pot holders, at least a foot high, sat in the middle of the table, just waiting for Mandy's suitors to claim them. Noah's mouth quirked downward at the sight of them. More than one boy in Bonduel would gladly chase after pretty Mandy Helmuth. With that many potential boyfriends, Mandy was bound to find somebody she liked. Although Mandy professed her indifference, in the end, she might be taken in by Adam Wengerd's perfectly straight teeth or that blasted cleft in Freeman Kiem's chin.

Anna leaped from her chair as if she didn't have one arthritic joint in her entire body. "My goodness, Noah. What happened to your lip?"

He self-consciously raised his hand to his mouth. "Ach, it's nothing."

"A boy who works with tools always has one injury or another," Mandy said. "Look at his thumb."

Noah let out the breath he'd been holding.

"Ach, du lieva, Mandy," Anna said. "Such excitement here tonight and you missed all of it." Her eyes twinkled with delight and just a hint of scolding. "I invited four boys to dinner and you never showed up."

"It's my fault, Anna," Noah said, not all that sorry that Mandy had missed a fresh batch of young men. "I needed her help with my buggy and then we got to talking about freckles."

Freckles? That was the worst excuse he'd ever thought up. But at the moment, thoughts of Mandy and those cute freckles crowded everything else out of his head.

"Annie used to have freckles in primary school," Felty said. "She was the prettiest girl I ever saw."

"Now, Felty," Anna said. She looked at Noah as if she thoroughly forgave him for every bad thing he'd ever done. "Noah, you are such a gute boy. I'm sure you didn't mean to keep Mandy out so long. It's just that we are running out of time. It's been eight days, and Mandy hasn't so much as gone on a picnic with a boy."

Felty stared into his mug of pink juice. "She's been out with Noah. That's something."

"Now, Felty. She can't be wasting her time helping people with their buggies with only four weeks left."

"He also pulled her from the river," Felty added, not taking his eyes from that mug.

Anna nodded as if she wanted to move on with the conversation. "And we're very grateful."

"I'm real sorry," Noah said. "I forgot my manners. I should have brought her home earlier."

Mandy laid a hand on Anna's arm. "Noah had nothing to do with it. Kristina's mamm had some trouble at the hospital, and she has to stay overnight. I thought I should be with Kristina. Then on my way home I ran into Noah, who needed help with his buggy."

"Oh dear," Anna said, seeming to forget about the quartet of suitors she'd entertained at dinner. "Is Ruth all right? Did they have to take out more than her gallbladder?"

"She had some reaction to the anesthetic. She will be right as rain by morning."

"I'm glad to hear it," Anna said. "I should do something to help her feel better. Should I take a casserole or knit something?"

"Knit something," Mandy and Noah said at the same time. Mandy glanced at Noah and winked. He felt as if he'd been knocked upside the head with a two-by-four. Had she meant to wink or did she just have something in her eye? Whatever it was, it shouldn't have made him feel as if he were taking a sudden drop on a roller coaster. Why was he acting like a child?

Anna nodded. "What does one knit for someone when they've had gallbladder surgery?"

"A pillow," Felty said.

Anna looked up to the ceiling and thought that idea over. "I've never knitted a pillow before. Maybe it's time to learn how. The doctor says if you stop learning, your brain will turn to mush." She motioned to two empty chairs at the table. "Cum, Mandy. Cum, Noah, sit. We must put our heads together to figure out how to find Mandy a husband."

"I should be going," Noah said. "I'm coming back in the morning to start on the roof."

"Now, Noah, relax for a minute," Anna said, pulling two mugs out of the cupboard. "You work too hard. Besides, we need your opinion. You know all of the boys in Bonduel."

Mandy sat and smiled at him apologetically. Her mammi was hard to say no to. Reluctantly, Noah slid into the chair next to Mandy. He'd rather not talk about the eligible boys in Bonduel. He wasn't sure why, but he didn't want Anna actually finding a boy for her granddaughter.

Anna poured a steaming mug for each of them from a

saucepan on the stove. It looked milky and pink and had lumps of something floating in it that Noah hoped were raisins.

"What is that, Mammi?" Mandy said, an uncomfortable smile twitching at her lips. Noah sensed that she was feeling more discomfort for him than she was for herself. She needn't have worried. He'd eat anything to spare Anna's feelings.

"It's cranberry-raisin eggnog," Anna said. "My own recipe."

"Delicious," Felty said, raising his mug and taking a hearty swallow. "It's got real cranberries and raisins."

Anna gave a mug to each of them, sat down, and scooted her chair closer to the table like she meant business. "Tell me, Noah. Who is a gute match for our Mandy?" She took a sip of her pink eggnog. "And it's not going to be one of those four who came to dinner."

Noah wanted to pump his fist in the air and shout hooray. Instead, he opted for a furrowed brow and a concerned frown. "Why is that?"

"It was the strangest thing, but after we ate, each and every one of them told me they wouldn't be able to come to our house for dinner for the whole rest of the year. Can you imagine? They're all busy with plans."

"Plans?" Mandy said.

"That's what they said. They were all such nice young men. I made my special potato, lentil, and green bean cheese soup, which was a little cold since we waited for over an hour for Mandy to come home."

"It was food fit for a king," Felty said.

Noah didn't know what king Felty was talking about, but potato, lentil, and green bean cheese soup sounded slightly unappetizing, even to Noah, who ate his own cooking every night. He looked into his mug and had no trouble guessing what had driven those four boys away. He felt a surge of gratitude for Anna's cooking skills. If Mandy's disinterest didn't keep the boys away, Anna's potato, lentil, and green bean cheese soup probably would.

He took a hearty swig of his eggnog and let the raisins and cranberries slide down his throat. "What boys came over tonight?"

Anna looked sideways at Mandy. "I hired a driver to bring them up from Wautoma."

"Wautoma?" Mandy looked positively astounded.

"But I can't keep recruiting boys from out of town," Anna said. "There isn't enough time or money. That's why I need your help, Noah. What boys from Bonduel would you recommend?"

Mandy's eyes flashed with amused defiance, as if daring him to speak.

Against her mint-green dress, her green-blue eyes seemed even bigger and momentarily made him forget the question. "Um, a gute boy for Mandy . . . um . . . Adam Wengerd has gute teeth."

Mandy kicked him under the table. He grinned at her.

"I like a gute mouth full of teeth," Anna said.

"I have one fake tooth yet," Felty said, "but all the rest are real. And one root canal. And thanks to Mandy's cousin Ben, my septum isn't deviated anymore."

Anna put down her mug and laced her fingers together. "It would help to narrow it down if we knew what qualities you like in a boy, Mandy."

Noah couldn't hold back a full-blown smile. "She likes muscles," he said, propping his elbow on the table and flexing his biceps several times for Mandy to see.

She quickly turned her face away from him. It was glowing bright red. "I do not."

Anna, serious about finding a suitable boy, didn't pick up on the fact that he was teasing. "Muscles. Well, that's at least something to go on. Wallace Sensenig's dat is a blacksmith.

Blacksmiths are famous for being able to lift anvils and such. It wonders me how strong Adam Wengerd is."

"I already told you, Mammi," Mandy said. "Adam Wengerd is not for me."

Noah's ears perked up at this good news. What did Mandy have against Adam Wengerd? Whatever it was, Noah was grateful.

"I think you should give him another chance, dear."

Felty got up from the table to pour himself more eggnog. "Noah is as strong as an ox."

"And she needs someone who can swim," Noah said.

Mandy kicked him under the table again. He had to bite his tongue to stifle his laughter.

"Most of the boys around here can swim," Anna said. "But I'm not sure how to determine who the strongest is."

Mandy finally chimed in. "Mammi, I really don't want to impose on you like this. You said it yourself. There's not enough time. I hate to have you do all this worrying when you should be enjoying life."

Anna waved away Mandy's concerns with a flick of her wrist. "Stuff and nonsense. This *is* what makes my life enjoyable. It's so exciting to see a romance bud between two young people. What other excitement could a middle-aged Amish woman expect to have?"

Noah smiled to himself. Anna had to be at least eighty years old. If she considered herself middle-aged, then she could expect to live for nearly another century. He eyed the cute little lady across from him. If anybody could live that long, no doubt it would be feisty Anna Helmuth.

Anna scooted her chair away from the table and retrieved a pencil and notebook from one of the drawers. Sitting back down, she licked the tip of the pencil and began writing. "Let's see. I've got muscles and a gute swimmer. What else do you want in a husband?"

"Freeman Kiem has a cleft in his chin," Noah added.

"I would think she wants a godly man who knows how to work hard," Felty said.

Anna nodded and jotted notes in her notebook. "Of course. And what about teeth? Do you like teeth?"

Mandy looked daggers at Noah before turning to her grandmother. "I like teeth, Mammi."

His heart thumped like a like a drum beating double-time. He was bowled over every time she looked at him, no matter the kind of look she gave him.

Anna added to her list. "I'll also put young and baptized and honors fater and mater. Every girl wants a boy who honors his parents."

Noah felt as if his chest caved in, and the doubt buried him like an avalanche. Did he honor his parents? He hadn't been able to make peace with the answer to that question for three years. Did he dishonor his mamm by honoring his dat? But if he abandoned his dat to care for his mamm, where was the honor in that?

Mandy glanced at him, and her smile drooped. He never had been very good at hiding his darkest emotions, and any mention of his parents dredged up feelings he usually buried at the bottom of his heart. Mandy knew, and right or not, he hated the fact that she had witnessed his shame.

"I need to go," he said, scooting his chair back and making a horrible racket as the chair scraped against the floor. "In the morning, I have to go to the bishop's to take a look at his milking machines, and then I'll be up to start on the roof. Probably around eleven."

Felty stood and shook his hand. The warmth in his expression made Noah feel a little better. Felty valued Noah's work and seemed to genuinely respect his abilities. And surely good-hearted Felty would know that Noah tried hard to honor his parents. If he wasn't always successful, Felty would never think the less of him for it. "I waited till September to start on the roof," Felty said. "So it won't be as hot up there. But it will still be mighty hard work."

Noah couldn't smile but he nodded and firmly clasped Felty's hand. "I'm glad for the job. I'm not afraid of hard work."

"I know you're not," Felty said, glancing at Mandy. "You work harder than anybody I know."

Noah eyed Mandy before donning his hat and coat. She looked extremely unhappy, as if she'd accidentally stepped on Noah's dog. He wanted to smile, to wink, to do something to reassure her that he was fine and that Anna's unintentional words hadn't stung like a nest of hornets. But it was all he could do to keep the hitch in his throat from choking him. "Good-bye," he muttered. "I'll see you tomorrow."

"See you tomorrow," Felty said.

"Good-bye," Mandy said, almost as if she were asking a question.

He slipped out the door and into the night. It would be better when Mandy went back to Ohio so he wouldn't feel like he was forever in a state of swirling emotions.

He climbed into the buggy and snapped the reins, knowing that it wouldn't be better at all. Mandy Helmuth might have been annoying, bossy, and prone to stick her nose where it didn't belong, but he adored those freckles. Maybe she could overlook the worst of him and agree to be his friend.

Perhaps he could talk her into five weeks instead of four.

Chapter Nine

Mandy drained the dirty water from the sink and then rinsed and wrung out the mop. The entire house took over two hours to mop. Unlike *Englisch* homes, there was no wall-to-wall carpeting, just yards and yards of wood and linoleum floors that needed to be cleaned. Mammi kept her house tidy. Mandy hated to think that she was doing all that mopping every week. Even though she protested whenever anybody called her old, Mammi was getting up in years. Mopping couldn't be the easiest task.

Mandy gazed out the window for about the hundredth time. No sign of Noah yet. She glanced at the clock. Only ten.

That morning she had gathered eggs, milked the cow, and picked what was left of the ripe tomatoes. After breakfast, Mammi and Dawdi had been in a very great hurry. Mammi had left the dishes for Mandy and wrapped up in her royal-blue sweater. Mammi had many sweaters of assorted colors, none of them the traditional Amish black. She loved her knitting so much that not even the bishop had the heart to tell her that non-black sweaters were against the rules.

Mammi had told Mandy that she needed to make some urgent calls, but hadn't said what was so urgent that she needed to leave right after breakfast at six o'clock.

After Mammi and Dawdi had left, Mandy had done up the dishes, strained the milk, oiled the furniture, and mopped the floor, and still the minutes had crawled by. Was Noah having success at Yoder's dairy? She hoped he wouldn't be late. Surely Dawdi's roof was just as important as the bishop's milking machines.

Mandy shook out the mop and shook her head at the same time. Why did she care when Noah arrived? He wasn't coming to see her.

Her face grew warm. But she would certainly like to see him.

She scowled to herself and shoved the mop into Mammi's broom closet. Nope. Nope, she didn't care about seeing Noah. She was only here for three more weeks and didn't want to form any attachments, especially not with a brawny, ornery Bonduel boy who growled at her frequently and teased her mercilessly.

Not to mention the fact that her best friend was still in love with him. That put a significant damper on things. Kristina would be loudly indignant if she knew Mandy was entertaining any thoughts about Noah or pining for his arrival on Huckleberry Hill.

Even though she had resolved not to be the least bit excited when Noah finally did show up, her heart skittered about when she heard a firm knock at the door. That could only be Noah.

He stood on the porch, frowning as if he'd just come from a funeral. He held a paper plate covered in tinfoil. She couldn't figure out if he was frowning because he didn't want to see her or because he was more than usually grumpy this morning.

Neither.

He handed her the paper plate. "I'm really sorry about last night. I said some very rude things that I didn't mean."

"What's this?" she said.

"It's a gift. A food gift. To show you how truly sorry I am."

"Another one? You don't have to bring me food when you want to apologize. Since you do something to offend me every two or three minutes, you'd have to bring an entire grocery store to make amends."

He winced, but there was amusement in it. "Don't remind me."

She peeled back the plate and tried not to laugh. "You brought me an egg salad sandwich?"

"I haven't gone to the grocery store this week. All I had was bread, mayonnaise, and eggs. And horseradish. I put horseradish in it. My special recipe. You'll like it."

Mandy didn't waste any time. Her stomach growled as if somebody had suddenly awoken it from a long nap. She snatched one of the halves and took a big bite. The horseradish mixed with mayonnaise and a pinch of mustard made her taste buds dance a jig. "Mmm, this is delicious."

He quirked his mouth into a sheepish grin. "I'm glad you like it."

She took a bigger bite, and he waited as she savored then swallowed. "You are a very gute cook, Noah Mischler."

"Well, it's not technically cooking."

She finished the first half and picked up the second. Hesitating, she held the sandwich out for him. "I'm sorry. It's rude to eat in front of you like this. Do you want some of this?"

He shook his head and stepped back. "I'm thoroughly enjoying watching you eat it."

She didn't offer a second time. She took another voracious bite.

He gazed at her with a boyish grin on his face. "Eggs Benedict again this morning?"

"Oatmeal." Mandy shuddered. "With bacon bits."

He chuckled. "I'm beginning to fear you might starve before you go back to Ohio."

"Not if you keep doing things to offend me. You're good at apologizing." She finished the sandwich and brushed her hands off. "Now that you can't possibly take back your gift, I want you to know that you have no reason to feel bad. If anybody should apologize, it's me."

"That's not true," he said. "I don't usually talk to girls the way I talked to you last night."

She wanted to wipe that concerned look off his face. She opted for a diversion. "How does your lip feel this morning? The swelling's gone down."

"Fine. My dat . . . It feels fine. I didn't get hit that hard." He backed away from her and down the porch steps. "I better start on that roof. I don't want Felty thinking he's paying me for doing nothing."

She nodded, surprised at how disappointed she felt. Noah would be eight feet above her head all day, but she wouldn't even be able to see him. At the moment, spying sounded like a pretty good idea.

"I brought Chester," Noah said. "He doesn't often get a chance to go on an adventure. Do you think it's okay if I let him out of the wagon?"

"Jah, of course," Mandy said. "Would he like a playmate?"

Noah nodded.

"Sparky," Mandy called. "Come and play with Chester."

Sparky waddled down the hall as if she'd just awakened from a long nap. "Sparky, do you want to play outside with a new playmate?"

Sparky wagged her tail, paused long enough to let Mandy run a hand across her back, and padded outside to meet this new friend. She hopped down the steps and stopped, sniffing the air, looking for the new playmate with her nose.

Noah walked to an old and creaky wagon pulled by a team of Percheron draft horses. How could he afford the workhorses and the two for his buggies? His dog Chester perched faithfully on a box in the back of the wagon, waiting for Noah to give him permission to get down. That was the most obedient dog Mandy had ever seen. Noah gave the word, and Chester seemed to spring to life. He bounded from the wagon and romped around the yard as if he'd just been freed from prison. When he passed Sparky, he nudged her with his nose, and Sparky sprang to life, bounding after Chester in a game of doggie tag.

Noah's wagon was laden with several bundles of asphalt shingles for Dawdi's new roof plus a configuration of boards and metal pipes that would be fitted together to make scaffolding. She watched as Noah hefted a bundle of shingles and started a pile of them to the side of the house. They must have been heavy. She could see the muscles of his arms and back tighten under his shirt and the sweat beading on his forehead after only two trips to the wagon.

He glanced at her as he made his third trip to the wagon, and she realized that she couldn't stand on the porch and stare at him all day.

No matter how much she wanted to.

"Can I help?" she called.

He shook his head, not exerting more energy than he needed to.

Mandy had run out of excuses to stand there. She turned to go into the house when Mammi and Dawdi rolled up the hill in their buggy. Dawdi stopped the buggy in front of the house and Mammi practically jumped from her seat and came racing toward Mandy as fast as her eighty-three-year-old legs would let her.

"Oh, Mandy," she panted, looking like a child about to open a Christmas present. "We've only got three minutes before they'll be coming. We need to make a pitcher of lemonade and grab a stack of paper cups." She raced into the house. "And where's my clipboard? I need my clipboard."

Mandy inched into the house where Mammi frantically

searched for her clipboard among Dawdi's newspapers and magazines at the side of his recliner.

"Is everything all right?" Mandy asked, not really wanting to know what Mammi was up to. She had a sinking feeling it involved pot holders, teeth, and prospective husbands.

"Mandy," Mammi asked, reaching into her knitting closet and pulling out four, five, *six* pot holders. Mandy swallowed hard. Mammi was expecting a crowd. "Run out to the buggy and get the lemons. Only fresh-squeezed will do."

Mandy slumped her shoulders and trudged outside. She couldn't muster any of Mammi's enthusiasm. Six fewer pot holders. They'd be knitting until Ascension Day.

Chester, who had been sniffing patches of dirt, ran to her and expected a greeting. She patted him on the head and scratched his neck. "You'll run the unsuitable ones off for me, won't you?"

The buggy had already disappeared. Dawdi must have taken it into the barn. She walked into the dim space and found Dawdi unhitching the horse while singing one of his many cheerful ditties, with lyrics that didn't quite fit the tune. "*I know there is a land of beautiful flowers, where you and I will meet when we're dead. We'll sit and while away the long, long hours, In heaven's bright eternal land.*"

"Pretty Flowers" had never sounded quite like that before.

"I'm here for the lemons," she said, with as much excitement in her voice as if she'd said, "I'm here for my root canal."

Dawdi stopped singing, reached into the buggy, and pulled out a grocery bag. "We bought three dozen," he said, winking at her. "Your mammi is planning on a lot of thirsty boys."

"I know," Mandy said. "She brought out six pot holders."

Dawdi's eyes twinkled as he stroked his beard. "Those are only for the boys who haven't already gotten one."

Mandy grimaced. "How many are coming?"

"A baker's dozen, at least."

Mandy went speechless, shocked into silence by the sheer numbers.

Dawdi handed her the bag of lemons, which was really quite heavy, and finished unhitching Pepper, the horse. "Your mammi always puts other people's needs ahead of herself. I love that about her."

Mandy took a deep breath and tried to look on the bright side like her dawdi always did. At least this batch of young men would get a nice, cool glass of lemonade for their trouble—whatever trouble it was that Mammi was planning on causing.

Well, maybe not. They'd run out of ice before they ran out of suitors.

Mandy followed Dawdi as he led Pepper out of the barn and released her to graze in the small fenced-in area north of the barn. She really didn't have a reason to follow him. She was just avoiding the inevitable gathering.

"Be sure to save a glass for Noah," Dawdi said as he closed the gate. "He'll be working hard in the sun all afternoon."

Mandy lugged her bulging bag of lemons back to the house. She encountered Noah along the way, going back to his wagon for another load of shingles.

"Here," he said, taking the bag of lemons from her before she even had time to protest. "Let me help."

She followed as he carried the bag into the house and laid it on the kitchen counter. "Trying to get rid of your warts?" he said, one corner of his mouth twitching upward.

She narrowed her eyes at him. "I don't have warts."

Mammi stood at the counter measuring cup after cup of sugar into a five-gallon cooler. "Noah," she said. "Would you like to help us pick a husband? They'll be here any minute."

Mandy winced and held her ground, although every

nerve in her body wanted to run down the hill and keep going until she got to Milwaukee. Surely in Milwaukee there weren't any mammis or Amish suitors or boys whose deep-brown eyes pierced through her skull every time they looked at her.

The muscles of Noah's jaw clenched, as they always did when he was irritated about something. "Nae, I'm afraid I can't spare the time."

Mammi didn't look overly disappointed. "All right then. We'll tell you how it turns out."

Noah crossed to the door and disappeared more quickly than Mandy would have thought possible. It was just as well. She'd rather that he not witness her humiliation.

"I thank the good Lord that I have two lemon juicers," Mammi said, pulling both of them from her bottom drawer. "Felty loves gadgets."

Even working together and as fast as they could, it took Mammi and Mandy almost twenty minutes to juice all the lemons. Mandy thought her hand might fall off by the time they finished. She glanced out the window as she poured the last of the lemon juice into the jug. "Mammi, I thought they were coming any minute."

She mixed water with the lemon juice and sugar in the jug. They didn't have a spoon long enough to reach the bottom of the jug, so she used the paddle from Mammi's old butter churn to mix the water, sugar, and lemon juice. Hardly anybody churned butter anymore, but Mammi held on to it just in case. Or rather, Dawdi held on to it. He loved gadgets.

Mammi furrowed her brow. "I can't remember if I told them ten-thirty or eleven. Maybe it was eleven. I'm glad I got the times mixed up. We wouldn't have been ready at ten-thirty."

"Just what have you planned for all these boys, Mammi?"

"Last night at three in the morning, I shot up from my

sleep with an idea. Felty thought I was having a heart attack. Noah said you like muscles, so we're going to give these boys a muscle test."

Mandy wasn't sure she wanted to ask. "A muscle test?"

"I think it's the cleverest idea I've ever had. That's what comes from sleeping on a problem." Mammi dumped all the ice cubes they had—one tray—into the jug and slid the lid onto the top.

Mandy winced. Nice tepid lemonade for the muscle test.

"Oh dear," Mammi said, taking hold of one of the jug handles. "This is going to be too heavy for me to carry out to the barn. Mandy, get Noah, would you?"

"Why do we need to take it to the barn?"

Mammi's eyes twinkled like a night of a million stars. "You'll see."

Mandy thought she might rather have a toothache than bother Noah, especially if he was going to be irritated again. "I can carry it, Mammi," she said, before actually trying to lift it off the cupboard.

Maybe not.

Mandy dragged her feet to the front door. If the jug was needed in the barn, Noah was the only one to carry it. No one else on Huckleberry Hill was strong enough. But he would never finish that roof if he had to be the fetch-and-carry boy.

She walked outside. Noah had set up the scaffolding in front of the house to the side of the covered porch so Mammi and Dawdi could still get in and out of the house. The wagon sat on the lawn next to the scaffolding for Noah to dump old shingles into the back of it. He had unhitched his team. They were probably in the small pasture with Pepper. They wouldn't be needed until later when he was ready to haul the old shingles away.

Mandy patted Chester on the head as she walked by. Wearing heavy work gloves and a slim pair of protective goggles, Noah stood on the scaffolding with a shingle fork, a four-pronged flat pitchfork, ready to scrape the old shingles off the roof. A plastic garbage bin sat next to him so he could throw the old shingles into it and then dump them into the wagon when the bin was full. His face was already dripping with sweat, even though it couldn't have been more than fifty-five degrees outside. She tried not to stare at the muscles bulging underneath his shirt or the agile way he maneuvered a shingle fork, as if it weighed no more than a stick.

Before he could turn around and catch sight of her, she marched back into the house. She couldn't, just couldn't, ask him to stop what he was doing and help her with the lemonade. If they must, they'd transport it to the barn one cupful at a time.

Mammi sampled lemonade from a little cup. "Is he coming?"

"I'll take it, Mammi," Mandy said, resolving to haul that thing all the way to the barn or die trying.

Without waiting for Mammi's protests, Mandy hefted the jug from the cupboard to the floor. It landed with a thud and probably left a dent in the wood, but nothing spilled and both Mammi and Mandy's toes were uninjured. Grasping one of the handles, Mandy dragged the jug across the kitchen floor, shoved it over the lip of the threshold, and tugged it across the porch to the steps.

With clipboard and paper cups in hand, Mammi followed to watch Mandy's progress. "Those stairs aren't going to be easy. You'll be all sweaty and wrinkled for your young men. Are you sure we shouldn't just ask Noah? He won't mind. He's such a gute boy."

Mandy reassured her mammi with a smile, grunted like a grizzly bear, and lugged the jug down the stairs. Taking a deep breath, she sat the jug on the grass and massaged her arms. Her muscles felt as if they'd been stretched beyond repair and she thought she might have pulled her shoulders from their sockets, but at least the lemonade was headed in the right direction.

After a brief rest, she grasped one handle with both hands and pulled the jug through the grass, walking backward and putting her back into it. Chester thought she was playing a game. He wagged his tail and yipped and tried to clean Mandy's face with his tongue.

"Chester, not now," she scolded. He stopped mid-bark, sat on his haunches, and gazed at her with that wise look on his face. Most obedient dog ever.

She was momentarily hindered when the jug met a depression in the grass that she couldn't wrench it out of.

"Do you want me to give you a push?" Mammi said.

She sensed him coming up behind her before she saw him. Noah placed his hand over hers around the jug handle. She turned her head and found his face within inches of hers. "Mandy," he said, frowning in concern, "you are going to kill yourself."

With heart racing too wildly to say anything coherent, she let go of the handle, stood up straight, and pursed her lips like a child caught stealing cookies from the jar. What did he mean smelling like leather and sweat and touching her hand like that? How could he expect a girl to make an intelligent reply with that concerned expression on his face and those arms that looked as if they'd been chiseled out of stone?

"Mammi and I are doing a test," she stuttered.

"A test?" he said as he grasped the jug with both hands and lifted it as if it were empty. "A lemonade test?"

"It's all part of the plan to find Mandy a husband," Mammi said. "I'm glad you came along to help. I told Mandy to fetch you first thing to do the carrying."

"I didn't want to bother you," Mandy said, making a conscious effort not to let her eyes stray to his well-defined biceps. Who cared if Noah had muscles? Everybody had muscles. She flexed her own arm. She had muscles. No need to obsess about muscles.

He headed toward the barn. She followed him. "It's no trouble for me," he said, "while it could mean weeks in the hospital for you."

"Weeks in the hospital?"

"You could have dropped this jug and shattered every bone in your foot."

Mandy raised her eyebrows. "I'm not that weak."

"Of course you're not weak. But this jug is heavy. I know. I saw you try to drag it across the lawn."

They walked into the barn where Dawdi sharpened his pruning shears. "Where would you like this lemonade, Anna?" Noah asked.

Mammi pointed to the five-foot-high stack of hay bales that had been delivered three days ago. "Right here on one of these bales would be perfect. Denki, Noah. We couldn't have done it without you."

Noah placed the jug on the cement floor, pulled a hay bale off the tall stack, and set the jug on top of it. "Okay," he said, giving Mandy a quick smile. He turned on his heels and marched out of the barn as if he were running from a fire. Mandy was slightly disappointed. She knew he had to get back to the roof, but couldn't he have stayed just another minute or two to help Dawdi with the shears or to let her give him a tour of the barn?

Hearing voices, male voices, Mandy peered out of the open doors. Noah was standing just outside the barn shaking hands with a group of Amish boys. Her heart thudded like a sledgehammer against cement, and she thought she might be ill. They were gathered around Noah, so it was hard to tell how many boys there actually were, but she counted at least nine straw hats.

Oh dear. What was Mammi planning on doing with nine Amish boys?

"They're here," Mammi said, beaming as if all her grandchildren had come for an extended stay. "I must have told them eleven o'clock."

Dawdi looked up from his pruning shears. "How do you do it, Annie Banannie? You are a miracle worker."

"Now, Felty," Mammi said, giggling as if she were a little girl being teased by a cute second-grader.

Three more boys ambled up the lane followed by a buggy with at least two occupants.

Mandy stared at the herd of young men as her jaw slowly sank to the floor. "How did you persuade all of them to come?"

"Well," Mammi said, smoothing her apron and sitting on one of the sturdy hay bales, "we're blessed it's a Saturday. Most of them didn't have to take a day off work. I told them I am looking for somebody to do a job, and I needed them to come and do an interview."

Mandy sat next to her mammi. "You told a fib?"

Mammi looked horrified at the very thought. "Of course not. I *am* looking for somebody to do a job. The job is to marry my granddaughter."

Mandy regarded her mammi doubtfully. "You make it sound so unpleasant, like a chore."

Mammi patted her knee. "Oh, my dear. None of these boys would think it unpleasant to marry you. That's one of the reasons I was able to convince them to come. They think you're pretty. I told them that you would be here and that you would be helping me do the interviews."

Now she knew positively that she was going to be sick. How could she face anybody after today? While shaking hands with Davy Burkholder, Noah glanced back at her and then just as quickly looked away. What was going through his mind? Was he secretly laughing, or did he pity her?

Mammi cradled her clipboard in her arm and jotted a few notes at the top of her paper. "Your dawdi and I went to every home in both districts this morning to round up suitable boyfriends."

"I just can't believe they all showed up." And she couldn't believe this was happening. She now understood how it might be possible to die of embarrassment.

Mammi looked at her out of the corner of her eye. "I must confess, I also promised them each a plate of cookies."

This news made Mandy feel worse. No one would be lured to a "job" interview with the promise of a plate of Mammi's cookies.

"And a glass of lemonade."

Wearing a crooked smile, Felty concentrated on sharpening his pruners. "Be sure to save a glass for Noah. He'll be sweating something wonderful come suppertime."

Mammi set the paper cups next to the jug, clutched her clipboard to her chest, and cocked her pencil at the ready. "Felty, will you go out there and let the boys in one at a time?"

Ach, du lieva. Mandy would have rather been anywhere but here. The shame was absolutely unbearable.

She squared her shoulders. Noah said she was strong. She would bear the humiliation for dear Mammi, whose only goal in life was to make her grandchildren happy. Besides, it would give her and Noah something to laugh about later on.

In no hurry whatsoever, Dawdi shuffled out of the barn and closed the doors behind him.

Mammi grabbed Mandy's elbow and bobbed her head up and down excitedly. "Are you ready? This is going to be so much fun. I'm glad you wore the baby-blue dress today. It brings out your eyes."

Mandy swallowed hard. As long as her eyes didn't fall out of her head, she'd be okay.

The barn had two rows of small windows near the ceiling,

so Mammi and Mandy had sufficient light to see by, even when the doors were closed. But still, light flooded the barn when one of the doors swung open. Mandy's cousin Titus stuck his head into the barn. Mandy nearly giggled with relief. "Dawdi said I should go first," Titus said. The toothpick in his mouth bobbed up and down as he spoke.

Mammi sighed in good-natured exasperation. "Titus, what are you doing here?"

"Freeman says you're hiring somebody for a job." He walked farther into the barn and regarded Mammi, sitting on the hay bale like a queen on her throne. He furrowed his brow. "Aren't you happy to see me?"

"I'm always happy to see you, Titus," Mammi said. "But don't be offended. You are definitely not going to get this job."

"But why not? I'm a gute worker, and after the corn's in, I'll have more time on my hands."

"I'm sure you're a fine worker," Mammi said. "Your dat raised you, and I raised your dat. I made sure my *kinner* worked hard every day." She patted the hay bale next to her and Mandy. "Cum, sit, and I will tell you a secret."

Titus sat down and put his arm around Mammi. "You're matching Mandy, aren't you?"

Mandy groaned. If Titus had figured it out, then nobody else had been fooled either.

Mammi widened her eyes. "How did you know?"

"Your apron pocket is bulging with pot holders."

"Oh dear," Mammi said, pulling the bright pot holders from her pocket. "I'll have to hide these." She stuffed them into the crack between the two hay bales and smiled at Titus. "Since you've taken all this time to come up here, we can try our test on you. It will be gute practice when the real boys come in."

"I'm a real boy," Titus said.

"Ach, Titus, you know what I mean."

Titus pulled the toothpick out of his mouth. He only did that when things were serious. "What do you want me to do?"

"Stand up and scoot that hay bale to where you'll have a little more space," Mammi said.

Mandy was just as curious as Titus as to what Mammi had in mind. Titus did as he was told.

Mammi nodded. "Now I want you to lift that bale over your head."

Titus looked as if he'd swallowed a slimy frog. "What? Why?"

Mandy giggled at the look on Titus's face. Although tall—he was a Helmuth, after all—Titus was of a slight build. Noah's thick arms made Titus's look like twigs.

Mammi didn't notice his expression because she was making notes on her clipboard. "Can you do it?"

Titus's mouth fell open, and he looked at Mandy, appealing for help. "It's gotta weigh at least a hundred pounds."

Mammi smiled pleasantly at Titus and made her voice sweet and soft as she always did when one of her grandchildren needed a little extra encouragement. "You move hay all the time on your farm."

"Jah, Mammi, but not over my head."

"Just try it, dear."

Titus wrapped his fingers around the two pieces of thick twine that held the hay bale together. Grunting, he managed to raise the bale to the level of his shoulders before his arms gave out and he let go. The bale tumbled to the floor with a quiet thud and a swish, showing no evidence of how heavy it really was.

"That was real good," Mandy said, trying to be encouraging. "Those things are heavy."

Titus winced and massaged his back. "I think I bulged a disc or something."

Mandy understood what Mammi had planned for all those boys waiting in line outside the barn. A muscle test.

Her face felt as if it were on fire. Could things get any worse?

Jah, they could.

"Titus," Mammi said, studying her clipboard, "do you know how to swim?"

Titus gazed doubtfully at Mammi. "You know I do. Dawdi taught me."

Mammi made a few more notes on her paper while Titus watched her in confused silence. She tapped her pencil on the clipboard. "You did your very best. That's what counts with God. He doesn't look on outward appearance."

"Okay," Titus said. "Can I have a glass of lemonade now?"

Mammi looked at the jug and pursed her lips. "Oh dear. I think we should save it for the real boys."

"I'm a real boy," Titus protested.

Mandy stood and pulled a paper cup from the bag. "We should let him have a drink, Mammi. He worked hard."

"Of course you're right," Mammi said. "But maybe we should give him half a cupful, just in case. I don't want to run out."

"We won't run out." She filled Titus's cup to the brim and handed it to him.

He frowned as if he had just failed a test he hadn't studied for.

"Now, Titus," Mammi said. "You may send the first suitor in. And remember, don't tell any of them, not even Freeman, that we're choosing one of them for Mandy. I don't want them to feel bad if we choose someone else."

Titus downed his lemonade in three gulps. "Okay, Mammi."

She arched an eyebrow. "And don't give them any clues

about the test. We don't want anyone to have an unfair advantage."

Titus slumped his shoulders. "I won't, Mammi, but will you tell me if any of them get it over their head?"

Mammi drew a line clear across the paper just underneath Titus's name. "Do you think you could send them in in alphabetical order, dear?"

Titus shuffled his way to the door. "By first or last names?"

Mammi nibbled on the eraser and looked to the ceiling. "I think first is best, don't you?"

Adam Wengerd, the arrogant boy who used to have teeth like a beaver, strutted into the barn. His gaze darted between Mammi and Mandy, and he seemed on the verge of asking just what was going on here. Mandy kept her mouth shut and tried to blend into the hay bale she sat on. Wouldn't it be nice if no one could see her?

Mammi directed him to stand next to Titus's hay bale. "Adam," she said, "can you lift that hay bale over your head?"

"Do you need someone to get it into the hay mow for you?" he said, pointing upward at the small loft where they stored hay. Mammi's barn wasn't all that high, so the loft was only a couple of feet above Adam's head.

"Eventually," Mammi said. "Today we just want to see if you can lift it."

"Okay," Adam said, with a tentative note in his voice.

He managed better than Titus had. He still made a face as if his spleen would rupture, but he raised the bale an inch or two over his head before releasing it and letting it smash to the ground.

"Was that good enough?"

"Oh yes," Mammi said, nudging Mandy's leg with her knee and giving her a knowing look. "I have one question. Do you know how to swim?"

Adam raised his eyebrows. "Jah, I suppose. I never took lessons, but I go to the lake all the time."

"Okay," Mammi said.

Mandy found herself wishing she had a clipboard as well. She didn't want to write anything down. She just wanted to hide behind it.

To her horror, Mammi looked at her. "Mandy, do you have any other questions?"

Mandy pressed her lips together as if they were glued shut and shook her head.

Adam tilted his head to one side and regarded Mandy. "I'll see you next Friday night, then, okay?"

Still lacking the power of speech, Mandy nodded.

Adam nodded back and strode out of the barn as confidently as he had entered.

She'd agreed to another date with Adam because she hadn't wanted to hurt his feelings when she should have just told him no.

"Send the next one in," Mammi called before Adam had shut the door. She widened her eyes and smiled. "You didn't tell me that you and Adam are seeing each other again. I thought you'd given up on him."

"It's just . . . he asked me to go to the gathering with him on Friday."

"Is he the one? I can send all these other boys home if you want. Of course, then we'd have a lot of leftover lemonade. Titus would get his fill."

"Nae, Mammi. Adam isn't the one. I don't think anybody in Bonduel . . ."

Mammi consulted her clipboard. "He does have very nice teeth. He never took swimming lessons, but most of die youngie have never taken lessons. A lot of them swim just fine." She put a little checkmark by Adam's name. "I liked the way he lifted that hay bale. Did you notice his muscles?"

Mandy didn't know what to say. How could she tell her

Mammi that she was trying not to notice anything about any of the boys? "Um, he lifted it all the way over his head."

"Jah, but not with the arms extended. That could be a point against him."

Nae, Mammi. Please don't keep score.

"Oh dear," Mammi said. "We forgot to give him some lemonade. Do you think his feelings were hurt?"

Titus came back into the barn.

"Titus," Mammi said. "Where is the next boy?"

"He's coming. But I need a pitchfork. Do you have a pitchfork?"

Mammi gave Titus an exasperated huff. "There is one over there by Dawdi's workbench and two more in the tool-shed, and what do you need a pitchfork for?"

Titus found the pitchfork and practically raced out the door. "Denki, Mammi," he said as he closed the door behind him.

Mammi propped a hand on her hip. "Just what do you think that was about?"

Moments later, the next boy entered the barn. Well, maybe "boy" was not an accurate description. He looked to be well on the downhill side of thirty with a potbelly and a shiny bald head. He shuffled his feet and kept his eyes down, acting as timid as a church mouse. "I hear you're looking for someone to do some work."

"We have a job, yes," Mammi said. "I've never met you. How did you hear about this job?"

"Davy Burkholder called me. I have a wood shop this side of Wausau. I could use something extra on the side to help me start a goat business." He fiddled with the brim of his hat. "My name is Aaron Stutzman."

Mammi rolled her eyes. "Aaron? Doesn't Titus know what alphabetical order means?"

Aaron kept shuffling, as if standing in the barn talking to Mammi was the most uncomfortable thing he'd ever done in his life. "I don't know. He told me to come in, so I came in. Did I do it wrong?"

Mammi flashed him a smile that would have put a skittish horse at ease. "Of course not, Aaron. You're doing just fine."

Mandy nearly put a stop to the test before Mammi went any further. Aaron, who didn't look to be in any sort of good physical condition, might truly hurt himself if he tried to lift a hay bale over his head.

Mammi looked down at her clipboard. "Aaron, do you know how to swim?"

"Jah."

"And what is the condition of your teeth?"

Aaron raised his eyebrows and stretched his mouth across his face as if Mammi had said something slightly inappropriate. "I had two pulled three years ago and lost one last summer."

Mammi furiously made notes, as if Aaron had given a stirring speech and she didn't want to forget one word. After an awkward minute of Aaron shuffling and fiddling and Mandy trying to look anywhere but at him, Mammi tapped her pencil on the clipboard. "Denki, Aaron. That is all. We will let you know if we want you to do the job for us. Have a cup of lemonade on your way out."

Aaron rolled the brim of his hat in his fingers. "I am a gute worker, and I could ride the bus up here two or three days a week. I want to raise goats and sell milk."

Mammi handed Aaron a cup of lemonade. "That's a wonderful-gute occupation. Lord willing, you'll have a big herd."

Aaron took the cup from Mammi and slowly backed away, nodding and attempting to smile on his way out.

Half his lemonade spilled in the dirt as he shut the barn door behind him.

Mandy sighed. "No muscle test?"

"I'd rather not have to call an ambulance this morning."

Mammi's eyes twinkled. "I guessed that it would be a waste of time, unless you prefer older men."

"Um, nae. I prefer men from Charm."

She patted Mandy on the knee. "That's only because you haven't seen all that Bonduel has to offer yet."

The next boy strode into the barn as if he owned it. He wasn't tall, of medium build, with a shock of golden curly hair on top of his head. He truly couldn't have been more than sixteen years old.

Mammi leaned close to whisper in Mandy's ear. "I don't expect you to marry this one, but he's Adam's little brother. I couldn't very well invite Adam without inviting Zeb."

"Hello, Anna," Zeb said, grinning as if he were completely confident of winning whatever contest Mammi asked him to compete in.

Mammi picked up her clipboard, wrote his name, and huffed out a quick breath. "It wonders me if Titus ever learned his alphabet. Aren't there any *F*'s, *G*'s, or *H*'s out there?"

Zeb's self-assurance seemed to wilt a bit. "Is this a reading test? I'm not gute with my letters."

Mammi waved her hand around. "Oh, it doesn't matter. We're glad you're here, Zeb—spelled with a *Z*."

"Titus told me you need some heavy lifting done."

Mammi pursed her lips. "Titus doesn't follow instructions very well. Sometimes that boy . . ." She didn't finish her thought.

Mandy had a pretty good idea where it was going.

Mammi regained her smile. Titus might have been a little thick in the head, but he was her grandson. No mammi could love a boy more. "Well, now, Zeb. Here is the test. Can you lift this hay bale over your head?"

Zeb gazed at the bale at his feet. "Sure. Where do you want me to put it?"

"Just lift it and put it down again."

Zeb bent over and hefted the hay bale to the level of his knees. Then with a grunt, he swung it so hard that it sailed over his head and catapulted him backward. He let go before it took him to the ground, but he had to take several steps back to regain his balance. He glanced at Mandy and grinned sheepishly. "Sorry. It kind of got away from me."

"No need to apologize," Mammi assured him. "Would you like some lemonade?"

"Okay," Zeb said.

Mandy picked up a cup and filled it for Zeb. He flashed a bright smile when she handed it to him. Zeb Wengerd had very nice teeth, just like his brother. "Times like these, I wish I was just a little older," he said.

"Zeb, do you know how to swim?" Mammi asked.

"Jah, of course. Doesn't everybody?"

Mammi made her notes on the clipboard, even though she'd already told Mandy that Zeb was not a candidate. Mandy supposed she wanted to be fair. "Denki for coming, Zeb. You did a gute job with the hay. Would you ask Titus to send the next boy in?"

Zeb nodded, finished off his lemonade, and handed the cup back to Mandy. She gave him a wan smile, dreading the parade of prospective suitors standing in line outside the barn for their chance. Couldn't they just be done with it? Maybe she should fib to Mammi and tell her that she had settled on Adam Wengerd. Or perhaps she should fake a headache. At this point, with her face the temperature of a cup of coffee and the pounding right behind her eyes, she wouldn't have to fake very much.

Nae. Illness would only postpone the inevitable. Sure as rain, Mammi would invite them all up another day to pull the buggy around the yard or pluck tree stumps from the ground with their bare hands. Better to get it over with now and limit the embarrassment to another hour or so.

Mammi looked as if she could barely contain her delight.

"Isn't this fun? Just wait until you lay eyes on Luke Miller. He's got seven sisters. His family grows chrysanthemums to sell at the produce auction every year. And he only has nine toes."

Mandy tried for that smile again. How often did she get to meet a nine-toed man? It would be a day to remember.

They sat for nearly five minutes before the next boy made his entrance. It was Paul Zook, whom Mandy had met last week when he came to help move the stove. He looked as if he'd been playing in the dirt. A dark smudge ran down the side of his cheek and his navy-blue shirt was dusted with a fine gray powder.

"Paul, denki for coming today," Mammi said. "I'm sorry you had to wait so long."

Paul brushed off his arms and sent a cloud of dust into the air. "We're making gute use of the time out there," he said.

Even though Paul made a very valiant attempt to get the hay bale over his head, he managed to pull it up to his chest but no farther. Mammi asked him about swimming and hunting, and she even requested that he tilt his head back and open his mouth so she could inspect his teeth. Mandy wondered if he felt like a horse up for auction. A horse with a nice set of braces.

Another dozen boys paraded through the barn, and Mammi added a question or a task with each one. Maybe she sensed Mandy's resistance and felt she needed to get more information.

She requested Freeman Kiem's complete dental record plus inquired into whether he'd gotten a tetanus shot. She asked Davy Burkholder's opinion on the deer hunt before directing him to wiggle his ears the way he did when he wanted to entertain his younger siblings. LaWayne Burkholder, Davy's cousin, did that trick where he crossed his eyes and curled his tongue both ways.

Luke Miller, the nine-toed boy, lifted the hay bale clear

over his head before dropping it with a satisfying thud. Then he snorted air in through his nose and spat out the contents of his throat onto the ground next to Mandy's foot. Shuddering slightly, she quickly kicked some loose dirt over his spit with the toe of her shoe, followed by a handful of hay and then a napkin. She'd take a broom and scrub brush to it later. She tried not to think about it. After all, lots of nasty things lived on the barn floor.

Mammi gave Luke some lemonade. "Will you send the next boy in?"

The nine-toed spitter ambled out the door. "I'm the last one," he said.

Mammi glanced up from her clipboard as Luke shut the barn door. "He was strong. Maybe you could cure him of that little spitting habit."

"Maybe," Mandy said.

Mammi exhaled slowly. "That was an interesting experience. Titus never did get them in alphabetical order."

"Perhaps he was going for tallest to shortest."

She narrowed her eyes. "Nae. Luke is six-foot-two." Mammi leafed through her seven pages of notes. "I liked John Shirk's answer about the Confession of Faith, but Melvin Lambright seems to the know the Bible better yet. LaWayne has had his appendix out. I wonder if that's something you'll wish he had later in life." She laid her clipboard and pencil beside her. Eagerness was written all over her face. "Well, what do you think, Mandy? You've seen some very promising prospects today. Very promising."

Mandy didn't want to be mean. She really didn't. One word from her would dash all of Mammi's hopes, but she didn't have the slightest interest in one of those boys. As much as she hated to disappoint Mammi, she felt she needed to be truthful. "I'm sorry, Mammi. I know I told Davy I'd try to find his litter of kittens a new home and I promised to help Luke Miller's sister with her piecrust, but I really don't want any of these boys for a husband. I'm here to visit you and Dawdi and Kristina. Dating a boy is not in my plan."

The corners of Mammi's lips drooped, but she didn't lose the sparkle in her eyes. Mandy had forgotten the most important thing. Mammi never gave up hope.

"You're going to the gathering with Adam on Friday. And there's a couple of boys from Cashton we haven't spoken with yet. There's still time."

Mandy didn't even let her shoulders sag. "I'll only be here for two more weeks."

"Three weeks, dear. You know I've got my heart set on five weeks."

"We'll see, Mammi. We'll see."

The door creaked open, and Titus stuck his head into the barn. He looked like a ragamuffin, with smudges of dirt on his face and shirt. "How did it go?"

"Wonderful gute," Mammi said, putting her arm around Mandy and pulling her close. "We've had so much fun."

Mandy felt obligated to agree for Mammi's sake. "Jah, they lifted a lot of hay."

Titus shifted the toothpick to the other side of his mouth and walked farther into the barn. His trousers were covered with dust. "Is there any lemonade left?"

Mandy shot to her feet, ready to put this traumatic and unpleasant experience behind her. "Plenty. I'll get you a cupful."

"What have you been up to, Titus?" Mammi asked. "You look as if you've been through an avalanche."

Noah marched into the barn, looking as filthy as someone would be expected to look after working on the roof all morning. Mandy could see where beads of sweat had made tracks through the dirt down his face.

For some reason, she could tell he was trying to avoid looking at her. She didn't like his avoidance at all.

Noah took Mammi's hand and helped her from the hay bale. "How did it go? Did you find a husband for Mandy?"

A playful grin should have accompanied that question, but he seemed way too serious. Maybe scraping off shingles had worn him out.

Mammi patted Noah on the arm. "You are very kind to be so concerned. I'm getting a little concerned myself, but Mandy says she's not interested. Not even in Luke Miller. Nine toes just isn't exciting enough."

Noah nodded thoughtfully, but Mandy thought she might have seen his lip twitch upward. "Mandy has an exciting life. Maybe Bonduel is too small a town to find what she's looking for."

"Who else can I try, Noah? I'm at my wit's end."

"How is the roof coming?" Mandy blurted out. She'd die of embarrassment if she had to stand there and listen to Noah and Mammi discuss her prospects.

Noah finally looked at her. His smile was so bright, she could have counted all his nice, straight, white teeth. Did a smile really have the power to knock a girl off her feet? "The shingles are off."

"All of them? So fast?" Mandy said. How had he managed?

"It was Titus's idea," Noah said.

"It wasn't really my idea," Titus said, removing the toothpick from his lips. "They was getting bored out there, so we decided as a group to help Noah strip the roof. It seemed kind of silly for everybody to be standing around on the ground while Noah was up there slaving away. We used the pitchforks plus three hoes. Some of us scraped shingles while others picked them up and dumped them in the wagon."

Noah swiped his forearm across his brow. "Then they helped me get the felt underlayment laid down so there won't be any leaks if it rains before all the shingles are laid."

"Noah's got a wonderful-gute stapler with a hammer tacker. It didn't take any time at all to tack everything down."

"Titus," Mammi said, planting a kiss on his grimy cheek, "you're a gute boy."

Titus blushed and wriggled away from Mammi as best he could. "Now, Mammi, don't get mushy. I'm a grown man."

Mammi nodded. "I know, dear. Even if you are a little shaky with your ABC's."

Noah rubbed the back of his hand across his mouth to stifle a smile. "There's nobody better with a shingle fork."

"Besides you," Titus said.

"Once we finished with the felt paper, nobody knew if they should stick around to hear if they got the job," Noah said. "I hope it was okay. I sent them all home."

"Just as well," Mammi said. "Mandy won't have any of them."

Noah's gaze lingered on Mandy's face even as he spoke to Mammi. "Everybody's gone now, except for Freeman. He's playing with Chester and Sparky." He pulled his work gloves from his back pocket. "Adam says you need some hay moved."

Mandy glanced behind her at the substantial stack of hay bales sitting against the wall. "Nae. We weren't—"

"Should I heft it into the haymow, Anna?"

Mammi thought for a minute. "I suppose that's where Felty would like it. We had it delivered on Wednesday, and we haven't really talked about it."

"Titus, can you help?" Noah said, gazing upward at the haymow. He lifted a bale by the twine.

"I'm not very good at lifting," Titus said.

Waiting for Titus, Noah swung the bale back and forth like the pendulum on the grandfather clock. "Climb up, and I'll throw them to you."

Titus tossed his toothpick on the ground and climbed the ladder. Muscles she didn't know Noah possessed looked to be carved into his arms as he lifted the hay bale over his head and tossed it.

Oh my.

She averted her eyes and bent over the lemonade jug as if doing something supremely important with the lid, willing her heart to stop fluttering like a meadow full of butterflies.

With his arms over his head like that, the bale had about two feet to travel upward. It landed on the floor of the loft, where Titus grabbed it and stacked it in the corner of the haymow. Noah wasted no time. Mandy tried to move out of his way as he hefted another bale and threw it to Titus. At this rate, he'd have the stack moved in a matter of minutes.

Mammi picked up her clipboard and pencil. "Denki, Noah. Felty will be so pleased the hay is put away."

Breathing heavily, Noah tossed another bale and then glanced at Mammi. "I'll carry the jug back into the house when I'm done here."

"No need," Mammi said, lifting the jug with one hand. "It's all gone."

Ach. They hadn't saved any for Noah, and Dawdi had reminded her twice. Yet again, Mandy wanted to kick herself.

Mammi shuffled to the door of the barn. "Noah got the roof stripped, and we can now cross several boys off our list. It's been a very productive morning."

Mandy watched Mammi leave with the empty jug. "I'm sorry we didn't save you any lemonade, Noah. You're the most deserving one."

"What about me?" Titus called. "It wasn't easy organizing everybody into typographical order."

Noah stopped throwing bales with all those muscles of his and curled his lips into a very attractive smile. "It's all right. I'm glad there was enough for your future husband, whoever he may be."

Mandy groaned. "Believe me, my future husband did not drink lemonade today."

Noah chuckled. "I hope he's not thirsty."

His eyes were such a warm shade of brown, Mandy thought she could very well get lost in them. But really, she needed to tear her gaze from his and go into the house and . . . what was it she needed to do?

Noah kept up his steady pace with the hay bales. Did he ever tire?

She should march out of the barn and away from the sight of Noah's chiseled arms and milk-chocolate brown eyes and go help Mammi do . . . something. Certainly Mammi needed help with something.

Instead, she leaned against the wall of the barn and watched Noah toss every last bale of hay.

The something, whatever it was, could wait.

Chapter Ten

Mandy parked Dawdi's buggy in front of Noah's house, grabbed her heavy canvas bag, and trudged across the sparse grass. Chester lay in his usual spot on the porch, looking very much asleep until Mandy passed him. He opened his eyes and greeted her with a friendly yip. Being the most obedient dog in the world, Chester never barked at inappropriate times or too loudly.

The bag banged against her hip as she climbed the stairs. The jar inside was heavy, but she had wanted to make sure she brought plenty. If Noah was sick, it might cheer him up.

On Saturday afternoon, Noah, with his nail gun, had gotten a good start on the shingles on the north side of the roof and promised to return first thing Monday morning. But Noah hadn't shown up this morning, and Mandy had started to worry. If Noah was sick in bed, he'd need someone to nurse him back to health. The poor boy didn't have a mamm or a wife to tend to him, and Mandy was certain that his dat couldn't be much help. Mandy would have to be the one. Helping other people with their problems was what she did best.

Like Kristina said, Mandy liked to fix things.

She heard the sound of an air compressor coming from

behind the house. Probably from Noah's dat's woodshop, which was a dilapidated old shack east of Noah's equally dilapidated house. Lord willing, Noah's dat was having a gute morning. Or maybe it was Noah in the woodshop, finishing up some last-minute project before coming to Huckleberry Hill to work on the roof.

After climbing the stair, she plunked her bag down on the porch. It was too heavy to hold any longer. When she knocked on the door, Chester rose to his feet and stood by her, as if planning on paying a call to his own house.

"Who is it?" she heard Noah call from the other side of the door.

"It's Mandy."

Noah didn't reply. Hadn't he heard her?

She put her mouth close to the crack and raised her voice. "We got worried when you didn't come this morning. I told Dawdi I'd check to make sure you're okay. Are you sick?"

"Mandy." He paused for what seemed like a full minute. "Today's not a gute day. Will you tell your dawdi I'm sorry? I'll be by on Wednesday."

"What's wrong?"

"It's nothing," he said quietly. At least that's what she thought he said. His voice had sunk very low.

She tapped lightly. "Noah, I can't hear you. Open the door so we can have a proper conversation like two normal people."

"I'll come on Wednesday. Tell your dawdi."

He was definitely sick and obviously didn't want her help. He was so touchy about letting her do things for him. Wasn't he always telling her to stay out of his life?

Well, she wasn't about to let him get away with that. He needed her help, and she'd insist he take it, like it or not.

But first she must convince him to open the door. "I've got something really heavy out here I need you to carry for me." No response from the other side. "Please? You'll feel horrible if I rupture a blood vessel in my neck."

There was still no sound of movement from the other side, and Mandy feared he'd fallen asleep, being as sick as he was and all.

"Noah?"

Just as she was about to throw up her hands and storm off the porch, the doorknob turned, and Noah slowly opened the door. He wore his straw hat pulled low over his eyes, as if the light would blind him if it landed on his face.

She folded her arms. "You are the most stubborn . . ."

He lifted his head to look at her.

"Oh," she gasped, before promptly clamping her mouth shut. She was really wishing for that third leg now. Yet again, she wanted to kick herself. First the lip and now this. Her heart sank all the way to her toes.

Mandy didn't think she'd ever seen a ghastlier bruise. Splotches of midnight purple and grayish black surrounded Noah's left eye. He looked as if he were wearing an eye patch.

He met her eye and then turned his face away. "Satisfied?"

"Oh, Noah. I'm sorry. I didn't know."

"But you won't just go away when I ask you to go away."

She felt horrible. Once again, her persistence had made things worse. "I thought you were sick."

He wouldn't look at her as he raised his chin. "I'm not sick. You can go now."

"Have you put anything on it?"

He started to close the door. "I'll come to your dawdi's on Wednesday."

"If you think that bruise is going to disappear by Wednesday, you are gravely mistaken."

He gazed at her resentfully. "Then I'll wait until next Monday."

"And lose a week's worth of wages? Besides, those tarps aren't going to see us through a downpour. Do you want that on your conscience?"

He rubbed his hand down the side of his face. "What do you want, Mandy?"

"That is the stupidest question I've ever heard, Noah Mischler."

Her reprimand took him by surprise. He raised his eyebrows.

"I want to help you, of course," she said.

"Why?"

"Because that black eye is probably even more sore than it looks, and I know how to get the swelling down as quick as you please." She stared at him, hoping by sheer willpower to get him to relent. She couldn't bear to go away without tending to that eye.

He exhaled slowly and took off his hat. "Why not? I'm already as humiliated as I can be."

Trying not to show how glad she was that she'd gotten her way, she marched past him into the kitchen and pushed up her sleeves. "There's no humiliation in having a black eye."

His jaw tightened. "Jah, there is."

That look of shame and despair in his eyes made her want to weep, and she promised herself she'd try to make things better for him. But he must never see how upset she was because of the black eye. He'd think she was making judgments about his dat, when in truth, she was only sorry for Noah's pain.

She propped her hands on her hips and adopted her best matter-of-fact tone. "Do you have any potatoes?"

"Um, okay. In the cupboard down to your left."

Chester ambled into the house and planted himself next

to Noah, leaving Mandy's bag sitting by itself on the porch. Noah narrowed his eyes. "Is this the heavy thing you were talking about?"

"Jah."

"So you tricked me into opening the door."

She smiled weakly. "I didn't want to wait on the porch all morning."

"You could have gone home."

She lifted her chin and arched an eyebrow. "I wouldn't have done that."

He smirked. "I didn't really think you would."

"Besides," she said, "I didn't trick you. That bag really is heavy. Pick it up if you don't believe me."

Noah stepped outside. A look of surprise traveled across his face when he lifted the canvas bag. "You weren't lying," he said, bringing it into the house and setting it on the table. "But you were exaggerating."

"How else was I going to get you to open the door? I knew you wouldn't want to disappoint your mamm by leaving a poor girl to fend for herself."

The hard line of his mouth softened a bit. "What's in here?"

Mandy pulled a small sack of potatoes from the cupboard and set it on the counter. "I brought you a present."

"Why?"

"Never question why someone gives you a present. Just take it and be grateful." She pulled the gallon bottle full of lemonade from her bag. "You didn't get any on Saturday."

He cracked a smile. "Too much competition."

"And you put away our hay. If anybody deserved a glass of lemonade, it was you." She reached back into the bag and pulled out two strands of knitted yarn and a plastic bag full of marshmallows. She handed him the yarn. "These are knitted napkins rings. Get-well presents from Mammi.

She says when all the fuss has died down, she'll make you your own pot holders."

Noah fingered the soft maroon yarn. "I am honored. I know only very special young men get pot holders."

She cleared her throat and willed herself not to blush. "Jah. Well, of course. You are very special to Mammi."

"Denki."

She showed him the bag of marshmallows. "I didn't have time to bake anything, so I grabbed these on the way out. We can roast them at your stove."

"And start a fire?"

"If you like."

Noah chuckled. "I am tempted to burn this place down and start over again."

"Sit," she said, in the bossiest voice she had. "Let me take care of that eye."

To her astonishment, he did as she asked. Maybe this morning he felt too disheartened and ashamed to put up a fight. Maybe he knew she wouldn't take no for an answer. She rummaged through a few of his tidy cupboards until she found a glass and poured Noah some lemonade. Without a word, he downed half of it and set it on the table.

He sat quietly with his eyes downcast and his hand wrapped around the glass while Mandy peeled a potato and cut it into thick slices. She arranged the slices on a plate and took them to the table. "Here," she said. "Let me put one of these on."

He hissed as she laid the potato slice over his black eye. "Isn't this supposed to be a steak?" he said.

"Do you have a steak?"

"Nae."

"I didn't think so." She grabbed his hand and raised it to his eye. "Hold the potato in place."

"For how long?"

She pinched her lips together to keep from breaking into a grin. "Three weeks."

He flinched in surprise and pulled the potato away from his eye. "Three weeks?"

She laid her hand over his and nudged the potato back in place. "It's a joke, Noah. Give it twenty minutes." Her hand lingered over his for just a second. She loved the rough texture of his skin against her palm.

He cleared his throat.

She cleared her throat. . . .

And pulled her hand away. What had she been thinking?

"When did this happen?" she said, her voice barely above a whisper.

"Last night."

Mandy bit her bottom lip.

He slid his gaze from her face and stared faithfully at a long, crooked crack in the table. "He never used to drink on the Sabbath."

"Did he hit you when you tried to take him home?"

"When my dat gets that drunk, I can usually deflect the blow. This one caught me by surprise." He clenched his jaw. "He's even stronger when he's had something to drink."

She could see the tension in his fingers as he clutched his glass. So much pain. For a boy who found humiliation unbearable, he was certainly bearing more than his share.

She couldn't resist laying her hand on his arm. He stiffened at her touch but didn't pull away. "You have nothing to be ashamed of. No one in the community thinks any less of you."

He still refused to look at her as he pulled his arm from under her hand. "That's because they don't know how bad it is."

"Even if they knew, they wouldn't blame you."

He pulled the potato slice from his face and fixed his eyes on her. They looked to be on fire as his gaze pierced her skull. "Look at me, Mandy. Do I look like a godly man? What will everyone think when they see this? What did you think?"

She stared at him until he felt compelled to meet her eye. "I am heartbroken that you must bear this trial. That's what I think."

He stared at her as if trying to decide if she was telling the truth. "Then you're the only one."

She was telling the truth. He had to see that. "Your patience and devotion to your fater astonish me."

Sitting back, he folded his arms and looked out the window. "I'm not devoted. I'm ashamed."

"God is good, Noah. Please don't be ashamed. It makes my heart sick to hear you say it."

He shifted in his chair, making it creak under his solid weight, and swiped some moisture from his eyes. He flashed her a pathetic smile. "I'm not a crybaby."

"Nae."

"But you've seen me bawl twice."

She shrugged her shoulders and grinned. "I do that to people. I was kind of disappointed that I didn't make you cry that first day I came to your house."

His grin grew in strength. "I cried when you left."

"I'm sure you did."

"Cried for joy," he said.

Giggling, she cuffed him on the shoulder. "Put that potato back on your eye, or it won't get better."

He positioned the potato over his eye again and took another swallow of lemonade.

"If you want to be embarrassed," she said, "think of how silly you look with a potato stuck to your face."

"I'd rather have a steak."

She opened her mouth like a fish gasping for air. "I'm appalled by the ingratitude."

Any hint of cheerfulness fled from his face, and he

reached over with his free hand and took hers. Little sparks traveled from her fingertips clear up her arm. "Despite my rudeness, I am very grateful. Denki for the potatoes."

For a moment, she forgot how to speak. "It's nothing."

"Nae," he said, squeezing her hand and sending sparks clear to her toes. "It means everything."

"I tricked you to get you to open the door. You didn't really have a choice."

The corners of his mouth twitched. "Next time I'll leave you on the front step with Chester."

"And I would deserve that."

The front door opened suddenly, and Mandy started and slid her hand from Noah's grasp. Noah's dat stepped into the house carrying a wooden basket shaped like a heart. He immediately caught sight of Mandy sitting at the table. "Ach, du lieva," he said mildly, trying to pull a smile onto his face. "We have a visitor."

Noah glanced at Mandy with evident concern on his face. She smiled and gave him a reassuring nod.

His dat wasn't quite as tall as Noah, but he looked almost as strong. He had kind, intelligent eyes like his son, and he walked slightly stooped over, as if he been beaten down by life a few times too many.

His gaze darted to Noah, and Mandy thought she had never seen someone look so ill at ease.

Noah tossed his potato on the plate, stood, and put a hand on his dat's shoulder. Mandy rose to her feet too. "Dat," Noah said, "this is Mandy Helmuth. Mandy, this is my dat Wayne."

"Have we met before?" Wayne asked.

Mandy's face flushed, and she saw the muscles in Noah's jaw twitch. She would never in a million years say yes to that question. He'd been too drunk to remember their first meeting, but Mandy would never shame Noah or his dat by mentioning it. "I'm from Charm. I'm here visiting my grandparents."

"Felty and Anna Helmuth?" Wayne said, self-consciously glancing again and again at Noah's face. "Very gute people. Felty gave me my first job harvesting his soybeans." His gaze strayed one more time to Noah's black eye before he lowered his eyes and fell silent.

Noah eyed Mandy doubtfully. "Dat, we—"

"I just got finished scolding Noah," Mandy blurted out, desperate to spare Wayne's feelings. "I told him he shouldn't wander around in the dark. It's too easy to bump into something and end up with a black eye."

"What?" Wayne raised his head, and his face seemed to light up from the inside. She'd opened a door for him. He walked through it. "Oh, jah. We all need to be more careful in the dark. Noah doesn't like to waste the battery, so he seldom switches on the light at night."

Noah peered at her with unmistakable tenderness in his eyes. She thought she might burst at the pure joy of that look.

"Mandy cut a potato for me," Noah said.

Wayne nodded. "I wish we had some tobacco for that bruise." He took off his hat and hung it on the hook in the entryway. "But we are very grateful for the potato." He gave Mandy a genuine smile. He and Noah looked most alike when they were happy.

"I could go to the store for some chewing tobacco," Mandy said.

"That will get the tongues wagging," Noah said. "People will spread rumors that Helmuths' granddaughter chews tobacco."

Mandy giggled. "I don't think anybody would believe it. I'm not a gute spitter."

Wayne laid the heart-shaped wooden basket on the table. "I came in to show Noah what I made. I've been cutting round baskets for years, but the tourist shop in Green Bay asked me to try a heart."

Mandy smoothed her finger over the wood. The Amish made collapsible baskets like this all the time. The body of the basket was a single piece of wood cut with a jigsaw and then fitted with a handle. Mandy was always fascinated at how one piece of wood could be cut to form such a clever thing.

"It's very pretty," she said. "I'm sure tourists will love the new shape."

"It turned out well, Dat."

Mandy could tell Wayne was pleased even though he only smiled with his eyes. "I might try some other shapes now that I know how to make a heart template." He picked up his basket and placed it on the counter behind them. "Would you like some *kaffe*, Mandy? I'll make all of us a cup."

"How about some lemonade, Dat?"

Wayne looked at the jug on the table. "Even better."

He pulled a cup from the cupboard and all three of them sat down. Chester planted himself next to Noah and peered at Noah's plate of potatoes as if he thought they might be good enough to eat.

Wayne poured himself a full glass and took a drink. "Gute lemonade," he said. "Did you make it?"

Mandy nodded. "I promised Dawdi I'd save some for Noah, but we ran out. I wanted to make sure he got his fair share."

Wayne scooted his chair closer to the table. "It's very pleasant having you in our house, Mandy. It's not often Noah invites girls over."

Noah got a funny look on his face. Was he blushing? "I never invite girls over, Dat."

Wayne propped his elbows on the table and stared at Mandy with a kind expression on his face, much like the one she often saw from her dawdi. "At any rate, I'm glad you've stopped knocking on our door and running away before we could open it."

Mandy tried to hide her confusion. Should she know what Noah's dat was talking about? "Knocking on the door and running away?"

Noah's laughter rumbled in his chest. Soon it exploded from his mouth. He pulled the potato from his eye and laughed uncontrollably while Mandy and Wayne stared at him in amused silence. "Nae, Dat," he was finally able to squeeze out of his mouth. "This isn't that girl."

It only took Mandy a moment to realize who it was who had been knocking at Noah's door and running away. Was there anything Kristina hadn't done to try to win Noah's heart?

Wayne sprouted a good-natured smile. "We always knew it was her because we could hear her giggling as she ran away."

Mandy wasn't sure why her face felt warm, except that maybe she was embarrassed for Kristina. Kristina never seemed to be embarrassed for herself.

"She did it three or four times a week over the summer," Wayne said. "Since August we ain't heard a lot from her."

"I'm sorry," Mandy murmured, feeling compelled to apologize on Kristina's behalf. She was her best friend, after all. Didn't she bear some of the responsibility?

Wayne must have sensed her distress. He studied her face and patted her hand reassuringly. "Mind you, I don't bear her no ill will. Noah's a handsome boy. I don't wonder that the girls get *ferhoodled* over him. This girl who knocks is probably head over heels in love with Noah. She just doesn't know how else to express her affection."

"She . . . it's not the best way. . . ." Mandy stuttered, not wanting to be disloyal to her best friend but believing that Wayne was being very forgiving of Kristina's behavior when in reality she probably deserved a gute spanking.

"Noah keeps to himself. The girls just don't know what to do about that." Wayne leaned back in his chair. "There's another girl who sneaks over and spies on Noah from the shelter of the trees across the road."

Mortified, Mandy slapped her forehead as Noah chuckled softly. "Same girl, Dat."

Mandy couldn't help it. A giggle escaped from her lips. Her best friend, the spy. She was soon laughing harder than Noah was.

"Did I say something wrong?" Wayne asked, with more distress than was warranted.

"Nae," Mandy managed to say between giggles. "It's just . . . that . . . Kristina is my best friend."

Wayne raised his eyebrows. "*Ach*. I'm sorry if I offended you."

"It wonders me how she ever gets her chores done, chasing Noah around all the time," Mandy said.

Noah studied her face, and his eyes smoldered with warmth. Her whole body seemed to tingle like a glass of bubbly soda. She had to look away.

The giggling finally subsided, and to avoid Noah's eyes, Mandy glanced at Noah's fater as he took another drink of lemonade. He was not what she had imagined about a man who got drunk on a regular basis and gave his son dark, ugly bruises. She had expected him to be more like the man she'd met outside the bar on a cool autumn evening. Belligerent, unstable, and wicked beyond saving. This meek, gentle man sitting next to her wasn't any of those things.

She thought of Jesus's admonition in Matthew: *If a man have an hundred sheep, and one of them be gone astray, doth he not leave the ninety and nine, and goeth into the mountains, and seeketh that which is gone astray?*

Surely God had not given up on Noah's dat. He still had time to turn his life back to God. And she still had time to help him. She formulated a plan before she stood from the table.

Getting to her feet, she grinned at her hopeless patient. "Noah, your eye is never going to get better if you don't keep that potato pressed to it."

He groaned, picked up a new slice of potato from the plate, and laid it over his eye. "I'm not going to get a lot of work done wearing a potato."

Noah's dat finished his lemonade. "Will you stay for supper, Mandy? Noah makes gute sandwiches."

"Jah, I know he does," she said, winking in Noah's direction.

He seemed to catch his breath and hold it.

"Since Noah is hurt," she said, "why don't I make supper?"

Noah stood up and marched to the fridge. "I can do it. You're our guest."

"With one hand?" Mandy teased.

He grinned. "If you can find me some tape, I'll attach this potato to my head so I'll have two good hands."

"You fed me on Saturday," she said. "It's my turn to feed you."

"You brought lemonade."

"I'm cooking supper." Mandy scooted next to Noah and nudged him with her shoulder, pushing him away from the fridge and out of her path. He chuckled and cheerfully glided in the direction she nudged him. She was glad he cooperated. If he hadn't wanted to move, she and a Clydesdale horse couldn't have made him go anywhere.

She opened the small fridge to see what they had on hand and flashed Noah a look of mock horror. The inside of the fridge was immaculately clean and astonishingly empty. Half a gallon of milk, a jar of horseradish sauce, some pickles, and a stick of butter sat in the door while six apples and a carton of eggs sat on the shelves.

She slowly turned her head and looked at Noah with raised eyebrows. "I see that you don't have steak."

Noah twisted his lips sheepishly. "I was going to go the store tonight."

"I'm glad to hear it," she said, rolling her eyes. "I wouldn't want you to starve."

"We don't starve," Wayne said. "Noah knows how to make *yummasetti*."

Mandy closed the fridge and leaned against the counter. "Let's start with a list of what you do have. Do you have flour and salt?"

"Jah," Noah said, his eyes gleaming with amusement. "And we have sugar and horseradish."

"I saw the horseradish. Do you have yeast?"

Noah looked through a few cupboards. "I don't think so."

"Please tell me you have vinegar and baking powder. I think I will die and go to heaven if you have vinegar and baking powder."

"Then I hope we don't have them. I don't want you to die."

He chuckled as she rolled her eyes a second time. He rummaged through a few cupboards and, with a wide smile, pulled a gallon jug from under the sink. "Vinegar."

"Very gute," she said, speaking to him as if he were a little boy who didn't know how to follow directions. "Now do you know what baking powder looks like? It is a fine white powder usually in a white and blue tin."

It was his turn to roll his eyes. He pulled a bright orange box from the cupboard. "Here it is," he said, as if he'd just discovered gold.

"Nope," she said. "That's baking soda."

"Is there a difference?"

"Jah, and if you want to truly be an expert cook, you've got to learn the difference or your quick breads will be ruined."

"I would be horrified if my quick breads were ruined."

He peered at the label on the soda box. "We couldn't use this anyway. It expired in 1997."

Mandy took it from him and poured it down the sink. "It will help your sink smell better."

He arched an eyebrow. "Since when do you go around smelling people's sinks?"

"It's one of my hobbies."

He chuckled and continued his search through the cupboards. "Aha," he exclaimed as he pulled out a small white tin labeled *Baking Powder*. He looked at the label. "It expired in—"

Mandy held up her hand to shush him. "What I don't know can't hurt me. Now go sit by your dat and put another potato on your eye."

Mandy pushed her sleeves up. She didn't have a lot to start with, but she could make do. After preheating the oven, she mixed up a quick batch of drop biscuits. While they baked, she decided to make an apple pie. Apple pie and biscuits wasn't the most nutritious meal in the world, but she had an inkling that Noah liked pie. It would be good enough.

They didn't have a pie tin, so Mandy formed the crust onto a cookie sheet. It would be more of an apple tart, but hopefully it would taste good.

Noah's dat went back to his woodshop while the biscuits baked, and Noah fed Chester and tried to sweep with one hand while she made the pie-tart.

Mandy pulled the biscuits out of the oven when they turned golden brown. Noah sniffed the air. "I don't think anything made in this kitchen has ever smelled so gute."

"I know it's greedy of me to ask," she said, "but do you happen to have any jam?"

He pumped his eyebrows up and down as if he had a great secret, and disappeared down the hall. Did he hide jam in the bathroom?

Soon he reappeared, still pressing the potato to his eye

and cradling two jars of jam in his arm, one purple and one orange. "This is huckleberry jam from your mammi," he said, motioning to the first jar. "And this is apricot jam from a very spindly tree we have out back."

"Jam grows on trees?" she said.

He nudged her with his elbow. "The bigger question is, does Noah know how to make jam? And the answer is, yes, I do."

"I'm astonished," she said, putting her hand to her heart as if he had truly shocked her.

"I know how to read directions. You can do anything if you just read the directions."

Mandy scooped the biscuits onto a plate with a fork and set the table while Noah fetched his dat from the woodshop. Noah and his dat didn't own a matching set of plates, so she set the table with a white plate with pink flowers, a plain yellow one, and a light-blue plate with stripes and a small chip on the edge. She set the butter and jam on the table along with a bowl of olives from a can she'd located while rummaging through Noah's cupboards.

She paused before laying out the silverware. Was it rude to rummage through people's cupboards?

Probably.

Noah and his dat couldn't have been more pleased with their meager meal of drop biscuits, olives, lemonade, and apple pie. Noah ate like a starved man, and her heart did a little flip-flop every time he paused long enough to give her a warm look and a compliment about her cooking.

Mandy cut herself a tiny slice of pie and watched with pleasure as Noah and his dat polished off almost the entire thing. Noah cleaned his plate, put down his fork, and picked up the cookie sheet. "Mandy, you should eat the last piece."

Knowing how much he loved it and how much of a sacrifice it must have been for him to offer it to her, she couldn't help but be charmed by his kindness. "Nae, I wouldn't dream of it. Finish it."

"Dat?" Noah said.

"I am stuffed," Wayne said, waving the cookie sheet away.

Noah didn't need more encouragement than that. He picked up the last piece like a slice of pizza and downed it in four bites. Mandy propped her chin in her hand and gazed at him. She couldn't think of anything more pleasant than watching Noah enjoy her cooking. Unless it was watching Noah toss bales into the haymow.

That was an extremely pleasant thought. A bolt of electricity skipped up her spine. No wonder Kristina liked to spy on him. Mandy could have watched Noah for hours without even taking time out for meals. She loved the fluid movement of his hands and arms as he worked with his tools, the solid arch of his back when he picked up a shovel, and the strong set of his jaw when he puzzled over a problem.

Their arms nearly touched when Noah propped his elbows on the table. "Would it be rude if I licked my plate?"

Mandy giggled. "I'm afraid so."

After lunch, Wayne ambled back to his workshop. He wanted to experiment with a new star basket template. Mandy wiped cupboards while Noah did up the dishes. She laughed when his eye-potato fell into the dishwater and he gave up on it altogether. It was too difficult to wash cups properly with one hand.

They dried the dishes together while Noah, who didn't like talking about his family, told her about the time that he and his brother Yost got chased by a moose.

When the dishes were washed up, Noah stashed the three mismatched plates in the cupboard and set his dish towel on the counter. "Shall we have dessert?"

"You're almost out of sugar and the apples are gone. There's nothing for dessert."

Curling one side of his mouth, Noah reached into her canvas bag on the counter and pulled out the bag of marshmallows. "Do you still want to burn down the house?"

A smile leaped onto her face. "I forgot about those."

He picked up the lighter sitting next to the stove, held it near the burner, and turned on the gas. The burner lit with a hiss and a whoosh.

She reached into the drawer and pulled out two forks. "Roasting sticks."

"Hmm," he said, pursing his lips. "They're not very long. I wouldn't want to singe my finger hairs."

The laughter just seemed to bubble out of her mouth. "Well, I do have another idea, but Mammi might not approve."

"I wouldn't want to do anything to upset your mammi."

Mandy reached clear into the bottom of her bag and pulled out a ball of blue yarn with two knitting needles sticking out of it. "Mammi insists I carry these everywhere. If I go places where I have to sit and wait, she wants me to knit pot holders."

"For all your boyfriends?"

Mandy cuffed him on the shoulder.

"Ouch," he said, grinning from ear to ear. "That was completely uncalled for."

"Jah, okay, you're right, but our pot holder supply is very low. Sometimes I'm tempted to pick a boy just so I don't have to knit any more pot holders."

A shadow passed across his face, but it was so fleeting that Mandy wondered if she had really seen it. "Surely your mammi knows that all those boys don't need pot holders as an encouragement to date you. Your freckles are encouragement enough." The way he looked at her, as if he found it impossible to take his eyes off those freckles, made her knees a little weak.

For a moment she forgot where she was and just stared into his eyes. If he weren't so handsome, she would have been able to think of something clever and amusing to say in return. But nothing was coming to her.

Instead, she did what any girl with her wits about her would do. She gave a little cough, as if something tickled her throat, and changed the subject. "These knitting needles would make great roasting sticks."

The corner of his mouth twitched, and he slid the needles from her ball of yarn. "But your mammi might have a heart attack if she knew?"

"It would be the same as if we used your flathead screwdriver to open a can of paint."

"The one with the keystone tip?"

"Jah."

He winced. "We should use the forks. I don't need my finger hairs."

Mandy giggled. "Let's see what else we can find."

She and Noah rummaged through the drawers. "There's not much here," she said. "You might own twenty different kinds of wrenches, but you don't even have a ladle or a turkey baster."

"Twenty-seven," he said.

"Twenty-seven what?"

"Twenty-seven different kinds of wrenches."

"Look at these," she said, pulling a carving fork and a long metal utensil from the bottom drawer. The utensil that she didn't recognize looked like a very long safety pin with no clasp at the top. She held it up for him to look at.

"That's a kabob skewer," Noah said.

"What is a kabob skewer, and why do you have one in your bottom drawer?"

"I have no idea."

"And why do you have a kabob skewer but don't own a spatula?"

He shrugged and chuckled. "I was going to buy a spatula but some locking-jaw pliers caught my eye."

She shook her head in exasperation. "You are incorrigible."

He pulled two marshmallows out of the bag. She skewered the carving fork into one of them, and he used the kabob skewer for his marshmallow. She didn't know what a kabob skewer was, but it was the perfect size for roasting marshmallows over the stove flame.

They stood close to each other and watched as their marshmallows slowly turned golden brown. Mandy savored the feel of Noah's strong arm brushing up against hers. She felt so bad for Noah and his dat. Noah didn't like to talk about his family, but Mandy thought she might be able to help them fix their difficult situation. But would he be open to her help? He hadn't been before.

"Noah," she said, turning her marshmallow around and around so it cooked evenly. "Have you ever thought about getting your dat some help?"

She felt him stiffen beside her. "He doesn't want help."

Knowing what a touchy subject this was for him, she probably should have stopped right there, but she knew she could help if he would just listen. She forged on. "There are places he can go. Places where they help people overcome their addictions."

His knuckles turned white around the carving fork. "If my dat went into one of those places, how long before the whole community knew about it? My shame would be ten times worse than it is right now."

"Noah, this is your community. You have nothing to be ashamed of."

He shoved his marshmallow too close to the fire, and it burst into flames. Without flinching, he flung the fork and burning marshmallow into the sink and turned on the water. "I have everything to be ashamed of."

Her mouth felt dry as dust. She didn't want to upset him, but if he'd just listen . . . she knew she was right. She laid her golden brown marshmallow on the counter next to the stove. "A counselor might be able to come to your house. Your dat wouldn't even have to go anywhere. If you just talked to somebody. Just looked at your options."

"Four years ago, my mamm tried to get help for my dat. Do you know what happened? The community found out. People started avoiding us. They whispered about us behind our backs. The elders had no choice but to put my dat under the ban. You know what shame follows the family of a person who is shunned."

Scowling, he turned his back on her, grasped the edge of the counter with both hands, and pushed against it as if he were trying to tip it over. With the strength of his arms and the condition of house, he just might have been able to do it. "Mandy," he said, his voice betraying smoldering anger and something deeper. Something that sounded like profound grief. "You must understand. Some things can't be fixed."

"I really think this can be fixed. My cousin's best friend—"

He whirled around to face her, and she thought for a split second that he was going to lash out at her. Instead, his voice was mild but restrained like a team of well-disciplined horses. "I've tried, Mandy. You have to believe I've tried."

"I believe you."

"I won't let myself be shamed again." He seemed to deflate instantly and leaned against the counter he'd just tried to push over. "My dat won't change, and I won't let myself hope that he will."

"There is always hope through Jesus."

"But not hope for my dat."

With his hands balled into fists, he clenched his jaw tight, as if he were trying to grind all his problems between his teeth. Wishing she could take some of his pain to herself, she reached out and caressed the side of his face.

Closing his eyes, he turned his face to her touch and exhaled slowly. He reached up with one hand and gently wrapped his fingers around her wrist as if to hold her hand against his cheek.

"I'm sorry," she whispered.

Opening his eyes, he slid his other hand around her waist and tugged her closer to him. Her heart was humming instead of merely beating. She looked up into his eyes as he pulled her even closer and stared at her lips as if they were his destination. Was he going to kiss her? Did she want him to?

Her heart hammered against her chest, demanding to be let out. Of course she wanted him to kiss her. More than anything.

He bent his head toward her. She wrapped her hands around those hard biceps and lifted her face to him. Suddenly, she felt him stiffen as he growled from deep in his throat, smiled feebly, and nudged her a few inches away from him. "I'm sorry. My mamm raised me better."

Better than what? What was wrong with a little kissing? She wanted a kiss. Didn't her wishes count for anything?

The heightened color in his face made his eyes look even browner. He released her as if she were hot to the touch and turned to the sink to retrieve his charred marshmallow. He picked up the carving fork and held it out for her examination. "I think I need another marshmallow."

"Here," she said, pulling hers from the skewer. "Eat mine. I can roast another one."

"I can roast another one."

"How many are you planning on burning? I only brought eight."

He glanced at her with a sheepish smirk on his face. "The rest will be golden brown as long as you don't distract me."

"Me? It's not my fault you don't know how to roast a marshmallow."

She handed him another marshmallow from the bag, and he skewered it with his fork. She could see the concentration etched on his face as he leaned closer to the flame and carefully held his marshmallow over it.

"Is it okay if I eat mine," she said in an exaggerated whisper, "or will that distract you?"

"Only if you chew loudly."

"How does anybody chew a marshmallow loudly?" She popped her perfectly cooked marshmallow into her mouth, leaned close to Noah's ear, and clacked her tongue as she chewed. "How about this?"

He chuckled quietly, trying not jiggle his fork in the process. "If I ruin this marshmallow, it will be on your head."

She stood up straight and spread her hands wide. "I am completely innocent."

Noah's marshmallow soon turned a toasty brown color. Smiling in satisfaction, he slid the crispy brown outer layer off the inner marshmallow and popped it into his mouth. Imitating Mandy, he clacked his tongue while he chewed, making both of them laugh. He finished off the gooey center of his marshmallow by sticking the roasting fork into his mouth and sliding it out again without the marshmallow attached.

"We really should get another potato on that eye," she said. "Do you want me to roast while you soak?"

"If you'll stick another marshmallow on my fork, I'll do both." She watched as he picked another potato slice from the plate and placed it against his eye. "Do you think I'll be better by tomorrow?"

She shook her head. "I'm afraid the eye isn't going to look much better for another week or two, even with a whole bag of potatoes."

He exhaled a slow breath. "I can't stay away that long. I need the money."

Mandy slid another marshmallow onto his roasting fork. "I have an idea to help you not draw attention to yourself."

"What?"

"Come to work tomorrow, and I'll show you."

"Tell me. How do I know I'll like your idea?"

She grinned. "You'll just have to have a little faith."

He cocked an eyebrow playfully. "I can't reroof the house with a paper bag over my head."

"I don't want you changing your mind. I'm hoping your curiosity will get the better of you, and you'll feel compelled to come."

He looked sideways at her. "No need to worry. I definitely feel compelled to come."

Chapter Eleven

Mandy threw the door open before he even knocked. "You came," she said, as if Noah's arrival were the best thing to happen to her since battery-operated sewing machines, although Noah knew that couldn't have been true. A girl like Mandy, who probably had a dozen boys buzzing around her all the time in Ohio, could never be interested in someone as unworthy and backward as Noah. She knew about his dat. She knew about his troubled family. He'd ordered her out of his house at least twice and snapped at her practically every time they got together. It was a wonder she could even stand the sight of him.

Even with all that pressing down on him, Noah couldn't help but smile at the sight of her. She was so pretty, and seemed so enthusiastic, as if she'd been eagerly waiting for him to show up.

She reached out and brushed her fingers across his eyebrow. His whole face started tingling. "Your eye looks better than it did yesterday. It's not as black."

He grinned and instinctively massaged his eyebrow right at the spot where her hand had just been. "It doesn't hurt so bad today, thanks to your potato remedy."

"Gute," she said, stepping back from the threshold. "*Cum reu*. Come in."

"I need to get started on the roof."

Felty sat in his recliner holding a pair of knitting needles and a ball of pink yarn. "Noah. Good to see you."

Noah turned his face slightly to the side so Felty wouldn't notice his black eye, but he couldn't help but smile at the sight of Felty holding a pair of knitting needles as if he were trying to saw through a very tough steak. "Are you knitting, Felty?"

Mandy shook her head and let out a puff of air. "Mammi has enlisted Dawdi to make pot holders. She's sure we'll never have enough."

"I don't really know how to knit," Felty said. "But if I hold the needles like this and look like I'm trying to figure it out, that seems to satisfy Annie." He stabbed one of the needles into the ball of yarn and waved it above his head like a flag. "She'll get suspicious when her pot holder supply doesn't get any bigger."

"I'll knit a few secretly for you, Dawdi," Mandy said.

Felty tossed the ball of yarn into the air and caught it. "Come in and sit, Noah. Anna made her famous gingersnaps."

Two years ago, Noah had chipped a tooth on one of Anna's gingersnaps. They were famous, all right.

"She's made dozens of gingersnaps," Mandy said, motioning to the table where several plates of cookies sat. "For all the boys who came on Saturday."

Noah did his best not to frown. "Denki, but I should probably get to work."

Felty rocked back and forth a couple of times until he gave himself enough momentum to stand up. He set the yarn and knitting needles on his recliner. "That's a wonderful-gute shiner you got there. Mandy told us all about it."

Noah clenched his jaw. What had she told them?

"That happened to me once," Felty said, eyes twinkling. "Except mine was a rake, not a hammer. I broke my nose and got two shiners."

Noah glanced at Mandy. Had she told her grandparents a fib and risked her soul to save him from embarrassment? He exploded with gratitude. She merely curled her lips as if Felty were talking about the weather.

"It's better today than it was yesterday," Noah said.

"Come in and have a sit," Felty said again as without warning, he shuffled toward the hall. "Mandy will give you a cookie while I take a nap."

"A nap, Dawdi? It's seven in the morning."

Felty was halfway down the hall. "There's never a bad time to take a nap."

Noah's lips curled upward as Felty disappeared. An eighty-five-year-old man could take a nap whenever he pleased.

"I'm glad you decided to come this morning," Mandy said, "because I have two presents for you."

"Presents? You don't need to give me presents." Even though he tried to rein it in, his heart galloped at the thought that she cared enough about him to give him a gift. He ground his teeth together and told himself that Mandy was just being kind. She was a nice girl, and she was sorry for him. That was all.

On the other hand, he'd brought *her* a present because something he'd buried deep inside himself a long time ago seemed to come to life every time she looked at him. She didn't even have to smile. Even when her lips twisted into a scold, his heart did a clumsy flip-flop and his stomach seemed to turn itself inside out.

He studied her face. Her aqua-blue eyes could have brought on a hot spell in January.

He was in big trouble.

Trouble or not, his mamm had taught him to show appreciation where it was due. He stepped into the house, reached into the pocket of his jacket, and pulled out his small tinfoil-wrapped package. "I brought you a present too."

A grin played at her lips. "Is it food?" She took it from him, and she widened her eyes. "It's warm." She unwrapped it and gasped when she saw the marshmallow and melted chocolate squished between two graham cracker squares. "What have you done?" she giggled.

His heart raced wildly at the sound of her laughter. "I know you like marshmallows. I thought you might like a s'more."

"The chocolate is melty. How did you keep it warm?"

"I packed it in a box surrounded by baked potatoes hot out of the oven. You should eat it now before it gets cold." He furrowed his brows. "Unless you don't want it. You don't have to eat it."

She looked as if she were ready to burst with delight. "Are you joking? Of course I want it." She took a big, crunchy bite, and the expression on her face was pure bliss.

"Gute?"

"Uh-huh." She held it out to him. "Have a bite."

"It's all yours," he said.

She nudged it closer to him. "You've got to taste this, Noah. Just one little bite."

He put his hand over hers and tugged the s'more to his mouth. Up against her soft skin, his fingers probably felt like sandpaper, but he wasn't about to let go. He kept his eyes glued to hers as he took a bite.

An attractive pink overspread her cheeks. She quickly pulled her hand away. "You are a very gute cook, Noah Mischler."

"Well, s'mores are at the top of my skill level. I can't even begin to make biscuits like you."

A smile played at her lips as she took another bite. "This reminds me of going camping and sitting around the camp-fire roasting marshmallows and making banana boats."

"Banana boats?"

"You've never tasted a banana boat? Oh, Noah. I'm so sorry. It's like never having seen a sunset."

He chuckled. "I've lived a very dull life."

There was one bite left. She hesitated for a second before offering it to him.

He waved her away. "I like watching you enjoy it."

Her cheeks grew even pinker. "I'm not a timid eater. Mamm says girls should be more demure in their enjoyment of food." She popped the last of the s'more into her mouth.

"Then you wouldn't be half so fun."

She probably couldn't get much redder, but he wished he knew the words to find out. He loved the way her freckles danced across her nose when she wrinkled it like that.

He realized he was staring when she cleared her throat and lowered her eyes. "Denki for the s'more. My stomach is very grateful."

"No breakfast?"

"Tuna quiche."

Noah winced. She didn't need to elaborate.

Clapping her hands, Mandy went to the fridge. "I need to give you your presents." She pulled out a white paper package and handed it to him.

He unfolded it. "Two steaks," he said. "For my eye?"

"I originally went to the store thinking I'd buy a steak for your eye, but when I got there and looked in their meat section, the thought of you holding a dripping, raw piece of meat against your face almost made me gag. So I bought the steaks for you and your dat to eat and more potatoes for your eye." She pointed to a bowl on the table with potato slices immersed in water. "It's probably impossible to lay a roof while holding a potato against your eye. I thought you'd like to take them home with you."

He couldn't keep a smile from his face. "You're very kind."

"And there's another present."

He eyed her suspiciously. "You said there were two. The steak and the potatoes."

She rolled her eyes. "The potatoes don't count as a present. I'm not that bad a gift giver."

"The potatoes are a gute gift yet."

She reached into her apron pocket and pulled out a pair of reflective sunglasses, the kind that made people look like insects instead of humans. "Wear these while you work, and nobody will even catch a glimpse of that eye. You'll look like a policeman, but no one will have to know about the shiner."

The warmth swelled in his chest. How much money had she spent on those outrageous sunglasses so he could keep his dignity intact? The pleasant sensation traveled into his arms and hands, legs and feet. Who was this girl who brought him homemade lemonade in a jug she could barely lift and knew what a crescent wrench was, but stuck her pretty nose into his life and thought she knew how to solve everybody's problems? When they had first met, he was more than happy to slam the door in her face. Now he thought he might burst with the need to gather her into his arms and kiss every one of those adorable freckles.

He pressed his lips together and clenched his teeth before the longing overpowered him. It didn't matter what he wanted. His mamm had taught him self-control. His dat had given him a healthy dose of humility. Mandy would never want a boy like him to kiss her. She'd probably run screaming for the hills.

She studied his face, and her expression drooped. "You don't like them."

He couldn't let her believe that for one more second. "They're perfect."

"I know they're a little fancy, but they're the darkest ones I could find."

His voice cracked with emotion, but he cleared his throat and forged ahead. "I couldn't have chosen better myself." He lowered his eyes. "I don't know how to thank you."

She flipped the sunglasses open and slid them onto his face. "The best part is that when people look at you, they'll see their own reflection. They'll be so busy checking their hair, they won't even wonder what's really behind those glasses."

And they wouldn't ever know that he was staring at them. Unashamedly and unrepentantly staring.

Unable to resist, he took her hand and squeezed her fingers before she stepped away from him. The surprise on her face was evident before she gave him a little laugh and squeezed his hand in return. Would heaven feel any nicer than this? Would his heart pound and his body feel lighter than air and his mouth curve into a smile without even trying?

The front door opened and Anna bustled into the room with a basket of pinecones and her dog Sparky at her heels.

Mandy pulled her hand from his grasp faster than Noah could have driven a nail into a sheet of corkboard.

"Ach, du lieva," Anna said. "Oh my goodness, Mandy, I had no idea you were entertaining a visitor." She beamed so widely that Noah thought he might be able to count all her teeth. That is, if he weren't wearing dark sunglasses indoors. It made counting teeth a little difficult.

"He's here to work on the roof," Mandy said, smoothing imaginary wrinkles from her apron.

Anna walked right up to Noah and studied his face with narrowed eyes. "Is that you, Noah?"

He nodded.

She laughed and tapped him on the arm. "I didn't recognize you behind those strange spectacles. I thought it was someone here to court Mandy."

Anna, who didn't have a speck of guile in her, didn't mean anything by it, but his heart plummeted to the earth like a block of lead. Anna was looking for a husband for her granddaughter, and it wasn't him. The sooner he came to terms with his place in Mandy's life, the better. He was just on Huckleberry Hill to replace the roof.

Mandy tilted her head to one side and gazed at him with a tease twitching at her lips. He couldn't return her amusement. He didn't feel like he was in on the joke anymore.

"Felty doesn't need spectacles," Anna said. "He got Lasik in August when Ben was here." She glanced at the empty recliner. "Where is Felty? He's supposed to be making pot holders. I gave him my special pink yarn."

"He went to take a nap," Mandy said.

The wrinkles around Anna's mouth bunched together. "A nap? At seven in the morning? It wonders me if he isn't coming down with something." She laid her pinecones on the table and headed down the hall. "Come on, Sparky. Let's go see what's ailing Felty."

The fluffy white dog padded down the hall after Anna. Sparky hadn't even waited for Noah to give her a pat. He might as well have been invisible, to both Sparky and Anna. That was what happened when you had a dat who shamed his family and the whole community. Nobody wanted you to marry their granddaughter.

The glint in Mandy's eye disappeared. "Is something wrong?"

"Nae," he said, adjusting his handy sunglasses. She wouldn't be able to read the storm clouds in his eyes. "I should start on the roof."

"If I can do anything to help, let me know. Lunch is at noon." She took the steak package from his hand. "I'll keep this in the fridge until you're ready to go home."

"Okay."

"Are you sure nothing's wrong?"

He crafted a convincing smile on his face. "I'm wearing a fearsome pair of Englisch sunglasses. What could be wrong?"

She relaxed her concerned expression. "Jah. You could scare small children away."

Small children and Amish mammis.

Chapter Twelve

How could she concentrate on knitting knowing Noah was mere feet above her hefting shingles and driving nails, and she wasn't there to see it? All that muscle flexing going to waste while she was stuck in the great room knitting pink pot holders for boys she wasn't interested in.

How long had he been up there? It couldn't have been more than an hour, could it? Still, he might be terribly thirsty yet. The weather was cool, but reroofing a house had to be backbreaking, throat-parching work. He was probably dying for a drink, and she would be selfish not to take him an ice-cold glass of water this very instant.

She set down her needles and practically raced to the kitchen, where she popped some ice into a cup and filled it with water. It wouldn't be easy climbing a ladder with a full glass in her hands, but Noah needed her. She'd do her best.

Mammi stood at the counter studying her recipe book. "Have you ever eaten potstickers, Mandy?"

Mandy hesitated, wondering which answer would make it more likely Mammi would try to make them. "I don't think so."

"I haven't either. Maybe we should try them for supper tonight."

Mandy glanced at the page in the recipe book. The picture didn't look too bad. But in her experience, it was how the recipe turned out after Mammi got hold of it that was the problem. "Do you have all the ingredients?"

"Not a one, except for brown sugar, oil, and eggs. I might have to try this later when I can get to that specialty store in Green Bay."

Mandy secretly hoped that a trip to the specialty store would take place after she went home to Charm. "Potstickers" sounded like a three-day stomachache.

She carried her glass of water outside, patted Chester on the head when he ran up to greet her, and stepped carefully up the ladder that leaned against the side of the house. Standing on the second rung from the top, she would be visible to Noah from the waist up. Although she couldn't see him, she could hear his nail gun spitting out nails on the other side of the roof. Somewhere amongst the trees, she heard a crow or some other such bird let out a mournful caw. Should she try to climb onto the roof? It might be next to impossible with a glass in her hand.

"Noah," she called. The nail gun didn't break its steady rhythm. "Noah!"

The rhythmic pop and swish of the nail gun stopped, and she heard his measured steps as he trudged up the steep pitch of the roof to the ridge. His frown seemed to be carved into his face until her saw her, and then his expression relaxed. Was he happy to see her? Dying of thirst? She couldn't tell. He had those aggravating sunglasses on.

The air caught in her throat when she made note of his muscular arms swaying back and forth with the movement of his muscular body and saw his strong fingers wrapped around his bulky air gun. She probably shouldn't find him so attractive. He was sweating, for goodness' sake.

He stepped over a bundle of shingles as he made his way to her down the slant of the roof.

"Mandy," he said gently, almost as if seeing her made him sad. "You're going to fall."

"I know my way up and down a ladder." She held out the glass to him, although at the moment, it seemed like a horribly lame excuse for bothering him when he was only trying to finish his work. "Nice sunglasses," she said.

He cracked a smile, sank to the surface of the roof, and sat cross-legged next to Mandy. "You know I have a water bottle, don't you?"

She bit her bottom lip and wished she didn't feel the heat traveling up her neck. He'd have an easy time guessing her thoughts. "Oh . . . well . . . I didn't know. I was afraid you might be thirsty."

He smiled an easy smile, as if he didn't suspect any ulterior motives from her. "It's very nice of you." He took her offered glass and drained it in five swallows.

That loud crow cawed again as Noah gave back the empty glass. His lips twitched slightly, but since his eyes were covered, she didn't know if he was amused or annoyed. "I'm sorry to bother you," she said.

"To tell you the truth, it's a welcome interruption."

She couldn't see his eyes, but there was warmth behind his voice. The warmth was contagious. It moved into her chest and took up residence there.

"I'm wondering if you could help me with something," he said.

"Of course. Anything. I'm gute with a hammer."

He gave her a half smile. "I'm sure you are. But I don't want you getting on the roof. It's too easy to fall." He kept his face turned toward her but gestured to his right with his head. "I know how you like to fix things. I need you to take care of a bird problem."

She started to turn her head as she heard another birdcall coming from the thicket across the lane.

"Don't look," he said. "It only encourages them."

Mandy nearly fell off the ladder. He reached out a hand to steady her. "What," she hissed quietly. "Do you mean to tell me that Kristina is spying on you? At my house?"

Noah exhaled slowly and nodded.

Her utter disbelief was only matched by her indignation, but she was able to keep her voice low and her face relatively expressionless. "She's my best friend. How could she?"

He shrugged. "It's what she does."

She wilted like a flower in the hot sun. "I suppose I should have recognized the birdcalls, but they sounded so real."

"Dori Rose is with her. Dori does a very good crow."

The expression on his face struck her funny bone. She nearly choked on her urge to giggle. "When I get my hands on her . . ."

The laughter rumbled in his chest. "Remember you've taken a vow of nonviolence."

"But how could she come to my mammi's house and spy on you? Why doesn't she just knock on the front door?"

"I have no idea what goes on inside a girl's head."

Mandy glanced in the direction of the birdcall, her indignation foaming like water in a raging river. "I'll take care of it. Where are they exactly?"

"You know the path that leads to the other side of the hill?"

"Where the huckleberries grow?"

He nodded. "They're behind the maple directly to the left of the path, unless they've moved in the last few minutes. They've been making an awful lot of noise. Like two bulls trampling the cornfields."

Mandy covered her smile with her hand. Noah's description wasn't very flattering even if it was accurate. Kristina wanted to be noticed. Of course she'd make as much noise as possible. "Can you keep their attention focused so I can sneak up on them?"

He arched an eyebrow so it peeked over the top of his glasses. "How should I do that?"

"I don't know. Go stand on the ridgeline and flex your biceps or something."

"You like my muscles, don't you?"

Familiar heat crept into her cheeks. "I do not."

He swiped his hand across his mouth to wipe off his mischievous grin. "Okay. I'll stand on the ridgeline and do a little dance. Do you think that will keep their eyes in this direction?"

With his good looks, he could lie down and take a nap and still hold Kristina's attention. "Whatever you do, don't fall."

He propped his chin in his hand. "I could do a hand-stand."

She couldn't keep the grin from taking over her face. "You are incorrigible. Now get up there." She took a step down the ladder.

"Be careful going down," he said. "Next time you need me, stay on the ground and I'll come to you. Your grandparents wouldn't look kindly on me if you broke your neck."

"I don't think they'd be mad at you."

"It's my ladder."

With empty glass in hand, Mandy stepped slowly down the ladder. She turned her back on the house, and with all the bearing of someone who had somewhere very important to go, she marched into the barn. After closing the door behind her, she walked out the back opening, around the small orchard of peach trees, and tiptoed into the thicket, making a wide arc so as to be able to approach Kristina and Dori Rose from behind.

It didn't take long to circle around behind them. There they were, pressing against the thick trunk of a sugar maple, peeking out from behind the tree and breaking into giggling fits whenever they caught a glimpse of Noah.

Holding her skirts so they wouldn't swish against the bushes and undergrowth, Mandy quietly stepped up behind the two girls, but they were laughing so hard, it wouldn't have mattered if she had tromped right up to the tree singing "Life's Railway to Heaven." They wouldn't have heard a team of horses.

"Oh, Dori Rose, look at those muscles," Kristina sighed.

They leaned their heads out from behind the tree to look.

Partially hidden by an unruly bush, Mandy shifted her gaze to the roof. Noah balanced on the ridgeline with one hand propped on his hip. He flexed his arms as he took a slow drink from his water bottle. Mandy smirked. He knew exactly what he was doing. Could he blame any girl for wanting to spy?

She ripped her gaze from the rooftop. No matter how attractive Noah might be, Kristina should not stoop to this. It was absurd and immature and made Noah extremely uncomfortable.

She stepped out from behind the bush and folded her arms. "Enjoying the view?"

Kristina squealed and jumped as if she'd been stuck with a pin. Dori Rose sucked in her breath and clutched her hand to her heart.

"Mandy," Kristina squeaked. "You gave me a heart attack."

Mandy's eyes traveled from Kristina to Dori Rose and back again. "Why are you spying on Noah?" she said, as if she were speaking to two very naughty little girls. "Krissy, you should be ashamed."

Kristina's prayer covering sat askew on top of her head. She straightened it, pursed her lips, and looked positively mulish. "It's no shame to look."

Dori Rose pressed a wide, uncomfortable smile onto her face. "We like to look."

Mandy frowned, making sure they knew she was not

amused. "You're not eight years old anymore. If you want to develop a relationship with a boy, you have a conversation with him. Bake him a pie. Meet him at a gathering."

Kristina put on her best pouty face and leaned against the tree. "You're no fun anymore, Mandy."

Fun? Mandy didn't remember ever having this kind of "fun" with Kristina. "Just . . . Krissy . . . please don't spy on him anymore." *And please leave him alone.*

Mandy's chest tightened. Was it fair to her friend, who was madly in love with Noah, to spend so much time with Noah herself? And to enjoy it?

It didn't matter. It wasn't as if she and Noah were courting or anything. She'd be gone in two weeks. Her spending time with Noah didn't hurt Kristina at all. Besides, he was fixing the roof. They inevitably spent a lot of time together. If Kristina loved him so much, she should convince her dat to hire Noah to fix her roof.

Mandy swallowed the bitter taste in her mouth. She didn't want Noah to fix anybody's roof but hers.

"He won't text me," Kristina said. "How can I have a conversation?"

Dori Rose nodded vigorously. "He won't answer her calls."

Mandy tried to soften her tone. "Why spend all your energy on a boy who isn't interested?"

Tears puddled in Kristina's eyes. "Why are you defending him? I'm the one who got my heart broken. Don't you care about your best friend's feelings? You should be helping me get him back like Dori Rose is doing."

"By making birdcalls and watching him from behind a tree?"

Kristina wiped her eyes. "You could let me bring him the water. I'm as good at smiling at him as you are."

Mandy's stomach sank. What had Kristina seen in her

smiles? "I was being nice. He's fixing Mammi and Dawdi's roof."

"You should have invited me over when you knew he was going to be here. It seems like you're trying to keep him all to yourself."

"He's fixing the roof."

"Then you should invite me over every day."

This time her stomach splatted onto the ground. She should be ashamed of herself, but she'd rather eat Mammi's cooking for the rest of her life than invite Kristina over while Noah worked on the roof. She would have liked to say that it was for Kristina's own good, that she was only protecting her friend from inevitable heartache. She could even have justified to herself that she wanted to shield Noah from her overbearing friend.

But she knew her motives went deeper than that. She wanted to be the one to give Noah steaks and marshmallows and unnecessary glasses of water. She wanted to be the girl who petted his dog and appreciated his muscles and drove his buggy home after a night at the bar—the only one he roasted marshmallows and carried tomatoes for.

Guilt grabbed her by the throat this time.

Oh sis yuscht!

What kind of girl wanted her best friend's boyfriend all to herself?

She pressed her lips together. Noah wasn't Kristina's boyfriend and never had been. But Kristina wouldn't see it that way.

Not so sure of herself, she put an arm around Kristina's shoulder. "You could have your pick of any other boy in Bonduel."

"Nae, Mandy. *You* can have your pick of any boy in Bonduel. They're all talking about how pretty you are."

Mandy narrowed her eyes. "They are not."

Dori Rose made a face. "Jah, they are. I heard them at

gmay. We call them the Pot Holder Club because they carry pot holders in their pockets."

The three of them giggled and any tension among them dissipated like fog from the lake on a warm day.

Mandy took a deep breath. What would it hurt to invite Kristina and Dori Rose into the house? Noah would be on the roof. Neither girl would be able to get a good look at his eye. No harm done.

Of course she'd have to deliver his lunch to him on the roof. He wouldn't be eager to set foot in the house while Kristina was over, especially with the black eye. Lord willing, Kristina and Dori Rose would grow tired of sitting in the house while Noah worked on top of it. Kristina's attention span wasn't that long. Mandy might have Noah all to herself by midafternoon.

A thread of guilt crawled up her spine again, but she pushed it down by telling herself that she was only here for two more weeks. How could she help her best friend win Noah's heart in two short weeks? It was impossible. She wouldn't even try.

In the meantime, she would enjoy Noah's company and eat his s'mores and try to fix his life, and Kristina would be none the wiser.

Chapter Thirteen

The pan sizzled as Noah cracked six eggs into it. He scrambled the eggs with a fork and added a hearty amount of cheese, a spoonful of mayonnaise, and a few drops of milk. He probably made scrambled eggs for dinner three or four nights a week. They were nutritious, fast, and easy. Dat seldom complained. Since he didn't do any of the cooking, he usually ate what Noah put in front of him. Thanks to Mandy, they'd eaten steak on Tuesday night. Scrambled eggs did get old after a while.

He had been tempted to accept Anna's invitation to dinner tonight, even though she was making something called couscous, but if he weren't home to feed Dat, Dat wouldn't eat. No matter how much Noah wanted to sit at the table next to Mandy and stare at her cute freckles, his most important job was taking care of Dat.

Noah pressed his fingers into the ridge where his neck met his shoulder. Three full days of hammering shingles had left his neck stiff as a board. He smiled to himself. The pain didn't bother him. Mandy lived under that roof, and just thinking about her in the house doing laundry or washing dishes or knitting pot holders made the labor seem effortless.

Today, she had spent the entire afternoon outside hanging

laundry within view of his perch on the roof. Her movements mesmerized him as he watched her out of the corner of his eye. He had even stopped hammering at one point just to stare at her while she pinned laundry with those graceful fingers and tugged the line to send the wet clothes higher into the air. The lack of hammering from the roof must have caught her attention, because she had looked up at him and waved, gifting him with a smile that put the shine of a new circular saw blade to shame.

During his long days on the roof, he found himself wishing that he hadn't told Mandy about his water bottle. Her visit with the glass of water had been the best part of his week. She'd even taken care of his Kristina problem. Maybe she liked him just a little bit.

He pressed his lips into a rigid line. Who was he kidding? Mandy was nice to everybody. He'd be a fool to think she was giving him any special attention.

"Dat," he called. "Dinner's ready."

Noah didn't know exactly how, but he could always tell instantly when Dat was in a low mood. Tonight was one of those nights. He shuffled into the kitchen with slumped shoulders and a scowl on his face. His beard and hair were tangled and matted, and his hands shook as if he couldn't calm his nerves.

Noah's heart sank. It had been good for a few days, ever since Dat had given him the black eye. Dat always felt horrible after striking his own son, even if he didn't remember doing it. The black eye had been a visible reminder of his weakness. After a drunken fit, Dat always promised Noah that he'd clean up his life, but the transformation only lasted until the irresistible need for a drink overtook him again.

The only reason Dat made those wooden baskets was to earn enough money for his next drink. Noah kept a tight hold on his own money, paying their rent, sending what he could spare to Mamm, buying feed for the horses, but he couldn't forbid Dat from making baskets or spending the money the way he wanted. Noah closed his eyes and reminded himself that no matter how much he wanted it or how hard he prayed, his dat was never going to change. Noah would square his shoulders and do what needed to be done for his dat, even if that meant trekking to the bar three or four nights a week to fetch home his drunk father. Some things just couldn't be fixed.

He divided the eggs between two plates and put a piece of toast and an apple slice next to them. He put the plates on the table, sat next to his dat, and bowed his head in silent grace. He never looked to see if his dat prayed. Noah always said an extra prayer for both of them, just in case.

They ate without conversing until they heard a knock on the door. Noah's heart leaped to attention. The only people who ever came to visit were the bishop and—since about two weeks ago—Mandy Helmuth. With his dat in such a sour mood, he was hoping for the bishop. He'd be mortified for Mandy to see his dat like this.

Noah opened the door and caught his breath. Mandy, smiling and looking like a daisy in winter, stood on the porch with an Englisch woman Noah didn't recognize. Her blond hair was cropped short, and she looked to be about his mamm's age or a little younger. The Englisch woman stuck out her hand, and Noah took it out of habit. Then he maneuvered his body so that neither Mandy nor the Englischer could see into the kitchen and catch sight of his dat.

"You must be Noah," the woman said. "I'm Jessica Trumble. Mandy said you could use my help."

Noah glanced doubtfully at Mandy. She smiled with all the confidence of someone who thought she was right.

Just what did she think she was right about?

He self-consciously ran his finger along his eyebrow. The bruises around his eye had faded to pinks and yellows, but they were still visible and still spoke of his shame. Had the

Englischer noticed them? "Who are you?" he managed to ask, even though he felt he had a mouthful of sawdust. He didn't care who she was. Mandy should know better than to bring a stranger into his home.

Shouldn't she know better?

"I'm not here to do anything but talk to you about the situation with your dat. Can we come in?"

"No," he said, the pressure building inside his chest. Mandy pressed her lips together, and something like uncertainty flashed in her eyes.

The woman gave Mandy a sideways glance. "Mandy said this is very hard for you. I understand completely. I used to be an alcoholic. When I was trying to get sober, I wouldn't have made it through to the other side without help from mentors and friends. And professionals. I'm a volunteer for a program through Al-Anon, and I want to help you explore treatment options for your dat. Maybe we could talk for a minute."

His heart pounded against his chest over and over again like an iron-cold sledgehammer. He nearly winced at the pain. What had Mandy done? "Who else knows you're here?"

"No one," the woman replied. "We keep everything highly confidential." She laced her hands together in front of her. "Look, I know this is hard, but Mandy is worried about you. She thought you might appreciate knowing you're not alone."

"I like being alone," he said. He clenched his jaw and ground his teeth until they ached.

Dread wrapped an icy hand around his chest as he heard his dat rise from the table and come to stand behind him. "What do you want?" Dat said.

"We want to help," Mandy said. Her smile had disappeared along with that smug confidence she'd worn only a few minutes before.

Dat pressed into Noah, and Noah stood his ground to keep his dat from getting too close to Mandy. He jabbed his finger in Mandy's direction. "We don't need your help." Dat spat the words out of his mouth much as he did whenever the bishop came over. "They took my Rosie. I don't want help from nobody."

Noah turned around and pressed a hand to Dat's chest as he became increasingly agitated. "Dat, sit down."

Dat always resisted any attempt Noah made to rein him in, but Noah was stronger than his dat and had been for several years. He wrapped one arm tightly around Dat's back and firmly clasped his arm as he shoved him back to the table and pushed him into his chair. Dat withered the minute he sat down, as if he were too tired to fight anymore.

"Finish your eggs, Dat."

"I'm not hungry."

Noah glanced at Mandy and the other woman standing on the porch gazing with pitiful curiosity into his tiny, run-down shack. Into his pathetic, run-down life. Shame and anger nearly tore him in half. Mandy had seen too much. Mandy knew too much.

He wanted her out. He wanted her out now.

Mandy and the other woman stepped back as Noah strode out of the house and closed the door behind him. He wanted to yell, to hurl the words out of his mouth like a thousand sharp daggers. Instead, he tightened his gut and kept his voice low as he pointed to the white sedan parked on the road. "I want you to go. And please don't come back." He looked pointedly at Mandy. "It only makes things worse."

An ocean of pain pooled in Mandy's eyes. Why should she feel hurt? He was the one humiliated beyond repair. "I thought you might want to—"

"You thought wrong," he said, controlling his voice and disciplining his expression.

The woman gave Noah a resigned half smile and put her

arm around Mandy. "I'm sorry we bothered you," she said. "I didn't really understand the situation."

He scrubbed his fingers through his hair. "You can't do this to people."

"Come on, Mandy," the woman said. "Let's go."

Mandy and the other woman finally stepped off his porch. At that moment, Chester ran from around the side of the house and nudged his nose against Mandy's hand as she walked away.

"No, Chester," Noah barked.

Chester obediently changed directions, bounded up the steps, and sat down next to Noah. Mandy dared a glance back at him. Her look, heavy with uncertainty and ache, was like a knife right to the heart. He folded his arms across his chest to keep the pain from seeping out. He'd done the right thing.

But had he lost Mandy's friendship because of it?

A few hard words between them, and it suddenly felt like his heart had been torn from his chest.

It had never felt so rotten to be right.

Taking a deep, shuddering breath, he laid a hand on Chester's head. At least he still had his loyal dog. Chester would never try to fix Noah's *dat* or stick his nose in other people's business. Chester didn't even stick his nose in the toilet.

"I'll drive you home," he heard the *Englischer* tell Mandy.

"Thanks anyway," Mandy said, her voice so dull that Noah barely recognized it. "I'd like to walk."

She'd like to walk? What could she have been thinking? It was almost dark, and Huckleberry Hill was a forty-five-minute hike from here. She didn't even have a coat.

"Are you sure?" the *Englischer* said.

Noah didn't hear Mandy's reply, but the woman got into her car and drove away. Foolish *Englischer*. She should have insisted on driving Mandy home. Didn't she know what a long walk it was?

Without a second look at Noah, Mandy wrapped her arms around herself against the chill and trudged up the road in the direction of her grandparents' house.

He'd just kicked her off his porch, and she probably wouldn't want him within a hundred feet, but he couldn't let her walk home by herself. His mamm had raised him better than that. Growling in frustration, he bolted into the house.

Dat sat at the table with his face buried in his hands. This little incident would send him running for a drink tonight. Alcohol made him forget. These days he had more that he wanted to forget than he wanted to remember.

"I'm going out, Dat," he said, grabbing two coats from the hook and the toast from his plate.

"So am I."

Noah hesitated for only a moment. There was nothing he could do to stop his dat. Hopefully his trip to the bar wouldn't turn into another black eye by morning.

He slid his arms into his coat as he vaulted off the porch and jogged in Mandy's direction. "Come on, Chester," he called, snapping his fingers for his dog. Sometimes a man needed his trustworthy hound tagging along.

Trudging as slowly as she was, Mandy hadn't gotten far. The gravel and dirt crunched beneath his feet as he approached her.

"I like being alone," she said without turning around. She picked up her pace like she thought she could outrun him. She couldn't. Her legs were far shorter than his. Chester bounded along beside him as if they were embarking on a grand adventure instead of chasing an aggravatingly stubborn girl who didn't even have the good sense to get a ride home when she had the chance.

"You need a coat," he said, taking a few long strides to catch up with her.

She kept walking and refused to look at him. "I'm fine."

"Don't make me more irritated than I already am, Mandy. Take a coat so you won't freeze to death."

"Oh, jah. I wouldn't want to make you irritated." She stared straight ahead and scowled with her whole face. "Why don't you stay away from me if you find me so irritating."

"Because you need a coat."

Chester jogged beside her as if he were playing a game with her. She was practically running now. "Go away, Noah."

Noah grabbed her arm. She yanked it away from his grasp. "Why are you mad at me?" he said. "You're the one who brought that Englischer to my home."

"I just wanted to help. I thought you'd appreciate it."

He eyed her as if she were crazy. "Mandy, you know me. Why in a million years did you think that I would want help from anyone? You completely humiliated me when I've already told you, some things can't be fixed. My dat can't be fixed."

"With God, all things are possible."

He frowned. If she wanted to quote scripture, he could quote contradicting verses all day long. "The scriptures also say to be still."

She halted suddenly and turned on him. "I know. You don't want to be bothered." Her tone was thick with bitterness. "So why are you still following me?"

He clenched his teeth and thought seriously about turning around and leaving her to her own devices. But he couldn't do it, no matter how angry he was with her. "Because you need a coat."

She exhaled slowly and snatched the coat from his hand. "Fine."

Unfortunately, Noah and his dat didn't own any small-sized coats. The sleeves fell past her hands, and the body of the coat probably could have gone around her twice. She looked kind of cute, like a child stuffed into a puffy snowsuit, until she glared at him and marched away from him as if he had a contagious disease. She couldn't go as fast with his coat hanging halfway to her knees.

He followed a few paces behind.

"I put the coat on," she said, turning her head slightly to her left as she trudged along. "You can go away now."

"I have to make sure you get home safely."

"Why should you care?" She threw the words behind her.

"A girl should never walk home alone."

"If I get run over by a car or fall into a ditch, at least I won't be able to bother you anymore."

He shoved the air out of his lungs in irritation. "Mandy, my dat's life is none of your concern."

She nearly tripped as she tried to go faster. "Follow me home if you must, but don't lecture me."

"Why would I lecture you? You don't listen."

Her steps faltered before she quickly recovered and crossed to the other side of the road. Walking on the opposite side parallel with Mandy, he could see her profile. Her face looked drawn and bleak, like a barren tree in the dead of winter.

He shouldn't have said that. He'd hurt her feelings when all he wanted to do was talk some sense into her. He was justified in his anger, after all.

Noah started to breathe heavily as he tried to keep up with her. She moved extremely fast for a girl in a long coat and a dress. "If you don't slow down, you're going to keel over from exhaustion."

"If you're worried about having to carry me home," she snapped, "don't be. I'd rather crawl on my hands and knees than let you touch me. I wouldn't want to be any more of a nuisance than I already am."

"I'm just saying, it's a long way home and—"

She stuck her nose in the air. "If I die along the trail, just call the bishop and have him send a buggy. Leave Chester to watch over my body. You need not be bothered."

"Now you're being silly."

"Leave me alone, Noah."

He stopped trying to reason with her and fell back a few paces. Chester fell back with him. The only sounds between them were the crunch of their footfalls on gravel and their shared labored breathing plus Chester's panting. At least Chester was getting some good exercise.

No communication at all was better than a quarrel. All he needed to do was see her safely home, and then he'd never have to speak to her again.

That thought slammed into him, and he nearly tripped over his own feet. What was he thinking? He might be ferociously angry and acutely humiliated, but he might shrivel up like a grape in the sun if he wasn't able to see Mandy again.

In the two weeks since she'd shown up on his porch looking like a wet hen with an entire tail of ruffled feathers, his whole world had changed. He went to bed at night looking forward to waking up the next morning. He caught himself smiling when nobody was looking and dreaming up ways to make her laugh when she was near. He whistled at work and bristled at the sight of knitted pot holders.

She had suddenly become very important to him. Essential, really. He couldn't imagine doing without her.

Even as angry as he was, he loathed the invisible wall of silence between them. He wanted to hear her voice more than any other sound in the world. He didn't even care if she snapped at him. And what could he do to get her to flash one of her adorable, freckle-garnished smiles?

His hopes went south when he glanced across the road. Her posture was stiff and unyielding, her face turned from him as if he didn't exist.

What if she never wanted to talk to him again?

A lump of coal settled in the bottom of his gut.

After about fifteen minutes, Mandy began to slacken her pace. Gute. She probably wouldn't faint.

Not that he would mind carrying her home, even if she had promised to crawl all the way. The last time she'd been comfortably tucked into his arms, she'd been soaking wet and hostile. He hadn't truly appreciated the experience. He wouldn't make that same mistake twice.

She slowed to a stroll, and he noticed she limped slightly. Had she sprained her ankle?

"You're limping," he said.

She turned her head and looked at him as if she was surprised he was still following her. "I'm not limping."

"Did you hurt yourself?"

She shook her head as if she were completely fed up with him. "I have a pebble in my shoe."

"Why don't you take it out?"

"I wouldn't want to inconvenience you by taking the time to do it. I know you've got more important things to do than babysit Mandy Helmuth."

"I can wait." When she didn't show any signs of stopping, he added, "You'll get a blister."

They walked alongside a fenced pasture where a stile with wide steps cut over one of the fences. Mandy veered toward it. After shrugging out of her oversized coat, she sat on the second stile step and removed her shoe.

Chester ducked under the fence and ran around the pasture, then ducked back out and ran a few paces down the road as if impatient to be going again.

Mandy frowned at Noah when he came up beside her and then grimaced when she took off her shoe. Even through her black stockings, Noah could see the dark spot of blood at her heel. "Blister?" he asked.

"Sharp pebble."

"Can you walk okay?"

Her head was lowered so he couldn't see her face and couldn't tell how much pain she was in. She'd walked fast and hard. Who knew how long the pebble had been cutting into her skin.

"I don't mind carrying you, Mandy," he said, knowing she wouldn't give him satisfaction by saying yes.

She turned her shoe upside down and dumped out, not one, but a handful of pebbles. "I . . . I'll crawl." She sniffled quietly.

Was she crying?

He nudged her chin up with his finger. Yep. A few tears etched meandering trails down her face. His gut clenched. He couldn't stand to see her cry. "How bad does it hurt?"

His touch seemed to break whatever dam held all those tears back. She dropped her shoe and scrunched her face into a frown. "Oh, Noah," she said, disintegrating into a pitiful sob.

Whatever anger he was still harboring melted like a marshmallow over a hot flame. How could he keep from softening into a gooey hunk of sugar when the tears glistened in her eyes as brilliantly as young leaves in the springtime? He squatted beside her and laid a hand over her arm. "It's okay. Don't cry. I promise to get you home."

She buried her face in her hands and wailed louder. "It's not that."

"I won't make you crawl, and I promise not to gloat about it." By some miracle, there was a clean tissue in his coat pocket. He handed it to her.

"I only wanted to help your dat," she said, smoothing the tissue with her hand. "I didn't mean to humiliate you."

"I know," he said. He wanted to be honest, even at the risk of inciting more tears. "But it still stings, even when you mean well."

Her lips quivered as she took a gulp of air. "When I met Jessica, I got carried away in all my excitement. My cousin's best friend almost died of a drug overdose. A counselor and a rehab program got him back on his feet. Now he's a pastor in Ohio."

"That's never going to be my dat."

Her lips twitched upward. "Well, he'll probably never be a pastor." She dabbed at the moisture on her face. "I feel so deerich. The last thing in the world I would ever do is purposefully hurt you or your dat. Do you believe that?"

He nodded. "You don't try to humiliate me. What other girl would buy a strange pair of sunglasses to keep my secret safe?"

She sprouted a weak smile.

He couldn't resist any longer. Not many girls could manage to look so pretty with a runny nose. He slid his hand down her arm and laced his fingers with hers. She leaned back slightly but didn't pull away. "It hurts me when you won't take my requests seriously," he said. "My family is my business."

She pursed her lips and stared at her hand in his. "But is this how you want to live the rest of your life? Taking care of your dat? What happens if you want to marry and raise your own family?"

If she only knew how these questions tortured him. Mamm had tried again and again to convince Dat to stop drinking. The pleading always ended in arguments, heartache, and shame. Noah could live with the heartache and dat's drunken rages, but he couldn't bear the shame.

"Mandy, God said to be still," he repeated, in case she hadn't believed him the first time.

"That doesn't mean to do nothing. Your dat can't get better without help. Why don't you want to help him?"

She couldn't know that her accusation felt like a slap in the face. "I've suffered enough humiliation."

One shoe off and one shoe on, she got to her feet and

stood on the first step of the stile so they were nearly eye-to-eye. "You haven't done anything wrong."

He couldn't tear his gaze from her face. "It doesn't matter."

"You are a godly man, Noah. Of course it matters."

He reached up and brushed his thumb across her lower lip. He had meant it as a gesture to persuade her to stop talking, but when his rough skin met her petal-soft mouth, he felt as if someone had set him on fire. His breath caught in his throat.

She held perfectly still as he grazed his thumb lightly along the line of her bottom lip and imagined what it would be like to breathe her in with every breath and feel the soft curve of her mouth on his.

The fire raged inside until he thought he might melt. Was it right to stand this close? To entertain these overpowering feelings? Struggle as he might, he couldn't remember one lecture from his mamm, although there must have been dozens knocking around in that brain of his. At that moment, it didn't matter what Mamm had taught him. Mandy smelled like roses and ice cream and looked more beautiful than pink tulips blooming on the hillside. She was the sun, the moon, and the stars.

Slowly, gently, he slid his arms around her waist and pulled her close to him. She placed her palms flat on his chest and lifted her face to his. With supreme gentleness and unquenchable thirst, he brought his lips down on hers. In the dimming light of sunset, his world seemed to explode with the brightness of a thousand stars. Her lips were softer than he could ever have imagined, and her embrace proved warmer than a summer's day. She snaked her hands around his neck.

Without surrendering his claim on Mandy's mouth, he tightened his arms around her. He stepped back so that her feet slid off the step and he held her in his arms, completely and unyieldingly. A sigh came from deep in her throat.

Her touch, her warmth, only served to stoke the fires burning wildly inside him. The more he drank, the thirstier he became. "Mandy," he whispered. There would never be any other words left for him to say. She filled every space inside him.

Just when he thought he might burst into flames, he felt the wetness of her tears against his face. He pulled away slightly and looked into her eyes. She smiled at him through her tears.

His heart sank to his toes as he relaxed his grip and let her feet find purchase on the stile step. "I'm sorry if I've done something I shouldn't have. I didn't mean to make you cry."

"Nothing like that," she whispered as she pulled him back into a tight embrace. "I'm just happy you don't hate me."

"Hate you? I'm turned every which way in love with you yet."

"Even though I'm irritating and nosy?"

"Enough talk. Is it okay if I kiss you again?"

She arched an eyebrow. "I'll be annoyed if you don't."

He pulled her close again and slanted his lips over hers. She felt so good in his arms, as if she belonged snugly close to his heart. Right now, it didn't even matter that he wasn't good enough for her or that a girl like her would never, ever consider a boy like him. She didn't pull away from him, and he'd be ungrateful to wish for more.

The fire inside him burned until he should have been reduced to a pile of ashes. He took Mandy's arms and gently nudged her away.

She frowned at him. "I'm not ready to be done yet."

He laid an affectionate kiss on her forehead. "My mamm told me never to go so far that I can't find my way back, and I don't know about you, but I'm a little disoriented."

She giggled. "I'm lost in a thick forest somewhere in Canada."

"I'm in China."

"I hear China is very interesting."

He squeezed her arms. "It's amazing."

Smiling, they stared at each other for a few seconds trying to regain their bearings when Chester nudged his nose against Mandy's hand. She gave Chester an affectionate pat on the head before sinking to the step and picking up her shoe. "I should get back. Mammi said she'd hold dinner for me. Couscous with clam sauce."

Noah reached into his pocket and pulled out the cold, dry piece of toast crumbling to pieces at the bottom of his pocket. "I saved this for you."

She shoved her lips to one side of her face and arched an eyebrow. "How long have you been saving it? Since Christmas?"

"I snatched it from my plate as I ran out the door. I'm not sure what I was thinking except that food seems to soften you up."

"Well, maybe not a stale piece of toast that's been sitting in your linty pocket." She finished lacing her shoe and stood.

He dangled it in front of her face. "It's either this or couscous with oyster sauce."

"Clam." She hesitated for mere moments before plucking the toast from his fingers and taking a big bite. "I hope nothing unsanitary has been in that pocket."

"Does a frog count?"

She stopped chewing as her tongue lolled out of her mouth.

He chuckled, taking delight in every expression on her face. "I'm joking. I haven't kept frogs in my pocket since I was about ten."

She held the piece of bread out for him. "Want a bite?"

He shook his head. "You need it more than I do."

She shrugged. "This toast isn't bad, but you should use more butter. Toast is only delicious when it's slathered with about a quarter stick of butter."

He made a face. "I like my toast dry."

"Jah, I can see that." She offered Chester the last bite, and he gobbled it up without even questioning whose pocket it had been in. "I'm full now. Let's go. I've been avoiding the clam sauce long enough."

He cupped a hand over her elbow. "Can you walk okay?"

"If you hold my hand, I'll be all right," she said, a tease glinting in her eyes. "What does your mamm say about holding hands?"

"I might still end up in China."

Her smile nearly knocked him off his feet. "I hear China is amazing."

He laced his fingers through hers. A pleasant sensation tingled all the way up his arm. "I'm willing to risk getting lost."

"Me too."

Chapter Fourteen

What was she going to tell Kristina?

Only the worst kind of friend would steal her best friend's boyfriend.

Only, it wasn't stealing if he hadn't really been the best friend's boyfriend to begin with. And she hadn't set out to steal anything. She'd sort of stumbled into Noah and had lost her heart in the process.

With a lump in her throat, Mandy did up the breakfast dishes while Mammi sat at the table and perused her cookbook. "Chinese noodles with ginger sauce," Mammi said, adjusting her glasses and leaning in for a better look. "Do you like Chinese food, Mandy?"

"I've never had Chinese food," Mandy said. But she'd heard that China was amazing. Despite her misgivings about Kristina, her lips curled into a smile. Amazing. If she had known that being kissed by Noah was that heart-stoppingly breathtaking, she would have asked him to do it two weeks ago. Of course a little more than two weeks ago she had been standing on his porch wagging her finger at him and making all sorts of wild accusations. She probably couldn't have talked him into it. Besides, Kristina had been watching from the buggy.

"Do you know what five-spice powder is?" Mammi asked.

"Nae. Is it Chinese?" Mandy glanced at her mammi doubtfully. It sounded like she was going to jump in over her head again.

Mandy's heart skipped an uneven rhythm when she looked at the clock. Almost seven. Noah would be here any minute. Would he wear the white shirt or the blue? Would he smile or put on his normal down-to-business expression?

Maybe he'd smile. He'd told her he loved her, hadn't he? Well, he'd said he was turned every which way in love with her. Was it the same thing?

She hoped so, because she was beginning to feel turned every which way in love with him too, even though he got mad at her on a regular basis. Even though he wasn't about to see reason when it came to his fater and even though she still had a secret she hadn't shared with him.

And even though . . . Kristina.

She adored that look he got on his face when he tried to solve a problem and the way he persistently stuck to a job until it was finished. He didn't let something he didn't know stop him from accomplishing his task. She loved the way he teased her and spoke plainly and felt so protective of girls. And yes, she had a preference for boys with muscles. Was that so wrong?

She rinsed out the sink and dried her hands, then touched her fingers to her lips. Every time she thought of Noah's kisses, her lips tingled pleasantly and her unbridled heart galloped like a racehorse. At this rate, she'd be breathless all day.

All month.

Probably all year.

". . . just sandwiches, don't you think?" Mammi said, looking at Mandy as if she expected an answer.

Mandy pulled her hand from her mouth. Had she been puckering? "I'm sorry, Mammi. What did you say?"

Mammi eyes danced. "My dear, your head has been up in the clouds all morning, but I can't say as I blame you. Paul is a very promising prospect, even with braces."

Mandy pasted on a fake smile. "Paul Zook?"

"Don't you remember, dear? He's coming at noon to take you to Cobbler Pond for a picnic, but I think it will just have to be sandwiches today. I used all the clams in the couscous last night."

Mandy's smile sagged slightly. Oh, yes. Paul Zook. The boy with braces who couldn't lift a hay bale over his head.

She scolded herself for that unkind thought. Most boys didn't have Noah's sculpted arms and strong back. That didn't mean they weren't gute potential husbands.

Except it *did* mean that they weren't potential husbands for her, because there was only one kind of husband she wanted. The realization crashed into her like a charging bull even as she tried to hold it back. She'd only known Noah for two weeks. She'd only liked him for one. Did she really want to marry him?

Hoping her expression didn't betray her wild thoughts, she cleared her throat and tried to focus on what Mammi told her. "I don't remember planning a picnic with Paul Zook."

"Well, dear, since you are going to a gathering with Adam Wengerd tonight, but I knew you had the afternoon free, I set an earlier date with Paul. He came over yesterday while you were at Noah's house. I knew you'd be thrilled, so he and I planned a picnic for you. You don't have plans, do you?"

Plans? She had planned to make up reasons to be outside all day gazing up at the roof and thinking about Noah's lips. It wouldn't really have been spying, but sometimes she wondered if she were as bad as Kristina.

Oh, no! She'd also forgotten about Kristina.

"Kristina is coming over this morning to help in the yard."

"The yard? What are you doing in the yard?"

Mandy wasn't exactly sure, but she had promised Kristina on Tuesday that if she would stop spying on Noah she could come over today and help Mandy do something in the yard. Kristina hadn't cared what the activity was going to be. She just wanted something, anything to get her within sight of Noah Mischler. Mandy's nagging conscience had gotten the better of her on Tuesday.

Her conscience wasn't nagging anymore. It was howling. Kristina would feel completely betrayed if she knew that Noah had kissed her supposed best friend. And Mandy should probably feel guilty for not feeling guilty about the kiss.

Someone tapped lightly on the door, making Mandy's heart do a double backflip with a twisting leap. "That will be Noah," Anna said, closing her dangerous cookbook. She bustled to the door. Mandy held her breath.

She couldn't see him, but she heard that low, silky voice of his. "Gute maiya, Anna. Just wanted to let you know I'm here."

"How nice to see you, Noah," Mammi said. "Be sure to join us for lunch."

There was a slight pause. "Is Mandy here?"

"Of course," Mammi said. "She barely finished the dishes."

Mandy practically leaped across the room to the front door. "Hello, Noah."

He wasn't smiling. His frown cut jagged lines into his face. "Can I talk to you outside for a minute?"

She didn't like that look. He was either still mad at her for interfering in his life or he regretted kissing her and had come to tell her not to get her hopes up. If she had a phone, would he have texted her the bad news?

She stepped onto the porch, gave Mammi a weak smile, and shut the door behind her. Chester stood obediently at Noah's side, regarding Mandy with a look of pity in his eyes. She shook her head. Surely she was imagining things. Dogs couldn't communicate their feelings like that, could they?

Her heart sank. She always knew when Chester was happy to see her. If Noah had confided in his dog, it wasn't all that strange to think that Chester would feel sorry for her.

Noah reached into his jacket pocket and pulled out a small brown paper bag. He clenched his jaw and forced a smile. "I made this for you."

Mandy opened the bag and pulled out a pint jar with a creamy light yellow substance inside. "Homemade butter?" she asked.

He nodded. "It's really easy to make. You just pour whipping cream into the jar and shake it until it turns to butter." The corner of his mouth twitched into a grin. "I know how much you like butter."

She opened the jar, scooped out a dab of butter with her finger, and popped it into her mouth. "Mmm. This is delicious. Do you have a spoon?"

His eyebrows rose higher on his forehead. "You eat butter plain?"

"When it's really good, I do."

Reaching into his pocket, he shook his head vigorously. "Please don't do that." He pulled out a small bag of crackers. "At least have it with a cracker."

She took a cracker from his bag and dipped it into the butter, scooping out a healthy teaspoonful. He grinned in amusement as she popped the whole thing into her mouth.

"Would you like a little cracker with all that butter?" he said.

She giggled. "I love butter. How did you know?"

His smile seemed to falter, as if it took great energy to keep it going. "You said as much last night."

Ach. Last night.

This was the part where he was going to tell her that the kiss was a mistake and that he hadn't really meant it when he said he loved her and would she please get a cell phone so he didn't have to face her when he delivered bad news. The butter suddenly tasted thick and heavy in her mouth.

"I'm sorry that I got carried away last night," he said, "and I promise it won't happen again."

"Oh," she said, feeling as if someone had cut the porch out from under her. "Okay."

"I know I'm not good enough for you." He lowered his eyes. "It was nice of you to kiss me back even though I don't deserve it from someone as wonderful as you are."

She forgot to breathe. He thought he wasn't good enough? He didn't want her to stay out of his life? A smile crept onto her lips. "You don't hate me?"

He furrowed his brow. "I told you that last night, didn't I? But I didn't give you any choice about kissing me, and you were too polite to push me away. I'm sorry."

Mandy glanced at the window that looked out onto the covered porch and then toward the woods in front of the house. It would be best to avoid any spies that might be lurking about. She laid the butter and crackers on the floor of the porch. "Don't eat these, Chester," she said. Boldly, she grabbed Noah's hand and pulled him down the porch steps and around the corner of the house to where the new shed stood. If Mammi truly wanted to spy, she'd have to jog down the hall and peek out her bedroom window.

Surprise flashed in Noah's eyes as she led him behind the shed. If Kristina was spying from the woods, she wouldn't be able to see anything. Mandy tried not to think about her best friend. There would be enough time for confession later.

"Noah," she said, "I do not regret kissing you. And that

thought about you not being good enough for me is nonsense. *You* are too good for me. I'm the one who should be worried."

He shook his head and tried to pull his hand away. She squeezed it tighter and wouldn't let him go.

"My dat is an alcoholic and my mamm left us. I don't deserve you."

"What about me? I go to people's houses who I don't even know and get mad at them for things they didn't even do. Then I spy on those same people, and they are nice enough to pull me out of the river. You saved my life. You take care of your dat. I don't deserve you."

"But my family is a mess. I haven't seen my mamm or my siblings for three years. My dat goes to the bar three or four nights a week. What gute Amish girl wants a boy like me?"

"I do." She bent her elbow and pulled his arm around her back, bringing him gratifyingly closer in the process. Stiffening, he leaned away. She countered by leaning closer to him. He stared at her lips as if he dared not hope to come in contact with them again. She saw where his gaze was focused. "If you don't kiss me right now," she whispered, "I'm going to be very irritated with you."

His eyes danced as he curled his lips. "You shouldn't whisper like that. It makes me forget every lesson my mamm ever taught me."

He wrapped his arms around her waist and brought his lips down on hers. They were smoother and more delicious than butter. Her heart thumped a powerful rhythm as she slid her arms around his neck and let herself be kissed until she couldn't remember which way was up.

He pulled away and then laid a kiss on her cheek and three on her forehead. "The bishop would never approve of this."

"Your bishop might not approve, but my bishop is not so strict. I've never heard him say anything against kissing."

"Let's pretend we're in Charm." He winked and kissed

her again, leaving Mandy wondering how something so simple as lips touching could catapult a girl to the roof even when she wasn't moving.

She pulled away to catch her breath and felt a catch in her throat. Should she tell him about the letter? She'd sent it over a week ago. There was no taking it back now. She studied his smiling face. She would wait. Nothing might come of it anyway, and they were getting along so nicely for a minute. She just couldn't spoil the mood.

Mandy had never been so glad for the bell on Kristina's bike. It certainly was annoying how often she rang the thing, but it was also a gute warning that Kristina was almost to the top of the hill. Today, Mandy needed plenty of warning.

He reluctantly released her as she took a step away from him. "Kristina's here."

He made a face and groaned. "Why?"

"She's my best friend."

"I know, but that doesn't mean you actually have to invite her up here." He tempered his scold with a smile. "It seriously cuts into our kissing time."

Mandy sighed. "I promised her we could work in the yard so she could gaze at you."

His smile faded. "You want me and Kristina to get together?"

"Of course not, but she promised to stop spying if I let her come today."

"Are you sure you're not trying to get rid of me?" He tried to act flippant about it, but she could tell there was real worry behind his question.

She rose to her tiptoes and brushed her lips across his. He softened like putty. "Do you want to get rid of me?"

"Not a chance."

"Then you're stuck. She'll think I'm the rottenest friend ever, but I'm going to tell her."

"You're not a rotten friend. It's not your fault she can't

see what's plainly in front of her." He took her hand and pressed his lips against her fingers. "Does this mean I'll be eating lunch on the roof yet? I want to eat with you, but not if Kristina's still here."

She tried for a carefree smile and failed miserably. "I'm going on a picnic with Paul Zook."

"Paul Zook?"

"Mammi set it up."

A dark shadow crossed his features. "I'm not good enough for you. Even your mammi and dawdi think so."

"Mammi also tried to arrange a date with Menno King. He's thirty-seven years old, Noah. It has nothing to do with who's good enough. It has everything to do with Mammi's desperation to marry me off."

Huffing the air out of his lungs, he looked away but seemed to relax. "Paul Zook got braces because his mamm said he'd never get a wife with those teeth."

"You have a thing about teeth, don't you?"

"I have a preference for freckles. I don't care about teeth."

"You do so. First Adam Wengerd and now Paul Zook."

He cracked a smile. "The real question is, do you have a thing about teeth?"

"I like your teeth."

His smile couldn't have gotten any wider without stretching beyond his face.

Mandy nearly jumped out of her skin when she heard Kristina's bicycle bell again, much closer this time. With a quick backward glance at Noah, she adjusted the navy-blue scarf around her hair and brushed the wrinkles from her apron. Putting an extra lilt in her step, she strolled around the corner of the house and greeted Kristina, who had parked her bike on the sidewalk and was putting down the kickstand.

Chester sat on the porch, guarding Mandy's butter and crackers, looking as if his waiting there was the most important job in the world.

Kristina giggled and took both of Mandy's hands. "Is that

Noah's dog? Is he here already? Oh, Mandy, I love him so much. If he sees me planting flowers and looking pretty, I just know he'll remember what we once felt for each other."

The lump in Mandy's throat felt like a stale piece of butterless toast. Jah, she was a rotten friend.

Should she mention that nobody planted flowers in September?

"Cum into the house," she said. "I think we should make some cookies first."

"For Noah?" Kristina said, nearly squealing her delight.

"Jah, okay, for Noah. And we need to talk." Making cookies was a gute activity. It kept their hands busy but still gave them a chance to talk about things like how they were in love with the same boy and what a rotten friend Mandy was turning out to be.

Kristina had insisted on sugar cookies shaped like hearts for the only boy she would ever love. Mandy's heart grew heavier and her throat got drier and drier as Kristina prattled on about how much she loved Noah and how if she didn't marry him, she would probably shrivel into a little ball and die at the ripe old age of nineteen.

Kristina beamed from ear to ear as they mixed the dough. They could hear the rhythmic pop of Noah's nail gun, interrupted by the occasional stomp of boots above their heads as Noah moved about on the roof. Noah was close enough to touch, a fact that had not been lost on Kristina. Or Mandy. She felt almost selfish for wanting Noah all to herself.

Breaking the bad news had to be done, and it had to be done quickly before Kristina made a complete fool of herself, if she hadn't already. But Mammi sat in her rocker knitting pot holders, and Dawdi read the paper in his recliner. Should she suggest they go out and gather eggs so that she and Kristina could be alone?

"It's a bit chilly out," Mammi said. "I'm glad I can be in a nice warm home yet."

No gathering eggs for Mammi.

Dawdi glanced up from his paper. "Mandy, do you think Noah will be warm enough out there? He might like a nice cup of that delicious hot cocoa you make."

"He'll like our warm cookies," Kristina said, nudging Mandy and giggling. "Made with extra love."

Under no circumstances was Mandy going to allow Kristina on that roof to pass out heart cookies to Noah. "He brought a thermos of kaffe, Dawdi."

"You might want to check on him, just the same," he said.

Kristina kept right on giggling. "We'll be sure to check on him."

They rolled out the cookie dough, and Kristina insisted being the one to use the cookie cutter. "They're like cutting pieces of my heart and giving them to Noah, one cookie at a time."

Under no circumstances was Kristina going to be allowed on that roof.

"We need to take a walk," Mandy said.

Kristina raised her eyebrows. "And look at Noah?" she whispered.

"Nae. I want to talk to you." She inclined her head in Mammi's direction. "Privately."

Kristina's eyes got wider. "Privately?"

Mandy nodded. Kristina's eagerness would crumble soon enough.

"Let's finish the cookies first. I want to have an excuse to go on the roof with Noah."

The popping rhythm stopped, and they heard more stomping. No doubt with every movement from above, Kristina's hopes soared higher. Mandy hooked her elbow with Kristina's and pulled her firmly to the door. "We need to let the dough sit. Let's go for a walk."

"Okay," said Kristina, elongating her vowels as if she were indulging Mandy merely because she was her best friend.

Mandy handed Kristina a jacket and put on her own black coat. Both girls donned their black bonnets before heading out the door. Chester and Sparky ran around the yard, chasing each other's tails. Once again, Mandy hooked her elbow around Kristina's and nudged her in the direction of the garden. If they walked amongst the bare peach trees, the barn would block their view of the roof. Kristina wouldn't be distracted by the sight of Noah, and no one would see if Kristina melted into a puddle of tears.

Mandy hoped that Kristina wouldn't melt into a puddle of tears. Even though she only imagined her feelings for Noah, infatuation was a powerful thing.

Kristina didn't take her eyes from the roof as they trudged across the yard. "Do you see him, Mandy? You are such a gute friend to let me come. The days I can't see him are the saddest days of my life. I love him so much."

Mandy took a deep breath. There would be tears. Lots and lots of tears.

"Where are we going?" Kristina asked when they passed the barn and walked among the trees in Dawdi's tiny peach orchard.

Mandy glanced behind her. They were out of sight of the roof. "Right here," she said. "I need to tell you something."

Kristina walked to her left and strained her neck to see over the roof of the barn. "I can't see Noah anymore. Let's talk in the front yard."

"Nae. I don't want anyone to see us."

"Will it take very long?"

Mandy laid her hands on Kristina's shoulders. "We have been best friends for a long time."

"It seems like forever. I thought I'd die when we moved

to Bonduel." Kristina frowned as doubt traveled across her face. "Is something wrong?"

"I wouldn't ever want to hurt you." Mandy pursed her lips.

For a split second she considered breaking things off with Noah. Wasn't her friendship with Kristina more important? She thought of Noah's kisses, of his gentle spirit and loyal heart. She couldn't let him go, not even if it meant losing Kristina.

Kristina narrowed her eyes. "What do you mean?"

"I mean that you know how important our friendship is to me."

"Of course I do. You invited me here today, didn't you? That is the act of a true friend. Because of you, I know I can work up the courage to talk to him. Maybe even ask him to take me to a gathering. Who knows what can happen after that? He'll grow to love me if he just gets a chance."

It was nearly impossible to breathe with the icy hand of guilt clamped around her throat. She felt as if she almost had to cough the words out of her mouth. "Krissy, there's something I need to tell you. I'm afraid some things have happened. I . . . the thing about it is . . . Oh, Krissy, I feel horrible, but I think Noah likes me. And I like him. We like each other."

Kristina narrowed her eyes. "You would never do that to me."

A hole yawned right in the middle of Mandy's chest. "I'm . . . I'm sorry. I didn't mean for it to happen. He's just so wonderful."

Kristina scowled. "I warned you."

"You did?"

"All the girls like Noah. He's handsome and polite. I warned you not to get yourself pulled in. He won't return your affection."

Oh dear. Kristina wasn't going to make this easy. What

could she do to make Kristina see the truth? "Nae, he likes me as much as I like him."

"How do you know? How could you possibly know that? He doesn't like you. He likes me." Kristina's voice rose in pitch.

Mandy had to stop her before she worked herself into a frenzy. "He kissed me yesterday," she blurted out. She hadn't wanted to share that bit of information, but she wanted to be very clear about where she and Kristina stood. They were, after all, still best friends. At least for another minute or two.

Complete silence as Kristina held her breath and stepped away from Mandy. Her mouth fell open, and she looked at Mandy as if trying to make out her shape through a clouded window. Before Mandy even knew what happened, Kristina drew back and slapped her hard across the face.

Gasping, Mandy stumbled backward, more out of shock than pain. She'd expected a fierce reaction, but nothing quite so violent. A river of tears sounded quite tame next to a blow across the face.

Kristina immediately blanched as white as Mammi's hair. "Oh sis yuscht. I didn't in a thousand years mean to do that." Mandy hoped Noah wouldn't hear the racket and come running.

Mandy laid her hand against her cheek. "I . . . I probably should have broken the news more gently."

Kristina seemed to forget about her short-lived remorse. She scowled. "How could you, Mandy?"

"I'm sorry."

"I shouldn't have let you go to his house. I knew as soon as you saw him you'd fall in love, just like every other girl in Bonduel."

"That's not what happened."

Kristina took a step toward her, and Mandy immediately took two steps back. She'd rather not get socked in the chin. "I should have known you'd try to steal him."

Mandy held out her hands in surrender. "If I thought you two really had a relationship, I would have stayed away. But you know you don't have a relationship and never did. You and Noah are practically strangers."

Kristina folded her arms. "What do you know about it? We saw each other every day last summer."

"Because you spied on him, not because you dated."

"He took me home from a gathering."

Mandy tried to say it gently, but there was no nice way around the truth. "That doesn't mean he was interested in you. You wanted to believe he loved you, but he never did."

Kristina puckered her lips as if she'd just eaten three lemons. "You want to believe he never loved me so that you don't feel so bad about betraying your best friend." She sat down in the dirt and buried her face in her hands. "You tricked me into showing you where he lives."

"Why would I have tricked you?"

"Because you wanted to steal Noah."

Mandy felt simply horrible. Was there any way to make Kristina see reason? "It's not stealing if it doesn't belong to you in the first place."

Kristina wailed louder. "It's not fair. You're prettier than me and smarter. How can I win his heart now? I'll never get a husband if you don't go back to Charm."

Mandy exhaled slowly and sat next to her friend, but not close enough to get an elbow to the kidneys. Kristina had worked herself into a tizzy. There would be no reasoning with her now. Still, she had to try. "You are a very beautiful girl. And your wheat bread is so much better than mine. Of course you'll get a husband. Any boy would be blessed to have you for a wife."

Kristina jumped to her feet. "Even Noah?"

"I'm sorry, Krissy. Noah doesn't love you."

"Because you stole him." She kicked the dirt at her feet. A few flecks landed on Mandy's dress. "You couldn't possibly love Noah the way I love him. You only even met him two weeks ago."

"Two and a half," Mandy said weakly.

"I'll get him back, wait and see." Kristina marched out from under the shelter of the peach trees before pausing to turn around and glare at Mandy. "And I will not invite you to our wedding."

"If you'd try to understand—"

Kristina turned on her heels and refused to look back. "Go back to Ohio and leave me alone."

Mandy sat in the dirt, feeling like dirt, as she watched Kristina slam her kickstand with her foot, jump on her bike, and ride down the hill as fast as she could go.

She stood and brushed the dirt from her dress. Would poor Kristina ever recover from her broken heart? Would she ever speak to Mandy again? With Kristina, things were either wonderful or horrible. Maybe she'd wallow for a few days and then see fit to forgive her best friend. Maybe she'd give up on Noah and give the other boys in the community a chance.

Mammi had a long list of potential suitors. Was the list transferable?

She walked out from among the trees. Her heart skipped a beat when she glanced up and saw Noah standing on the ridgeline staring at her, obviously unaware of what had passed between her and Kristina. He grinned and waved. She waved back.

Just the sight of him made her feel a hundred times better. No wonder Kristina loved him so.

Her stomach clenched. And a hundred times worse.

"Did Kristina have to leave early?" he said.

"Jah," was the only answer she could muster.

"At least you can stay inside until lunch. It's getting cold yet."

"We made cookies. I'll bring some up."

"I'd like that," he said, swinging his hammer in the air. He turned to get back to his shingles but reversed direction just as quickly. "I almost forgot," he said. "Have fun on your picnic."

Any happiness she felt upon seeing Noah hissed out of her like air from a leaky balloon. Instead of eating Noah's butter for lunch, she was going on a picnic with Paul Zook.

Someday he'd have really nice teeth.

At least she could look forward to that.

Chapter Fifteen

Noah cleaned his tools before stowing them in his toolbox and loading them on the small trailer he'd fashioned out of some old rubber tires and a few boards. Now that the old shingles were cleared from the roof, he hadn't needed to borrow Shirk's team and wagon. He could barely afford to keep his own two horses as it was.

Even though the sunset chilled the air, sweat trickled down the back of his neck. He'd put in almost twelve hours today. A gute day's work, even if it had been tinged with bitterness.

Wiping the moisture from his forehead with his sleeve, he gazed at the half-finished roof. He would have liked to work longer, but dusk had forced him down and turned his thoughts toward home, where nothing but silence, frustration, and heartache awaited him.

One more week and Felty's roof would be finished. Then what would be his excuse for coming around to see Mandy every day?

He frowned as he gazed up at the overcast sky. The shroud of darkness fit his mood perfectly. Mandy might have liked his kisses, but he could never hope to compete with the parade of suitors that Anna had lined up for her granddaughter.

And he had been unfortunate enough to witness the spectacle from the roof today.

It was bad enough that Paul Zook had taken her out for a lovely picnic at the pond early this afternoon. Noah knew it had been "lovely" because Paul had told him so when he and Mandy had returned. Then less than an hour ago, Adam Wengerd and his brilliant white smile had taken Mandy to a gathering with some of die youngie in the east district.

Watching the girl he loved ride off with someone so ir-resistibly charming set Noah's teeth on edge. Why was Anna so enthusiastic about Adam Wengerd? His smile wasn't that electrifying.

Noah secured the toolbox to the trailer, trying not to frown so hard that he cracked his jaw. Mandy was planning to return to Charm in two weeks, three if Anna had her way, but still, it wasn't enough time, especially when she was wasting so much of it with other boys. If he spent every waking hour with her for the rest of his life, it still wouldn't be enough time.

When she left, there would be a hole in his chest where his heart had been. He hadn't realized there was such a huge void in his life until Mandy had come to fill it.

He'd probably gotten three hours of sleep last night, toss-ing and turning and wondering what he could do to convince her to stay for another three or four weeks. Or to stay forever.

He shook his head at that silly notion. There was no possible way he would convince her to accept his hand in marriage. They'd only known each other for two weeks yet. And despite her protests, she really was too good for him. He lived in a run-down shack with a fater who was so drunk most nights that he couldn't even put on his own night-clothes. What girl in her right mind would want to marry into that trouble? Hadn't she said as much last night when she'd brought that counselor to his house?

Do you want to take care of your dat for the rest of your life? What happens if you want to marry and raise your own family?

It was a sure bet no girl would willingly take that on, even if she was in love with him. If he asked Mandy to marry him, she'd laugh. It was a sin to be prideful, but he didn't like to be laughed at.

Maybe if he were the bishop's son with five hundred acres of land and a whole stable full of horses, things would be different.

He wanted to marry Mandy. He couldn't marry Mandy. The end.

He swiped his hand across his mouth as if that could erase the memory of Mandy's sweet lips or her perfect freckles. His gut clenched. He loved her. After only two weeks, he loved her. But she was going to leave him, just like Mamm had left. Just like Yost and Lisa had left.

The pain was so thick, he nearly choked on it. He should never have let his feelings run so far away from him. They weren't coming back anytime soon.

"Come on, Chester," he called as he climbed into his homemade wagon with the old courting buggy seat he'd salvaged from a rummage sale. Chester hopped into the wagon and sat on his haunches next to Noah. His ears twitched at the prospect of a ride.

The horse was already pointed in the right direction. Noah jiggled the reins and the horse took a few steps forward. Noah heard a car crunching its way up the gravel lane and pulled back. Better to let the car up the hill first before he tried to go down. He didn't want a collision.

Who was coming to Anna and Felty's in a car? Mandy and Adam had left in a buggy.

Even though it wasn't completely dark yet, the headlights

led the way as the car crawled up the lane. Cars always took the road to Huckleberry Hill slowly. If they went too fast, they'd just spin their tires on the gravel, not to mention risk hitting a horse or a bicycle coming the other way.

Noah recognized the car as it came closer. It was Peggy Lofthouse's. She often drove the Amish around town. Peggy pulled next to Noah's wagon and rolled down her window. It was too dark to see much inside her car, but Noah could see that someone sat next to her in the passenger seat. "Noah Mischler. I thought you'd be up here. How's the roof coming?"

He managed a smile. Peggy didn't need to take the brunt of his sour mood. "About half done. Should be another week or so."

"I brought you a visitor."

Noah glanced behind him wondering if she were talking to somebody else. "Me?"

The car door opened, and shock like a bolt of electricity hit Noah squarely between the eyes.

"Yost?"

With his hand leaning against the roof, his brother stood with one foot still in the car as if unsure he should have been there. "Hey, Noah. How are you?"

Considering he hadn't seen his brother for three years, he was completely stunned. That's how he was. "I am gute. How are you?"

"I . . . um . . . I . . ." Yost's voice cracked into a million pieces. "I've missed you."

"I've missed you." Noah's eyes stung with sudden tears. Yost was back, looking older but still so young and so unsure of himself. Noah wasn't about to let him stand there wondering if he was welcome or not.

Half laughing, half sobbing, he leaped from his wagon, strode around to the other side of the car, and took his brother into a rib-crushing embrace. Yost laughed as if his heart would break and returned Noah's hug with a powerful embrace of his own.

Noah pushed Yost to arm's length. "Look at you. You're probably four inches taller."

A wide grin exploded onto his brother's face. "And you're probably four inches thicker."

The laughter overflowed and left both of them breathless.

"What are you doing here?" Noah asked, the astonishment clear in his voice.

"I rode the bus to Shawano, and Peggy was kind enough to pick me up."

"Where are you sleeping? Do you want to stay at my . . . the house?"

Yost nodded and there was a tinge of sadness in his voice. "Of course. Peggy took me there first, but no one answered when I knocked. She thought we might find you up here."

"Do you need me to drive you back to the house?" Peggy asked.

Noah leaned over so he could see Peggy inside the car. "Nae. He can go with me."

Peggy propped both hands on the steering wheel. "Okay. Call me when you need another ride."

Yost pulled a small leather bag from the floor of the front seat and gave Peggy some cash. "Denki for the ride."

Peggy put the car in reverse, did a four-point turn, and disappeared down the lane.

"I'm glad we found you up here," Yost said. "I wasn't sure if that house was really where you lived. I've never been there."

Noah slung an arm around Yost's neck. "You won't hurt my feelings to say it."

"Say what?"

"It's a shack."

Yost's eyes flashed with pain. "I just didn't realize. I thought . . . I guess I didn't know what I thought. You've been sending a lot of money to Mamm. Maybe more than you can afford."

"We do okay. There's a shed where Dat can work."

Yost's voice cracked again as if he couldn't possibly keep it from breaking. "I should have known you'd send everything to us."

Noah didn't deserve anybody's thanks. "How's Mamm?"

"She's okay," Yost said, setting his leather travel bag on the ground. "The community accepts her, mostly. She has a job cleaning houses."

"I know," Noah said. "She told me."

"Lisa thinks she's in love with a boy named Joe Mast, but he's stringing about five girls along at the same time."

Noah gave Yost a half smile. Lisa was all grown up now, and he was missing it. "Tell her not to worry. I'm saving a little extra for her wedding."

Yost nearly catapulted himself into Noah's arms once again. "I'm sorry, Noah," he sobbed. "I missed you so much."

Noah couldn't speak. Not with this overpowering emotion threatening to burst from his chest.

"I was so mad at you," Yost said. "I wanted you to pick me over Dat. He chose to drink. I thought he should bear the consequences of his drinking. I wanted you to love me more than you loved him."

"I do, Yost." Tears trailed down his cheeks. "But I couldn't leave him to himself like that. Even when we sin, even when our trouble is of our own making, Jesus doesn't abandon us. I couldn't abandon Dat. He needed me."

"I needed you."

"I know, but God wanted me to stay. I knew you would be okay. I knew you were strong enough."

Yost covered his eyes with his hand. "I can never be as strong as you."

"Jah, you can."

"You're so good, Noah, and I'm so stupid."

"No brother of mine was ever stupid."

"I've held on to this grudge and cut off all contact. I should have written. I could have visited. Even from long distance, I needed you, but I was too proud to admit it. You could have helped me in so many ways if I had let you. The letter finally made me realize that."

"The letter?"

"From your friend Mandy."

Yost might as well have socked Noah in the mouth. "Mandy wrote you a letter?"

"Didn't you know?" He furrowed his brow. "Maybe I misread the letter. I thought you wanted me to come."

"Of course I wanted you to come. Just because I didn't know about it doesn't mean you're any less welcome. I'm surprised, that's all."

He didn't know why he felt surprised. Mandy couldn't resist sticking her nose into his business. She thought he needed fixing.

"What did the letter say?" Noah asked.

"She told me that you are taking gute care of Dat, like the Good Samaritan. Like the Lord Jesus would have wanted you to. She said that staying behind with Dat was the hardest decision you ever had to make, and you shouldn't have lost your family because of it." Yost put a hand on Noah's shoulder. "She set me straight, that's what she did. She told me that as a Christian, I needed to forgive you, and as a brother, I needed to make amends. It wasn't anything I didn't already know. I suppose I just needed a kick in the pants."

"Mandy can do that to a person."

"I took some days off work and got on the first bus to Wisconsin."

Noah eyed his brother. Praise the Lord, Mandy had sent the letter before he'd gotten mad at her last night. She probably wouldn't have sent it after his reaction, but this time her meddling had never been more appreciated.

"She went on and on about what a godly man you are and a devoted son and how gute you are with a hammer and how you can fix any machine ever built. Three whole pages about how wonderful you are." He grinned. "She likes you."

Noah couldn't stifle a smile. Just thinking about Mandy made him goofy. "She's exaggerating."

"Do you like her? Or is she a forty-year-old spinster with knobby knees?"

Noah took Yost's bag from the ground and laid it in his wagon. "No knobby knees. She has freckles."

Yost rubbed his chin as if deep in thought. "Freckles? She sounds cute."

"She's beautiful."

"So you like her."

"If you think I'm going to spill my guts to you when you've only just come, you're crazy," Noah said.

Yost thumbed his suspenders. "Spill your guts? It sounds serious."

If Yost knew that he had only known Mandy for two weeks, he would probably have serious doubts about Noah's sanity. And if he guessed how deeply Noah was already in love, he'd know for sure his brother was crazy. Noah sobered slightly. He was crazy, because Mandy was never going to love him like he loved her, not with Adam Wengerd coming around so often.

Noah pushed down the sadness that threatened to overtake him and smiled. He'd forgotten that mischievous grin of Yost's. "I bet you'd like to know."

"I've got some time. I'll wear you down."

Noah gave Yost a friendly shove. "How long are you going to be here?"

"A week is all I was able to get off work."

"It's not enough, but it's something," Noah said.

Yost pumped his eyebrows up and down. "Will I get to meet the girl with freckles?"

"Not if I can help it."

Yost threw up his hands in protest. "Hey, we're practically old friends. She sent me a letter, remember?"

Noah pointed to his wagon. "You'll have to sit in back."

"Is this because you're afraid I'll steal your girl?"

"It's because there's only one seat, and I'm a better driver than you."

Yost shrugged and jumped into the small wagon bed. He wrapped his arms around Chester's neck. "Chester. You're not a puppy anymore." Chester whined and licked Yost's hand. Yost scratched behind Chester's ears and nuzzled his face close to Chester's.

"We'll be home in about half an hour," Noah said. "You don't mind scrambled eggs for dinner, do you?"

Yost leaned back on one hand while resting the other hand on Chester's neck. "How's Dat?" he asked quietly.

Noah lowered his eyes. "About the same."

Yost took a deep breath. "I'll try not to be mad at him."

"It doesn't do any good and only makes him feel worse."

Light spilled from the house as Anna opened the front door. "Noah," she called. "I'm so glad you're still here. I've got dinner ready on the table." She put her hand to her face as if shielding her eyes from the sun. "Who is that you've got out there with you?"

"This is Yost, my brother. Do you remember him?"

Anna bloomed into a smile and clapped her hands. "Remember him? He used to play hide and seek in the haymow with Titus." She crooked her finger to summon them closer. "Let me have a look at you."

Yost and Noah marched up Anna's steps for inspection.

Anna reached up and patted Yost's cheek. "Lo and behold, you're all grown up. How old are you?"

"Three weeks shy of twenty."

"What a fine young man you've turned out to be. Come in. I want to give you something."

Anna ushered them into the house and shut the door, then she bustled to her long closet and pulled out a pink pot holder. "I've been saving these for Mandy's special boys, but I don't see that it can hurt to give you one as a welcome present."

"Denki, Anna. I love your pot holders," Yost said. He nudged Noah lightly with his elbow. "But who are Mandy's special boys?"

"I've been working on finding her a husband. I thought maybe the pot holders would give the boys an extra push."

Yost glanced at Noah, his expression a mixture of confusion and doubt. Noah shook his head slightly, making sure Yost knew this wasn't the time to ask questions. Anna didn't think he was good enough for Mandy. There'd be plenty of time to explain all that when they got home.

"Dinner is ready," Anna said. "We're just waiting for Felty."

Something smelled very appetizing. Maybe Anna had found a reliable recipe. "I wish we could," Noah said. Mandy might come home early from the gathering. Eating Anna's cooking would be worth it if he got to sit next to Mandy at dinner. But Dat needed to eat too. "We've got to get home to see Dat."

"Oh, I see. We'll have to invite your dat to dinner so you boys can eat with us. Felty likes to talk with your dat about fishing. And license plates. Felty plays the license plate game every year, you know." Anna pulled a small calendar from the little drawer next to the sink. "What are you doing next Tuesday night? All three of you could come for dinner."

"My dat doesn't feel well most nights," Noah said, letting his eyes dart between Anna and Yost. "We probably shouldn't make any definite plans."

Anna stowed her calendar back in the drawer. "I'll ask Felty to talk to your dat. Felty can talk people into anything."

Noah shook his head. "I don't know." It was too risky for Dat to come to dinner, especially at night when he trembled with the need for a drink. Felty and Anna must never see his dat like that. It was bad enough that Yost would have to witness it, but Anna and Felty were people he loved and respected, and they respected him. He couldn't risk losing their good opinion.

Hearing a noise outside, Anna stood on her tiptoes and peeked out the kitchen window. "Well. I wouldn't have expected that."

"Is something wrong?"

"It's Adam and Mandy. I didn't think they'd be back for hours."

Noah's pulse sped up. Mandy was back from her date with dazzling-smile Adam. Maybe it hadn't been such a gute date. Maybe that didn't make Noah sad at all.

The door opened, and Mandy and her cousin Titus walked into the room. Titus was unexpected but very welcome. Mandy had lost Adam somewhere between the gathering and Huckleberry Hill. Her eyes locked on Noah, and her genuine smile melted his heart.

Titus, with a toothpick hanging from his mouth, followed Mandy into the house. "We're here," he announced.

Anna wilted slightly when she realized that Adam wasn't with them. "Titus," she scolded. "Mandy was supposed to ride home with Adam."

Titus acknowledged Noah with a nod and a smile and pulled the toothpick from his mouth long enough to speak. "Mammi, aren't you ever glad to see me?"

Anna patted Titus on the cheek. "I'm always glad to see you, Titus. You just seem to show up at the most inconvenient times."

"But, Mammi, if it weren't for me, Mandy would have had to walk home."

Noah frowned. Had Adam abandoned Mandy at the gathering? How dare he? Annoyance simmered below the surface. No boy should treat a girl that way.

Anna propped her hands on her hips. "Where's Adam?"

"A volleyball hit him in the face," Mandy said. "He was afraid that one of his teeth was loose. Freeman took him to the emergency room."

"One of his teeth?" Noah said, raising a significant eyebrow in Mandy's direction. She pursed her lips in an attempt not to smile.

"I left the gathering early and brought Mandy home," Titus said. "Wasn't that nice of me?"

Anna went to the cupboard and pulled out a stack of plates. "Very nice, Titus, but you should have let one of the other young men bring her home. She's only got two weeks left."

Titus raised his hands as if stopping traffic. "It's not my fault, Mammi. Davy, John, and Melvin all offered to take her home. She asked me to do it."

Noah winked at Mandy. She turned a light shade of pink. *Good girl. Keep all those other boys away.*

Anna sighed. "Mandy, what were you thinking? If I didn't know better, I'd suspect you didn't want to find a husband."

"I'm sorry, Mammi," Mandy said, not sounding all that sorry. "I didn't want to impose on anyone, and Titus didn't mind. I promised him a large helping of yummasetti."

Titus, who wasn't always real quick to clue into things, finally looked, really looked at Yost, and his eyes nearly fell out of his head. "Yost Mischler? I didn't even recognize you." He whooped and hollered as if his horse had just won the derby, then cast his toothpick on the floor and pulled Yost in for a back-slapping hug. "What are you doing here?"

"Mandy sent me a letter," Yost said.

"That must have been some letter," Titus said. "I've been asking you to come back for three years."

"I'm only staying for a few days."

"That's better than nothing," Titus said.

The color traveled up Mandy's neck as she made a point to keep her gaze away from Noah.

Noah recognized the look. Just yesterday he'd taken her to task for meddling in his life. She was afraid that she'd offended him once again. She looked uncertain and wounded, and her distress was all his doing. Would anyone notice if he thumped his palm against his forehead?

"Mandy," he said, compelling her to look at him. "Can I talk to you alone?"

"I don't think so," Mandy said.

His gut clenched. It was worse than he thought. "Please? For a minute?"

She expelled the air from her lungs and nodded. In plain sight of everybody, Noah grabbed her hand and pulled her toward the front door.

"Are you coming back?" Anna asked.

Noah gave Anna a reassuring smile. "I wouldn't miss that yummasctti."

Mandy went along reluctantly. No doubt she was anticipating a lecture. Noah closed the door behind them and led her down the steps.

"Where are we going?" she asked.

"I don't want anybody listening in on our conversation."

She dragged her feet. "How loud are you planning to yell?"

They went to the side of the house next to the propane tank. It was becoming their favorite meeting spot. She turned to face him. Without another word, he gathered her into his arms and kissed her thoroughly. She gave a surprised squeak before softening in his embrace and kissing him back. She felt so good in his arms, and for a few seconds, he let himself believe that she belonged there. How would he ever go back to normal life when she was gone?

After a breathless, heart-stopping kiss, she pulled away and studied his face. "That wasn't quite the lecture I expected."

He chuckled. "I know. After my reaction last night, you are wise to be wary."

"I want you to know I wrote Yost that letter more than a week ago. I'm sorry if you're upset. I meant what I said yesterday. I won't interfere in your life anymore."

He put his hands on her shoulders. "Mandy, it's okay. You were right."

She narrowed her eyes. "I was right?"

"I mean, not about everything. Not about most things."

Her lips twisted into a wry grin. "Oh, well, you wouldn't want to make me feel any worse, would you?"

"I still don't want you meddling in my life, but I haven't seen my brother for three years. I could kiss you for sending him that letter."

"Why don't you?"

He folded his arms so he wouldn't give in to the temptation. Mamm wouldn't approve of all that unbridled affection. "I'm trying to thank you for getting my brother to come to Wisconsin."

She got on her tiptoes and whispered in his ear. "You're welcome."

He pulled back as if he'd been burned. "Don't whisper, Mandy."

She giggled. "You are so strange."

He raised his eyebrows. "Is that gute?"

Her eyes danced, and he could tell she was teasing him.

"The good news is that if it's not a gute thing, at least I'm brave enough to tell you and not just talk behind your back."

"You talk behind my back?"

Mandy took Noah's hand. "If you're not going to kiss me, we should get back before Mammi starts to worry."

"Wait," he said. "I need your help. Your mammi wants to invite Dat to dinner on Tuesday."

She kept her eyes glued to his face. "Noah, believe me, I didn't have anything to do with that."

"I know. Your grandparents are trying to be thoughtful, but it's impossible for my dat to go anywhere. I don't want anyone to see what he's really like. He doesn't want anyone to see him like that either."

Mandy's brows inched together. "Maybe it would be good for him. He should get out and be with other people besides you and Chester. My mammi and dawdi might be able to help him."

Noah frowned. "You weren't going to meddle, remember?"

"It's not meddling to have an opinion."

"It is when your opinion is about my life."

Mandy took a step back and laced her fingers together. "Don't be cross with me. I know you think it's none of my business, but what are you going to do when somebody in the district discovers how bad your dat's drinking has become? What if your dat decides he wants to go to gmay next week? Or someone else catches you at that bar trying to drag your dat home? Someday, whether you want them to or not, people are going to see your dat as he really is. What are you going to do when that happens?"

She was right about one thing. He didn't like the question. He ground his teeth together until his jaw ached. "I've got things under control. Nobody has to know anything."

"It takes a lot of work keeping a secret." She reached out and cupped his face in her hand. "Aren't you exhausted?"

"It's my choice, Mandy. I'd rather do this than be buried in shame. Yost hasn't seen Dat in three years. How ashamed do you think he'll be?" He felt as empty as a fifty-gallon drum, like he always did when he thought about Dat. Two weeks ago, Mandy had come into his life and made him forget. He hated that she was the one to remind him of how unworthy he really was.

She withdrew her hand and sighed. "I'm afraid that one day all your secrets will come crashing down, and it will be more painful than you can imagine. I never, ever want to see you hurt like that."

"Shame is what hurts." He wanted to wipe that look off her face, as if she pitied him. He curved his lips and shoved his hands in his pockets as a gesture that he didn't want to argue. "Denki for caring about me."

She cracked a smile. "You're stubborn, and you're welcome."

"I'll never be able to thank you enough for asking Yost to come back."

"A kiss would be a gute thank-you gift."

He brought his lips over hers and kissed her gently, all the while trying to smother the fire that threatened to consume him whenever they touched. Only an ungrateful son would forget what his mamm had taught him.

She melted into his arms and kissed him back, then pulled away and smiled at him. "You're welcome," she said dreamily.

He couldn't help but laugh. Even though she liked to pry into his life, he'd never felt so happy.

Chapter Sixteen

Mary Lambright, Melvin's younger sister, who couldn't have been more than sixteen years old, handed Noah a warm, soft pretzel. "Denki," he said. "Did you make these?"

Mary glanced at Yost and blushed down to her toes. "Me and my sister," she said, handing Yost a napkin and a pretzel significantly bigger than Noah's.

"Denki," Yost said, giving Mary a smile that no doubt made all the girls in Missouri swoon.

Mary's blush traveled to the tips of her ears. She mumbled a reply that Noah couldn't decipher, probably "you're welcome," and marched back into the kitchen as if there were pretzels burning in the oven.

When she turned her back, Noah poked Yost in the ribs. "I think you have an admirer."

Yost, who had always been oblivious to girls fawning over him, let his gaze travel around the room. "Who are you talking about?"

"Mary Lambright gave you the biggest pretzel I've ever seen."

Yost grinned. "Are you saying I got a bigger pretzel because I'm better looking than you are?"

"Not better looking. I think she felt sorry for you."

"You've always been jealous that the girls love me so much."

Noah tilted his head and smirked. "Giggly schoolgirls? You can have 'em."

Yost rubbed his jaw as if deep in thought. "Except that one girl at Helmuths' house. That one likes you something wonderful."

Noah's heart thumped in his chest. "I don't know who you're talking about."

"What she sees in you, I'll never know."

"She doesn't see anything."

"Oh, she's ferhoodled all right. She looks at you like you're made of lollipops and gingerbread. It's disgusting."

Yost couldn't know how welcome those words were to Noah. Did Mandy really look at him that way?

Of course Yost had been curious about the Helmuths' pretty granddaughter when he first arrived. Noah had filled him in about Mandy, but he hadn't told Yost that he was in love with her. Yost might laugh at him for daring to even hope for such a girl as Mandy Helmuth. Best keep his feelings to himself.

That didn't stop Yost from teasing him. Yost was smart enough to recognize that there was something more than acquaintance between Noah and Mandy. He simply didn't need to know how deep Noah's feelings ran.

If only Yost could stay forever, then Noah might feel sure enough to confide in him again. Still, it felt so gute to have his brother back if even for a short time.

On Saturday they had gone fishing with Dat, and then Yost had helped Noah fix the washing machine and build a worktable for Dat's woodshop. Yost had offered to help Noah finish the Helmuths' roof this week. Noah had declined his help, saying that it was Yost's vacation and that he didn't need to do any work while in town. Yost had insisted that he'd rather be up on the roof spending time with his brother than doing just about anything in the world.

On Friday night after arriving in town, Yost had treated Dat like a distant acquaintance, not showing him any particular affection but not showing contempt either. On Saturday, he had made more of an effort. He and Dat hadn't spoken in three years. Clearly Yost still resented Dat's drinking and his inability to get sober, but Noah could tell he was trying to understand and at least be patient with Dat's weaknesses.

Yost and Noah had attended gmay together this morning. Noah's black eye had faded to nearly nothing, so he had felt it safe to go to church.

It had been hard to concentrate on the sermon with his favorite brother sitting next to him and the most beautiful girl in the world sitting across the way. He'd never been so glad that the benches were set up so the men were sort of turned toward the women during church. Whoever thought of that seating arrangement must have never been distracted by a pretty girl during worship services. But Noah wasn't complaining. Mandy's presence certainly made church that much more pleasant.

Noah wasn't quite sure how he did it, but Yost had convinced him to come to the *singeon* tonight. Noah seldom went to singings or gatherings. He was usually looking after his dat or hoping to avoid prying questions about his family. He'd only agreed because Yost wanted to see old friends, and Noah didn't want him to get bored with just him and Dat as company. Mandy hadn't come to the singing. Anna and Felty had invited some family for dinner. Mandy had stayed home to be with them.

Unfortunately, Kristina Beachy was at the singeon, but Noah had managed to avoid her like a bad case of the stomach flu. How could she and Mandy be so different and still be best friends?

Noah and Yost ate their pretzels while Yost let his eyes

roam around the room. "Looking for pretty girls?" Noah asked.

"It doesn't hurt to look," Yost said, grinning mischievously.

"Do you think you might be taking one back to Missouri with you?"

"Only if she's pretty enough, like Mandy Helmuth."

Noah spied Dori Rose, one of Kristina's silly friends, out of the corner of his eye. She stepped sideways toward him, all the while keeping her eyes trained in another direction. Was she trying to sneak up on him? He almost groaned out loud. Not another featherbrained girl he had to dodge! Kristina had been persistent all summer. He didn't think he had the patience to put up with another spy. Maybe Dori was interested in Yost. Yost could be the one to try to avoid her.

Dori Rose tiptoed across the rug until she stood only a few feet away. He didn't think he would be able to be nice to her if she spoke to him. He drained his cup of lemonade and set it on the end table. "Are you ready to go, Yost? We should probably get home."

Yost raised an eyebrow. "Okay," he mumbled with his mouth full of pretzel. "If you want to."

Dori Rose clasped her hands behind her back, stepped directly in front of Noah's escape route, and widened her eyes as if ready to spill a marvelous secret. "Noah, there's someone who wants to talk to you."

Noah attempted a pleasant look on his face even as he deflated like a balloon. She had him cornered. "You?" he asked.

Dori Rose covered her mouth with her hand and giggled nervously. "Noah Mischler, that would be just silly. She's in the barn waiting for you."

Noah furrowed his brow. Out waiting in the barn? Sounded like an ambush. "Who is it? Tell her to come in if she wants to talk to me."

Dori Rose looked uncertain. "I don't know. She says it's a matter of life and death. She really wanted to talk to you without people around."

Noah glanced at his brother. Yost had no idea what was going on. He merely shrugged. No doubt Kristina Beachy or someone equally giddy stood in that barn just waiting to attack. He wouldn't go anywhere near it.

"Tell her that I will talk to her on the front porch if she really wants privacy, but I'm not going all the way out to the barn. Yost and I need to get home."

Dori Rose puckered her lips doubtfully. "She really wanted the barn."

"Front porch or nothing."

He could see the wheels in her head turning frantically. She probably hadn't expected him to resist, though Kristina must certainly have known there'd be at least a little reluctance on his part. Of course, Kristina had never been one to take a hint.

"Okay," Dori said. "I will tell her to be on the front porch in three minutes. Is that enough time?"

He clenched his teeth. Three minutes wouldn't give him enough time to sneak out the back door and drive away in his buggy. "Jah. I will be there."

Dori Rose giggled, nodded, and raced out the door. Noah exhaled slowly. If Kristina thought it was a matter of life and death, he would at least try to be nice. He'd give her two minutes, and then he'd crush all her hopes and dreams. Some girls just wouldn't take no for an answer. He'd have to be blunt. Again.

He picked up Yost's lemonade and took a swig. "Yost, I've got to—"

Yost smirked. "I heard. Does this happen often with girls? I don't know what they see in you."

Noah gave Yost a weak shove. "They don't see anything. They're bored."

Yost pointed to the clock in the wall. "You've only got two minutes left. You better get out there. I'll wait here."

"If I'm not back in three minutes, come and fetch me. She might try to kidnap me or something."

Yost chuckled. "That poor girl, whoever she is, deserves at least five minutes."

Noah growled. "You're no help."

"You can take care of yourself."

He grabbed his jacket from the small pile of overcoats next to the sofa. "What if there are seven or eight of them? I don't do well when girls gang up on me."

Yost's eyes flashed with amusement as he folded his arms across his chest. "It's sad there's not enough of you to go around."

"Oh, be quiet."

"You're turning green. I think it's very entertaining." He picked up his cup and discovered it was empty. "Noah," he snarled.

"I was thirsty."

Yost made himself comfortable on the sofa. "I'll be right here if you need me, *broodah*. Be sure to let them down easy."

Noah lifted his eyes to heaven. "No help at all."

He trudged to the front door as if he were going to his own funeral. He'd already told Kristina to leave him alone. What more did he have to do? He didn't know the words to make her go away permanently.

He opened the door and stepped onto Lambrights' wrap-around porch. The family obviously liked to sit out here often. There were six patio chairs and a porch swing. As he expected, Kristina stood with her hands resting on the porch railing staring into space as if she'd been waiting there ever so long. Dori Rose must have raced to the barn and brought Kristina back here, both of them sprinting all the way.

His mamm had taught him to be polite, even to people

who sorely tested his patience. "Do you need something, Kristina?"

She snapped her head around, as if his presence surprised her. She probably hadn't expected him to show up. It wasn't like him to actually come when she called. "Noah," she said, crossing the wide porch and throwing her arms around him before he had time to avoid her.

He gently but firmly pried her arms from around his waist. "Kristina, if you're going to do that, I'm leaving right now," he said, grateful that he hadn't let Dori Rose talk him into the barn.

With urgency flashing in her eyes, Kristina dropped her hands and took three steps back. "Nae, nae. I'm sorry. Don't leave. I just want to talk."

"Maybe," he said. "But I'd rather you let me alone."

The disappointment on her face was almost tangible, but she soon recovered. She laced her fingers together and regarded him as if she were giving him permission to stand on the porch. "I know you're still mad at me about what I said about your dat."

Noah crossed his arms over his chest and tried not to think about the shame. Kristina had thought she was being funny when she called his dat a drunk and a bum. After that cutting comment, his forbearance had snapped. That was when he had admonished her not to text or call anymore. And that was when Mandy had shown up at his door to scold him for breaking up with a girl he'd never actually been with. "I'm not mad about that anymore."

She burst into a smile. "That is wonderful gute."

"But I don't want to date you, Kristina. We're not really a good match."

A divot appeared between her eyebrows. "How do you know if you won't talk to me? Mandy said I should talk to you so we can get to know each other."

Noah peered at her doubtfully. "This was Mandy's idea?"

"She'll be gone next week, you know."

Noah didn't know why this prompted him to contradict her. "Two weeks. She might stay for two more weeks."

Kristina scowled as if he'd just insulted her. "It was Mandy's suggestion that I should have a conversation instead of spying on you."

"I don't like to be spied on."

Kristina pinched her lips and squinched her eyes as if she were trying to milk out a few tears. "I had to spy," she whined. "You won't talk to me."

Like the stub of a candle, his patience was just about spent. "I'm talking to you now. What do you want?"

"I want to know why you let my best friend kiss you."

Noah felt as if someone had beaned him in the head with a rock. "She told you that?"

Kristina narrowed her eyes resentfully. "She tells me everything."

Dread crawled into Noah's veins. Kissing Mandy had been one of the most wonderful-*gute* experiences of his life, and she had told Kristina about it? Silly, childish Kristina who couldn't keep her mouth shut with a whole roll of duct tape?

"Why . . . would she tell you?"

"Don't get upset about it. I don't blame you. Who knows how many boys she's kissed in Charm? Dozens and dozens, I suppose."

Were their kisses so cheap, so meaningless to Mandy that she had shared their experience like a piece of bubble gum? Were his deepest emotions reduced to items of gossip for Mandy and her friends to giggle about? The kisses had meant everything to him. Apparently they hadn't meant quite that much to Mandy. He felt ill.

"I think it's pretty rotten for a best friend to kiss the boy I've loved for a whole year. She knew how much I loved you, and then she comes into town and steals you."

"It's nobody's business," Noah stuttered.

"How can you date a girl who treats her friends like that?"

Noah felt increasingly breathless. "You and I were never together."

"She'll be gone in a week. Do you really think she kissed you because she loves you?"

Noah didn't know what to think. Why had she let him kiss her? Why had she asked him to kiss her? She knew as well as he did that she was leaving. What did she want from him?

Kristina batted her eyelashes as if a whole fireplace of ashes had fallen into them. "She told me she came to town to be with me, but I think she came to lure you in and break your heart. If I'd known, I wouldn't have invited her to come."

Could this be true? Was Mandy toying with him, determined to collect his broken heart like a souvenir? He clenched his teeth and rubbed his hand down the side of his face. Mandy was leaving soon. She had never hidden that fact from him. Maybe she had known from the beginning that their relationship had an expiration date, like milk from Yoder's dairy. And maybe she didn't care that Noah would be crushed when she was gone.

He bridled his galloping imagination and considered the source of this information. He'd never heard one sensible word from Kristina's mouth. Maybe her jealousy colored her understanding and made her say things that weren't true. Still, Mandy had told her about the kiss. What else had she shared with Kristina, and were they laughing at him even now?

Kristina must have sensed that something she had said hit the mark. She studied her fingernails with disinterest even as her eyes blazed with intensity. "I'll forgive her, of course.

That's what best friends do. But she doesn't deserve your love, Noah. It doesn't mean anything to her."

Noah tried to keep any emotion out of his voice. "How Mandy and I feel about each other is none of your business." His life was none of anybody's business. Why wouldn't everybody leave him alone?

"But I love you," she whined at the perfect pitch to set his teeth on edge.

"I don't love you," he said. "I . . . don't love anybody." He felt as if he were choking as he shoved the lie from his mouth.

She balled her hands into fists and glared at him. "I've been loyal to you ever since we met. It's useless to wait for someone prettier. No girl but me would ever marry a boy whose fater is a drunk."

Noah flinched. She should have known how much he hated that word.

"Remember when you dragged your fater out of that bar? He was drunk, and he smacked you. He hit his own son."

This time Noah felt as if he'd been sliced right through the heart with a carving knife. There was only one way Kristina could have known about the incident at the bar. "How do you know about that? Did Mandy tell you?"

Kristina stuck out her lower lip. "Everybody knows about it."

Noah thought back to gmay this morning. Four people had asked him about his dat. Nobody ever asked him about his dat. He caught his breath. Kristina was right. Everybody knew. Just like Mandy wanted.

"No girl would stoop to marry into such a family," Kristina said, reaching out to grab his hand. He stepped back. "No girl except me. My love is strong enough to help us through the bad times."

Even though it was a cool night, Noah felt the sweat

trickling down the back of his neck as an oppressive vise squeezed the air out of his lungs and threatened to suffocate him.

How could she do this to him?

She'd promised. Mandy had promised him that she wouldn't tell a soul about that night at the bar, and like a fool, he had believed her. He pressed his palm against his forehead as their last conversation played over and over in his head. On Friday she had seemed so concerned for his well-being.

What are you going to do when somebody in the district discovers how bad your dat's drinking is? What if someone sees you dragging your dat home from the bar? Someday, whether you want them to or not, people are going to see your dat as he really is.

She must not have been satisfied with his response, because she was apparently trying to force his hand. Maybe she thought if she told everybody about his dat, Noah would feel compelled to admit the truth and shove his dat into a rehab center whether he wanted to go or not.

Mandy couldn't help herself. She stuck her nose into other people's business like bees stuck their noses into flowers, but Noah never thought she'd stoop this low.

Mandy knew that this wouldn't help his dat. It would only serve to compound Noah's already deep humiliation.

Had she purposefully wanted to shame him to teach him a lesson?

"You know it's true," Kristina said.

He'd forgotten what Kristina had been saying. He didn't know what was true anymore.

"I would be the best wife you could wish for," she said. When he didn't respond, she added, "I make yummy pie. You like pie, don't you?"

Mandy made pie. Huckleberry pie with mild, sweet

berries. Apple pie with cinnamon and nutmeg. It was the best thing he had ever tasted. No other pie would ever, ever measure up. But that was all over now. He'd never eat pie again.

Kristina must have found his silence encouraging. "I also make really good pretzels. Much better than Mary Lambright's."

Mamm probably wouldn't consider it good manners to tell Kristina that he'd be happy to never lay eyes on her for the rest of his life. And what about the girl who had taken his heart and thrown it on the pavement? What would his mamm say about a girl who'd put his secrets on display like laundry on a clothesline?

His legs would no longer support him. He stumbled to the nearest chair and sank into it, burying his face in his hands to cover his despair.

"Kristina," he whispered. "I really want to be alone. Could you please just go?"

"Is that all you have to say?"

"I don't want to talk right now. If you go, I'll text you later."

With his face in his hands, he couldn't see her expression, but her voice rose to an almost fevered pitch. "You will?"

"Jah." He would have said just about anything to get her to leave.

"Do you promise?"

"I promise. I will send you a text." One text, and at the moment, he couldn't promise her it wouldn't be a rude one.

Kristina gave a little squeal. He heard her skip down the porch steps, and soon the sound of her footsteps faded in the distance. She had probably gone back to the barn to lie in wait for some unsuspecting boy who had the misfortune of wandering in there.

Noah did his best to breathe. Was this really happening? Was kind, adorable Mandy really this calculating—so bent on getting her own way that she would reveal his most carefully guarded secrets?

Because of Mandy, everybody knew about the night at the bar. How many of his neighbors were laughing at him behind his back or horrified by what they knew about his fater? How could he face anyone ever again?

He heard the front door open, and someone walked out onto the porch. Should he stand up and try to act as if nothing were wrong? It didn't matter. Now that everybody knew about his family's disgrace, they knew how unworthy he was to be living among them. He wanted to crawl into a hole and never come out.

"I know that was a lot longer than three minutes, but Mary wanted to tell me all about her new kittens."

Noah exhaled in relief. It was Yost.

"Noah? Are you okay?"

Noah lifted his head to see Yost peering at him anxiously. He hastily stood and swiped his fingers through his hair. "We need to go."

Yost placed a hand on Noah's shoulder. "What's wrong? What did she say?"

"Nothing. It doesn't matter."

Yost frowned. "I know you, Noah. Whatever it is, it matters a lot."

Noah jumped off the porch and marched in the direction of their buggy. "If you want a ride home, you'd better come now. I'll not stay here another minute."

"Okay, okay. I'm coming. Just let me get my coat."

Noah didn't slacken his pace. If Yost couldn't catch up, he'd have to find his own ride home. The front door opened and closed, and Noah heard Yost's quick steps close behind him. "Noah, tell me what's wrong."

Noah made the mistake of searching his brother's face. He saw the innocence of youth and the blissful ignorance of hope. Yost could return to Missouri without having to endure the shame of a fater's downfall or the gossip that circulated around the Mischler family. Yost could go home and live his life and be happy. Noah would never be happy again.

Everything was different now.

Something inside him crumbled, like the walls of Jericho. He yanked Yost to him and sobbed until he was too weak to cry anymore.

Chapter Seventeen

Mandy looked up toward the ceiling. She couldn't see them, but she could hear Noah and his brother tromping about on the roof like two lumbering moose in the forest. It was gute that Noah had his brother to keep him company, but two people working on the roof meant that it would be finished twice as fast. What would she do when Noah didn't have a reason to come to Huckleberry Hill?

What would she do in less than two weeks when she had to go home?

Maybe she should spend the rest of the week outside gazing at the boy on the roof who had become the center of her universe. Could she convince him to make her the center of his? Would he care when she left? Might he ask her to stay?

Dawdi tromped up from the cellar with a box of empty canning jars in his arms. "*Some morning yonder, we'll cease to ponder, O'er the trouble life's brought to our eyes. All will be clearer, my love will be dearer, In that lovely heav'n in the sky.*"

Dawdi placed the box on the table. "Applesauce canning day is my favorite time of year."

Mandy smiled. "I'm glad I'm here to help this time."

"You can turn the crank. Once I turned eighty, my elbow froze up every time I did it. Young people should always be the crank turners."

"I'd be happy to turn the crank. I like seeing the applesauce come out one side and the peelings come out the other. I love applesauce day too." Even though it would mean less time outside dreamily gazing at Noah.

"Annie wants us to put up three dozen quarts of applesauce, but I bet we've got enough apples for five dozen. Do you want to take some bottles back to Charm with you?"

"I might not be able to carry them on the bus."

Dawdi fingered his beard. "Too bad Noah can't go with you. He could carry a whole suitcase full of jars as easy as you please."

"We could give some to Noah and his dat. They don't do any canning of their own. They'd probably appreciate it."

"Very gute idea. It's the least we can do for all his work on the stove. It saves your mammi a lot of labor." He nodded thoughtfully. "Noah sure is a smart young man, to know how to install a stove and fix our roof. I don't think there's nothing he can't fix."

"Jah," Mandy said. "I think I'll go take him some cookies."

"The way to a man's heart is through his stomach, your mammi always says." His eyes twinkled. Did he suspect something between her and Noah? "You should save some for Luke Miller. Your mammi's invited him to dinner tonight." Dawdi didn't suspect anything. He was probably hanging his hopes on the nine-toed boy.

Mandy snatched the small bag of snickerdoodles from the counter, donned her sweater, and stepped outside. It was nearly ten o'clock. Noah and Yost had been up there for almost three hours yet. Maybe they'd like a cookie break.

She'd baked them early that morning in hopes of giving them to Noah before he started working. He usually came to say hello to her before going to the roof. It was always the best part of her day, especially when he brought her something to eat. But this morning, he hadn't knocked, and she hadn't known he was here until she heard the clunky footfalls above her.

Chester and Sparky frolicked around the yard like two puppies, wagging their tails and nudging each other with their wet noses. Mandy gave each dog a little love before ambling far enough away from the house to be able to see the boys working on the roof.

Yost, following behind Noah with a pile of shingles and his own nail gun, glanced in her direction. He didn't seem inclined to acknowledge her. That was strange. On Friday, he hadn't seemed like the timid type.

"Gute maiya, Yost."

He turned and gave her a half smile. "Gute maiya."

All of Noah's attention was focused on nailing shingle after shingle into place. The muscles of his shoulders and back seemed to work in one fluid motion whenever he raised the nail gun. He was laying down shingles so fast, he didn't even turn to look at her. She didn't want to be a nuisance and interrupt his hard work, but she simply had to see that smile at least once. "Noah," she called, "try not to work yourself to death. I wouldn't want to have to carry your body down the ladder."

He didn't even turn around. Could he hear her over the popping of the nail gun?

Yost sprouted a sheepish grin. "He's in a hurry to finish before the rains come this weekend."

Uncertainty tightened around Mandy's chest. Something was wrong. Noah wouldn't look at her. What didn't he want her to see?

She felt a catch in her throat. Two Sundays ago, Noah's dat had given him a black eye. What was it this time? A broken nose? A goose egg on his forehead?

Dear Heavenly Father, not now. Not when his brother has come for a visit.

What could she do? She didn't want to embarrass him, but if she knew what his injuries were, she was sure she could fix them. Why didn't he trust her? She already knew the worst about his dat.

Her insides plummeted to the ground when she heard the familiar sound of a bicycle bell behind her. *Oh sis yuscht!* Kristina couldn't have picked a worse time to pay a visit. Wasn't she still mad at Mandy? She had told Mandy to go back to Ohio and leave her alone. Her righteous indignation should have kept her away for at least another day or so.

Kristina appeared around the bend in the lane, walking her bicycle with an extra spring in her step and ringing her bell over and over as if she were playing a song. Apparently, she was in a very good mood. Mandy couldn't decide if that was a good or a bad thing.

Kristina waved her arm back and forth over her head as if she were trying to signal an airplane. "Yoo-hoo, Mandy."

Mandy followed Kristina's lead and pretended there was nothing amiss between them, even though Kristina had accused her of vile betrayal only three days ago. "Hi, Krissy. How nice to see you."

Kristina's gaze traveled to the roof where Noah was still trying to lay down all the shingles in a matter of minutes. "Hello, Noah," Kristina chirped in that flirty, singsong voice that was sure to annoy him.

Noah didn't acknowledge her. The steady sound of his nail gun driving nails into the roof was all the response they got. Yost glanced at them and stretched an apologetic smile across his face. "We're pretty busy," he said.

Kristina pulled her phone from her apron pocket and jiggled it in her hand. "Noah, I got your text," she called, gushing as if there was something private and personal between her and Noah.

Noah had texted Kristina? That was surprising. He certainly shouldn't be encouraging her. She'd double her efforts if he gave her any reason to.

There was nothing to do but distract Kristina and get her into the house as quickly as possible. Mandy couldn't risk letting her best friend catch a glimpse of Noah's injured face. Whatever the injuries were, Noah would be mortified if anyone saw.

"Let's go in the house," Kristina said, before Mandy had a chance to suggest it. She cradled her phone in her hand as if it were a *buplie*, a baby.

Mandy cupped her hand over Kristina's elbow. "Jah. You can help me lay out some quilt squares. I'm making a top for Mammi."

Kristina marched into the house with purpose, as if she wasn't just there for a friendly visit. As soon as Mandy closed the door, Kristina grabbed her hand and pulled her to sit on the sofa. "Come here, Mandy." She was overjoyed about something, but Mandy could tell she was trying to temper her enthusiasm. She practically shoved her phone in Mandy's face. "Look what Noah texted me. And don't say I didn't warn you."

Doubtfully, Mandy took the phone from Kristina. "I don't see it."

Kristina snatched the phone away and pushed some buttons. "Here," she said.

Mandy studied the screen. It said, *I need you to deliver a message to . . .*

Mandy turned to Kristina. "Who are you supposed to deliver a message to?"

"Oh, for goodness' sake," Kristina said, not trying to mask the exasperation in her voice. "Don't you even know how to use a cell phone?" She pointed to a tiny arrow on the keypad. "Push this, and the message will scroll down. You can't see the whole message at one time."

Mandy pushed the arrow button and the words scrolled up the screen. *I need you to deliver a message to Mandy for me. Tell her that I agree with you that a best friend should never betray a confidence. Tell her that I don't want to talk to her or see her again, and I don't want to be her friend.*

The room began to spin. Mandy found it nearly impossible to breathe. "I don't understand," she said weakly. What was Noah about?

Kristina took her phone and flipped it shut. "You read it. It sounds plain enough to me. Neither of us can trust you."

She didn't even know where to begin to try to understand what was happening. "But . . . why?"

"He's mad, Mandy. Real mad." She patted Mandy's hand, but Mandy didn't even feel it. She was numb. "I'm your best friend. There is forgiveness in my heart. But Noah might never forgive you."

"Forgive me for what?"

Kristina looked at Mandy as if she were an idiot. Maybe she was. "Noah doesn't approve of you trying to steal your best friend's boyfriend. He's very honorable that way."

"He was never your boyfriend."

"And he was never yours, even though you kissed. He agreed with me."

Mandy's stomach dropped at the idea that Noah had agreed with Kristina about anything.

"He seemed particularly upset about the kiss," Kristina said.

Upset that they had kissed?

Her heart skipped a beat. Nae. He must have been upset that Kristina knew about it. He hated when other people knew anything about his personal life. Did her telling Kristina feel like a betrayal to him?

The room pitched about wildly. She felt light-headed and dizzy. Maybe she shouldn't have told Kristina about kissing Noah, but at the time, she had wanted to convince Kristina that Noah didn't love her. Horrible, horrible mistake.

Noah was sensitive about such things, she knew, but to never want to see her again because of a careless word to a friend? It seemed so final, so extreme. She thought she meant more to him than that. More than to toss their relationship aside in a text message.

She'd made a lot of mistakes with Noah, but she wasn't about to roll over and play dead. She loved him, and she was going to fix this, for the both of them.

Standing up, she grabbed the phone from Kristina.

"Hey," Kristina protested.

"I need to borrow this," Mandy said. "I'll be back."

"Are you going to talk to Noah? He said not to, remember?"

Mandy stormed out of the house. She would not let Noah break her heart in a text message, and she certainly wouldn't let him do it without a fight.

They seemed to do a lot of fighting. He was probably expecting it.

Kristina burst from the house, ran down the steps, and followed so closely that she almost stepped on Mandy's heel. "I'm coming with you. Noah is my boyfriend. He sent me the text."

Pretending Kristina wasn't right behind her, Mandy marched around the corner of the house and climbed the ladder as if she lived on the side of a cliff.

"Mandy, I don't like ladders. Come back," Kristina said. "I need you to help me up."

Feeling a twinge of guilt, Mandy ignored her best friend. Kristina, in all her annoying eagerness, had done nothing wrong, except maybe to fail to see how her behavior drove boys away. Mandy would fix things with Kristina later.

Fixing things with Noah was an emergency. Surely she could leave Kristina waiting on solid ground in an emergency.

Noah's nail gun did not stop as Mandy got to the top rung and stepped onto the roof. She sucked in her breath as she tried to steady herself on the incline.

The brothers were intent on their work, no doubt attempting to finish the roof in record time so they could leave this terrible place and never come back. Neither of them noticed her until she spoke. "Noah Mischler," she said, trying to lend steadiness to her voice. She loved Noah, and she felt deep remorse for telling Kristina about the kiss. If she couldn't convince him of that, all her hopes of happiness would come crashing down around her.

He glanced at her, hesitated for a second, and then resumed laying shingles as if all the nails in the world still needed to be driven. Why he thought he could get away with that behavior was beyond her. Hadn't he known her long enough to understand how persistent she was?

If he wouldn't come to her, she would go to him. She took a couple of steps on the steep incline, raising her arms to balance herself. He refused to look at her as she made her way toward him tottering unsteadily with every step. She was doing very well until she stepped on an errant nail and her foot flew out from under her. She squeaked in alarm as she fell hard on her backside with her feet dangling precariously over the edge.

That got Noah's attention. Frustration gathered on his face as he cast his nail gun aside, leaped to his feet, and took four giant steps to reach her. He slid next to her, hooked an arm around her waist, and held on tight as if she were a fence post and he was the cement anchoring her to the ground. "Mandy," he hissed. "I told you to stay off this roof. You could have broken your neck."

Mandy panted for air and willed her heart to slow to a

gallop. It felt so gute to be close to him, even if he was a little prickly at the moment. "You wouldn't even look at me. You broke up with me in a text. I had to come up."

"And risk your life?"

"For you, I'd risk anything." She did *not* want to melt into a puddle of tears. She sniffed them back.

His expression didn't soften. If anything, the lines around his eyes could have been cut into his face, and the muscles of his jaw tightened as if his mouth were fastened shut. He slid his hand from her waist and wrapped his fingers around her arm with an iron grip. Pulling her to her feet, he steered her away from the edge of the roof and toward the ladder. "You need to get down. Your dawdi would be angry if you fell."

"My dawdi doesn't get angry."

"Then I would be angry if you fell."

Kristina stood below with one foot propped on the bottom rung of the ladder as if gathering the courage to climb. "Stay down, Krissy," Noah said. "Nobody is allowed on this roof except for me and my brother. Go, Mandy."

He didn't release her arm. She knew he wouldn't let go until she was securely on the ladder.

Gute. She could be stubborn as well.

"I came up here to talk to you. I'm not climbing down until you explain yourself."

His eyes darkened like a looming storm. "I don't have to explain myself to anybody, least of all you. You're a stranger to me. Stay out of my life."

An oppressive ache pressed into her chest. "Noah, please don't push me away like this. Whatever it is, whatever I did, we can work it out. I'm ready to apologize over and over again. Please talk to me. Let me apologize."

Still holding on to her arm, he turned his face from her with an uncompromising lift of his chin. "I said everything I needed to say in that text."

Hadn't she scolded him about this very thing already? He was so maddeningly headstrong. "I'm not going to let you break up with me over a text message. Your mamm would say it's very bad manners."

He whipped his head around to look at her. "What do you know about my mamm? Don't talk about my mamm."

His sharp reaction shocked her to the very core. What had she done? She lowered her eyes. "I'm sorry, Noah. I didn't mean—"

"Yes, you did. What do you know about any of us? You came into town thinking you could fix us, when all you've done is ruin our lives."

Noah glanced at Yost, who had abandoned the shingles and stared at both of them, his eyes brimming with concern. With her arms folded across her chest, Kristina eyed them from the ground with a smug frown on her lips.

Mandy felt as if she might suffocate as the pressure on her lungs became unbearable. "I've . . . I've ruined your life?" Because she told Kristina about a kiss?

Kristina grabbed onto the ladder. "I still love you, Noah. I promise I'll never spy again."

Noah shook his head as if he didn't have any disgust to spare for Kristina. "Get down. And don't come up again."

"If you want me to go, you'll have to push me off." A fall from the roof couldn't have hurt any worse than how she already felt.

His expression was one of barely contained rage. If she didn't know him so well, she might truly be afraid that he *would* push her off the roof. He swiped his hand down the side of his face and seemed to pull his anger deeper inside himself. Taking a deep breath, he said, "Then you can stay, but sit down so you don't fall."

Mandy nodded. She'd rather speak to him without Yost or Kristina listening in on their conversation, but at least he was willing to talk.

Once he saw her safely sitting on the roof, Noah stepped over her legs and onto the top rung of the ladder.

Mandy couldn't believe it. "What are you doing?"

"If you're not going to leave, I am."

Kristina's face bloomed into all kinds of smiles as he quickly climbed down the ladder. She tried to grab his hand, but he stomped away before she could latch on. "Where are you going?" she said.

Noah glanced in Mandy's direction. "When she's gone, I'll come back."

Mandy thought she might be ill as tears sprang to her eyes. He might as well have shoved her off the roof. How had he come to despise her this much in three short days?

He strode across the lawn, snapping for Chester to follow him. Was he going to walk all the way home?

"Noah, wait," Kristina called as she picked up her skirts and ran after him.

He'd think he was being attacked, but Mandy was determined to chase him down right along with Kristina. She couldn't let him go like this, not when there was so much to say. Not when her heart broke at the thought of losing him. She leaned over and clutched the top of the ladder and swung her foot onto the first rung. He had a head start. Would she be able to catch up to him and his long legs? And what would she do when she did catch up with him? She lifted her chin. She might break an arm, but she'd tackle him if need be.

Whom was she fooling? She, together with every school-girl in Bonduel, couldn't bring Noah Mischler down.

She sighed in relief as Dawdi, oblivious to the tempest swirling about him, came out of the house and stopped Noah halfway across the yard. Noah was too polite to dart past Dawdi without acknowledging him. Kristina nearly bumped into him as he abruptly halted.

Dawdi reached out a hand to him. "I'm glad to see you're taking a break. Did Mandy give you the cookies?"

"Um, nae."

By this time, Mandy had made it down the ladder. Dawdi motioned for her to come closer. "Do you have those cookies?"

Still struggling to draw air into her lungs, Mandy took the small bag from her pocket and handed it to Noah. He wouldn't look at her, but he pulled a cookie from the bag and took a big bite. "They're delicious," he said, as if he were loath to admit that Mandy knew how to cook.

"I want one," Kristina said.

The muscles in Noah's jaw twitched as he held out the bag for her. As if she hadn't just witnessed the destruction of Mandy's heart, she giggled as she made eyes at Noah and took a bite.

Mandy stared at her friend in disbelief. Poor Kristina, so immature, so ignorant and insensitive. Could someone like that really have ruined all her hopes with Noah? Over a kiss?

Granted, it was a stunning, head-spinning kiss, but it appeared that Noah had already forgotten it.

Noah handed the bag to Dawdi. "I have to go home now. Yost will finish up."

Dawdi looked confused. "You walking?"

"Jah. I need to clear my head."

"Okay then," Dawdi said. "We will see you tomorrow. Mandy will give you some applesauce."

Noah nodded curtly, turned on his heels, and trudged down the lane.

Dawdi patted Mandy's shoulder. "That is one of the finest boys you'll ever meet." He raised his eyebrows. "Your eyes are watering."

She stood as stiff as a pillar. Was she just going to let him go? What would Dawdi think if she took off running after him?

She watched Noah put distance between them with his long, fluid stride. At that moment, it didn't matter what Dawdi thought. Without a second glance, Mandy sprinted down the lane and left Kristina munching her cookie. "Mandy!" Kristina called. "Wait for me."

"Don't go, Kristina," Mandy heard Dawdi say. "Mandy made lemon shortcake. Would you like some?"

"Yes, but I need to . . ."

"Best let Mandy have her say with him, don't you think?"

Kristina made no answer. She was probably having quite a time deciding if it would be better or worse to leave Mandy and Noah alone with each other.

"If you don't eat it now, sure as rain, one of Mandy's special boys will eat it up in two shakes of a lamb's tail."

Mandy was too far away to catch Kristina's response, but she didn't hear footsteps behind her or a loud, obnoxious bell zooming in for an attack, so lemon shortbread must have been a temptation sufficient enough to keep Kristina from chasing the man she loved all the way down Huckleberry Hill.

Noah must not have expected Mandy to follow. Up ahead, he kept a steady pace, but he didn't run like a man being chased. Wonderful gute. She'd have a chance.

She got close enough to ambush him. "Noah," she said breathlessly. "Please stop. I'm not going to give up until you hear what I have to say."

To her surprise, he stopped in the middle of the lane, dragging his feet in the gravel and sending a cloud of dirt into the air. He didn't say anything, just frowned resentfully and folded his arms, patiently awaiting her explanation.

His rigid posture and harsh expression called forth fresh tears, and she made no attempt to staunch them. She might as well try to hold back the Wisconsin River with her hand. He really looked as if he despised her, and she couldn't bear his contempt.

"Please tell me what I've done to hurt you."

"You won't leave me alone. That's what you've done." He started walking again.

She stepped in front of him as her profound pain gave way to anger. "Don't dismiss me like that. After all we've shared with each other, don't you dare dismiss me."

He scowled right back. "Don't tell me what to do. I'll never allow you to tell me what to do again. And I'll certainly never trust you."

"I've only wanted to help."

"You don't really want to help. You want to be right."

"That's not true. I care for you. I want—"

"You told Kristina that we kissed." He spit the words from his mouth like a bitter pill.

Mandy closed her eyes and shook her head. She was going to be sick. "I did. But she wouldn't—"

"I bet you had a gute laugh about it."

"No. I would never. How could I laugh about that? I will treasure that kiss until the day I die."

"That sounds like something Kristina would say. Funny and insincere."

Mandy stared at him with her mouth wide open. Noah's emotions frequently boiled over, but it wasn't like him to be cruel or react fiercely.

"I was right about you all along," he said. "You're only going to be here for four weeks. You came to have a little fun, maybe see if you could get some stupid boy to fall in love with you. Maybe stick your nose where it didn't belong and ruin someone's life in the process. You should be proud of all you've accomplished, and your month isn't even up yet."

The sharpness of his tongue made her tremble. "Kristina wouldn't believe me. She said I was imagining things. I told her you kissed me in hopes that she'd finally give up and leave you alone. Leave *us* alone."

"Why should you expect Kristina to leave me alone? You don't."

A sob came from deep in her throat. "If I had known you'd be so upset, I never would have said anything to her."

"You know she can't keep her mouth shut. About anything." He narrowed his eyes into slits. "In fact, you were counting on it, weren't you?"

"Counting on what?"

The pain and vulnerability flashing in his eyes cut her to the quick. "You must think I'm so stupid. Kristina knows all about what happened at the bar. Did you think I wouldn't find out?"

Mandy forgot to breathe. Could things get any worse? She'd hoped to keep Noah from finding out that Kristina had been there that night. "I didn't want you to find out. I knew it would upset you."

"You wanted Kristina to tell the whole community."

"Why would I want that?"

"Because you wanted to be right. You wanted to force my hand. You told me yourself that someday someone would find out about my dat. You thought that if news like that spread to the community, I'd be shamed into calling your counselor or checking my dat into the hospital. You wanted to get your way with me and my dat, and you didn't care how you embarrassed us in the process."

For a moment, Mandy was at a loss for words. Is this what Noah thought of her? "That's not true. I promised you I wouldn't tell anybody."

"Your promises are as cheap as tissue paper."

Tears trickled down her face. "I can't understand this. I love you. Can't you see I love you?"

He flinched as if she had struck him. "And so you think you know what's best for me?"

"It breaks my heart to see how tightly you've tied yourself into knots. You're so afraid of the truth that you shut out the very people who could help you. You've even shut out God."

He glared at her. "You don't know anything. I would never shut out God. He is my only strength. You're so sure you're right that you want to force me to do what I won't do. To shame me in the eyes of my community."

"I don't want to shame you. I want to help you. You don't even know how the community would react because you won't let them see. You'd rather ignore it or run away."

He took off his hat and raked his fingers through his hair. "Tell that to my brother who I haven't seen in three years. I didn't run away from my fater. I stayed. I'm the only one who stayed." His voice cracked, and he nearly lost his composure. She gently placed her hand on his arm. He jerked away from her. "Go back to Ohio, Mandy. I was so much better off before you came."

He turned and stomped down the lane, giving a short whistle that summoned Chester to his side. He didn't look back. She didn't try to stop him.

What had she done? She had wanted to tell him she was sorry, but her apology sounded more like a rebuke. *You're so afraid of the truth that you shut out the very people who could help you. You'd rather run away.*

How could she have said that to him when he had cared so faithfully for his fater for all these years? Noah was the bravest person she knew.

He was right. He'd be so much better off without her.

Raw and empty, she stood silently in the lane and watched Noah until he disappeared from sight. A pathetic sob involuntarily escaped her lips. She felt profoundly lonely, as if she were the only person left in the whole world.

For the first time since she'd come outside, she noticed how brisk the air was. A light breeze teased wisps of hair across her face, and she shivered as a chill ran down her spine and tears spilled down her cheeks.

She'd lost him, and she wasn't even sure how it had happened. All she knew was that a cavern gaped in the place where her heart used to be, and it hurt to breathe.

How long did she stand there? It could have been minutes. It could have been hours. She trembled as the wind picked up and seeped underneath her sweater.

She had learned her lesson. She would never try to fix anyone's problems ever again, never try to help girls with their broken hearts or boys with their broken families. Noah had made her see that her help was unneeded and unwelcome.

But the lesson had come too late. Noah was gone.

Chapter Eighteen

The dry leaves skipped along the ground and cackled as the wind picked them up and swirled them in a dancing spiral. Mandy squinted against the dust that blew into her eyes. Lord willing, the wind would not make mischief of the loose shingles on the roof. Yost was working as fast as he could to finish the roof before the weather turned downright hostile, but if the wind kept blowing his shingles around, his job would take much longer. If only Noah hadn't left Yost to do the job by himself.

Noah had been fully aware of how little time they had left to finish the roof before bad weather hit. Only the deepest kind of hurt and anger would have kept him away when Yost needed his help so urgently.

Mandy swallowed the lump in her throat. She'd really fixed things gute this time. Mammi and Dawdi's roof might not get done, and Noah Mischler hated the very sight of her. Her heart ached so badly that it hurt to breathe.

Turning her face away from the wind, she searched for green tomatoes on Mammi's vines. If they got the tomatoes in before the first frost, they could ripen on the counter, and her grandparents would eat fresh tomatoes for another month or two, even if Mandy wouldn't. Mammi wanted her to stay in Bonduel indefinitely, but Mandy wouldn't be here to eat tomatoes or make pot holders or roast marshmallows with any boys in the neighborhood.

If she had her way, she would leave immediately, go back to where she belonged, and forget that there was even such a place as Huckleberry Hill and such a boy as Noah Mischler. But she had promised Mammi that she would stay the full four weeks just in case there was a boy within a fifty-mile radius whom she hadn't yet met.

Mammi was planning a gathering at their house the night before Mandy's departure. Even if the thought of Yost Mischler working on the roof all by himself made her want to weep, she couldn't disappoint Mammi. She'd stay eight more days.

She hoped that once she got back to Ohio, she would be able to breathe again. Maybe she'd find a new and exciting boy who wouldn't be annoyed with her all the time. Of course, a new boy probably wouldn't have arms as thick as tree branches or hair the color of clover honey. He definitely wouldn't know how to fix the refrigeration system at the local market or how to install a gas stove without setting the house on fire. If he did know how to shingle a roof, maybe he wouldn't want a stupid girl bothering him, even if she did know how to use a crescent wrench and a Phillips screwdriver.

Mandy cleared her throat and made herself think about Eggs Benedict. Thinking about screwdrivers made her want to cry. She didn't want to be sniffling all day.

She picked up her two galvanized metal buckets full of green tomatoes and tromped toward the house. Before long, the snows would bury the hill in white drifts. Huckleberry Hill was so charming in the wintertime, but she wouldn't be here to see it.

The wind teased her hair from beneath the scarf she'd tied around her head as she made her way toward the house. The faint tinkling of a bicycle bell tripped along the breeze. It could only mean one thing. Kristina was coming for another visit. After yesterday, what could she possibly want?

Mandy threw her head back and growled. Oh, how she wished Kristina would quit bothering her!

Yost called to her from the roof. "Is everything okay?"

She quickly lowered her head. Yost did not need to see her pallid complexion or the red-rimmed eyes. "Jah. I am only making noises."

If Yost thought her strange, well, it probably wasn't the worst thing he thought about her. Noah's disdain certainly would have spilled over to his brother.

Standing on the first step, Mandy slid her buckets onto the porch and waited, once again, for Kristina to pop from around the bend with that self-satisfied grin she had worn yesterday. After Noah had gone, Mandy had come trudging back up the hill only to be greeted by Kristina coming the other way on her bike. She had held her head as if she had a whole bouquet of flowers in her hair while she pedaled slowly down the hill. "It serves you right," was all she had said as she passed Mandy coming the other way.

As devastated as she had been, Mandy had been tempted to stick out her tongue.

What would Kristina do today? Had she come to gloat?

Mandy wouldn't stand for that. Kristina could just turn that bike around and ride down the hill, because Mandy would not put up with any smug remarks from her best friend. Former best friend.

With friends like Kristina, who needed enemies?

Kristina came into sight marching up the hill with a purposeful stride, ringing that bell for all she was worth. When she saw Mandy, she scrunched up her face, as if she'd just eaten a crab apple.

Mandy balled her hands into fists. She felt bad enough as it was. She did not need Kristina's righteous indignation to make her feel worse.

"Mandy," Kristina said, quickening her pace when she saw her, "I am so sick of boys, I could just spit."

Mandy's brows inched together. "Sick of boys?"

Kristina didn't even bother with the kickstand. She let her bike fall to the ground, reached out for Mandy, and pulled her in for an embrace. "Noah especially," she said, loudly enough that Yost working on the roof could hear her.

Mandy let herself be hugged and then pulled away to study Kristina's face. "I thought you were mad at me."

"Best friends can never be mad at each other for long. Besides we've got to stick together against those stupid boys who break our hearts."

Could Kristina even begin to guess at the depth of Mandy's broken heart?

Kristina pulled her cell phone from her pocket and waved it in front of Mandy's face. "Not one word from him since yesterday. Not one. And that text wasn't even meant for me. I thought he'd at least text me back. But ten texts is my limit. If he won't answer me after ten texts, then he's had his chance."

"You don't want to look desperate, I guess," Mandy said weakly.

"That's right, because I'm not desperate. A boy who breaks up with two girls over a text message isn't worth your time. Or mine. There are plenty of other boys. I'm through with Noah Mischler."

Mandy's reaction bordered on astonishment to hear her own advice spouted back to her from such an unlikely source. Had all those lectures she'd given Kristina finally sunk in?

She exhaled slowly. "That's right. A boy like that doesn't deserve our affection." She felt even less convinced than she sounded. She was the one who didn't deserve Noah Mischler, the ill-mannered boy who broke up with girls over text messages. "What made you change your mind about him?"

"I chased him down the hill yesterday on my bike."

Mandy nearly choked on Kristina's words, but she restrained herself from showing any reaction. "Did you?" Didn't this girl ever have chores to do? She seemed to have a lot of time for idle notions.

"He was halfway home by the time I caught up to him. First he tried to convince me that he wasn't good enough for any girl. You know, because of his dat. Then he got impatient and told me that he wasn't interested in me or you ever, and that if I kept pestering him, he'd speak to my fater and tell him to take my phone away." She scowled and wrapped both hands protectively around her phone as if to guard it from Noah even now. "I told him I wouldn't marry him if he got down on his knees and begged me to, even if he were the richest man in the world. Even if he were the bishop, I'd never even dream of marrying him. I told him off right good."

"What did he say?"

"He said 'gute.' That's all. Just 'gute' and stomped away. But I'm sure he regrets it now."

Well could Mandy imagine Noah's reaction. He would have frowned, clenched his teeth, and when his back was turned, breathed a sigh of relief.

"Good riddance," Kristina said. "He's caused me enough trouble. You almost drowned because of him."

Nae. She had escaped from the river because of him. She had smiled a thousand different times a day because of him. She had eaten French toast because of him.

She had fallen in love because of him.

"My one comfort is that you didn't get him either," Kristina said.

Mandy shouldn't have expected anything better from her friend, but her heart hurt all the same. Nope. She didn't get him either. But it didn't give her any comfort.

Kristina folded her arms and pursed her lips as if she

were trying to be strong. "I'll never meet another boy like Noah Mischler, and now I've lost him."

Better him than the cell phone.

Kristina burst into tears, just as Mandy had expected her to, and threw herself into Mandy's arms. She was the friend who could fix things. Kristina depended on her, but she probably didn't know or even care about the ache in Mandy's heart.

For once, Mandy was grateful for Kristina's insensitivity. Mandy probably would have melted into a puddle if Kristina had shown her any sympathy at all. And Mandy was determined not to be a puddle until she got back to Charm. Mamm wouldn't mind puddles on her floor.

Mandy led Kristina to the porch steps to sit. She wrapped an arm around her to shield her from the cold and let her cry it out. The crying lasted a few minutes longer than Mandy expected, probably because Kristina was crying over the thought that she had almost lost her cell phone. That would have been a tragedy indeed.

The wind rushed through the trees, pulling leaves from their branches and sending them whirling into the air like tiny birds. "It's getting cold," Mandy said. "Should we go in and make some tea?"

"Have you got some of that lemon cake from yesterday? It was really good."

"Jah, I have a little left over."

"Okay. I'll come in." They stood, and Mandy led Kristina up the stairs like an invalid. Kristina halted on the porch and wiped her eyes. "I want you to know, Mandy, that I forgive you for what happened with Noah."

Mandy didn't even bat an eyelash. "Denki. I appreciate that."

Over the sound of the wind, Mandy heard a horse coming up the hill. Both she and Kristina turned as Davy Burkholder rode up the lane and waved at them.

"What's he doing here?" Kristina said, probably put out because she'd have to share her lemon cake if Davy decided to stay.

"Do you know Davy Burkholder?"

"Jah. He isn't in my district, but I sometimes see him at gatherings." The corner of Kristina's mouth drooped. "He's short."

Mandy eyed Davy as he jumped off his horse. He wasn't that short. And Mammi thought he had nice teeth. And according to Noah, he had three stuffed elk heads hanging in his living room. What girl wouldn't find that charming?

Davy led his horse to the tree at the edge of the lawn that served as a hitching post of sorts. He secured the reins around the tree, looked up on the roof, and yelled. "Yost Mischler, how are you?"

Mandy heard movement above her. "Trying to keep from blowing away," Yost called. "And you?"

"Not too bad. We're working on getting the corn in before the wind takes it." He gazed at the roof for a moment. "Where's Noah?"

"Working at Yutzys' today," Yost said.

"Tell him not to work too hard. If he wears out, nothing will ever get fixed in Bonduel again."

"I will," Yost said.

Davy smiled and removed his hat before the wind took it. "Hullo, Mandy. Hullo, Kristina. *Wie gehts?*" Davy did have sort of a cute smile.

Kristina stood a little taller as she peered at him. "We're just fine." She must have forgotten that she had been bawling her eyes out not two minutes ago.

Davy ambled up the porch steps. "Are you okay, Kristina? Your eyes are red."

Kristina self-consciously brushed at the hair at the nape

of her neck. "Oh, I . . . dirt is flying every which way in this wind."

"Nae, you've been crying. I know when a girl's been crying. I have sisters."

Davy hadn't mastered tact yet. Well, he was young. If enough girls disapproved of him, he'd learn when to keep his opinions to himself.

"What brings you to Huckleberry Hill?" Mandy asked. Surely Davy wasn't here to talk about Kristina's puffy eyes.

"Your mammi asked me to take you kite flying tomorrow. It seems she's got two homemade kites, and she wants us to see how high they'll fly."

Dear Mammi. There was no end to her schemes. "Okay. I can go with you. What time?"

"I get off work at four. I'll pick you up at five."

"It might be too windy," Mandy said, hoping beyond hope that they would have to cancel.

"It depends if Anna made a strong kite," Kristina said. "If it's made of paper, the wind will rip it up."

"We don't have to fly kites for very long. Then we can go shooting. I really want to take you shooting."

"Okay," Mandy said, with even less enthusiasm. She'd tried shooting before and came back with a bruised shoulder. "I'm sorry you had to come all the way up here to ask me."

Kristina perked up and held her phone for Davy to see. "Next time, you can call me. Mandy and I are always together, and I have a phone. I can get a message to her without you having to make a trip."

Davy seemed to take a greater interest in Kristina. "You have a phone? That's wonderful gute. All my friends are either baptized or nearly so. Nobody has a phone anymore. Well, Noah does, but he won't text me."

Kristina caught her breath. "Me neither! It's so annoying when you text somebody and they won't text you back."

"I know. It's like they're ignoring you," Davy said.

"I have unlimited texting on my phone."

Davy's eyes got big. "Me too!"

Realization popped onto Kristina's face. Mandy was surprised how long it had taken her. "Why don't we text each other? I always answer my texts."

Davy bloomed into a smile and pulled his phone from his pocket. "That would be wonderful gute. Let me put your number into my phone."

Kristina giggled as she and Davy exchanged phone numbers and compared service providers. Mandy couldn't have cared less about data plans, but it seemed that when it came to phones, Davy and Kristina were kindred spirits.

Mammi and Dawdi emerged from the house. Dawdi wore a bright yellow scarf around his neck and carried a box containing half a dozen bottles of newly canned applesauce. Mammi had on a lovely lavender sweater. She looked quite spectacular.

"Davy," Mammi exclaimed. "I didn't know you were here. Is today kite-flying day?"

Davy looked up from his phone. "Nae. I'm coming tomorrow."

Mammi's eyes danced in delight. "How nice to have you here two days in a row. Cum reu and have a piece of Mandy's lemon cake."

Davy looked at Kristina. "Do you want to come in with me? I can show you all my games."

Kristina nodded. "Do you have Angry Birds?"

"Jah. And Angry Birds Star Wars and Bad Piggies."

"Go on in," Mandy said. "I'll be right there."

Kristina and Davy strolled into the house with their eyes glued to their phones. They wouldn't care one whit if Mandy joined them.

Mammi smiled her best grandmotherly smile at Mandy. "How nice of Davy to come up today. Once I sparked his interest with my kites, I knew he'd come through for me." Mammi turned to Dawdi, who waited patiently while she buttoned up his black jacket. "Your dawdi and I are going out for a bit."

"Do you want to come?" Dawdi asked, winking at her as if she were in on a secret.

"Now, Felty," Mammi scolded. "Mandy can't come with us. We might be gone for hours, and Junior Schwartz and Junior Shrock are coming for lunch."

Mandy lifted her eyebrows. "They are?"

"They both go by 'Junior,' so try not to get confused," Mammi said. "On the counter, I left a list of questions to ask them. Be sure to inspect them thoroughly. You've only got two weeks left."

Mandy wasn't quite sure what Mammi meant by "inspect them thoroughly," but Mandy had no intention of doing any such thing. "One more week, Mammi. Only one." Staying a full five weeks was out of the question. Noah Mischler was here. She didn't want to be anywhere near him.

She exhaled slowly. In truth, she wanted to be by his side forever, but he didn't want her and she wouldn't put herself through the torture of being so close to him and yet feeling so distant. He hated her. She wanted to get as far away as possible.

Mammi's disappointment was as thick as smoke. "Are you sure? There are still dozens of boys to meet. An extra week would give us time to bus them in from Cashton and Augusta."

"I'm sure, Mammi. I need to get home and help Mamm with the canning."

"The roof will be done by then," Dawdi said.

Mandy had no idea what that had to do with her leaving.

Her only concern was that Mammi and Dawdi would get a sturdy roof over their heads. "Lord willing."

"I'm sorry I didn't get time to make something for lunch," Mammi said, "but there are chicken wings in the fridge. Junior Number One has a big appetite, so be sure to make extra." She furrowed her brow. "Oh dear. Chicken wings will never do for a boy with a big appetite. Do you want my spicy meatball recipe?"

Mandy smiled in resignation. She dreaded the thought of having to entertain more boys and "inspect them thoroughly," but cooking something would help take her mind off Noah. "Chicken wings will be fine, Mammi. I'll make a big potato salad to go with it."

Mammi nodded. "That will fill them up. Be sure to invite Yost to eat with you. He can't be on that roof all day with no nourishment."

"I will."

Mammi reached into her canvas bag. Among other things, she carried her knitting with her wherever she went in case she had an extra minute or two to make a pot holder.

"We should be home before dinnertime. Be sure to get rid of the lunch boys by four o'clock because John Shirk is coming at five."

Mandy's stomach felt like a pile of rocks. "John Shirk?"

"We've only got one more week, dear." Mammi found what she had been looking for in her bag and pulled out four knitted creations that looked like oversized, stuffed pot holders. "I thought about making lentil stew tonight for dinner, but if you've got something else you'd like to make, I'll save the lentil stew for later."

Even though Mandy was in no way interested in a relationship with John Shirk, she didn't want him to have a stomachache as his only remembrance of Huckleberry Hill. "I will make fried chicken, Mammi. You can relax."

With her pot holder–like bundles in her hand, Mammi

tagged along behind Dawdi down the porch steps and out onto the lawn. Both of them stopped and gazed up at Yost on the roof.

"Yost," Dawdi called. "How is the work coming?"

"Slow," Yost called back.

Mandy followed her grandparents so she could get a good view of Yost.

Dawdi shielded his eyes against the wind while he looked up at Yost. "And Noah says he's not coming back?"

Yost studied the nail gun in his hand. "That's right. He's mighty busy with other repair work."

Mandy ignored the way her heart thumped in her chest.

"Where is he today?" Dawdi said.

"At Yutzys' fixing their egg sorter. At least that's where he was going this morning."

Mammi waved her yarn creations around her head. "Yost, I made these for you and Noah. They're knee pads so your knees won't get sore kneeling on that roof all day."

Yost raised his eyebrows. "Denki, Anna. I'm sure they'll come in handy."

Too bad one pair of knee pads would go unused.

Mandy took the knee pads from her mammi. "I can take them up to him if you want."

"That would be very kind of you, dear."

Dawdi took Mammi's elbow and led her to the barn to fetch the buggy. Mammi waved at Mandy. "Have fun with the Juniors. Pay special attention to their teeth."

Mandy climbed the ladder. Yost met her at the top so she didn't have to set foot on the roof and took the knee pads from her. He gave her a doubtful smile. "Denki." Who knew what Noah had told him about her? He was probably reluctant to be in the same state with a girl who ruined people's lives.

"How much longer do you think the roof will take?" Mandy asked.

"Three or four days. Lord willing, the weather will hold off until it's done."

"What's left to do besides the shingles on this side?"

Yost wiped the back of his hand across his forehead. "After that, I need to do the ridge cap. It's a lot of cutting." He examined Mammi's knee pads, trying to figure out how they fit on his leg.

A very gute idea began to formulate in her brain. Yost needed more time. Noah wasn't going to come back. "Could you use some help?"

The corners of his mouth turned down. "Noah's not coming back. I'm happy to finish it for him."

"What would you say if I knew someone who works for free, is really gute with a nail gun, and has two hours to kill?" She hadn't actually ever used a nail gun, but she was sure she'd be good with one. How hard could it be?

Yost nodded. "Any little bit helps."

"Gute. I will go and put on my sweatpants."

Yost's mouth formed the words before his tongue took action. "What? You?"

"Jah, me."

"I could never allow a girl to help me. Noah wouldn't like it. Neither would my mamm."

Mandy hoped she'd get to meet this mamm who had drummed the manners into her sons such that they wouldn't dare go against what she'd taught them. Rose Mischler must have been a very strong woman, and her sons must have loved and respected her for it.

"Neither Noah nor your mamm has to know," Mandy said.

She stepped halfway down the ladder before Yost stopped her. "I don't think this is a gute idea."

"That's okay. I'm not offended."

She ran into the house where Davy and Kristina sat at the

table studying Davy's phone. "Slide your finger like this to see how many pieces of fruit you can slice in half," Yost said.

"I got a watermelon," Kristina said, bursting with excitement.

"Be careful. They start to come really fast."

In her room, Mandy put on a pair of sweatpants she wore when she rode horses, plus another sweater under her jacket. It would be cold on that roof. She retied her shoes and buttoned her jacket and ran outside mere minutes after she had gone in. Working on the roof sounded like the most exciting thing she'd done all day—maybe because she needed to feel useful. Maybe because Noah would be furious if he found out. Gute. Let him be furious. He had no right to tell her what to do. She didn't care what he thought.

If she kept telling herself these lies, she might forget the truth.

After a quick visit to the toolshed for an extra hammer, she bounded up the ladder with less caution than she'd ever used. *Take that, Noah Mischler.*

Dawdi walked the horse and buggy out of the barn. Mammi sat inside with her knitting already wrapped in her fingers. Dawdi glanced up. "Mighty late in the year to try to get a suntan, Mandy."

Mandy made sure she was securely planted on the roof before she lifted one hand and waved at Dawdi. "I want to be sure you to have a tight roof over your heads before I leave for Charm next week. Yost is teaching me."

Dawdi wasn't one to fuss when one of his relatives did something out of the ordinary. "Okay," he said. "Don't fall in the bushes behind the house. They're stickery." He climbed into the buggy, and it rolled down the lane. Mammi never looked up from her knitting.

Yost pulled a shingle from the bundle. "Are you sure about this? Have you ever laid shingles before?"

"You can teach me."

He shook his head, reluctant to do anything that might get him into hot water. "Noah won't like it."

She took the shingle from his hand. "I don't want to talk about Noah. I want to talk about your sister Lisa. Has she thought more about wedding colors?"

Yost stared at her. "Wedding colors? Lisa's not engaged."

"Every girl thinks about wedding colors. I might do something daring and go with pink plates."

"Are you engaged?"

"Not at the moment, but there's probably a boy somewhere in Ohio who will have me."

Yost cracked a smile. "I don't doubt more than one. There's more than one in Bonduel who'll have you too."

He meant it as a joke, but to Mandy, it was like the poke of a pin in her heart. The boy she wanted didn't want her. She pretended to be amused. "Show me how to fit this shingle, and I'll tell you all about my wedding plans. I'm sure you're dying to know."

He chuckled uncomfortably. "If you show me how to put on these knee pads, I'll show you how to match up the shingles."

They determined they needed to tie the knee pads around the back of their legs. Yost's were navy blue and Mandy's were deep purple. "We look adorable," Mandy said.

Yost seemed to relax more and more the longer they sat on the roof together. "I hope not. Here, slide away from the edge." He picked up a shingle and pointed to a notch at the top. See this? You have to match this with the line and the shingle already down."

With only the slightest misgivings, he showed her how to fit the shingle into place and how to use the nail gun. Soon they were working side by side, Yost with his nail gun and Mandy with Noah's. He moved twice as fast as she did, but she had to believe that her help did him some good.

At least her help was of some value to somebody.

After a few minutes of not talking about wedding colors, Mandy said, "Yost, do you mind talking about your family? I'd love to hear all about them."

The question took him by surprise. "Of course I talk about my family. Who doesn't?"

Who doesn't, indeed. She pinned him with an earnest gaze. "Tell me about your mamm."

Chapter Nineteen

Noah stepped back from the conveyor belt, careful not to step on one of the two dozen wire baskets of eggs on the floor near his feet. The Yutzys' eggs were piling up for sorting, and he wasn't anywhere near figuring out what was wrong with the sorting machine. There were so many moving parts and so many places where something could go wrong, he almost had to examine the machine inch by inch to figure it out.

It didn't help that it was nearly impossible to keep his mind on the task at hand. Mandy's stricken face, her pleading, her declaration that she loved him, all worked against him until he felt as if his grief would bury him. He barely knew which way was up.

He tried to ignore the twist of pain in his chest at the thought that she didn't really love him. If she loved him, she would stay out of his business. She wouldn't bring this horrible, paralyzing shame down on his head simply because she wanted to be right.

He'd be better off rid of her so he could pick up the pieces of his reputation in the community and try to move on with his miserable life.

He took a hex wrench from his toolbox and loosened a

bolt at the front of the conveyor belt. Mandy might know how to use a hex wrench, but she knew nothing about fixing people's lives. She'd made a mess of his. Who cared if she could wield a screwdriver with the best of them? It didn't matter anymore.

Barbara Yutzy and her daughter Lizzie squatted near a basket of brown eggs sorting them by hand until Noah could get their machine up and running. "What do you think, Noah?" Barbara said. "Can you fix it?"

"Not yet," Noah said, jiggling the wrench to loosen the bolt. "I'm working my way around it yet."

"Well, if anybody can fix it, you can. I've never seen a mind better suited to figuring things out. Amos is good for nothing when it comes to machines."

Noah let the praise slide off him like he always did. The Plain people tried to avoid the temptation to be proud. "I thank the gute Lord for my talents."

"The Lord gave you your talents. You have sense enough to know how to use them."

The bolt fell to the floor, and Noah scooped it into his hand and dropped it in his pocket. The floor of the barn where the Yutzys sorted their eggs was sparkling clean. Not an easy task on a chicken farm. A large window in the wall to his left revealed the main warehouse area where over two thousand chickens pecked at grain from dozens of feeders. Those chickens put out about two thousand eggs a day. The Yutzys needed their sorter something wonderful.

With his attention centered on the conveyor belt, Noah heard someone step into the barn.

"Come to help sort eggs?" Barbara said.

Noah looked up. Felty and Anna Helmuth stood in the wide doorway, grinning as if the idea of thousands of eggs made them ecstatic. Felty carried an old, heavy-looking apple box. Noah immediately stepped around the egg baskets and took the box from him. No sense in Felty pulling a muscle.

"Hullo," Felty said, gladly giving the box to Noah.

The box contained six quart jars of something yellowish brown. Probably applesauce. Hadn't Felty said something about doing applesauce yesterday?

"Barbara," Noah said. "Do you want me to take this into the house?"

"Nae, Noah," Anna said, folding her hands together. "The applesauce is for you. Mandy thought you might like some."

Of course Mandy thought he might like some. She'd been to his house. She'd seen the condition of his cupboards. By now, everybody in Bonduel probably knew the condition of his cupboards. Anna and Felty's offering was probably only the beginning of the food donations. Since Mandy couldn't keep her mouth shut, his neighbors would feel sorry for him and probably start dropping off all sorts of food.

"Denki," Noah said, even as the bitterness grew in his heart. What was everybody thinking about him now that Mandy had spread his private business all over town? "How did you know I was here?"

Felty walked farther into the room, eyeing the overflowing baskets of eggs that filled every corner of the room. "You could make a lot of Eggs Benefit with these, Annie Banannie."

"Now, Felty," Anna scolded.

"We heard you was having trouble with your egg sorter," Felty said.

Barbara nodded while slipping eggs into their carton compartments. "Do you want to help sort, or what?"

Felty thumbed his suspenders. "I think we could spare some time to sort eggs, couldn't we, Annie?"

"Jah. We would love to help," Anna said, surveying the room with a subdued grin on her face. "This room is lovely, Barbara. It reminds me of the barn where I was born."

Noah was pretty sure Anna wasn't born in a barn, but he didn't say anything. And there wasn't much lovely about the egg sorting room. The walls were painted a very light blue, but other than that, there wasn't one thing in the room that wasn't functional to the process of packing eggs. Was Anna trying to butter Barbara up for something? Noah had known Anna long enough that he knew she always seemed to have a plan.

"It don't matter how lovely this room is if we don't get that egg machine fixed," Barbara replied.

"We are ready and willing to sort eggs," Anna said. "With my knitting experience, I'm sure I'll be very quick at it. But first we need to talk to Noah."

Noah wanted to avoid any such thing. There was no possible way that Anna and Felty would talk him into coming back to Huckleberry Hill to finish their roof. Yost could manage on his own.

Barbara stood and propped her hands on her hips. "Well, he's busy. My egg sorter's got to be fixed."

Barbara was blunt like that, and she didn't give an inch if she thought you didn't deserve it. Maybe he wouldn't be forced to explain himself to Anna and Felty after all. He said a quick prayer of thanks for Barbara Yutzy.

"Of course it does," Felty said. "But we come all this way. Could you spare fifteen minutes for a jar of applesauce?"

Barbara wanted to say no. Obstinate annoyance was written all over her face. But the applesauce must have softened her up. Either that or she thought better of rubbing her neighbors the wrong way. Some of the lines around her mouth disappeared. "Okay, but make it quick. The eggs ain't getting any younger."

Felty's eyes twinkled as if he were about to burst into laughter. "I'd say those eggs are about as young as they can get."

Barbara didn't laugh. She didn't even crack a smile. "If you're gonna go, go. Time's a-wasting. And leave the applesauce on the table over there."

Anna pulled a jar of applesauce from the box and laid it on the table as directed. "There's a lovely willow outside, Noah. Shall we sit under it?"

Noah felt guilty as soon as he walked outside. The wind whipped through the trees, sending leaves tumbling to the ground like rain and making a fantastic racket. Yost would be having a terrible time getting the last of the shingles on.

He'd cook an extra nice meal for dinner to make it up to him. Yost understood why Noah couldn't return to Huckleberry Hill. He loved his brother and didn't begrudge him the extra work.

Noah still carried the box of applesauce. "I'll put this in my wagon," he said.

He tromped to his wagon while Anna and Felty ambled to the giant willow that sat in the Yutzys' front yard. With the wind blowing branches every which way, they wouldn't be able to hear a thing under that tree. Gute. They didn't need to hear what he really thought of their granddaughter.

Noah laid the box of applesauce in the bed of his wagon and turned to see Felty and Anna pointing to a small tool-shed behind the tree. "It's too noisy," Felty yelled over the din of the wind. "Let's go to the shed."

Anna and Felty still weren't going to hear what Noah really thought about Mandy. He'd keep his mouth shut, like he always did.

First Anna and then Felty disappeared inside the shed. Noah came last, opening the door and letting it swing shut behind him. He gasped as he nearly plowed Anna over. The shed was almost pitch black with dim slits of light squeezing between a few loose slats. They stood in a small circle facing each other. With tools, shelves, and bags of feed lining the walls, there wasn't much room for them to spread out.

Felty held up a penlight and shined it at the ceiling in the center of their little circle. "It's a little cramped in here," he said.

Anna clapped her hand over her mouth and giggled. "Barbara won't know what became of us."

"That might buy us an extra five minutes," Felty said.

Taking a deep breath, Anna wiped the smile off her face. Even in the dim light, Noah could see her intense gaze. "Noah," she said, "the Bible says that if my brother has aught against me that I need to go and be reconciled to that brother."

He held his breath, ready for a lecture. Mandy, who didn't seem to know how to keep quiet about anything, must have told them how he'd yelled at her yesterday, and the Helmuths didn't like how their granddaughter had been treated.

He clenched his jaw. They were probably justified. He hadn't been very nice. In his anger, he'd forgotten everything his mamm had taught him about how to treat a girl. She would be ashamed if she ever found out.

But what did one more person matter? The shame already smothered him like a pile of dirt. What was one more stone on the heap?

Anna rummaged through her big canvas bag, which she had managed to fit in the shed with them. Felty nearly fell backward into a stack of fertilizer bags when he tried to make room for Anna's oversized purse.

She pulled something from her bag and slipped it into his hand. He raised it to the light. It was a pot holder. "Noah, dear, I'm afraid I have offended you."

Noah stuttered as the honor of receiving a pot holder rendered him speechless. "I . . . I don't understand. You think you've offended me?"

"When Yost came to Huckleberry Hill this morning, I sensed right away that something was wrong. Noah Mischler would never walk away and leave a job undone unless he had a very gute reason."

Warmth pulsed through Noah's veins, replacing the ice that had hardened his heart for the last twenty-four hours. Was that what people thought of him? That he always finished a job he'd committed to do? They knew about his *fater*, didn't they? Why would they still hold a good opinion of Noah?

Anna raised her eyebrows and nodded emphatically. "Felty pointed out, and very rightly so . . ."

"*Denki*, Banannie," Felty said.

"You're welcome, dear. Felty pointed out, very rightly so, that I have been handing out pot holders to complete strangers while ignoring you and all the gute work you've done on our house." Anna was close enough to reach out and cup her hand over Noah's cheek. "I never meant to make you feel unimportant."

Noah was quite dumbfounded. They weren't going to scold him? "I . . . I don't deserve this," he finally managed to say.

I made your granddaughter cry.

"We really, really want you to have the pot holder," Felty said, as if pot holders were as valuable as gold.

Noah let out a breath he'd been holding for a long time. "Okay. Thank you. I'm very grateful."

"And you forgive me?" Anna said.

"You didn't do anything wrong."

Anna clicked her tongue. "Tsk, tsk. What a sweet boy you are." She zipped her canvas bag shut. "And now, much as I'd enjoy spending the rest of the morning in this shed with you, I did promise Barbara I would help sort eggs until her machine is fixed. I wouldn't want to disappoint Barbara." She lowered her voice. "Much as I love her, she can be a might testy yet." Anna nudged her way around Noah and out the shed door. "Come on, Noah. The sooner you get back to work, the sooner Barbara will get her machine back. I'd rather not wash chicken poop off the eggs by hand. It will ruin my appetite."

Noah and Felty followed Anna out of the shed. The wind blew as loud as ever, but Noah welcomed the fresh air and the wide-open space.

Anna walked ahead of them as Felty clapped a hand on Noah's shoulder. "So, you've got your pot holder. You never said if you'd come back."

Noah turned his face away. He'd hoped in all the kerfuffle about pot holders and applesauce and chicken poop that Felty would forget about the roof. Even though Anna had sacrificed one of her precious pot holders for him, he couldn't come back. Felty would never understand why.

"Yost's a fast worker."

Felty stroked his beard. "I'm not worried about the roof. Yost is working hard, and now that Mandy's helping him, they won't be working past Friday."

Noah coughed as if a bug had flown into his mouth. "Mandy?"

"She got on the roof and started hammering away this morning."

Noah felt the anger build inside him. "She shouldn't be up there. It's too dangerous."

"I don't wonder but she'll be okay. She's not one to take risks, and she has the Helmuth sense of balance."

Not one to take risks? Noah recalled having to pull her out of a river once. "She still shouldn't be up there." He clenched his teeth together. Someday he'd wear them down to nubs. Had she gone up there just to irritate him? Or to compel him to come back?

His teeth screeched as they ground against each other. The thought of Mandy lying in a heap on the ground buried under a pile of shingles made him want to jump in his wagon and ride as fast as the wind to Huckleberry Hill.

He shook his head. He'd never let Mandy dictate what he did and didn't do with his life. If she thought putting herself in danger would force him to come back, she was greatly mistaken.

If she fell, it would be by her own choice.

He ignored the fact that he felt as agitated as a swarm of bees. Any more of this jaw clamping and he'd give himself a headache.

"Are you hungry?" Felty asked.

"What?"

"Are you hungry?"

"I guess." Noah motioned toward his wagon. "But I brought a lunch."

Noah followed Felty to his wagon, where Felty reached into the applesauce box and pulled out one of Noah's five remaining jars. Felty unscrewed the ring, popped off the lid with his fingernails, and took a swig of applesauce like it was a glass of water. "Annie's applesauce is nice and runny. I always drink it instead of eating it with a spoon. It saves time."

He handed the jar to Noah who, after only a second's hesitation, took a drink and found the applesauce pleasantly sweet and decidedly lumpy. Not quite as smooth as water but tasty enough.

Felty took out a handkerchief and wiped his mouth. "Do you know the Kaufmanns?"

"Mose and Beverly? Jah. Mose is one of the ministers in the other district."

"Did you know their son died in a car accident last year because he was driving drunk?"

"Everybody knows it. I went to the funeral. They had a benefit supper for his widow and children."

"How do you think Mose felt when it happened?"

Noah shrugged. "I'm sure he grieved like any fater would grieve for a son."

Felty nodded sadly. "After that, did you keep your distance from Mose and his family?"

"Why would I do that?"

"What his son did was shameful, a humiliation to the family. Don't you think his family should have hung their heads in shame for what their son did?"

"Nae," Noah said. "They are members of the community. They have nothing to be ashamed of."

Felty took another drink of applesauce. "But do you think less of them for raising such a son?"

Noah blew out a puff of air as he realized where Felty was headed with his questions. "I don't think less of anybody."

"Amos Bieler's daughter ran off with an Englischer. Matthew Zook used drugs. What about their families? Should they be shunned?"

The ever-present shame overwhelmed him. He wished he'd never met Mandy Helmuth. Noah sank to the ground and sat with his back propped against the wagon wheel. "How much did she tell you?"

"Who? Anna?"

"Mandy. What did she tell you about my dat?"

Felty grunted and slowly sank to the ground. "A middle-aged man should not sit on the ground like this. I might not be able to get up." He scooted next to Noah against the wagon wheel. "Now, you were saying something about Mandy."

Noah didn't want to talk about it. He already knew the answer. "It wonders me what she told you about my dat."

"Mandy hasn't told me anything about your dat."

"Oh," Noah said. "I thought she would have told you everything."

Felty laid a hand on Noah's knee. "Noah, I see your dat

every Monday, so I suppose I know better than most what is going on, but it don't take a fool to see that your dat is struggling. It wasn't a secret the reason your mamm left him. The Plain people are the biggest gossips in the world. News spreads faster than dandelions on the wind."

Noah tightened the muscles of his jaw. "I know."

"When your mamm left, she asked the whole district to watch out for you. But you haven't wanted any watching out for."

Noah traced his finger in the dirt at his feet. "I had hoped everyone would forget about our troubles or think that things aren't so bad anymore. Most people have forgotten. If they hadn't, they wouldn't hire me to do jobs for them or treat me like I'm one of them."

"You are one of us."

"Not anymore. I'm not worthy to be one of you. My shame follows me like a bad smell."

The line between Felty's brows deepened into a furrow. "Noah, it's not your shame."

"Yes, it is. If I were a better son, my dat would stop drinking. If I were a better son, my mamm wouldn't have left. Noah Mischler can't cast the beam out of his own eye."

Felty folded his arms and shook his head. "Jesus chose all twelve of his apostles. Shouldn't he have been more careful about choosing his friends? Is it his fault that Judas betrayed him?"

"Of course not. It was Judas's own evil choice."

"It is not your fault that your fater drinks."

The hole in his heart widened until he could have parked a buggy in it. He bowed his head and rubbed his eyes so the tears wouldn't start. "After little Edi died, he came home with five bottles of whiskey. He went through the first four in a matter of days. Mamm hid the last one. When he ran out of liquor, he lay in bed sobbing. The whiskey seemed to calm him down, so I found the hidden bottle and gave it to him. I wanted the wailing to stop, but I did a horrible thing."

Felty nudged Noah with his elbow. "Noah, one bottle of whiskey didn't start your dat down that road. You were how old? Fifteen? Sixteen? You showed your dat some compassion in the only way you knew how."

"I lost Mamm because of it."

"How long are you going to punish yourself for the sins of your father? Your dat drove your mamm away, not you. You have been a gute son to him. There is no shame in that."

Noah took a deep breath, hoping it would ease the pain in his chest. It didn't. "I have tried to do everything right so people would forget about my dat. I think it was working. But now because of Mandy, everybody knows the worst."

Felty raised his finger in the air. "Now we come to it."

"To what?"

"The reason you're pushing Mandy away from you. She knows too much about you, and you're ashamed that she knows."

Noah turned away from Felty's perceptive gaze. "What I think about Mandy doesn't really matter. She'll be gone in a week."

"And you're not happy about it, no matter what you want to tell yourself."

"I'm more than happy to see her go." His heart flopped over in his chest. How could he convince Felty if he didn't really believe it himself? "Before Mandy came to town, nobody knew about the bars and the black eyes. My business was my business. Now I'll be the boy people talk about behind their hands at gatherings. People will think less of me because my fater has sunk so low."

Felty inclined his head. "Maybe they will. One thing's for sure. You're so afraid of the humiliation that you pretend there isn't a problem, and everybody pretends right along with you. This isn't Mandy's fault. You think you're gute at hiding the truth, when really, everybody knows about your dat. They just pretend not to know because talking about your dat makes you upset. But, Noah, the very people you are trying to hide from are the very people who could help you if you let them."

Bitterness filled his mouth. Shame threatened to engulf him like a dead tree in a raging forest fire. "I don't need any-body's help."

"Now you're being stubborn for the sake of being stub-born."

Fine. He'd hold on to his dignity any way he could. Mandy would never humiliate him again. That was all he cared.

"Ask God. He will show you the way if you let Him. Maybe He'll show you the way back to Mandy."

Anna stuck her head out of the door of the warehouse. "Noah, there you are." She tiptoed out the door and closed it behind her. "Remember that thing about chicken poop? It's getting bad in there. Would you mind taking a look at this egg sorter? I'm afraid it's an emergency."

Noah jumped to his feet even though he felt as heavy as a whole truck full of chicken poop. He didn't want to talk to Felty any more. He wanted to finish his work, go home, and be left alone.

He was halfway to the warehouse when Felty called him back. "I know you're irritated with me," he said, "but if you don't lend a hand, I'll never rise from the ground again."

Chapter Twenty

Chester wagged his tail so hard he fanned up a breeze. His enthusiastic greeting usually put Noah in a good mood, no matter how bad a day it had been, but he didn't think he'd be in a good mood ever again. "Hey, boy," Noah said, patting his dog on the head and hanging his jacket on the hook in the hall.

Shadows from the floor lamps danced on the walls as Noah stuck his head into the kitchen. Yost stood at the stove tending to something in their frying pan. He glanced at Noah. "It's fried chicken."

"You know how to make fried chicken?"

"There's chowchow, corn, and yams with brown sugar. It's almost ready."

Noah cocked an eyebrow. "You know how to make fried chicken?"

"I didn't make it."

"Kentucky Fried?"

Yost gave Noah a smug glance. "Nae, homemade. But I promised the cook that I would keep it a secret because she said you wouldn't want to eat it if you knew who cooked it."

Noah wanted to scowl. He opted for a disinterested

frown. She just couldn't resist interfering in his life, could she? "She's right," he said.

Yost grimaced. "You're not going to refuse the only decent meal we've had since I got here?"

"I said I didn't want to eat it. I didn't say I wouldn't eat it." The heavenly aroma made his mouth water. He'd be a fool to send it back where it came from, even if he didn't appreciate Mandy's interfering. "Why did she send it over? Does she think we don't know how to feed ourselves?"

"Yep, that's exactly what she thinks. I told her the sad story of everything I've eaten since I've been here. I think she was concerned I would die of starvation."

"That's Mandy. She thinks she has a right to help people even if they don't need it."

Yost eyed him as if he were crazy. "We need it. In case you haven't noticed, the only thing in the fridge is a half a gallon of milk, a bottle of horseradish, and a jar of pickles. She made dinner for her grandparents and for some boy. She said it was not trouble to make dinner for us."

No doubt she had been oozing with pity when she said it. "Felty tells me she was on the roof this morning."

"I told her you wouldn't like it, but she refused to get down."

Noah reminded himself that he didn't care if Mandy fell and broke her neck. If she was going to be stubborn, she could suffer the consequences. That didn't keep dread from creeping into his bones.

Yost turned off the stove, covered the pan, and moved it to a cool burner. "I thought I might as well put her to work if she was going to be so insistent about it. I hope you're not mad."

Of course he was mad. What could he do about it?

"She caught on real well to the nail gun, and she's a fast worker. Once she got the hang of things, she was a big help."

That first day on Huckleberry Hill, she'd been so eager to help with the stove. He wasn't sure why he had agreed to let her, unless it was those cute freckles that tempted him in a moment of weakness. She proved she could wield his tools with skill. He'd been completely impressed and completely undone.

"The only bad thing is that she talked and talked. She wanted to know my opinion on wedding plate colors. I don't know anything about wedding plate colors. Do you?"

Not much except that Mandy wanted her wedding plates to be pink and blue. The ache in his chest grew. Pink and blue would be real nice for a wedding.

"Did the wind give you trouble?"

"A little, but it died down in the afternoon. Mandy and I should be able to finish by Thursday."

Mandy and I. It sounded like they were a couple, a team. Friends. "Just don't tell her any secrets."

Yost retrieved a quart bottle of chowchow from the fridge and peered at Noah. "I know you're mad at her because she told her friend about Dat and the bar, but I think she's a wonderful-gute girl. She's prettier than a bluebird and very sweet. And she makes gute fried chicken. Is it worth rejecting her just because she gossips about people? All girls gossip."

"She knew how important the secret was to me. She wanted to hurt me. It wasn't harmless gossip."

"Still," Yost said, "if I didn't have a strict policy of not dating girls my brother has dated, I'd take her to a gathering. She has freckles."

Noah should have put his brother's mind at ease—*Oh, I don't care if you date Mandy Helmuth. She's nothing to me*—but he couldn't do it. He couldn't pretend that it didn't matter who Mandy went out with. There was only one boy he wanted Mandy to date, and he hated himself for wishing it.

He squared his shoulders and shook off his sour mood. Yost needed to stay away from Mandy for Yost's own protection. What secrets of his would she eventually spill?

"Would you do something for me, Yost?"

"Sure."

"Don't let Mandy on the roof anymore. She'll get hurt."

"I'll do what I can, but I won't promise anything."

"I guess she'll do precisely what she wants to. She always does."

Yost sighed and wiped his hands on a dish towel. "Did you fix the egg sorter?"

"Jah, and the Bielers' sewing machine and the Kings' water heater. On the way home I stopped by Baker's and looked at his car. He needs a new battery."

"You want to set the table?" Yost said, pulling two plates from the cupboard.

"Where's Dat?"

Yost slumped his shoulders and frowned. "Gone."

Noah understood the meaning behind the look. "Gone" could only mean one thing.

"I'm sorry, Noah."

"It's not your fault."

"This time I think it is. I tried to talk to him."

Noah clenched his teeth. "About what?"

"I told him he was ruining our lives with his drinking. I told him if he loved us kinner and Mamm that he'd give it up so we could come home."

Noah bowed his head. "Oh, Yost."

"I shouldn't have said anything, but I came home and he was just sitting there waiting for one of us to get home and cook him dinner. After working like a dog all day, I didn't think he deserved it, and I told him so. How can you stand it, Noah? It makes me sick."

"What did he do?"

Yost set the plates on the table. "He threw his kaffe mug at me and started yelling like I've never seen. Then he left."

"You shouldn't provoke him like that."

"I know," Yost said, "but I couldn't just go along like nothing was wrong. Everything is wrong, Noah. Everything."

"Nae, that's not true. I have things under control. I know how to handle him."

"You never really had control, Noah. You've got to hand it over to God."

Before Noah could give Yost the same arguments he'd given Mandy, he felt his cell phone vibrate in his back pocket. He pulled it out and looked at the screen. The call he was expecting, but three or four hours too early. His stomach dropped to the floor.

"Hullo," he said.

Yost riveted his attention to Noah's face. Noah must have been wearing a very dark look.

"Noah? It's Pete. Look, I'm real sorry. He was here before the shift change. I didn't realize how much he'd already had."

Noah's whole body felt heavy with the burden of holding up his dat. "Is he throwing pretzels?"

"You gotta believe I'm real sorry. He passed out on the floor. A couple of guys helped me haul him to the buggy. I'm real sorry, but if the authorities knew I'd served somebody enough drinks to pass out, they'd shut me down."

Noah's pulsed raced. "Where is my dat, Pete?"

"He's in his buggy. In the parking lot, but you gotta get him to the hospital. He's still breathing, but I don't know how much he had before I got here. That's the thing. People can die of alcohol poisoning."

"Call an ambulance."

"I'm real sorry, Noah. You gotta come down here and get

him. If the authorities found out, I'd be in big trouble. You understand, don't you?"

Noah pressed the END button and cut Pete off. His mind raced, and he felt sick to his stomach like he always did when Pete called. Except this time, he might be violently ill.

"Is it Dat?" Yost asked.

"He passed out in his buggy," Noah said.

Yost's eyes flashed with pain. The kind of pain Noah felt every time he made a trip into town to get his dat. "We need to go get him."

Noah nodded. Maybe he should have felt guilty about it, but in his head, he calculated how much an ambulance and a visit to the emergency room might cost. The numbers slipped from his brain as if they were grains of sand in a sieve. It didn't matter the price. He would not be responsible for his fater's death. He'd find a way to pay for it. "I'm going to call an ambulance."

"Why?"

"Pete says he could stop breathing."

Yost snatched his jacket from the hook next to Noah's. "You call. I'll hitch up the buggy. We can meet the ambulance at the hospital."

Noah braced a hand on Yost's shoulder. "It'll be ugly."

Yost wrapped his fingers around Noah's forearm and gave him a somber, no-nonsense look. "Maybe it's about time you shared some of the ugliness with me."

Chapter Twenty-One

Noah glanced up at the threatening sky and filled his lungs with the crisp air. A thunderstorm was rolling in from the west, sure as you're born. Good thing Yost had finished the roof yesterday. The Helmuths wouldn't need to worry about a leaky roof, and Noah wouldn't have to worry about Mandy breaking her neck.

He put Yost's suitcase in the trunk. "Have you got the money and the letter for Mamm?"

Yost nodded. "I still don't feel good about taking half the roof money. You did most of the work."

"It wouldn't have gotten finished without you."

"Me and Mandy."

"I knew you wouldn't be able to keep her on the ground," Noah said. "At least she won't have a reason to get on the roof again."

Yost smirked. "She was only up there those three days. And I kept a close eye."

"It's a real blessing that you came into town when you did. For more reasons than one."

Yost slung his arm around Noah's neck. "Don't forget the reason I came into town."

Noah ignored the stab of pain right between his ribs. "I should have written to you myself a long time ago."

"Why didn't you?"

"I guess I was afraid you wouldn't come." *You don't want to let people into your life. You'd rather run away.*

Noah clenched his teeth. If he could just get Mandy out of his head, he'd be able to think more clearly.

Yost put his other arm around Noah, and they squeezed the wind out of each other. "Is it ever going to change, Noah? Will Dat stop drinking? Will we ever be able to come back?"

Noah pinched his eyes shut. Dat was never going to change. And Noah would give his life over to his dat because he couldn't risk giving it over to anybody else. Trusting your heart to another person hurt too much. He didn't need or want it.

"He's not drinking as much as three years ago. It's been better lately."

Yost grunted derisively. "Better? I was at the hospital, Noah. Is that what 'better' looks like?"

Noah turned his face from his brother. He pictured his dat, pale and delirious, lying in that hospital bed with an oxygen mask over his face and formidable tubes and wires attached to his body. The doctor had warned Noah that if his dat didn't stop drinking, there'd be more terrifying visits to the emergency room. More bills to pay. More shame to bear.

Noah thanked the Lord that no one from the community had seen them. Mandy hadn't appeared out of nowhere to stick her nose into his business. All in all, it had turned out okay. Noah rubbed his eyelid, where his black eye was just a memory. Was he imagining things, or did he always feel better with Mandy's nose in his business? He diverted his thoughts away from that place in his head where Mandy lingered. The ache was unbearable.

"We're going to be okay," Noah finally said. "From now

on, I'll watch him more carefully. Dat won't let it go that far again. He likes the hospital less than I do."

Yost didn't look convinced, but he didn't press the issue. There was nothing he could do about it anyway. Surely it was obvious to him that the answer was no. He and Mamm and the siblings were never going to be able to come back.

Noah pulled Yost in for one more bone-crushing bear hug. "I love you, broodah."

"I'll come in January and bring Lisa."

"I'd like that," Noah said. A visit would be welcome after another lonely and miserable Christmas. And a lonely and miserable autumn, made extra miserable by the hole in his heart left by Mandy Helmuth.

Yost climbed in the passenger seat. Noah went to the driver's side of the car and handed Peggy some money.

"Thanks, Noah," Peggy said, stuffing the cash into her purse as if she were shoving trash into the garbage can.

"Thanks for taking my brother to the bus."

She smiled. "Call me anytime. Ralph is making me crazy." Ralph was Peggy's husband, and he'd just retired. Word was that he dogged Peggy's every step during the day because he didn't know what to do with all his free time.

Peggy draped her arm across the steering wheel and furrowed her brow. "How's your dat doing?"

Noah felt his shoulders tense. What did Peggy care about his dat? What did she know about his dat? "He's fine. He's been making lots of baskets for the gift shop in Green Bay."

"I love those baskets," Peggy said. "I've got four of them at home yet." She fiddled with the keys in her hand. "I don't mean to pry or anything. I was just wondering how he's been doing since that night at the bar a couple of weeks ago. My dad struggled with the bottle. I know how hard it is."

"It's real hard," Yost said.

Noah pushed the words from between his clenched teeth. "Mandy told you about that?"

"Told me? I was there. The three of us saw it. I took Kristina home while Mandy stayed to help."

Noah didn't mean to stutter, but his surprise rendered speech nearly impossible. "Kri . . . Kristina was with you?"

"We drove by just as you came out of the bar with your dat. We saw him sock you in the mouth. I haven't told a soul." She reached out of the car and placed a hand on his arm. "As far as I know, nobody else saw but us, and Mandy made Kristina promise not to tell anybody what we'd seen. I'm sorry if I upset you. I just hope the best for your dat."

The world swirled around his head like a swarm of yellow jackets, only louder. Kristina knew about the night at the bar because she'd been there, not because Mandy had told her. Mandy hadn't broken her promise. She hadn't betrayed his trust.

He felt dizzy with relief.

He felt sick with remorse.

He'd chastised her, yelled at her, rejected her for something she hadn't done. He was a fool. A stupid, self-righteous, indignant fool who couldn't see past his own troubles. The world did not revolve around him, as he sometimes behaved like it did.

He couldn't form a reply to what Peggy had told him. He merely stepped away from the car and raised his arm in the air in what passed for a wave. He didn't even see them leave. His sight was already turned inward to the small pebble that was his heart. The thought that he might have already lost Mandy shattered the pebble into a thousand pieces, sending shards of stone into his chest and making his bones ache.

He had to apologize.

Now.

It had been a simple, stupid mistake. Would she forgive him? Would she let him back into her heart? Hope spread through his veins like warm honey. He loved her. Surely she wouldn't reject that.

He marched into the house with a greater sense of purpose than he'd ever felt. He'd need something spectacularly delicious to soften her up.

What could he do with half a gallon of milk and a jar of pickles?

Chapter Twenty-Two

As far as Mandy could tell, there was only one leak in the barn roof, and it appeared almost directly over her head. She shifted her milking stool to the right so she wouldn't get dripped on and kept right on milking. Dawdi might need to hire Noah to fix the barn roof next. He would probably be glad for the work. Her heart felt as heavy as a bucket of milk. He'd be glad for the work after Thursday, when Mandy wouldn't be here to bother him.

With only the sounds of the rhythmic ping-ping of the milk in the bucket and the occasional swish of Iris's tail, the inside of the barn seemed eerily quiet buried beneath the sound of the rain pounding on the roof outside. Good thing she'd brought the umbrella. She'd be soaked to the skin if she tried to make it back to the house without one.

Thunder rumbled in the distance, and Iris took a stuttering step forward. She turned her head as if to figure out what Mandy was doing back there. Mandy put a comforting hand on Iris's belly and cooed until Iris stopped fussing.

Mandy usually found the sound of rain comforting. Like a river tripping against the boulders or waves lapping against the shore at the lake, there was something peaceful about the sound of rushing water. But today, drops pelting the roof only reminded her of the sound of Noah's work boots clonking overhead as he had worked on Mammi and Dawdi's roof.

She sniffed and stubbornly blinked back a delinquent tear that threatened to escape. Noah didn't love her, didn't trust her. He didn't even particularly like her. She shouldn't waste one drop of water on that boy.

She finished with the milking and let Iris loose. Mandy's breath hung in the moist, pungent air of the barn as she opened her umbrella, tightened her coat around her, and picked up her bucket of milk. She'd miss Bonduel more than she'd ever admit to Mammi. She had many relatives here whom she loved dearly, as well as her best friend Kristina. And after a gute long time, she'd even fondly remember her time with Noah, even though he hadn't turned out to be the boy she'd thought he was. Even though he'd twisted her heart beyond recognition when she'd only wanted to help.

Before she could reach the handle, the door of the barn opened a crack. Her heart banged against her chest as Noah stuck his head inside. Water dripped off his hat, and his shirt looked to be soaked through.

She exhaled slowly. Didn't he know what an umbrella was? "You're going to catch your death of cold," she said.

Holding a plastic grocery bag in one hand, he slid into the barn, shut the door, and took off his hat. He hung it on a nail that already held a gute piece of rope and a horse bridle. He glanced at her tentatively as he wiped some of the moisture from his face with his equally wet sleeve.

Instinctively, she took a step back. She never wanted to be caught close to Noah Mischler again. "What are you doing here?"

He winced. She must have sounded as wounded as she felt. "Oh. Mandy . . . I'm really . . . Oh sis yuscht, I'm really sorry."

He might not have liked her very much, but the pain in his brown eyes was real enough. She resisted the urge to try to fix it for him, but she softened her expression, put down her bucket of milk, and collapsed her umbrella as a sign that she was at least willing to remain in the barn while he explained himself. She could always bolt if he tried to make her feel guilty.

He held out the bag, probably wanting her to come closer to take it so he wouldn't have to strain his throat when he yelled at her. "I made these for you."

"Why?"

His eyes pleaded with her. "To tell you I'm sorry about what I said."

She was tempted to raise an eyebrow as a sign that she didn't believe him, but it wasn't in her heart to be cynical. And it certainly wasn't in her heart to hurt him, though surely it would be impossible to do that, knowing how he felt about her. She finally gave in and took the bag. She let it dangle from her fingers as if she couldn't have cared less what was inside. "It doesn't matter, Noah. I'll be gone in less than a week."

He clenched his jaw. "I don't want you to go."

"I've done nothing but bring you trouble. You told me so yourself." *Ach, du lieva.* She couldn't keep the bitterness from her voice.

He closed his eyes and grimaced, as if her words had slapped him in the face. "Mandy, I made some assumptions I shouldn't have. Kristina told me she knew about that night at the bar. I thought you had broken your promise and told her about it. Just like you told her about our kissing."

A dull throbbing started behind her eyes. "You must think very badly of me to believe I would break a promise like that."

"Nae. I was devastated to think that you, of all people, would do that. It hurt so bad because of how I feel about you."

"How you feel about me," she repeated, her voice quivering. He didn't love her, and she would be a fool to let herself believe that he did.

"Can you blame me for jumping to conclusions? Ever since I met you, I've been acutely aware of the shame I bear because of my dat. What Kristina told me was just one more shovelful of dirt on my head. I wasn't thinking clearly. You told her about the kiss. It wasn't much of a leap to believe you told her about the night at the bar."

"So it is my fault once again."

"That's not what I mean. I get defensive when it comes to my dat. It's not your fault." He took three steps closer and reached out his free hand to her. She ignored it. The look on his face was pure agony. "Mandy," he said, in a whisper barely audible above the sound of the rain falling outside. "Mandy, please forgive me. That day, the things I said, I pushed you away. Please forgive me. I love you."

There they were. The words she would have given anything to hear a few days ago. She didn't believe them, but the knowledge that he believed made it harder to do what she knew she had to do.

Mandy pursed her lips to keep the memory of his kisses from making her lips tingle. "Yost told me about the hospital," she said.

Noah shoved his fingers through his damp hair. "I told him not to say anything. We agreed it would be better for Dat."

"How is he feeling?"

"He's fine. We'd be fine, if . . ."

"If people would just leave you alone."

Understanding flashed on his face, and his gaze pierced hers. "I don't mean that," he murmured.

"Yost didn't blab your dat's troubles to the community, if that's what you're worried about. He thought that since I am close to your family, I might want to know." She exhaled a deep breath and stifled the sob that wanted to come with it.

"But he doesn't know that I'm *not* close to the family. You won't let me get within a mile of your problems. You're so afraid of being hurt and embarrassed that you've built a very thick wall around yourself and won't let anyone in, even the girl you claim to love."

"I do love you, Mandy. It's just that I don't want you to suffer too."

"Nae. It's that you don't want to compile your shame. Not even for me." He started to protest, and she turned her face from him. "Yost told me some wonderful things about your mamm. She is an amazing quilter. Her quilts sell for hundreds of dollars. And she loves flowers."

"I know."

"She planted a half acre of roses when she lived here. Pink are her favorite. She once sewed your dat a whole new shirt in two hours, and she can quote passages of scripture from memory. She must be an wonderful-gute mamm."

Noah slumped his shoulders. "She is."

"But you kept her from me. You're so ashamed, you didn't want me to know anything. Not even that your dat used to take you and Yost ice fishing, or that he never failed to tell your mamm and Lisa they were beautiful every day for as long as you can remember."

Noah gazed at her resentfully. "Talking about it won't make my dat the man he used to be."

"But it would make you vulnerable. You close yourself off to me because you would do anything to avoid looking weak or pitiful. Talking to Yost made me realize something. You made me feel guilty for wanting to be a part of your life. For caring." The tears couldn't be stopped now. "Maybe I am too nosy, but maybe I wanted to share your life. Maybe I pushed harder because I wanted you to let me in. But I can't get in. You've locked that door and thrown away the key."

"If I show you who I really am, you'll stomp all over my heart."

She felt as if she'd been slammed against a wall. He was so wrapped up in himself that he refused to give her the gift of his trust. He loved his safe, private misery more than he would ever love her. "Maybe you're right. Nothing is worth the risk of getting your heart stomped."

He held out his hands to her, pleading with his eyes, his face, his whole body. "Mandy, please, you don't understand."

If she lingered any longer, she'd melt into a quivering mass of tears and sobs. "I'm sorry, Noah. I want someone who'll give me his whole heart, not just the safe, convenient part of it. I deserve to be loved that way."

Clutching his bag of food to her chest, she bolted out of the barn, leaving her umbrella and her heart behind. Soon her weeping would become uncontrollable. Better to do that in the privacy of her own bedroom. She ran through the torrential rain, made it into the house, and shut herself in her room. Sniffling back the tears, she opened Noah's carefully wrapped tinfoil package to find six warm, brown circles. Furrowing her brow, she picked one up and took a bite.

Fried pickles.

Delicious.

He hadn't had the time, or probably the money, to go to the store, so he'd used his imagination with what he had on hand. She'd definitely miss Noah's creative food. And his solid arms and honey-colored hair. And the smile that could charm the wings off the bumblebees and make her heart leap out of her chest. She'd be very sorry to never see a smile like that again.

The tears came like a cloudburst. She collapsed across her bed, wet clothes and all, and cried herself into numbness.

Chapter Twenty-Three

Noah couldn't remember how he got home. Maybe the horse knew the way and, eager to be out of the rain, had trotted home without any direction from Noah. It didn't matter that he'd taken the enclosed buggy; just walking from the buggy to Felty's barn and back again had been enough to soak Noah clear through. He drove down the back lane and unhitched the buggy in the relentless rain, then coaxed the horse to the shelter that did duty as a barn. The wooden structure was more like a shed, but it kept the rain and snow off his two horses and provided shade in the summer and a little warmth in the winter.

Someday he'd have enough money to build a proper barn, with a space for the horses and maybe a cow, plus all his tools. He'd start a business from that barn, and people would come to him when they wanted something fixed. Someday. When his dat stopped drinking and there were funds in his empty savings account.

Noah trudged out of the shed and stood gazing out at the road, letting the icy rain pelt his back and shoulders. Mamm would scold him, tell him to get inside before he caught his death of cold. Mandy would have ushered him into the house and brewed him a steaming mug of chamomile tea to ward off infection or made him a mustard plaster and insisted he wear it for three days. She was bossy like that, always thinking she knew what was best for him.

He loved that about her.

Well, it was better this way. Wasn't it? He had lost Mandy, but with her gone, he'd be able to retreat back into his private life, never living in fear that his secrets would be found out, never having to face the debilitating shame that followed him like a shadow.

It was good she was out of his life. She wanted a part of him that no one was ever going to get.

He swiped his hand down the side of his face and shook his head to banish Mandy from his mind. When he thought about her, the dull ache in his chest would flare into bitter, raw pain. He could only take so much.

Cold and weary, inside and out, he bowed his head and tried to remember what it felt like to be happy, what it felt like to breathe without the weight of the world pressing on his chest. He'd lost Mandy, and much as he wanted to deny it, he knew he'd never breathe properly again.

A light glowed inside the house. Dat was awake. He should be. It was almost dinnertime.

Noah wanted to walk into that house less than he wanted just about anything. He hated seeing his dat so broken, hated the burden of giving his dat all of himself until Noah Mischler had nearly ceased to exist. Hated to be reminded of what he had lost.

He slogged around to the front and opened the door. The smell of batter, deep-fat fried, accosted him. He'd made Mandy fried pickles. There wasn't a thing left in the fridge. Noah pulled off his soggy boots just inside the door. He'd change into dry clothes before fixing dinner.

Dat sat at the table with a beer can in his hand. How had he gotten that? He didn't look particularly drunk, but he was brooding. Tears trickled from his red-rimmed eyes.

"What going on, Dat?" Noah asked, moving slowly into the kitchen as if he were tiptoeing around a sleeping bear.

"Yost left me a note. He's gone."

"That's right. He could only stay for a week. He left this morning."

Noah jumped as Dat brought his fist down hard on the table, making the beer can bobble as if it would tip over. "What did you say to him?"

Dread pulsed through his veins. "About what, Dat?"

Dat sprang to his feet, sending his chair crashing to the floor behind him. He snatched a wadded piece of paper from the table and held it up like a torch. "He told me he'd only come back if I stopped drinking. He told me to be a man, as if I'm not his fater. As if I'm not the man who brought him into this world."

Noah had never seen Dat this angry without being staggeringly drunk. Dat, usually so meek and contrite, seemed to grow claws and fangs as he stood there, scowling at Noah with hatred flashing in his eyes.

"You are his fater. And he loves you."

Dat scowled and hurled his wadded note at Noah. It rolled near his feet. "What did you tell him?"

"Nothing, Dat. Let me fix you something to eat." He didn't mention that there was nothing in the fridge.

In one swift movement, Dat charged at him and slammed him backward against the front door. Noah grunted in pain as his head hit the wood with stunning force. "What did you say to him?"

Breathless and dizzy, Noah tried to focus as his dat pinned him against the door with his big hands. Noah was stronger. He could have laid his dat flat with a hard fist to the chin, but he had never hit anyone before, not even his dat when he was in a drunken rage. He was a Christian, and Jesus said to turn the other cheek. Jesus said, "Blessed are the peacemakers." What good was a vow of nonviolence if he didn't keep it?

"You drove Yost away," Dat yelled. "Just like you drove away your mother." Before Noah could dodge it, Dat drew back his hand and punched Noah in the face.

Pain exploded inside his head, and he could taste the salty blood that seemed to fill his mouth. He held his breath as bits of light flashed in front of his eyes.

"She's gone, Noah. She's gone." Dat swung his fist again but with less force this time.

Heartbroken and reeling, Noah grabbed his dat's wrists and held him back with an iron grip. His dat had never struck out at him when he was sober. "Please don't hurt me, Dat. I'm your son. I love you."

Dat seemed snap out of whatever violent mood had taken control of him. Taking two steps back, he looked at his hands as if they were foreign objects he'd never seen before.

"This isn't who you are," Noah said breathlessly. "This isn't who you are."

With horror written all over his face, Dat stumbled backward and managed to find a chair. He sat, buried his face in his hands, and began to weep. "I'm sorry, Noah," he sobbed. "I'm so sorry."

With an ache in his chest as wide as the sky, Noah found a dish towel to mop up the blood dripping from his mouth. He sat down next to his dat and gently massaged his jaw. Lord willing, nothing was broken even though it hurt something wonderful. Where was Mandy when he needed a cold potato?

They sat in silence until, after a few minutes, Dat cried himself out and the dish towel was stained with blood. Dat lifted his head, and his frown deepened as he examined Noah's face. "I'll get you some ice." He found a tray of ice in the freezer, dumped some of it into another dish towel, and handed it to Noah. "That one girl cut you some potato, but we're out. Whatever happened to her anyway? We never see her anymore."

Noah cleared his throat. "She's leaving for Ohio next week."

Dat sat down. "Just like your mamm left me." He waved his hand as if he were swatting a fly. "You and I, we don't need them. We're doing just fine the way we are. We don't need any of them."

That sounded like something Noah often told himself. "Nae, we don't," Noah murmured, placing the ice-cold towel on his face as he involuntarily tensed. Every muscle, every sinew, every tendon in his body told him it was a lie.

He closed his eyes and pleaded silently with God. *Heavenly Father, I'm stubborn and frightened and proud. My pride has kept Your grace from finding place in my heart. I'll do anything You require of me, but please, give me the courage I need to travel the road. I need You. Please, show me the way.*

Dat took another swig of beer. "If Rosie won't do what God wants her to do and come home, then we don't need her."

Noah lowered his eyes. It wasn't Mamm who was resisting God's will. God had given Dat plenty of chances. He simply refused to take them.

Noah caught his breath. Was he so shortsighted that he could see Dat's stiff-neckedness and not his own? God had already shown him the path and given him a nudge, but he had been too much of a coward to take the first steps.

How could he doubt that God had sent Mandy into his life? How likely was it that a girl from Charm and a boy from Bonduel would meet by coincidence? And yet, he'd squandered the gift. So afraid to let anybody into his heart, he'd held back, and she had sensed it. His fear of being humiliated had paralyzed him, and he'd lost Mandy because of it.

A girl like Mandy, with so much love to give, wouldn't be content with just a piece of him. She deserved his whole heart, his whole life, even the parts he kept carefully hidden. She deserved his unconditional faith. If he loved her, then he would entrust the deepest parts of his heart to her, even though it would give her the power to crush him.

He hadn't believed in the goodness of her heart or the power of her love. No wonder she had rejected him.

Noah gazed around the room. His dat sat at the table clutching a can of beer, the cupboards were bare, the fridge was empty, and he cradled a blood-soaked dish towel in his hand. His jaw throbbed painfully, and his heart ached as if he'd been impaled by a nail gun.

He didn't want to live like this anymore. No matter the consequences, he wanted Mandy. He *needed* Mandy.

Heavenly Father, I'm ready to open my heart.

He pressed against the gaping hole in his chest. Even though he had burned all his bridges with Mandy, he was strong. He would swim the divide between them. He would find the courage to win her.

No matter how terrified he was.

Chapter Twenty-Four

Mandy slumped in her chair, exhausted from trying to pretend that she was having fun at her own party. Truth be told, she wanted to shut herself in her room and wait for Peggy to take her to the bus station. She'd already packed her small suitcase. It sat expectantly on her bed with her coat and black bonnet, ready for the trip back to Charm tomorrow. The bus left at 11:10 in the morning. She wished she was already home.

The great room teemed with bodies. Mammi had ended up inviting twenty-two young people to the party. She had originally invited sixteen boys and no girls, plus Mandy's cousin Titus, who didn't count as a prospective husband. Mandy had talked Mammi into inviting at least a few other girls. "I can't marry all of them, Mammi, and the boys will get bored with only one girl to flirt with."

To Mandy's great relief, Mammi had agreed, albeit reluctantly, to pick out a few girls to attend Mandy's going-away party. She'd invited Kristina, Dori Rose, and the three Sensenig sisters. Katie Sensenig was well into her thirties, but Mammi couldn't be talked into inviting a wider selection of girls. She wanted to be sure that Mandy got her first pick of the boys, no matter what.

No matter that she'd met them all before and wasn't interested in a single one. No matter that the boy she wanted wasn't even at the party. He didn't dare go to parties. Too many people asked too many questions he didn't like to answer.

Mandy chastised herself for letting Noah Mischler creep into her thoughts when she still needed to muster a few smiles before the party ended.

The ending couldn't come soon enough.

Kristina sat next to Mandy, energetically punching buttons on her phone. Periodically, she would giggle hysterically and steal a glance at Davy Burkholder, who sat across the room on the sofa texting her back. Why they couldn't have a conversation like normal people was beyond Mandy's ability to comprehend. Still, they seemed to be enjoying themselves immensely. Who was Mandy to judge? It wondered her what would become of their relationship when one of them got baptized and was forced to give up the cell phone. Would they get bored with each other? Would they have anything to say face-to-face?

Mandy and the rest of die youngie were playing a wild and perilous game called Do You Like Your Neighbor. Dawdi had pulled out all the folding chairs they owned, plus all the chairs from around the table for the game. Everyone sat in a circle in the great room while one person stood in the center of the group.

Freeman Kiem happened to be in the center at the moment. He approached Arie Sensenig and asked, "Do you like your neighbor?"

Arie grinned as her eyes darted around the room. "Nae," she said, putting the rest of the players on alert.

"Whose neighbors do you like?" Freeman asked.

Arie grinned wider and batted her eyelashes. "I like Paul's neighbors."

The boys sitting on either side of Paul and the two people sitting on either side of Arie leaped to their feet. The object was to trade places with the neighbors without losing your seat. As soon as Titus gave up his chair, Freeman slipped into it. Benji Troyer, one of Paul's neighbors, ran as fast as he could, but Luke Miller beat him to the other available chair next to Arie. Benji was left standing in the middle while everyone else laughed at his expense.

Benji grinned and groaned. "Luke, you stole my seat." He walked up to Dori Rose, who exploded into a fit of giggles before Benji even asked her the question. "Do you like your neighbor?"

Dori paused for dramatic effect. "Yes!" she squealed.

The entire room seemed to erupt as everyone was required to jump up and find another seat. It was Musical Chairs times ten. Mammi and Dawdi did not play this game. One of them would have broken a hip. Instead, they stood in the kitchen watching the mayhem with amusement.

Mandy avoided the chaos by sliding into the seat next to hers, which was technically against the rules, but she didn't have the heart or the energy to actually stand up and scramble for a different seat. Titus, who seemed to like to run around and around just for the sake of running, ended up in the middle.

Laughter skipped through the room as the game players settled into their seats. At least everyone else was having a gute time at her farewell party. Hopefully, Mammi wouldn't even notice how miserable Mandy was. She felt as if gloom hovered over her like a cloud of gnats. It was all she could do to keep from ruining the night for everyone else with her dismal disposition.

They heard a knock, and Mandy felt nearly dizzy with surprise as Noah Mischler let himself into the house.

Longing and dread warred with each other inside her head. He was so handsome, so tall and muscular, she could stare at him for hours. But if he said one word to her, she'd disintegrate into a soggy pile of tears and hankies. Would it be too obvious if she sprinted to her bedroom with a sob on her lips?

"Noah!" seven or eight of the boys called at once. Oh yes. The whole community adored Noah. He was everybody's favorite person because he was smart and could fix anything and didn't have a selfish bone in his whole body.

When she dared a glance at his face, her heart sank. She tried to talk herself out of caring, but it was no use. Noah sported large purple bruises around his mouth. They looked a few days old, but were still clearly visible. She blinked back the tears.

The corner of Noah's mouth curled slightly and his gaze landed on Mandy, piercing through her skull and compelling her to look away. She wished she could swat his gaze away like a fly. Why was he looking at her like that? Why had he even come? He hated parties, and a party where Mandy Helmuth was in attendance was to be avoided at all costs. Especially with a battered face.

"Noah, it's so gute to see you," Dawdi said, stepping forward to take Noah's hand and slap him on the back. If only Dawdi knew that Noah was responsible for the dull, throbbing ache that was Mandy's constant companion, he wouldn't have been so friendly.

At least Mammi didn't gush. She had no inkling that Mandy and Noah meant anything to each other. Mandy sniffed and studied her fingernails. They *didn't* mean anything to each other. There was nothing for Mammi to see. "Cum reu, Noah," Mammi said. "Pull a chair into the circle. They seem to be playing some sort of game."

Nobody said anything about the bruises as Noah took a few hesitant steps closer.

"Jah, Noah," Titus said. "Come play."

Noah took off his hat and fingered the brim. He shuffled his feet nervously as if deciding whether he should stay. "What are you playing?" he said.

"Do You Like Your Neighbor," Titus said. "Have you played before?"

Noah swallowed hard, as if forcing down his fear, and pulled the last chair from under the table. Paul and Melvin made room for his chair between them. "I know how to play."

Mandy folded her arms and did her best not to stare. If Noah could be comfortable being in the same room with her, then she could endure being in the same room with him. Maybe he'd already moved on without her. Maybe he didn't care anymore.

She bit her tongue to keep from losing her composure and reminded herself that this was the way she had wanted it. She deserved to be loved with Noah's whole heart, not merely what he was willing to share with her.

Titus wasted no time in strutting up to Noah. "Noah, do you like your neighbor?"

Noah's gaze traveled around the circle, alighting on hers and holding her captive with the pain and hope she saw there. Her heart did a cartwheel and three backflips.

Answer the question, Noah. Answer the question and leave me be.

"Yes," he finally said.

The room erupted again as people jumped to their feet and scrambled for a free chair. Mandy didn't move. She'd lost the strength in her limbs. If she was lucky, they'd banish her from the game for cheating.

When the dust settled, Noah stood in the middle of the circle slowly turning around as if to make sure everyone else had a seat. For such a crazy game, he appeared as calm as a lake on a mild summer morning.

He stood in silence for a moment, glancing at Mandy, glancing away. His breathing grew heavy as he pressed his lips into a rigid line and slid his hand down the side of his face.

"Come on, Noah," Titus said. "Pick somebody else."

With his feet securely planted, Noah turned his head in Titus's direction. "Can I interrupt the game for a minute?"

"Do you want to sing us a song?" Freeman asked, chuckling as he balanced himself on the two back legs of his chair.

Noah cracked a smile and turned back to face Mandy again. "Nae. I need . . . I just need to . . . tell you something. Can you spare a few minutes?"

Everyone nodded, curious as to what could be so important that he would interrupt the game. Everyone except Mandy, Kristina, and Davy. Kristina and Davy were glued to their phones. Mandy didn't breathe for fear of upsetting some sort of delicate balance.

Noah took a deep breath and cleared his throat. "Most of you know that my dat has been drinking ever since my sister Edi died. I appreciate all of you for pretending that nothing is wrong, for not treating me any differently than you would the bishop's son or daughter. I . . . I want to thank you for that. For sparing my feelings. For trying to protect me. You know how ashamed I am about it."

Everyone froze as if time had stopped. No one seemed to even be breathing. Mandy certainly wasn't.

"But most of you don't know how bad it's gotten for us. A week ago last Tuesday, my dat and my brother Yost had a fight about my dat's drinking. Yost was brave enough to confront him about it. I never am." He pinned Mandy with an intense gaze. "I've been a coward." He bowed his head and concentrated his gaze at the foot of Mammi's rocker. "After the fight, Dat got drunk and ended up in the hospital with alcohol poisoning."

Katie Sensenig gasped.

"He's okay." Noah brushed his hand across his mouth. "But on Friday he was so mad, he punched me in the face. He's done it before. A couple of weeks ago he gave me a black eye." He glanced at Mandy again, and the tenderness in his eyes stole her senses. "Mandy helped me hide it. She'll never know how grateful I was for that."

Breathlessly, Mandy stared at him. What was he doing? What gave him the courage to reveal his most horrible secrets?

"I don't say this to speak ill of my dat. He's had a hard time of it. Our whole family has. I've been hiding from everyone because I'm so ashamed."

"You don't have anything to be ashamed of," Freeman Kiem murmured.

Noah laid a hand on Freeman's shoulder. "Denki for saying that. But I should be ashamed. Ashamed that I haven't trusted any of you enough to share my burden. I feared you'd all turn against me."

Freeman shook his head. "We would never do that."

Noah looked at the eyes glued to his. "If any of you are uncomfortable being around me, I understand. I know that some of your parents won't want you to associate with me. I understand that also. But I'm hoping that you will help me with this burden. I'm tired, so tired, of carrying it myself."

Mandy couldn't help the tears that trickled down her face. *Noah, I want to help you carry this. Will you let me?*

Melvin Lambright spoke up. "What can we do?"

"I need to talk about it. I need you to ask me how I'm doing. I don't want anyone to tiptoe around the subject anymore. Denying that it's happening only gives it more power."

Several of die youngie nodded their agreement.

He turned his eyes to her again. "Mandy helped me find a counselor," he said, "and I've started going to meetings of Adult Children of Alcoholics in Green Bay. The bishop has approved it."

His brief glance told her he'd done this because of her. Because he didn't want to lose her. Because he loved her. An overwhelming feeling of tenderness spread through her body and pulsed in her veins. He had braved the shame and the humiliation for her. The thought took her breath away.

"Most of all, I need your prayers."

"We've already been doing that," Dawdi said.

Noah nodded. "And I've felt them. I haven't always listened to God's guidance, but I know He's tried to get through to me. It will be the hardest thing I've ever done, but I'm going to stop enabling my dat—that's a new word I learned in my first meeting. I've moved in with my horses. I might get stepped on, but at least I won't get hit."

Titus, her loveable, heart-of-gold cousin, stood up. "You're not going to stay in that shed all winter. Come home with me. You can have Ben's old room."

Mandy wanted to lay thirty wet kisses on Titus's face.

Noah shook his head. "I don't want to impose."

Titus hooked an arm around Noah's neck. "My mamm will be wonderful angry if you don't come. And you don't want to see it when she gets angry."

The gesture was too much for Noah. He let out a muffled sob and jabbed at the tears in his eyes. "Okay," he managed to say before speech became impossible. He tugged Titus in for a sturdy hug.

After a minute, Titus struggled free. "I'm too scrawny. You'll cut off my circulation."

Noah was soon surrounded by the boys who thought so highly of him, offering him support, housing, and groceries if he needed them.

Mandy stayed firmly rooted in her seat. Would she float off the ground if she tried to stand? Or maybe trip all over her shaky legs and end up face-first on Mammi's rag rug?

It appeared that the game was over. Kristina scooted next to Mandy. "Noah will never get a wife now. I tried to warn him. He lost his chance with me when he refused to answer my texts." She opened her phone and pumped her eyebrows up and down. "Davy Burkholder likes it when I text."

Mandy could barely keep a fraction of her attention focused on Kristina. She lost sight of Noah as more and more of the boys at her farewell party wanted to shake his hand and offer support. Mandy would have liked to kiss him, but she didn't think she was going to get her wish anytime soon.

Kristina's phone vibrated with another text. She opened it and gave a puzzled squeak. "Wha—what does this mean?"

She showed Mandy the screen. *My favorite color is brown, like chocolate.*

"I think it means Davy likes chocolate."

Kristina narrowed her eyes. "Nae. It's from Noah."

Another text showed up on her screen. Mandy eagerly grabbed the phone without even asking.

"Hey," Kristina said. "What if it's from Davy?"

When I was a little boy, I used to be scared of the dark. My mamm made me a stuffed bear, and my dat sang me to sleep every night.

Her heart beat double-time as she glanced in Noah's direction. She could see him in the midst of the surrounding crowd. He looked up from his phone and searched her face, all the while keeping up a conversation with Paul and Titus.

The phone vibrated again. *When Edi died, my mamm stayed in bed for a week, and my dat didn't utter a word to anyone. I felt guilty that I was still able to function. I made grilled cheese for the kinner every day until Mamm was on her feet again.*

Mandy sighed quietly, and her heart broke for the Mischlers all over again. She couldn't imagine the pain of losing a child.

Bursting with indignation, Kristina grabbed her phone

from Mandy's hand. "It's my phone, Mandy. Why is he texting all that stuff?"

Mandy felt as light as a feather. "He wants to tell me about his family."

Kristina snapped her phone shut and inclined her head in his direction. "Then go talk to him. He shouldn't be using up all my texts." This from a girl who texted Davy Burkholder even if he was sitting next to her.

Kristina's phone vibrated again. She lifted her eyes to the sky in exasperation. "There he goes again." She opened her phone and handed it to Mandy. "It's for you."

I'd do anything if you'd stay another week.

Mandy clutched the phone to her chest and found him in the crowd again. "You would?" she mouthed.

He nodded. Her heart flipped around like a circus tumbler.

He punched the buttons on his phone again. Kristina's phone vibrated.

I'd do anything if you'd stay forever.

Her eyes shot to his face. He gazed at her with so much love, she thought she might overflow with pure joy.

Kristina snatched her phone from Mandy's grasp.

"Krissy, please, I need to see it."

Kristina expelled every bit of oxygen from her lungs in an effort to communicate to Mandy how inconvenienced she was. With irritation written all over her face, she opened her phone and read Noah's text.

Her demeanor transformed instantly. Gasping, she bloomed into a smile that took over her whole face. She snatched Mandy's hand. "Mandy," she said, in what she must have thought passed for a whisper. "Is he asking you to marry him?"

Mandy put her finger to her lips. "I . . . I don't know."

Kristina sighed as if she'd held it in for ever so long. "How romantic. That's how I want a boy to ask me. Over text, like he just can't wait to do it in person." She clutched her phone in both her hands. "Oh, Mandy. He's so handsome. Now that I've found the only man I'll ever love, I want you to find happiness too. And if you're really set on Noah, I won't object. He doesn't deserve you, but what girl ever thinks of that when she falls in love with somebody."

Mandy smiled warmly. "Denki, Krissy. I hope you know that I never meant to hurt you. Noah and I just . . . happened."

She patted Mandy's arm. "I know. Just like me and Davy. There's no stopping true love."

Mandy and Noah met eyes. He stared at her doubtfully before resorting to his phone to communicate.

Will you marry me?

Mandy felt breathless and light as her heart thumped an uneven rhythm. She wanted to push all the boys aside and throw herself into his arms so he could kiss her with abandon. Instead, she handed Kristina the phone. "Would you text Noah something for me? I don't know how to do it."

"Okay," said Kristina. "But then you've got to promise I can have my phone back. Davy is getting lonely."

"It will be the last one," Mandy said. "Are you ready?"

"Ready."

Noah didn't take his eyes from her face as she quietly dictated her message to Kristina. "Text him this: *A boy should not ask a girl to marry him in a text message. I know your mamm taught you better than that.*"

Kristina's brows inched together. "Are you sure? What if he decides he doesn't want to ask you after all? You shouldn't be difficult."

Mandy stifled a giggle. "I'm sure."

Kristina punched her buttons with all the dexterity of a seasoned expert. That girl could generate a message without even looking. After she pressed SEND, she snapped her phone shut and took Mandy's hand. "I hope you won't regret it."

Mandy made eye contact with Noah across the room. He had turned a very light shade of green waiting for her reply. Was he truly that uncertain of her love? Their last encounter hadn't gone well, but surely he knew she loved him.

If he didn't, he would. Soon.

She had to wipe that look of distress off his face. She smiled and winked. He cocked an eyebrow as rosy red replaced the green pallor of his skin. Was he blushing? She'd never seen him quite so discomfited. Or so attractive. Her heart whirred like a hummingbird in flight.

His phone lit up, and he pushed the button that would allow him to read her text. Were his hands shaking?

He clenched his jaw as he read her message, and then rolling his eyes in exasperation, he curled his lips into a very attractive grin, stuffed his phone into his trousers pocket, and ambled toward her, nudging boys out of his way as he came.

As Noah approached, Kristina giggled and squeezed Mandy's hand until her knuckles cracked. Mandy could barely keep to her seat as he took her by the hand, all the while looking as if he might burst into laughter. "Everyone," he said, raising his voice above the chatter.

Oh, no.

Mandy's face felt as if it might burst into flame. He wasn't going to do it in front of everybody, was he? Well, she *had* told him he needed to show people his heart.

Noah looked around the room to make sure everyone was listening. No doubt about it, they were. "Since I've resolved to quit hiding from the people I love the most, I want you to be the first to know that I am in love with Mandy Helmuth. I adore her. I can't live without her. I want her to be my wife."

The Sensenig sisters sighed rapturously.

Mandy's heart had never been so full. She couldn't possibly utter a word when she felt this happy.

Noah got down on one knee and brushed his lips across

the back of her hand, causing her to tremble all over. Kristina squeaked and looked as if she might faint in a fit of euphoria.

"Mandy Helmuth, you know I don't have a place to call my own yet, but if you'll be patient with my weaknesses, I'll build us a house with my own two hands. A house where we can raise our children and grow old together. Will you marry me?"

Everyone paused breathlessly, staring at Mandy as if she held the success of the party in her hands.

Her heart raced as she squeezed his hand in hers. "Yes. It will be the happiest day of my life."

The room came to life once again. Noah pulled Mandy to her feet as their friends cheered and clapped. This was probably the most excitement they'd ever had at a party before, even a party with Do You Like Your Neighbor.

Dodging bodies, Noah hastily pulled Mandy through the group of friends and out to the porch for a little solitude. She shut the door behind them an instant before he captured her in his arms and kissed her urgently. She kissed him back with all the joy of having found something that she despaired was lost.

"Noah," she whispered. "You came back to me."

"I couldn't bear to stay away." He rested his forehead against hers. "I am nothing without you." His eyes glistened with tears. "I'm so sorry, Mandy. Can you forgive me?"

"That's a silly question. Of course I can."

"So I guess this means you'll stay an extra week?"

Mandy giggled. "Mammi will get her fondest wish. But then I'll have to go home and order plates for the wedding. How does October sound?"

His shoulders bounced up and down as he chuckled. "I want to marry as soon as the plates can be ready."

"We'll pick a time when your mamm and family can

come to Ohio." She kissed him on the cheek. "And what about your dat?"

Noah frowned and tightened his arms around her. "Things at home are very, very rough right now. Jessica says it's going to get worse before it gets better. With things the way they are, I shouldn't have asked you to marry me, but I couldn't bear the thought of not being with you. I don't know how this is going to end with my dat. I only know that I love you, and I'll do anything to keep you close to me forever."

She skimmed a finger across his bruised lips. He trembled. "Shh. We'll bear this together. No matter what happens, you can be sure of me."

She savored the feel of his strong arms around her. Arms like these had never known a day of idleness. Arms like these would cradle her babies, roast marshmallows, hammer thousands of nails, and hold her close. Noah would love and protect her, and God would watch over them both.

"And you can be sure of me," he whispered as he brought his lips down on hers.

She'd never felt more sure of anything in her life.

As the party went on behind them, Anna positioned herself at the kitchen window where she had a good view of the kissing going on outside on the porch. "I have to admit, Felty, I never saw that one coming. Who would have thought gloomy Noah Mischler would have caught the attention of our dear Mandy?"

"Who indeed," Felty said, his eyes twinkling like July fireworks.

"To be sure, it's a wonder."

Felty took another bite of one of the six different kinds of cookies Mandy had made for the going-away party. "You're not disappointed, are you, Banannie?"

"Disappointed? Stuff and nonsense. Noah is the best kind of boy I can imagine. I just don't see how I could have missed the fact that he and Mandy are perfect for each other."

Felty nodded. "They seem to suit quite well."

"Of course they do. Now that they're together, I can't imagine any boy better. He's got nice teeth, he's a gute swimmer, and . . ." Anna's mouth fell open. "Ach, du lieva, what muscles! No wonder Mandy fell for him."

Delight spread across her face as she leaned close to Felty so she could whisper in his ear. "And I don't have to bribe any more boys with pot holders. All these boys will just have to find their own wives without my help or my pot holders. I can get started on making you a Christmas sweater instead of knitting pot holders all day. This is wonderful gute."

Felty thumbed his suspenders. "Wonderful gute. It's not Christmastime without a new sweater."

Anna frowned as a sad thought came to her. "Felty, do you think I've lost my touch? I mean, Mandy and Noah came like a bolt out of the blue. What if I don't have the gift anymore?"

"Of course you have the gift. Look how many grandchildren you've been able to match up. I think we've more than done our duty as grandparents."

Anna brightened considerably. "You're right. Even though we didn't arrange the match, it was successful all the same. Mandy fell in love while she was here, and she did it in the four weeks we allotted her. Isn't that nice?"

"Very nice, Banannie."

"I feel so much better." She clapped her hands together. "I'm ready for a new project."

"My Christmas sweater?"

"Now that we won't be having guests for dinner every night, we'll have time to start thinking about our next match."

"But, Annie, I thought you were tired of knitting pot holders."

Anna squared her shoulders and raised herself to her full height of five feet zero inches. "I'm willing to sacrifice your Christmas sweater for the good of our grandchildren."

"Oh, okay," said Felty, squinching his eyebrows together. "I suppose I am too, if you think it's best."

"I'm quite worried about Cassie. She has so much love to give, and no one to give it to."

"Cassie? You're not going to try to pull her back into the church, are you? I don't think she'll come back, even though her mamm would jump for joy if she did."

Anna took one more peek out the window and closed the curtains on Mandy and Noah, whose lips were surely going to fall off with all that kissing. "Now, Felty," she said. "Cassie's mamm will work herself into an ulcer if she keeps fussing about Cassie coming back to the church. She's not coming back, but that doesn't mean we can't find her a gute match. Remember that new doctor at the hospital? He's young, he's single, and he has the light of God inside him."

Felty rubbed his beard. "The doctor seems nice enough, but how are you going to get him to come to Huckleberry Hill? And what about Cassie? She hasn't been home for months."

Anna patted her husband on the shoulder. "I have a very powerful gift, Felty. Leave it to me." She got that look on her face that she always did when she was thinking deep and sneaky thoughts. "But the doctor won't be lured here with anything less than a scarf, a beanie, *and* a pair of mittens."

"Knitted, I expect?"

Anna smiled slyly. "And a matching set of earmuffs. Let's send these youngsters home. I've got some knitting to do."

Please turn the page for an exciting sneak peek of

Jennifer Beckstrand's next Huckleberry Hill romance,

HUCKLEBERRY HEARTS,

coming in December 2015!

Anna Helmuth glanced up from her knitting long enough to study the top of Dr. Reynolds's head. "Doctor, I can see your whole head from up here, and I'm happy to say that you haven't got any bald spots."

"That's good news," the doctor replied. "My maternal grandfather was as bald as a cue ball."

Anna sat on the exam table with one shoe off and one shoe on knitting a baby blanket for the newest arrival in the Helmuth family, a baby daughter to her grandson Aden and his wife Lily. Anna's husband Felty sat next to her with a gift box in his lap.

The young, handsome doctor with the slightly crooked nose perched on his rolling padded stool carefully examining the bottom of Anna's foot, and that's why she had such a good view of the top of his head. He worked his thumbs around the edges of the black spot the size of a quarter on the pad of her foot. She squirmed and tried not to drop a stitch while he poked at her.

"Sorry, Mrs. Helmuth," the doctor said, applying firmer pressure so as not to make Anna jump out of her skin.

"Call me Anna. We Amish don't go by *Mister* and *Missus*."

One side of the doctor's mouth curled upward even as his eyes danced with good-natured humor. "Sorry, Anna."

His smile was one of the reasons Anna was considering him as a match for her granddaughter. Cassie needed a pleasant young man who would make her laugh and wasn't afraid to be laughed at. He had good teeth and a full head of hair, which made it more likely that Cassie would take a second look, and although Cassie wasn't Amish anymore, she needed a godly husband more than anything else. The doctor had a way about him that told Anna he was a man of God, deep down.

Anna's knitting needles clicked in an easy rhythm born from years of practice. "You're not married, are you, doctor?"

Felty drummed his fingers on the top of the box in his lap. "You asked him that same question at our last appointment, Banannie."

Anna raised her eyebrows at her husband. "It's been two weeks. I'm just making sure his situation hasn't changed."

Dr. Reynolds chuckled softly even as his fingers probed the bottom of Anna's foot. "Nope, not married."

"And what about a girlfriend? Do you have any girlfriends?"

"No girlfriend."

Anna winked at Felty as her smile grew wider. "You must be wonderful lonely yet," she said, starting a new row of stitches on her blanket.

The doctor let Anna's foot slip from his grasp and scooted over to the cart that held his computer. "I don't have much time for a social life. The hospital kind of owns me until I finish my residency. I live in a one-bedroom apartment with an ancient sofa and a turtle named Queenie. I don't get out much except to come to the hospital." He looked up from his computer long enough to give them a genuine smile. "But I don't mind. I've wanted to be a doctor for as long as I can remember, and I get to treat good people like you. You are the first Amish folks I've ever met."

"It's gute you met us first instead of David Eicher," Felty said. "He's a hard pill to swallow."

Anna nudged her husband with her elbow. "Now, Felty. Be careful what you say. David's daughter is married to our grandson."

The doctor looked like he was doing important work on his computer and she hated to interrupt him, but she had to know a few things before committing to him altogether. "Do you like children, doctor?"

"Children? I love 'em. I want a whole passel of kids some-day." His lips curved as he typed away at his computer. "Which is probably why I don't have a girlfriend. Talk of kids tends to scare women off."

"Not if you're Amish. We're determined to multiply and replenish the Earth."

"Single-handedly," Felty added with a twinkle in his eye.

"Now, Felty." Anna looped the yarn around her needle and eyed Dr. Reynolds. "Are you a hard worker, doctor?" Her mamm always used to say that being a hard worker was the best quality a son-in-law could possess.

The doctor stopped typing long enough to consider the question. "I hope so. You can't survive medical school with-out knowing how to work hard. My family owned a cherry orchard growing up. I used to work in the orchards with my dad. In the spring I pruned trees until I thought my neck would fall off. In the summer my brothers and I memorized Scriptures while we picked cherries."

"You memorized Scripture?"

The doctor sprouted a crooked, unnatural grin and nodded.

That was all she needed to hear. God had put the doctor in Anna's path, and Anna wasn't about to waste the opportunity. There wasn't even time to consult Felty. She had to act fast.

The doctor rolled back to the exam table and took Anna's hand in his. Sympathy flooded his expression. "Mrs. Helmuth—"

"Anna."

"Anna, I'm afraid I have bad news. We got the results from the biopsy we did at your last visit. That black patch on the bottom of your foot is cancer. Melanoma. It will have to be cut out."

Anna furrowed her brow. "Does this mean I need to come back?"

Dr. Reynolds nodded gravely. "Several times. We'll have to cut out the bad part of the skin, and if it's deep, you'll need a skin graft. Someone will have to come to your house several times a week to change the dressing and check the site for infection."

Anna burst into a smile. "So we'll be seeing a lot of each other."

The doctor raised an eyebrow. "Not exactly the reaction I expected."

"God moves in a mysterious way, His wonders to perform." Anna deposited her knitting in the canvas bag next to her, slid from the table, and took the box from Felty's lap. "You'll be the one operating, won't you?"

"I could do it, but I'm on my dermatology rotation right now. You might want the plastic surgeon to do your skin graft. I've only done six weeks of plastic surgery."

"Stuff and nonsense. You're being humble." Anna pursed

her lips and turned to Felty. "Another wonderful-gute quality in a husband."

The doctor's lips twitched. "I assume you want someone to operate on you, not marry you."

Anna pinned the doctor with the look she usually reserved for naughty grandchildren, complete with the twinkle in her eye. "*I* don't want to marry you, doctor. Felty and I have been very happy for sixty-four years."

"I'm glad to hear it," Dr. Reynolds said.

"But I'll only agree to the surgery if you do it," Anna added, standing firm so that not even a team of Percheron horses could move her.

A grin played at Dr. Reynolds's lips. "I'll have to check with Dr. Mann first, but it should be okay."

Beaming like a lantern on a dark country road, Anna handed Dr. Reynolds the box. "I made these especially for you, doctor. I know you won't disappoint me."

Dr. Reynolds opened the box and pulled out the navy blue mittens that went with the fire-engine red scarf and the red and blue beanie Anna had knitted, also in the box. "These are for me? Why would you knit a pair of mittens for me?"

Anna grinned. It was always gute to keep potential suitors a little off balance. "There's a beanie and scarf to go with it."

"It's an extraordinary gift for someone you barely know."

"My grandmotherly talents haven't led me astray yet. You're the one I've chosen to receive the special beanie."

The doctor looked as if he didn't quite know how to argue with that. Smiling, he picked up the red and blue beanie and stretched it onto his head. It fit perfectly over all that thick hair of his. "Thank you. It's very kind. Knitting reminds me of my mother."

"I want you to feel warm and cuddly when you think of the Helmuths."

Dr. Reynolds grinned as he wrapped the scarf around his neck. Anna had made it extra long. She didn't want a stumpy scarf to be the reason he wouldn't marry her granddaughter.

"Just in time for the coldest days of winter," he said.

Anna was sure he would have put on the mittens, too, if he weren't still working on the computer. He finished whatever he was typing, took Anna's hand, and guided her to sit in one of the soft chairs. Felty, bless his heart, waited on the exam table—probably keeping it warm in case she needed to sit there again.

The doctor, with his beanie and scarf, rolled his stool directly in front of Anna. "I don't want you to worry about this. There's no reason we shouldn't be able to get all the cancer during surgery. You're going to be just fine. And have a killer scar on the bottom of your foot."

Anna waved her hand in the doctor's direction. "Oh, I'm not worried. The good Lord has a purpose for everything. Isn't that right, Felty?"

"Yes, it is."

She patted the doctor's hand. "But if *you're* worried about it, we should pray together. God will comfort you better than even my beanie can."

A shadow flitted across the doctor's face. "I'm not worried. You'll be fine."

Anna didn't especially like that expression. "You're uncomfortable praying?"

"I suppose I am."

"But you said you used to memorize Scriptures."

"I did. Out in the orchard." The doctor lowered his eyes. "That was a long time ago."

Anna scrunched her lips together. "Oh, dear."

Dr. Reynolds swiped his hand down his face. "The truth is, Mrs. Helmuth—"

"Anna."

"Anna, God and I aren't on speaking terms, but if you want someone to pray with you, I can call Marla. She's one of the nurses, and she goes to Mass every Sunday."

Cassie might not have been Amish anymore, but she still needed a godly husband, and someone who didn't talk to God would not be a godly husband. How could Anna have been so mistaken about this one? He seemed like such a nice boy. And, *ach, du lieva,* she'd already given him the carefully knitted beanie and scarf. And mittens! Mittens were no small thing.

"Oh, dear," Anna said again. "Felty, I'm afraid I've cast my pearls before swine."

"No such thing, Annie."

Dr. Reynolds cracked a smile. "Am I the swine?" He pulled the beanie off his head, and wisps of his sandy blond hair stuck straight into the air. "If you'd rather offer this to someone more religious than I am, I completely understand. You had no idea what my relationship with God was before you gave it." His expression almost melted her heart. He truly held no hard feelings whatsoever. Maybe there was hope.

What kind of person would she be if she took back a gift simply because the young man might be unsuitable for her granddaughter? "Of course not," Anna insisted. "Even if you are a swine, I gave that beanie freely. I want you to have it."

Dr. Reynolds chuckled as his eyes danced with amusement. "I guess I'm not used to the Amish customs yet."

Anna wrung her hands. "Oh, dear. I didn't mean to call you a swine. It's just an expression."

The doctor patted her hand reassuringly. "I know what you meant. And if it makes you feel better, you're not the first woman to call me that."

Felty always seemed to be able to get to the heart of the matter. "So you don't believe in God?"

Dr. Reynolds frowned in concentration. "I'm not sure."

"That's better than a 'no,'" Felty said.

Anna tapped her finger to her lips. "So your faith is wavering, but not altogether extinguished. Felty can work with that, can't you, Felty?"

"I don't know what you're talking about, Annie."

"I mean that there's still hope for Dr. Reynolds," Anna said.

The doctor lowered his head to hide another grin. "Probably not."

"Just you wait," Anna said, nodding at the good doctor who'd misplaced his faith. "By this time next week, your faith will bloom like a cherry tree in springtime."

The doctor cocked an eyebrow. "What's so special about next week?"

Cassie was what was so special, of course, but Anna couldn't very well ruin the surprise. The doctor would take to Cassie like a fruit fly took to a mushy apricot. And Lord willing, he'd find his faith again.

Maybe the beanie was in the right hands after all.

Books by Bestselling Author
Fern Michaels

Available Wherever Books Are Sold!
Check out our website at www.kensingtonbooks.com